BOOK OF CREATION

Loyev Books

BOOK OF CREATION

A contemporary fantasy

Michael Winstrom and Ran Lahav

Loyev Books
Hardwick, Vermont, USA
PhiloPractice.org/web/loyev-books

ISBN-10: 1-947515-76-4

ISBN-13: 978-1-947515-70-3

Loyev Books

1165 Hopkins Hill Rd., Hardwick, Vermont, USA

PhiloPractice.org/web/loyev-books

A note on the historical context of the book

The *Book of Creation*, which is at the heart of the plot of this fantasy, is a real historical book; or, rather, a thin booklet by today's standards. Sefer Yetzirah (ספר יצירה), as the book is called in Hebrew, the original language in which it was written, is an ancient text whose origin and meaning are enigmatic. Scholars have devised a variety of theories to exaplain and interpret it, but these must be regarded as no more than learned speculations. Most likely it was written in the land of Israel by a Jew (or Jews) at the beginning of the first millenium, but even these basic facts are contestable. The authors of the present fantasy took the liberty to offer their own interpretation of the obscure pronouncements that make up the *Book of Creation*, without claiming historical accuracy.

Loyev Books

1

The small but elegant hotel room in London's financial district was filled with shadows. Two figures sat at a table. Two books lay open beneath a dim lamp. The pages of one were creased and browned from the centuries it had seen, although the ancient Hebrew script was still legible. The other was a dual-language version of the same text. Its cover read: "The Book of Creation."

The older of the men, Professor Jeremiah Eliezer, searched his friend's eyes, looking for strength. William Oleander stared back. Eliezer lowered his gaze and passed his hand over the book's pages, brushing aside an imaginary crumb. He hesitated, then pulled the old manuscript towards him. The same questions that had been torturing him now returned: Are we entitled to use discernment—our ancestral meditation—to awaken this ancient book? Are we certain what will happen when the powers of discernment are focused on these mysterious invocations? And if the Council discovers what we are doing? This might be deemed treason, and the penalty would surely be death.

"We are Keepers," Eliezer murmured, answering his own worries. "Our duty is to the Blessing, not blind obedience to tradition."

Oleander nodded as if his mentor had spoken to him. He trusted Eliezer's understanding of the Book of Creation but loathed hiding their endeavor from the Keepers' Council. As a monk he valued obedience. "Let's hope," he said, "we know what we're doing."

For a moment Eliezer was tempted to halt their endeavor. This is like tapping a dormant volcano. It's not too late to stop and study the Book more...

Eliezer rubbed his sweaty palms on his pants. No, he urged himself, we can't go on studying forever. "Let us start, William."

Each threw a last glance at the pages, then closed his eyes and quieted his thoughts. They sank into silence, then still further inward, to their Inner Depths. Some time later their minds were hovering at the edge of the great Void.

Eliezer began reciting, Oleander immediately joining him:

WITH THIRTY-TWO MYSTERIOUS PATHS OF WISDOM ENGRAVED GOD, THE LORD OF HOSTS...

This was only the Book's introductory passage, but already they were engulfed by a tender energy: it was unmistakably the Blessing they knew so well.

...AND HE CREATED HIS WORLD WITH THREE SFR'S: WITH SFR AND SFR AND SFR.

They pronounced these last words cautiously. Since the manuscript lacked vowel signs they could only conjecture which ancient Hebrew words the letters were supposed to designate.

The Book's opening verse completed, they were ready to plunge into its core: the first in a list of enigmatic statements, each starting with "Ten *Sefirot* of *Belimah*."

TEN *SEFIROT* OF *BELIMAH*, TWENTY-TWO FUNDAMENTAL LETTERS, TEN SEFIROT...

They felt the Blessing swell all around them. The suddenness of its pressure took them by surprise, knocking them off balance for a moment. It was only because they were experienced Keepers that they kept their focus.

...LIKE THE NUMBER OF TEN FINGERS, FIVE OPPOSITE FIVE, AND THE COVENANT OF THE ONE SET IN THE CENTER, WITH THE WORD OF THE TONGUE IN THE MOUTH AND WITH THE CIRCUMCISION OF NAKEDNESS.

The forces surrounding them mounted and deepened, held back by something they couldn't see. Had Eliezer been able to open his eyes he would have seen Oleander gripping the edge of the table so hard his fingertips had gone white. Eliezer breathed deeply, then whispered one Hebrew word: "*Mila.*"

Something stirred in the great energies around them. Then came an explosion of Blessing, breathtaking and powerfully sweet, surging through them into the Void. It was unlike anything they had experienced in all their years of discernment. They were galvanized. They gasped; they were fire, they were air, they were nothingness.

At last the almost unbearable intensity subsided. By degrees their consciousness left the edge of the Void and returned to their bodies. Slowly they uncoiled and slumped in their chairs, hollow, exhausted and damp with sweat. Their eyes met and they smiled. Their drained faces did not show their exhilaration: *They had succeeded.*

On their return to the airport they sat in the taxi quietly pondering. What exactly had happened? And the worry that weighed on each: Had they disturbed anything in the fabric of these mysterious forces?

2

Dina Carlini stepped from the train into the afternoon sun. Tall and lithe, her short brown hair stirring in the wind, she set down her luggage and shielded her eyes from the harsh brightness. As she waited for her vision to adjust a man approached her.

"Welcome to Lucerne, Miss Carlini." He was an older man in a dark suit and tie. "My name is Klaus Schroeder. I'm from the Frostburg Institute. Allow me." He picked up her suitcases. "This way please."

"Thank you."

The car was just beyond the platform. He placed her things in the trunk of the Mercedes and then opened the rear passenger door for her. The car smelled of new leather and luxury. She was uncomfortable at being chauffeured, and he said nothing more. As they pulled into traffic she thought again how little she knew about her destination.

She had gone to Father Binino last February about her visions or dreams or hallucinations—she didn't know what to call them. She'd had them on occasion all her life but in the last year they had become more acute, more *real*. She would find herself seeing—as if she were present herself—some familiar scene from the Bible, usually about the Patriarch Jacob and his twelve sons and one daughter, Dinah, her namesake. These experiences were wondrous but also very troubling, and she had begun to find them interfering with her ability to go about her life.

Had these visions been about something other than the Bible she would have sought a doctor. That afternoon, months ago, she had described them to Father Binino. She worried she was going crazy and said so.

"No, I can assure you that isn't true." Then he described details of certain visions impossible to know unless he also experienced them. "Very few people on Earth possess this gift," he told her. He was one of them, and this was how he recognized it in her. Further, he told her she possessed this gift to a degree unknown in his experience. "Dina, you cannot grasp how extraordinary you are."

"I'm like you, then?"

"No, my dear, next to you my gift is paltry."

She could see it pained him to admit this.

"What do these visions mean? Why am I having them?"

He stared at her a long moment as if making up his mind. "There is a place… there are people who can tell you about this, who can give you the answers you are looking for. And much more."

"You can't tell me?"

"It's in Switzerland. The Frostburg Institute for Biblical Studies."

"If you have this same problem, or gift, why can't you help me?"

"I am forbidden to say more. I've probably said too much as it is."

"Forbidden? By the Church?"

"No. Listen, Dina. I will make all the arrangements for you. But you cannot ask me any more questions. If you wish to understand who you are, what you are, you must trust me."

The Frostburg Institute, the public face of The Keepers' School for Externals, was located in Lucerne, Switzerland. Designed to evaluate "externals"—those candidates not yet initiated into Keeperdom—it was set apart from the compound that housed the Keepers' headquarters. While that compound was situated outside Lucerne, the school for externals sat in the oldest part of the city, along the River Reuss. Once a private residence, it had been purchased over two hundred years ago by the Keepers' Council and turned into the "Frostburg Institute for Biblical Studies." This camouflage explained to the curious the odd comings and goings while discouraging interest from outsiders. This was the traditional way of the Keepers, who always were mindful of shielding their activities from the rest of the world.

The car began to slow, and as it made the turn through the iron gates Dina noted the discrete brass plaque on the pillar.

"We are here, Miss," the driver said.

The tires thudded on the cobblestones of the drive as the car moved around to the rear of the house. It was almost too large to be called a house. It reminded her of a museum.

"The Frostburg family lived here for many generations," the driver said as if reading her mind. "Extraordinary, yes?"

"It's amazing."

This time, she did not wait for him to open her door.

"Please, this way."

As they neared the rear entrance the door opened and the frame was filled by a stout blond woman in a brilliant red dress.

"Welcome, Miss Carlini. May I call you Dina?"

"That's fine, yes."

"Good. And you may call me Miss Crumb. Klaus, would you put Miss Carlini's things in her room? Thank you."

Once in the spacious entryway, she turned to face Dina. "Now, let's have a look at you. You're even prettier than your photos." Photos? She had sent none. "Your Italian and French are quite good I'm told." She waited as if wanting proof.

"I've been speaking both as long as I can remember. My mother insisted, though we always spoke English at home, in New York."

"Yes, your mother is from Milan. You hold both Italian and American passports, is that right?" Dina nodded and wondered how she knew. "You may find it more comfortable to speak Italian or French at times, but of necessity we use English as our common language, which is conveniently similar to American." She winked, making Dina smile. "Let's go upstairs and I'll show you your room."

The house had three floors, but the ceilings were more than twice as high as in modern buildings, and the climb to the third floor took away her breath. She noticed that Miss Crumb, despite her size, appeared to enjoy the exercise. Once on the top floor, they stopped midway down the hallway. On the white door was stenciled in neat black letters "Miss Carlini."

"After you."

Expecting a dormitory room, she was taken aback by the grandness. Her whole apartment in New York could have easily fit inside the walls of the room. The furniture was modern yet blended with the age of the house. There was one bed, already made up.

"You'll have plenty of time to settle in. I'll show you the one shortcoming." Down the hall, she opened an unmarked door. "I'm afraid there are only two baths on this floor. You'll be sharing with four other young women. The young men share the one at the other end."

Downstairs, Miss Crumb explained that the formal welcome would be given when all the students were present. She was the first to arrive. Nine more were expected.

"Meals are served at eight, one, and seven o'clock. We dine together as a family. You are welcome to explore the house, but please do not leave the grounds. "I'm sure you have many questions. Be patient. We are very pleased to have you here."

Crumb again climbed the steps this time to the second floor, stopping at the office of the Director, Councilor Menach Peprini. She knocked.

"Come."

She entered and made the long trip across the Persian rug to a chair in front of his desk.

"She has arrived?"

"Just now." She sat down. "And there *is* something undeniably special about her."

"Because you perceive it? Or because you've read Binino's report and so expect her to be extraordinary?"

"I can't say. But anyone who had a visualization of Gates Ten or Eleven with no training…"

"So says Binino."

"You never raised any doubts when we discussed her admission."

"Binino is almost certainly exaggerating. Nevertheless, even if she visualized only Gate One, she belongs here."

"But if she really did…"

"Yes."

Joanna Crumb saw that Dina Carlini intrigued him more than he would admit.

3

The others began arriving. Most seemed in their early twenties, making Dina feel old at nearly thirty. All spoke English, though each with a different accent. She asked a bespectacled, serious-looking one what he had been told about the gift.

Alexi Samsov looked at her perplexed. "What gift?"

"Why are you here, then?"

"My professor in Kiev arranged my studies here. He knows the Director and I'm receiving full scholarship. And you? What's this gift you mention?"

Dina made a decision. "I'm on scholarship also. I think we all are." She smiled. "It seems we're all gifted."

After that, she did no more than introduce herself to the others. Those who spoke freely seemed to think this was simply a scholarly institution. Those she suspected knew more were quieter.

Joanna Crumb went to bed hoping the Blessing conditions would be favorable tomorrow. She had toiled for weeks preparing for the new class and hated the thought that something would go wrong.

The next morning Crumb perceived the Blessing to be on the rise. It was a glorious morning at the Institute—not from the perspective of an ordinary human observer who would have noticed only the overcast sky and damp wind. But for a Keeper who could perceive the flow of Blessing in the air it was indeed special. She wondered whether any of the new arrivals could feel it. A few might sense something, maybe simply as a good mood.

That afternoon Crumb was relieved to find the Blessing was stable at an acceptable level. The beginning of a course was an important event. It was advisable to wait for favorable Blessing conditions to ensure against adverse moods, unforeseen conflicts, and all kinds of mishaps—which ordinary people attributed to chance but only Keepers knew resulted from a diminishment in the Blessing. In previous years Class-Masters sometimes had to wait days, like mariners watching for the weather to improve in order to set sail. She sent Klaus to tell the candidates to join her in the conservatory at six-thirty that evening.

Ten chairs were arranged in a half moon around the fireplace. The newcomers were visibly tense. Crumb watched them take their seats, noting how the ambient Blessing flowed around the contours of their heads and bodies, creating soft auras. She was satisfied.

"This evening our Director, Mr. Peprini, will formally welcome you to the Frostburg Institute. But as your Class-Master, I wish to welcome you as well. No doubt you've realized this is no ordinary school. We do not accept applications. We do not advertise in any manner. Admission is by invitation only. Each of you has been very carefully selected. More so than you can imagine. There is no tuition. Your room and board, travel, indeed all your expenses, are provided. Why this generosity, you may ask?" She paused to make sure they felt the import of the question. "How does the saying go? 'From those to whom much is given, much is expected.' The sacrifice and duty of nobility. You see, much has been given to you."

Dina looked at Alexi and several of the others. It seemed they grasped, too, that Miss Crumb wasn't speaking of mere intelligence.

"You are here to nurture what you have been given. And though we understand you have a special ability, we can't be sure yet whether you have the character, the nobility that must also be present for this to be realized. Let us hope." Miss Crumb saw several worried faces and her mood brightened suddenly. "And now we'll adjourn to the dining room. I believe a wonderful dinner is awaiting us."

Each year, by centuries-old tradition the day of the autumnal equinox, a new group of candidates received from the Director their formal welcome. This autumn ten had arrived from ten countries around the world, an exceptionally large class. As always Menach Peprini insisted on giving the welcome himself, not from kindness, but because he wanted to ensure they were indoctrinated properly. The facts could be communicated well enough by his assistants, but the proper attitude to take towards those facts, well, that, of course, would be *his* attitude. He thought of these candidates as ducklings awakening to the world and wanted them to be imprinted with the image of Menach Peprini first. Those who advanced would be posted throughout Keeperdom, and he wanted them loyal to him above all others.

He looked at his watch. Leaving his office he walked down the hallway; it pleased him to hear only his footsteps. He paused outside the door to the conservatory. At precisely eight o'clock he entered. He walked across the large room until he was in front of the fireplace. The ten students instinctively sat straighter in their chairs. He moved to a position in front of the large fireplace.

"I am Menach Peprini, Director of the Institute. You have been summoned here because you have a gift. You are here because one of my colleagues—each of whom, I add, is an alumnus—recognized this quality in you. I'm sure something of the program was explained to you before you arrived. *Forget what you have been told.*"

The sternness of this order took them aback and they examined him more closely. He looked to be about forty-years-old. Actually, he was fifty-nine. Keepers lived significantly longer than ordinary human beings and aged more slowly. Those with exceptionally pure blood looked much younger than they were. They saw a slender, precise man, his dark hair neatly combed, his face freshly shaven even at this hour. Several marked him as vain, judging by the finely tailored suit and polished shoes. Peprini would have acknowledged his vanity. A man who admits no character flaws is lying to himself. The women noticed his manicure as well as the ruby ring he wore, the same one they had seen on all those at the Institute.

"The life ahead of you will not be an easy one."

The blond Australian boy with a face like a fox—Tiplady—silently snickered as his eyes roamed the beautiful room and took in again the Director's fine appearance. Peprini frowned. A lack of self-control was always unfortunate whatever the endeavor.

"Consider the upcoming week your probationary period. You may, of course, leave at any time. It is possible, as well, that you may be asked to leave should we determine you are unsuitable." He smiled at Tiplady.

He began to pace. This was a promising group. The Carlini woman… he had tried not to stare but it was difficult. Her aura was different from any he had seen. As for the others, the glimmer of Blessing in the air resonated around them agreeably. Alexi Samsov seemed good, and the Dutch Maria Jongsma was excellent, while Tiplady was likely a mistake. Aside from his dismally thin aura, if the boy couldn't mind his behavior for this introduction he would hardly make a devoted Keeper. Peprini made a mental note to reprimand the municipal judge in Adelaide who had recommended him.

He turned to face them. The need to ask questions was plain on their faces.

"Understand this above all else," he said imperiously. "We alone can teach you who you are."

Each felt this was true. Dina realized that in some way he knew more about her than she did herself.

"If you leave us, or if we ask you to leave..." He stared at them. For reasons none could put to words they feared beyond all proportion they might be told to leave. "You will never know who you are."

He sighed as if he had had enough of them. "Tomorrow morning we shall see."

4

Moments later Joanna Crumb returned. It was plain that Peprini had been unsparingly severe. "Tomorrow morning will begin your Verification—your entrance exam. This will verify whether indeed you have the gift. Please, your questions must wait until tomorrow."

As the students shifted uncomfortably at this announcement, the door opened and an older man entered. Tall, he had once been thickly built but with age was now both softer and thinner, the loose fit of his suit coat confirming this. His longish gray hair appeared combed back with his fingers. He nodded to the Class-Master and walked with measured steps to the front of the room.

"Tonight we have a treat," she continued. "A very special visitor from Israel has kindly agreed to stop here on his way back home from London. It is my pleasure to introduce Professor Jeremiah Eliezer from the Hebrew University of Jerusalem. He will speak to us this evening about the Book of Genesis. Let me say this now: This is a scholarly institution. You are welcome to continue practicing your respective creeds, if you have any. We are not here to convert you. In due time you will understand the profound importance of the Bible."

Crumb moved to an antique mahogany chest and opened the doors. Ten new leather-bound Bibles rested in two stacks. She took one pile and distributed them, then the other. Professor Eliezer faced the candidates and examined their faces, and they, too, appraised his: old yet vital, kind and yet aloof. In his left hand he held a worn Bible.

He opened the book and started reading, pronouncing the words in an archaic accent:

"And God created man in His own image, in the image of God He created him, male and female he created them. And God blessed them and said to them: Be fruitful and multiply and replenish the Earth...

"Genesis—the first book of the Bible—Chapter One. The first blessing: On the sixth day of creation, after God has created light and darkness, land and luminaries, plants and animals, he creates human beings. And He blesses them. Now, why does the author of Genesis mention the blessing here?"

They stared at him.

"Look, this is the very first chapter of the Bible—the creation of the world, the beginning of humankind. The text is ceremonious and precise. In the original Hebrew, not a single word is superfluous. Still, the author decides to include God's words to the Man and to the Woman. Why?"

"It must be," said Jorge Pinedo, the small Peruvian, "in order to say that God's blessing is very important."

"Precisely. God's blessing is an essential part of the creation of the world. In the Bible, a blessing is not just a string of words. It endows the blessed person with the powers of life itself."

Amira Tarik frowned in concentration. "It is saying, isn't it, that humanity depends on God's blessing."

"Indeed. But sadly, despite God's blessing, not everything goes well for humankind. Very soon afterwards, still in the Garden of Eden, Adam and Eve defy God. The father and mother of humanity are tempted by the serpent—the personification of evil—to disobey God's commands. They eat the forbidden fruit. The consequences are quick to come: the curse.

"God says to Adam: *Because you have listened to the voice of your wife and eaten from the tree about which I commanded you 'you shall not eat from it,' cursed is the ground for you; in toil you shall eat of it all the days of your life.*

"You see, life is not just a blessing. Life is a struggle between the powers of the blessing and the powers of the curse; between the powers of flourishing and order and the powers of destruction and chaos. Even the Garden of Eden holds not only beautiful things but also the serpent. This is no mere coincidence. The Bible tells us that the role of humanity—indeed the role of each one of us—is to help the blessing overcome the curse."

Eliezer continued. "Some time later, in the fourth chapter of Genesis, we find the story of Cain. Cain, Adam and Eve's son, murders his brother Abel. And God curses Cain: *What have you done? The voice of your brother's blood cries to me from the ground. And now cursed are you from the ground which has opened its mouth to receive your brother's blood from your hand. When you till the ground, it will not henceforth yield to you its strength. A fugitive and a wanderer you will be on the Earth.* Again the curse.

"Troubles keep coming. Humans continue to side with the powers of the curse. They do so much evil that God destroys them all with a flood. Only the virtuous Noah and his family survive in the Ark. And with these survivors God tries a new beginning, a new blessing. In the ninth chapter of the Book of Genesis, He gives again His blessing to the remnants of humanity: *And God blessed Noah and his sons and said to them: Be fruitful and multiply and replenish the Earth.*

"Nevertheless, humanity continues to fall. Humans turn out to be too weak-willed. So God changes his tactics. And now comes a new stage. God no longer blesses humanity as a whole—that has failed. Rather, He chooses one virtuous person and gives him His blessing to pass on to the rest of humankind. This extraordinary man and his descendants now become the conduits through which God's blessing is carried to the rest of humanity."

"Vessels of the Blessing," muttered Alexi Samsov.

Professor Eliezer turned to him. If the young Ukrainian only knew the meaning of what he had just uttered... "Yes," he finally said, "Vessels of the Blessing, if you wish. Now who, according to the Bible, was the first Vessel?"

There was silence in the room. Some lowered their faces to avoid his searching eyes.

"Boldness is a virtue," he urged them. "Open your Bibles to the Book of Genesis and find the answer."

There was a rustle of pages.

"I think," suggested Nalini Sing, a dark woman from Mumbai with a red dot on her forehead, "that it's Isaac's son Jacob. It says here in Genesis Chapter Twenty-Eight: *And Isaac called Jacob and blessed him.*"

"Exactly," interrupted Lev Bolski, a red-haired South African Jew. "Even earlier, in Chapter Twenty-Seven, Isaac blesses both sons, Jacob and Esau."

"Hold on," said Eliezer. "A human blessing means little. Anyone can say words of blessing. But God's blessing is a gift of life-powers. Look for blessings made by God."

Again there was a turning of pages.

"It's Moses, isn't it?" said Tiplady, pointing to his open Bible. "Right here, God says to Moses: *I have set before you life and death, the blessing and the curse, therefore choose life that you may live, you and your seed.*"

Professor Eliezer raised an eyebrow. "Are you sure we are talking about the same Bible? In mine, the verse you quoted appears some four hundred years after Genesis, in Chapter Thirty of the Book of Deuteronomy."

"Crap."

"I found it!" Jorge Pinedo's sing-song voice was shrill with excitement. "Genesis Chapter Twenty-Eight. God says to Jacob: *I am the Lord, the God of your forefather Abraham and the God of Isaac... In you and in your seed will all the families of the Earth be blessed.*"

"Good," said Eliezer. "*In you and in your seed will all the families of the Earth be blessed.* Jacob was a vessel of God's blessing to all of humanity. But not the first."

"Then it must have been his father, Isaac," suggested Lev Bolski.

"Can we do better than guess?"

Alexi raised his hand. "Here. Genesis Chapter Twenty-Six. God says to Isaac: *I will be with you and I will bless you... I will establish the oath which I swore to Abraham your father... And in your seed will all the nations of the Earth be blessed.*"

Eliezer nodded approvingly. "Isaac was a vessel of God's blessing before his son Jacob. But again not the first."

"Abraham," declared Maria Jongsma, the Dutch blonde, her voice soft but confident. "Genesis Chapter Twelve. God says to Abraham: *And I will bless you and make your name great, and you will be a blessing... And in you will all the families of the Earth be blessed.*"

"Excellent. Here we have the first three vessels of God's blessing to humanity: Abraham, his son Isaac, and then his son Jacob. I hope I don't need to tell you that these Biblical patriarchs, who lived about four thousand years ago, were the forefathers of the Children of Israel, the first persons to believe in one God. With these three, humanity enters a new historical stage. Before them, in the first eleven chapters of Genesis, human beings fail to use God's blessing to overcome the curse. But when Abraham appears humanity is blessed in a new way: through the special capacities of Abraham and his descendants. From that point on, they are the vessels of God's blessing."

Eliezer paused to let them digest these words.

"Is all this..." Dina asked hesitantly, raising her eyes from the pages of the book, "is there really a blessing that sustains our world?"

A strange depth glowed in her aura and he found himself tempted to tell her the truth.

"I am a scholar," he said instead, "not a Rabbi. At the moment we are analyzing what the Bible says."

"Are you asking us to believe," Tiplady said derisively, "that the world started five-thousand-and-something years ago?"

The old man ignored the provocation. "No, we are not. But that's not the point. A story can be true in many ways—as a metaphor, for instance, or as a symbol."

"What could Adam and Eve possibly symbolize?"

"Perhaps an earlier stage of human history—a stage of greater plenitude. Believe what you wish. After you pass your Verification you will understand more about all this."

Eliezer closed his Bible signaling the end of his lecture. "You have been blessed." He saw they thought he was still speaking about humanity in general. "More so than others. There will be times, as you embark upon your new path, that you will wish you hadn't been. But in these matters, we have little choice."

He had not planned to say this, but since his meeting with Oleander in London he had been feeling the weight of his lifetime as a Keeper and of the sacrifices he had made, and seeing their young faces he couldn't help but add this bit of honesty.

"I wish all of you the best."

The ten, still pondering this, watched him leave the room.

5

New York, three weeks earlier

William Oleander made his way through the line leading to security. He reached into his coat pocket and felt again for his passport and boarding pass.

His cellphone rang.

"Eliezer, can this wait? I'm at JFK and just about to go through security. My plane leaves in forty minutes."

"William, listen. Vessel David Wyatt's had an accident. It's serious. William?"

"That's impossible."

"Yes. Still, it's happened. The most ordinary of things. He fell down the stairs in his townhouse."

"Excuse me, please, I'm sorry."

"What?"

"Give me a moment, Eliezer." Oleander reversed direction and maneuvered through the line until he was clear. *"He fell down the stairs?"*

"Our people overheard the housekeeper talking to the paramedics before they took him away."

"Just how serious is it?"

"He's had a concussion, that's all we know at this point."

"Do you know what hospital?"

"Cedars-Sinai."

"I'm on my way there. I'll call when I know more."

The taxi jerked into traffic and Oleander took long, slow breaths. Vessels did not have accidents, certainly not the kind that put them in the hospital. *What could this mean?*

He got out of from the cab at the hospital entrance and two women approached him.

"Councilor?" One said cautiously. Away from the St. Raphael Abbey, Oleander dressed as a businessman; that combined with his youthful appearance explained the woman's uncertainty." He nodded. "I'm Master-Keeper McCleish and this is Keeper Golden. Councilor Eliezer said you'd be coming."

"Take me to him, please."

The elevator doors opened on the fourth floor. As he stepped into the hallway he was struck with a wave of nausea. This wasn't the normal hospital odor but something very different. He turned to the women. "Do you smell that?"

The two looked at one another. "I asked a nurse about it. She didn't know what I was talking about," McCleish said.

He focused intently on the strange sensation. "That's because… I don't think it's an actual *smell*." He sniffed the air and sensed nothing in his nostrils. "It's not something physical. It's something we are attuned to and the rest of the world isn't," he added, gesturing with his nose towards the people going about their business. "Something to do with the Blessing." He shook his head and turned to the women.

"He's this way, in 434."

The stench was thicker as they approached the door. Oleander looked in and was shaken by the figure in the bed. A bandage stretched across his forehead and his right arm was in a cast.

"Do either of you have ID that shows you are his family?"

"We both do, we are his sisters. But we didn't know if we should use it."

"It's fine, go ask. I'll wait here."

No Vessel in memory had experienced any significant illness or accident. It just does not happen. They are protected. If Vessel Wyatt could be injured, he could be killed. If it could happen to him, it could happen to the other Vessels. *What had changed?*

6

After his lecture to the candidates, Eliezer stepped from the building to find Klaus Schroeder waiting.

"Good evening, Councilor. You said you wanted me to take you to the Abbey after your lecture?"

"Yes, Klaus, but first I need a few minutes of rest in the gardens. A quiet viewing of the Blessing always restores me."

"It has been delightful today."

"Indeed."

"I'll wait for you by the black Mercedes."

"Thank you."

Eliezer turned towards the vast lawn that sprawled behind the main building of the Frostburg Institute. He walked across the grass and stopped near a fountain. On a pedestal in the center of the pool was a sculpture of a man dressed in Biblical robes looking into the distance: Esau watching his brother Jacob approaching after many years of separation.

Eliezer examined the evening sky, the stars just beginning to become visible. He breathed deeply, letting the silence percolate into him. Then, as if waking up, he took his cellphone from his pocket and turned on the encryption.

"Oleander."

"Eliezer. I've been waiting to hear from you."

"Where are you, Old Monk?"

Oleander, being quite young by Keepers' standards—thirty-eight and looking twenty-five—did not like to be reminded of his age. In Keeperdom, as in all ancient societies, there was a prejudice against the young. But he knew from Eliezer it was a term of endearment.

"I've just arrived at the monastery."

"Any after-effects?"

"I can't shake this worry."

"No one will know what we have done."

"Not that. We are prying open the Primordial Gate—we're interfering with the foundations of reality. I keep thinking there's going to be some backlash."

"The Blessing looks very nice here in Lucerne."

A sigh could be heard from his end of the line. "Anyway, how are you feeling?"

"Tired, William, very tired, but that's all."

"I'm exhausted."

"To be expected, I think. So if everything is well, let us talk again in a couple of days."

Eliezer turned off his phone, glad he had decided not to tell Oleander how worried he was too.

He strolled towards the parking area. His thoughts shifted to Julia—Councilor Julia Erna, only a few miles away. He longed to see her, and the thought of meeting her made him hasten his steps. But then another thought struck him. She would undoubtedly sense something different about him, that he was exceptionally tired, that something was weighing on his mind. She knew him too well. Besides, she likely knew he had flown here not from Israel but from London and would surely ask what he had been doing there. He wasn't ready to lie to her.

"Ah, Klaus?"

"Yes, Councilor?"

"Let's cancel the drive to the Abbey. I believe I'll remain at the Institute for the night."

"Very good, sir. Good night."

7

The next morning the ten candidates were assembled in the conservatory, visibly anxious, waiting for their Verification tests to begin. In an adjacent room, sunk in deep armchairs, sat three examiners: Councilor Eliezer and Master-Keepers Joanna Crumb and Alfonso Garcia. Garcia was bald, with a neat goatee, and the smallest of the three, dressed in his usual three-piece suit of a summer yellow with a matching kerchief in the suit pocket. He winked at Crumb. The friendship between Garci and Crumb went back to the time they had been novices together, and both were pleased to be working together. Being a Councilor—the highest rank in Keeperdom, which only ten men and women currently possessed—Eliezer naturally presided. The other two were high-ranking Keepers too, but as Master-Keepers were second in rank to Councilors. A fourth person was in the room, the Director of the Keepers' Training, Councilor Peprini, standing by the door.

"Let the Blessing alone make the judgment," Peprini uttered the ancient dictum. "The examination, Councilor Eliezer, is now in your hands." Involuntarily his face grimaced slightly.

It was not known why he disliked Eliezer. Even he was not entirely sure. There was something about the old man that irritated him—perhaps his casual manners or the fact that Eliezer had lived while his own father had died at a much younger age. He turned and left the room.

"Unfortunately," Eliezer said to his two colleagues, "you will have to start the Verification without me. I have some unfinished business to take care of. I will join you after luncheon." As a Councilor he wasn't required to offer an explanation, which was to rest from the exhausting session with Oleander in London two days ago.

The Verification was a tradition Keepers had been following for at least two millennia. It last had been revised twelve-hundred years ago. Following the death of Vessel Sarah Saladin of Persia and the subsequent Plague of Constantinople in the years 747-748, the levels of the Blessing protecting the Earth had dropped dramatically, resulting in the plague as well as numerous lesser known calamities. Panic grew among Keepers.

Councilor Palenaides the Bald instituted rigorous new laws. With his powerful personality and the help of new rigorous laws that touched upon every aspect of the Keepers' lives, Palenaides managed to reinvigorate Keeperdom. Among other things, he insisted on stricter control over admittance to Keeperdom. The enormous wealth and security of the Order tempted some Keepers to admit family and friends lacking the gift. He determined that every candidate be assessed by three high-ranking examiners, one of whom had to be a Councilor.

The Verification relied on the principle that only those of Keeper blood could sense the ambient Blessing in the air. Non-Keepers—which meant the vast majority of the inhabitants of the Earth—could not sense it at all, something that gave them the illusion the world turned according to the decisions of human beings and the laws of nature. Only Keepers knew the Earth depended on the protection of the Blessing, without which everything would quickly fall into disarray. This indeed was the very purpose of the Keepers: to protect the Blessing which protected the Earth.

Klaus entered the conservatory and the ten candidates turned to him expectantly. "Mr. Pinedo, your examiner, Mr. Garcia, is waiting for you in room number 6, on the first floor. Miss Carlini, your examiner, Miss Crumb, is in room 5 on the same floor."

Dina stood, relieved that her examiner would be a familiar face. Klaus smiled knowingly. "This is only the first round, Miss Carlini. Two other examiners will see you afterwards."

She entered one of the reading rooms; several library tables with lamps were surrounded by walls lined with bookshelves. A deep leather chair sat directly in front of a large window. Dina was disappointed to detect in Miss Crumb a more formal attitude.

"Have a seat right here. Now, do you see that mountain peak over there, the one with almost no snow on it? Focus your mind just above it." She chose that spot because at the moment it was especially rich with Blessing. "Attend to that point. If a thought comes to your mind, just ignore it. Let it pass. Don't fight it."

Dina nodded and focused on the indicated point.

"Relax, Dina. Open yourself to it as if you want to hear what it wishes to tell you. Be an empty vessel and let this spot pour into you whatever it wishes to give you."

An experienced Keeper in Dina's place would feel an influx of Blessing filling her with its sweet tenderness. But a candidate, even highly gifted, needed much training to reach that level. Miss Crumb's role was to boost temporarily Dina's sensitivity in order to learn whether she could sense the Blessing. This would verify that she possessed the Keepers' gift.

Crumb had little doubt. The unusual aura around Dina's head assured her the young woman was far from ordinary. She stood behind Dina, placing her hands on either side of her head and began the Keeper's meditation. In this way, Crumb augmented Dina's sensitivity to the Blessing.

Dina's aura brightened, indicating she was reacting strongly to the spot of Blessing above the mountain peak. At last, Crumb removed her hands. "You can rest now. Did you have any special feeling?"

"Well, it was nice to sit quietly and relax. And it is a beautiful view."

Crumb was puzzled. Most candidates were astounded when feeling the Blessing for the first time. It was an experience unlike anything else. How could Dina fail to sense this? She was certainly not blind to the Blessing— her aura reacted magnificently. Well, she thought, I suppose the important fact is that *something* in her reacted to the Blessing, even if unconsciously. She moved to the second trial: to see how Dina reacted to a lack of Blessing.

She scanned the sky, and finding a dark gap in the fabric where almost no Blessing shone, pointed to it. "Now, I want you to concentrate on the upper tip of this long cloud. Focus your eyes on it. Open yourself to that spot."

Again Crumb placed her hands on Dina's head. To her puzzlement, Dina's aura swelled just as before. *How bizarre*, she thought, her aura responds even to a spot with only a pale covering of Blessing. Crumb had never heard of such a thing.

Minutes passed and Dina's aura became strikingly vivid.

"Alright, that's enough. Tell me what you felt."

"Just like before, Miss Crumb. I almost fell asleep."

"You didn't sense an emptiness, a vulnerability?"

Dina could see what Miss Crumb was hoping for, and she reluctantly said, "I'm sorry, I didn't."

Crumb was at a loss. She had never seen a candidate shining with such a remarkable aura and yet feeling nothing. She continued with the procedure used for all candidates: Complete ten trials, and see whether Dina reacted differently to varying intensities of the Blessing. For two more hours they worked. Dina's aura grew splendidly on every single trial, regardless of where she was looking.

At the end of the session, Dina looked questioningly at Crumb. The Master-Keeper only smiled and led her to the door.

At lunchtime, Eliezer returned. They were not allowed to discuss the candidates until the end in order not to influence each other's assessment. Eliezer saw that Crumb was disturbed and thoughtful. Alfonso Garcia made an attempt at small talk, but finding neither Eliezer nor Crumb responsive, lapsed into silence himself.

The Verification resumed immediately after lunch, and again the candidates were called one by one.

8

Three days later the three examiners sat around a conference table in one of the Institute's reading rooms.

"A good group," Garcia said. "The only serious disappointment is Cabeza. His reaction to the Blessing is hardly noticeable.

"Indeed," Eliezer said. "The gift is much too diluted. Our woman in Mexico City—his college counselor, I believe? Obviously, she overestimated his capacities. And the others?"

"Tiplady, the Aussie, is borderline," Crumb said.

"And an arrogant little bastard," Garcia added. "I disliked being in the same room with him let alone placing my hands on him, I must say."

"On the other hand, Alexi Samsov is promising. Maria Jongsma is excellent."

Garcia nodded enthusiastically. "She is quite superb, yes. Sensitive to the slightest whiff of Blessing."

"And Dina Carlini… her aura was astounding. But…"

All three examiners had noted her magnificent aura and yet her strange insensitivity.

Eliezer frowned pensively. "What do you make of it?"

"All she needs is practice," Crumb said with conviction. "Her aura is the best I've seen in the nine years since I began as an examiner. She is simply not yet aware of what she is sensing."

"No," Eliezer said. "That may explain why she doesn't feel anything, but not why her aura reacts equally to both rich and weak areas of Blessing."

"Maybe she is extremely sensitive," Garcia suggested, "even to levels of Blessing we don't recognize. If she has had visions of Gates Ten and Eleven as Father Binino claims, who knows what she might be capable of?"

"Again, that still doesn't explain why her aura doesn't vary from sensing powerful levels of Blessing to barely any. The amount of ambient Blessing has no effect on her aura. She, my fellow examiners, is a mystery."

Menach Peprini sat in his second-floor office reflecting on the document in his hand. It was an ordinary daily report, one of many he regularly received from Keepers' headquarters around the world. In addition to being Director of Keepers' Training, he also effectively ran the Security Division. Technically, Councilor Rudolf Antioch was Director of Security, but in recent years the old man, approaching 138 years of age, had come to rely on Peprini more and more.

Peprini discreetly employed some four dozen men and women for what he called "special tasks." He had recruited them from among the more poorly performing novices and those deemed "borderline cases." The other Councilors were only vaguely aware of this group.

He left his office—the former drawing room of the Frostburg house had no windows—and stepped into the adjoining reading room. He peered out the bay window at the ten candidates on the lawn below. Their tension was evident in their movements. No doubt they knew their future was now being determined and their anxiety drew them together. It was also certain they were discussing the meaning of their experiences during the Verification: What had been the nature of the sublime feeling they had all experienced? And what had this to do with the Institute for Biblical Studies?

He noticed Eric Tiplady standing apart from the rest.   The boy was eyeing a silver Mercedes which stood in the parking lot thirty yards away. He glanced to make sure no one was looking and then moved towards the car. He circled it admiringly, took a quick look again, then opened the driver's door and got in.

Peprini grinned at the boy's nerve and made up his mind.

Later, Peprini sat behind his desk, brooding over the report of the examination team. Joanna Crumb sat opposite him.

"I approve. You will see to it that Mr. Cabeza leaves us tomorrow morning. The others will be assembled at the Novitiate tomorrow evening at six for the Rite."

"Including Tiplady?"

"Including Tiplady."

"Menach, the three of us doubt he will ever be able to discern Gate Two."

"A talented man can be used in many ways."

"And Dina Carlini? As Eliezer wrote here, she has some peculiarities. He recommended…"

"I know what Councilor Eliezer thinks," Peprini said dismissively. "Yes, including Carlini. I expect she will prove our trust."

He might have a special use for her as well, he thought. "That's all, Joanna."

9

In 634 A.D., after the Muslim conquest of the Holy Land, the surviving members of the Council of Keepers abandoned its headquarters in Jerusalem, resettling in Constantinople. For five hundred years this served them well. At the beginning of the 12th Century, the Council began thinking of a new home because of tensions between the Roman Catholic Church and the Eastern Patriarchs. Those Keepers who had sworn vows to one church were in danger from the other. The decision was made following the sacking of Constantinople by the Fourth Crusade in 1203. The Keepers needed a safer place. After much debate, they decided to look for a Benedictine abbey in Europe, mainly because each abbey was autonomous: Monks pledged devotion to a particular house and the Church rarely intruded.

They chose the Lucerne Abbey, built by the Benedictine St. Leodegar in the mid 8th Century and later given the name of St. Ignacio. A small group of Keepers swore vows in 1204. Each year saw one or two more join. As their numbers and control over the Abbey grew stronger, only *their* Keeper brothers were admitted.

During this period the Council began constructing a convent only a mile away to house the female Keepers. As nuns, they also had adopted the Benedictine rule, and Scholastica convents, an order named after the sister of St. Benedict, were found across Europe. St. Ignacio and St. Scholastica functioned as a monastery and a convent, at least in outward appearance, until the 1890's when the St. Ignacio Order broke from the Benedictines. A Keeper posing as a businessman then purchased both from the Church, together with the surrounding land. The convent was turned into the Novitiate—the home and school for Keeper novices. It was decided that novices were sufficiently advanced to be housed in the vicinity of their headquarters. The externals—candidates who had not yet passed their Verification exams—remained at the Frostburg Institute in the heart of Lucerne.

The Novitiate rested in a meadow surrounded by birch and aspen-covered hills. The medieval face of the granite-block buildings made newcomers surprised by the modern features of the interior. Keepers, despite their ancient roots, never turned away from what was new.

Master-Keeper Leo Pem sat in his office awaiting the nine new novices. The tenth candidate, Gabriel Cabeza, had been given a letter from the Frostburg Institute thanking him for his efforts and wishing him the best of luck in future endeavors.

Pem turned his head upon hearing the crunch of the gravel drive as the minibus arrived. He rose from his chair but this did little to increase his height. Barely over five feet, he had been given an exceptionally muscular body that required little effort to maintain. He considered this fair compensation for his short stature. But the Keepers' gift made all such mundane advantages and disadvantages insignificant. Being of indeterminate race, each person who examined his face concluded a different ancestry for him.

As Class-Master of the Novices, he was chiefly responsible for their training. But Menach Peprini, as Director of Keepers' Training, had the last word. Pem had always been scared of him. When as a twenty-year-old he had arrived at the Frostburg House, Menach, only a few years older, was already the Assistant Director to his father, Marcus Peprini. He could not help feeling that Menach found it distasteful to be in his company, as if he believed the little man belonged in a circus. Pem had battled this thought since he had stopped growing at age ten, and he shuddered to think what would have become of him had it not been for the Keepers. No, he was never happy to see Menach Peprini. Nevertheless, it had been Peprini's decision to appoint him as head of the Novitiate.

He returned to his desk and the novice files. Interesting, he thought, how the gift of Keepers' blood affects people in different ways. Some realize their experiences are unusual but say nothing. Some, like Jorge Pinedo, seek medical help hoping to rid themselves of the visions that made ordinary life all but impossible. His psychiatrist prescribed anti-psychotics and the result was his voluntary admission to a mental hospital in Lima, Peru. It was there that a Keeper, a physician who made the rounds of the mental hospitals in Latin America looking for such cases, recognized the cause of his trouble. Pem wondered, as he had before, how many of his kind fell into madness never understanding who they were.

Or take Natalie Norisot. Half French and half Vietnamese, she was at thirty-four the oldest novice in Pem's years at the post. She had almost escaped the Keepers' notice. It wasn't until her rich mother died without a will that the Parisian lawyer—who was also a Keeper—spotted her gift. It was impressive enough that despite her age she was summoned.

Lev Bolski was no such surprise. He had been marked by his rabbi early on, as had Nalini Sing. Her father happened to be a colleague of a university dean in Mumbai, India, who in fact was a Keeper. Indeed, each year the headquarters in Lucerne sent several graduates to cities around the globe to occupy social positions in which they could, in time, meet a large number of people, especially young ones who might possess the gift. Keeperdom was sufficiently rich and powerful to pave the road for its brothers and sisters to such central positions.

Pem's thoughts wandered to his favorite and no doubt the prize of the class, the frail Dutch Maria Jongsma. Her performance at the Verification had been exceedingly good. He chastised himself for the twinge of jealousy he felt. He had no designs on her, knowing that nothing could possibly happen between them. Rather, he was looking forward simply to being near her the coming year, living under the same roof and seeing her each day. His worry was that Peprini also had shown unusual interest in her. Last year at this same time Peprini had intervened and removed another novice, Pilar Diaz, saying he would personally train her. As a Councilor, this was his right and a great honor for the novice. But, Pem wondered, why now? In Pem's nineteen years at the Novitiate Peprini had never done this. It was obvious that both were quite attractive. But both were also exceptionally talented. Pem couldn't explain why, but he knew Peprini's interest wasn't sexual despite the whispers of gossip.

Peprini's car entered the narrow stone gates of the old convent. Dusk had settled and the bright lights in the windows appeared out of place in the medieval buildings. As he turned off the ignition, Tennier, the watchman, stepped from the shadows and opened his door.

"Good evening, Councilor."

"Thank you, Tennier. You are well?"

"Fine, sir, thank you for asking."

He closed the convent's heavy entrance door, and moments later Pem came striding on his stubby legs down the narrow hallway from the offices.

"All is prepared?" Peprini asked. He seemed to sniff the air. "This will do well," he said.

Pem was sure the Director would approve of the Blessing conditions for the ceremony but was still relieved.

"Yes, Menach. They are waiting in Founder's Hall."

Peprini turned without comment. Though the corridors had arched ceilings, he had to be mindful. The convent was built eight-hundred years ago, and parts of the original building still remained. The height of particular hallways and doorframes were such that women of 13th Century stature would have found them accommodating, but males of today had to be careful. Peprini thought again how Pem must enjoy scurrying down these halls as if they had been built for him. The doorway to the Founder's Hall was one of these legacies, and even with the stone floor worn to a shallow groove, Peprini had to dip his head to enter the small anteroom.

Their robes lay on a table. Each year Pem dreaded this moment. It was proper for him to help the Director first don his robe. But the difference in height made Pem unable to assist unless he stood on a chair, and this he refused to do (though he had never spoken of it). Peprini understood, of course, and moved away as he pulled on the burgundy silk to show no help was needed. Pem was grateful for this small gesture. He put on his own robe.

Founder's Hall, despite its grand name, was quite small. The nine novices sat together in their robes. They made a tight fit on the bench. It was not lost on them that a second bench would have made them more comfortable. They were pressed together for a reason.

Peprini and Pem stepped from the recessed doorway. All nine stood as one. Pem stopped and sat in a chair to the side, while Peprini continued until he stood in front of them. Without being told they sat down.

"You must have grasped by now that you weren't sent here to advance your scholarly pursuits. You left your family, friends, and plans because this was essential in coming to know who you are. *Who we are*. We are Keepers. You are here tonight because we have decided to invite you to join Keeperdom. We are the oldest society on Earth, having existed without interruption for four thousand years. You are here because of the blood you carry in your veins. No amount of study, no amount of faith can earn this invitation. Blood alone decides the matter.

"We have the most important duty among mankind. You glimpsed something of this during your Verification. You experienced the Blessing that God gave to Abraham, Isaac, and Jacob." Each looked as if told the answer to a riddle. "Our duty as Keepers is to protect that Blessing. That is who we are. None outside Keeperdom knows of us. And they must never know of us. Now you must make the most important decision of your life: Will you join us?" His eyes passed down the row of initiates. "If you decline, the door is forever closed to you. If you decline, you must leave now. A car is waiting outside to drive you to the city."

He smiled. "No, I am not worried you might reveal us. After all, who would believe you? Our story is quite fanciful." He turned his head malevolently. "Do you think that after four thousand years we have not thought of every manner by which we could be revealed? If you join us, you will learn that trust comes very slowly. And once you join, you may not leave us."

Peprini looked into the eyes of each, deliberately, one by one. He saw the expected fear. But it was mixed with excitement and a sense of belonging. He saw in them a newfound self-knowledge, made stronger by the luminous Blessing that gathered near them. He was confirmed in the choice of these nine. All would remain, including Carlini; despite her peculiarity, her aura was quite special. The Jongsma girl looked even paler than three days ago. He wondered whether she would be strong enough for what he had in mind. Pilar was healthier, yet the *project* (as he thought of his secret) had been very taxing on her. Perhaps he wouldn't need Maria Jongsma; perhaps he could bring his project to culmination with Pilar. But to be safe he would send for her tomorrow.

"I am very pleased. Pem?" he said, not looking. Pem appeared with a pillow of the same burgundy silk as the robes. Nine rings, each with a deep red ruby, rested on the pillow.

"Kneel," Peprini said.

10

Paris, France

Mark Gregor passed by the Georges Pompidou Museum as he had done countless times. It was only five blocks from his home, an apartment in the busy Beaubourg neighborhood of Paris. As he strolled he would hum the musical piece he was composing at the time, soon arriving at the corner of Boulevard Sébastopol, still humming, and wait with other pedestrians until the light changed. Walking was the best time for resolving difficult points in his musical compositions. As a young composer, he was under much pressure to produce.

But this evening Gregor's mind was not on his work. As he passed the museum, he noticed someone was following him. In fact, he now realized, the same footsteps had been clicking after him since he had left his apartment building. Someone was close behind, though he had to admit, not unusually so. He reminded himself that this was nothing odd in a crowded city, but couldn't deny his anxiety.

He turned and their eyes met. The man stared at him. He wore a tan suit that was soiled and wrinkled. His face was unshaven, his hair disheveled. There was something almost marionette-like about his posture. But it wasn't his appearance that unnerved Gregor. It was his eyes: the man's eyes were vacant, with no person behind them. Yet, Gregor believed he could see the man's single-minded purpose was to follow him. Or worse. He hurried his pace and the man kept up. His anxiety now turned into a visceral revulsion. He felt a feverish chill; his face and dark-blonde hair were already damp with sweat, and he wiped his face with his sleeve.

Traffic was heavy and he had to stop at the intersection of Boulevard Sébastopol. The shabby man followed and stood close by, still staring.

Behind him, he noticed two familiar faces. Since moving to the neighborhood he had often seen these two and several others like them. He imagined they were police or perhaps bodyguards of diplomats who lived in the area. For a moment he thought of enlisting their help, only to realize how foolish he would sound. After all, nothing had happened.

In some strange way, the shabby man made him feel exposed, as if a shield he had possessed all his life was gone. A sense of vulnerability choked him. The light turned green. Gregor hesitated and then leaped into the road. From the corner of his eye he saw his pursuer had not moved. Gregor smiled, almost giddily relieved, and then felt struck across the legs. He felt no pain but heard the *whump* of the collision, then screeching tires, then a thump as he landed on the concrete.

Time moved very slowly. His body no longer felt his. He remembered the face of the dingy man and wished it would go away. He heard shrieks around him. Above the voices, someone called his name. With great effort he opened his eyes for a moment. It was one of the "policemen" stooping over him. How does he know my name? The man's voice was shocked and full of dread. He cares about me, Gregor realized, as if he's always known me. *How strange; how strange…*

People gathered around the body, unable to take their eyes off the unnatural tangle of limbs. The man instructed everyone to stand back while another knelt beside the body and looked for a pulse. Then both men stopped what they were doing. They stared at the body but their eyes were glazed, their faces knotted in concentration.

"Do you see it?" said the one kneeling.

The other was entranced. "It's dying out," he murmured. "It's almost gone."

Moments later the two men came to, as if awakening. The younger one again searched for a pulse, refusing to believe what was obvious.

He stood up. "*The Vessel is dead*," he said with disbelief.

"*Keep your voice down*," the other whispered. "We need to call an ambulance. We have to be certain."

"Emil, he terminated!"

"*Keep your voice down*."

Half an hour later in a nearby hospital, a doctor formally pronounced Gregor's death. Emil Cordon put his hand on his friend's shoulder and shook it gently.

"LaPointe, we can't wait any longer. We have to report this."

"Do we call Master-Keeper Boudwain?"

"You do that. I'm going to call Lucerne and ask for Councilor Erna."

It was impossible. It… it simply could not be. Julia Erna's fingers tightened around the phone.

"Councilor Erna?"

Vessel's Wyatt injury three weeks ago was improbable enough, but this now... How can a Vessel of the Blessing die in a car accident? This couldn't be happening. She put both elbows on her desk and prepared herself.

"Tell me again."

"Vessel Gregor terminated. God help us... His Blessing went away with him."

"Yes," she murmured. "I heard you." How odd, on such an ordinary day. The Blessing has been quite pleasant today—the reverberations from his death haven't reached us yet.

"Councilor Erna, are you still there?"

"You realize what you're saying?" she said harshly. "Terminated means not just that he died, but that he died while possessing his inheritance: the Blessing! A Vessel dying before passing it on to his child... Listen carefully. There must be no doubt, none whatsoever, do you understand?"

"Of course I know that." Cordon was still shaken, otherwise he never would have spoken this way to her.

"You were the two Keepers responsible this morning for the Vessel, correct?"

"Yes, but...."

"If there has been a... lapse in your duty we must know. If you lost track of him for a time... no one will be angry with you. But nothing can be hidden, nothing else matters right now. Is there anything you need to tell me? Emil?"

"There was something strange around him, not the usual aura." She could hear him search for the words. "I mean, his Blessing was there, but he was surrounded by... a cloud of emptiness, I don't know how else to describe it. It made me sick to my stomach. LaPointe too, but... we didn't know what to do, and... then the car hit him. He died a few minutes later. But before that we...."

"Yes?"

"We saw the Blessing dying out." His voice was reverential. He waited but the other end of the line was silent. "It trembled in him for a minute..."

"Emil?"

"And then it was gone. He was just a body. LaPointe saw it too."

"Then it's true."

"Councilor Erna, I don't know how it could have been prevented. He stepped off the curb without looking and the car came out of nowhere."

"Listen to me carefully." She had more important duties right now but she couldn't help consoling him. "To witness a Vessel die with the Blessing... You have endured what very few Keepers ever have. I know you will feel responsible, and the guilt may become overwhelming." Even as she said this she wondered if she could withstand that burden. "Be strong."

"Yes."

"And return to Lucerne, all of you, as quickly as possible."

Erna put down the phone. First Vessel Wyatt's injury, and now Vessel Gregor's termination. Two impossible events three weeks apart. There must be some connection. Is it possible that the Blessing no longer protects them? She stood, slipping on her shoes, adjusting her dress and moving her hair, gray and just below the neck, away from the collar of the dress in a habitual motion. She removed her glasses, rubbed her eyes, and replaced them.

Her eyes were caught by two junior Keepers, both women, working in the flower garden outside the south window of the Rare Book Company building. They smiled and shared something funny. She felt sorry for them to have this happen at their beginning, when all was new. But then, in this regard they were all innocent.

She recalled her own arrival at the Frostburg House some fifty years ago. Having just returned from a summer vacation at her parents' home in Buenos Aires, Argentina, she made her first crucial step into the Keepers' world. Menach Peprini's grandfather, Alberto Peprini, then the school's head, welcomed her class. His stern words made it clear that Keeperdom would demand total devotion. But young Erna, having been given a strict Austrian education—her parents had emigrated from Vienna to Argentina during the Depression—was not afraid of discipline. It was on that day that she realized that in some deep, mysterious way she belonged to this world, not from choice but because of the ancient blood in her veins. She was not entering a new world but returning to her oldest home.

She had understood the sacrifice demanded of her, and this she accepted joyfully. Several years later she had become romantically involved with Eliezer. Eventually she agreed with him, though with more pain and reluctance than he displayed, to give up their romantic relationship for the sake of the deeper commitment to Keeperdom. She quickly advanced to the rank of Master-Keeper, faster than Eliezer, and when she became a Councilor, twenty-five years ago, she could not conceive of her life apart from Keeperdom. She no longer belonged to herself. She was a Councilor, a member of the governing body which controlled and directed the lives of the four-hundred or so Keepers around the world, and which watched over the five remaining Vessels—and through them the lives of all humanity. When she was offered the position of Head of the Council, she accepted matter-of-factly. She thought she was prepared for every imaginable challenge, but she could not have foreseen the death of a Vessel of the Blessing.

11

Peprini had left the hall after the ceremony. Pem, now more relaxed and cheerful, looked at the nine new novices as they congratulated one another and speculated what was to come. They hardly noticed the aristocratic middle-aged woman who entered. He stood and motioned to them to take their seats.

"For the past week," announced the Novice-Master, "you have been candidates, and as candidates you were unaware of the true reason you were summoned here. Now the time has come. In accordance with tradition, we will mark the beginning of your year-long novitiate with an opening lecture by a most distinguished Keeper. Today I am honored to introduce Councilor Theresa Fournier."

The Novice-Master grinned. "Don't worry, you will soon know what a Councilor is. At the moment let me say the Council is the governing body of all Keepers around the globe. Councilor Theresa Fournier is also the mother superior of an important convent in Colombia, South America. It is a great honor to have her with us."

"Thank you, Pem. Sit," she said to the students, obviously used to giving commands.

She stepped down from the altar and Pem brought her a chair. She did not take her eyes off them as she smoothed her long dark skirt and sat. Her erect posture, her bony face, and regal bearing made for an imposing presence. The nine moved uncomfortably on the bench as they were pierced by her gray eyes. She had been told this group was unusual. One of them, Maria Jongsma, the Dutch girl, exhibited some remarkable talents. Another, Dina Carlini, had an exceptional though peculiar aura. Two or three others were also promising. The others were average but solid.

"No doubt you have many questions. In due time you will learn the answers. Today I will reveal to you four secrets—you have proven yourselves worthy of them. These are the secret of the Bible, the secret of the Blessing, the secret of the Vessels, and the secret of the Keepers.

"Here is the first: The Bible—I mean here the Book of Genesis—is not just a book. It is certainly not a myth. *The Bible is a reality*. It is a reality not just as an account of the past. It is a reality right now, in the present, every moment. I don't mean that every element in the story of Genesis is *literally* true—certain events are metaphors, but as metaphors they reflect a reality that exists here and now. That is why the book has always been regarded as holy even by those ignorant of this secret.

"From this follows the second secret: If the Bible is a reality, then the Blessing that the Bible talks about is a reality too. Because like everything else in Genesis, the Blessing is not an event in the past. The Biblical Blessing flows to our world every moment. This very moment. Thanks to it the world flourishes and manages to avoid all kinds of potential threats— disasters and plagues and mishaps we know not what. Without it, humanity would quickly die out."

Fournier paused and let her words sink in. "But how does the Blessing flow into our world? Through what channels does it come to us? How does it pass from its Biblical source into our lives? The answer is the third secret: The Blessing comes to humanity through the Vessels."

Fournier's voice grew fuller and stronger. "Four thousand years ago God blessed Abraham, his son Isaac and his grandson Jacob—for the sake of humanity. As the Bible says: *In you will all the families of the Earth be blessed*. These individuals served as the channels through which the Blessing flowed into our world. They were the Vessels of the Blessing for the Earth.

"If you know your Bible, you know that God blesses them exactly twelve times. He blesses Abraham five times, Isaac—four times, and Jacob—three times. Twelve Blessings altogether. We Keepers call these the Twelve Gates. These are the twelve Biblical passages that reveal God's Blessing to the Patriarchs. These are the twelve points in the Bible World from which God's Blessing flows to our world."

She stood and wrote on the blackboard off to the side:

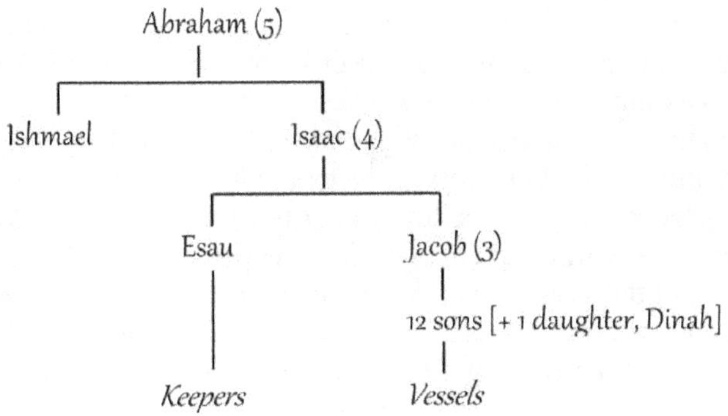

"Ms. Jongsma, I believe. You appear to have a question."

Maria started. "Well, in fact I do, Councilor. What happened after these Patriarchs—these Vessels—died? The book of Genesis doesn't mention God blessing anyone else after this, I think."

"You are right. The twelve blessings to Abraham's family are God's only blessings to humanity. The gift of Vesselship passed from Abraham to his son Isaac, then to Isaac's son Jacob, and so on."

"So, after the last of the Patriarchs died, the gift…"

"When Jacob died, the gift passed to his twelve sons. It split into twelve portions. These were the forefathers of the twelve tribes of Israel. But only we Keepers know these twelve sons had a much greater mission: to serve as Vessels. Indeed, these twelve were the forefathers of all future Vessels. *Because from then on the gift of Vesselship never split again.* It passed from mother or father to only one child. That is why there are exactly twelve Vessels, twelve channels of the Blessing that pass from parent to child through the generations, and who maintain God's Blessing to the entire world."

She paused and then added quietly, "*At most* twelve. Because a lineage can die out. If a Vessel dies before passing on the Blessing to a child—or 'terminates' as we call it—then…"

There was silence in the room. Fournier smiled wryly. "Some Vessel lineages did indeed end, but enough remain: five to be exact. Our world still flourishes."

"Are we these Vessels?" asked Natalie Norisot, who immediately recoiled at her own impertinence. "I mean… our gift… But we can't be… we are too many."

Fournier nodded. "Keepers are one thing and Vessels another. Of course, we too are children of Abraham and of his son Isaac. But we are not children of Jacob. We belong to a different lineage, a no less important lineage! We are the descendants of Jacob's older brother, Esau. But the gift of Vesselship passed from Isaac to Jacob, not to Esau."

She raised her head and declared proudly. "We Keepers are the children of Esau. You will remember Genesis Chapter 26. The Blessing was supposed to go to Esau—to us. But Jacob tricked his father Isaac and took the Blessing for himself."

Fournier had explained the magnitude of Jacob's trickery on numerous occasions but still felt bitterness at the loss of her birthright.

"We Keepers carry only a little bit of the gift in our blood. Not enough to maintain the world, but enough for some powers nonetheless; enough to take care of the Vessels and ensure the Vessels serve as channels for the Blessing. Our mission is of absolute importance. Because the people who are Vessels don't know they are Vessels. They don't know that the well-being of the entire world depends on them. Vessels are like innocent children. It is our job to take care of them—without letting them notice it. So this is the fourth and last secret for you today: It is the Keepers' job to watch over the Vessels, to care for these extraordinary children.

Fournier sighed. Another generation of Keepers who will work arduously all their lives for the good of humanity without recognition. The world will continue to laud politicians, generals, businessmen, movie stars, Church leaders—without ever suspecting that the real figures who sustain the world and make it flourish are those handful of men and women who will live and work and die in anonymity.

"You are novices now," she said quietly. "Now that you have been accepted into Keeperdom you are entitled to ask questions."

Alexi Samsov was quick to respond. "So what exactly are Keepers supposed to do? How do we make sure that the Vessels act as channels for the Blessing?"

"A very good question. The short answer is: we discern. By discerning the twelve Blessing passages in Genesis—the Twelve Gates—we ensure that the Vessels reach those sources of the Blessing. But," she added with a stiff smile, "don't ask me more about discernment. That's the fifth secret, and I promised you only four. I'll leave it for your teachers to tell you."

Maria Jongsma raised her hand. "Councilor Fournier, you didn't mention God's Blessing to Adam and Eve."

Fournier looked at the slender girl with kind eyes, enjoying the special qualities of the girl's aura. "We don't know what the world was like before Abraham. Abraham appears in Genesis Chapter 12, but the first eleven chapters of the Bible are a mystery to us. We can't visualize them."

"But… what about the stories in those chapters—the Creation, Adam and Eve, Cain and Abel, Noah's Ark?"

"No one is certain how to understand them. Most of us believe they are symbolic, that they symbolize millions of years of human evolution. You see, before Abraham the Blessing came to Earth in a different way, not through the Vessels but directly upon all creatures. This primordial kind of Blessing—what the Bible describes as God's Blessing to Adam and Eve at the world's creation—is much too powerful for any Keeper to discern. We call it the Primordial Gate. It is out of bounds for us. Even what the Bible describes as Noah's Blessing is beyond us."

Fournier examined Maria Jongsma's face. "But you have another question?"

"And God's Blessing to Ishmael?"

"Oh, yes, Ishmael," Fournier replied airily. "He was indeed Abraham's son but his mother was only a maid. Naturally, he didn't inherit from his father…"

The door to the hall flung open. A man stood in the doorway. Fournier's eyes narrowed disapprovingly.

"What is it, Masking?" she asked sternly.

"Councilor Erna needs to see you at once."

12

Peprini just passed through the Frostburg House gates when Johan Stahlburg came running, as best the old man could, up to the car.

"Menach." The old Finn licked his lips as he gathered himself to speak. "I'm sorry, I've tried but you haven't answered your phone."

Peprini sensed bad news and disliked waiting for it. "What is it, Johan?"

"Councilor Erna telephoned."

"Well?"

"Vessel Mark Gregor has terminated." Stahlburg could read his eyes. "Yes, that's what she said."

"Are we certain?" He didn't expect a Keeper of his rank to be informed, but he asked nevertheless.

"I overheard her saying there is no doubt." Stahlburg didn't see the reaction he expected. Instead of horror or grief, Peprini appeared as if just given a puzzle to solve. As the Councilor turned the car around, the old Finn believed he would never understand the man.

For the second time that evening Peprini drove through town, and once over the bridge the car began the climb toward the Abbey and Rare Book Company. Raising his eyes to the evening sky, he thought he could detect an attenuation of the Blessing's luminosity, though he couldn't be sure if this was only part of the normal fluctuation. He decided not to phone Councilor Erna, nor think about Gregor's death in the absence of any other information. It would be an exercise in discipline. Still, an anxiety started to grow in him.

Soon the Abbey's orchard on the south hillside appeared in the moonlight. The rich smell of ripening apples wafted through the car in the cool air. Unexpectedly he found himself becoming nostalgic. How long had it been since he had looked closely at the Abbey? He realized how little the grounds around the monastery had changed since he had been a boy. The trees were taller, and that was about all. The Abbey had been built to last centuries and the stone walls and slate roof showed no wear he could see.

This time at the fork he took the turn towards the Abbey. A short distance and he was in the courtyard. As he parked the car Theresa Fournier emerged from the building. Peprini stepped out expecting a greeting but Fournier only shook her head in resignation.

He turned his back to the Abbey and strode across the courtyard to the Rare Book Company Building.

Julia Erna was standing by the bay window of her office when Peprini entered.

"How did it happen?"

"A car accident." She went through the questions and answers with him as she just had with Theresa Fournier and several others. This required no effort of patience and she understood this was because she hadn't yet accepted the death.

"I want his minders here. Immediately."

"I've already ordered them to return."

He picked up the phone on her desk and entered a number.

"Just listen. You and five others will go to Paris tonight... I don't care. Just make sure they're all experienced with the Blessing surrounding a Vessel. I'll have copies of the latest field reports e-mailed to you... Yes, Gregor. Be quiet and pay attention. Go over his life. Look to every woman with whom he's been for more than passing contact. The reports will provide names and addresses... That's right. You are looking for any trace of the Blessing that might have passed from Gregor to his child... Perhaps, but more likely the Paris team was sloppy and missed its passing. You will act on the assumption that Gregor passed it to someone and you are to find that someone."

He put down the phone.

"You sounded convincing."

"They must be made to believe there's a chance. It's a fool's errand but must be done. The interesting job will be questioning LaPointe and Cordon."

He turned and left her office, going just down the hall to his own. She followed.

"You doubt them?"

"Does it matter? As responsible for security, Julia, I must question them regardless. Just as I questioned our New York team after Vessel Wyatt's injury."

"Are you saying there is some connection between Wyatt's injury in New York and Gregor's termination in Paris?"

"That is one thing I would like to know. And that is why I must interrogate LaPointe and Cordon."

"Interrogate? Menach, really. We are Keepers, not..."

"Inquisitors? It's you who must remember who we are. Are we not obligated to be utterly certain of its loss?"

"Alright. You and Albrecht may interview them."

"I will handle what needs to be done. Were the Council to meet this task would no doubt fall to me anyway."

Erna wasn't fazed by his reminder that her position as President was mostly titular. "I said interview, Menach, not interrogate. I don't want you brutalizing them. They've been through enough already."

He sat down at his desk, then looked up as if asking why she was still there.

"I want to see them when they arrive, Menach. Before you question them."

She closed the door. Peprini leaned back in his chair, taking in the silence of the room. His eyes were drawn to two photographs on the desk. He picked up the one showing an old man, a younger man, and an adolescent boy. His grandfather, his father, and himself. The three stood proudly in front of the Abbey, as if it were their ancestral home and they aristocracy. In a way, it was true. His father had been a Councilor before him, his grandfather also a Councilor as well as the second chairman of the Lucerne Rare Book Company.

Like his father before him, Menach did not undergo the traditional training of a novice. Both were perceived to have the gift of discernment when very young, and they had been trained by their fathers. This had been a violation in the case of young Marcus Peprini, Menach's father. But both Menach's grandfather and father were Councilors when Menach was born, and so it was permissible to begin training him as a small boy once it was established he possessed the gift.

Menach grew up never doubting he would be a member of the Council. It was virtually his birthright. He was also led to believe that because he was a third-generation Keeper—the only one known ever to exist—his gift, his power, was superior. Of course, this wasn't true; power is what it can do, no more, no less. Further, he had developed his ability to its fullest by the time he reached adulthood. While impressive and enough to earn him a place on the Council, it held no more promise. Most Keepers, having learned of their gift as adults, were still developing it, still had a curiosity and some even a passion for it. These qualities had been exhausted in Menach by his eighteenth birthday. He was envious of those yet to reach their potential even as he was irritated with them for not having done this by now.

He set the picture down next to its pair, this one of his wife and two children. The boy and girl had been disappointments. Neither possessed the power of discernment, neither would be Keepers. When it had become evident they were ordinary, Menach had cursed himself. In time he stopped blaming himself and concluded it must have been his wife's fault. His own blood was too pure to have failed; there had to be something about his wife's blood that blocked the passage of the gift. Years ago he had thought of divorcing his wife and remarrying in hopes of producing a child with the gift. But he knew he never would.

He went over to the bookcase and pulled out a thick binder. It contained photocopies of excerpts from the *Chronicles*, the Keepers' vast inventory of historical documents. He flipped through the pages and stopped at 1241-1242 B.C., shortly after the death of Jason of Padua, the sixth Vessel to terminate. The pages were in Latin, which, despite the fading ink, he could decipher with ease. Though he had read these passages many times years ago, a phrase now grabbed his attention: *...tamper with the sacred rules of discernment.*

It was minutes from the second Council meeting after Jason's death. The paragraph read: *Councilwoman Mother Agnus: A tragedy strikes only those who deserve it. The sin of arrogance is prevalent amongst us. Let us humbly remember that we are servants of the Blessing and that it is not for us to tamper with the sacred ways of discernment, nor to inquire about its secrets. We must in perfect faith follow the ways of our devout ancestors.*

"Superstition," he said. But something inside him remained unsettled. A worry had been nagging him since Gregor's death. Would Mother Agnus say, he wondered, that I have tampered with the sacred rules of discernment?

He scoffed, but at the same time was annoyed to sense a pang of guilt pecking at him.

The pages with the earliest date held a special fascination for him, as they did all Keepers. It was the earliest story he could remember his father telling him as a child, a story he was never permitted to tell his own son and daughter.

FROM THE CHRONICLES OF THE KEEPERS

Thebes, Egypt, the third year of the rule of Pharaoh Siamun
1014 years since the death of Abraham (s.d.A)
Recorded by Keeper Setnakht, servant of Vessel Intef

The fourth day of the month of Kahrka

My master Intef is getting weaker. Today the physician checked his symptoms and consulted the sacred books and prayed for an answer, but none came. All know this is a bad sign. The children want this kept secret from Intef. Tiaa, Kyenebu, Meketaten, and Mentuhotep take turns sitting at his bedside. Only I know that their father cannot die yet, not until he has passed on the Blessing. There are twelve Vessels in the world, twelve who are descendants of the twelve sons of Jacob, twelve lines of Blessing, and this number has never changed, nor will it ever change. Everyone in the household looks to me for strength.

The ninth day of the month of Kahrka

Vessel Intef's illness has worsened. Strong and vital, rarely in his life has he been even slightly ill, let alone confined to bed. Nedjem, my younger brother in Keeperdom, has been silent, but I believe he thinks as I do. Could Intef die? Just to write this seems a heresy. Intef still holds the Blessing, and so we have not believed it possible for him to die, not yet. But the unquestioned certainty I once had is gone. Perhaps it is seeing the change in Intef. He has lost a hundred deben of weight since the beginning of the season. If illness can ravage him thusly, can it not kill him? But even as I write this I cannot make myself believe he will die. One thousand years of history say it cannot happen.

The fourteenth day of the month of Kahrka

I have sent Keeper Nedjem to the Council in Jerusalem with a message about Vessel Intef's condition. The roads through the desert to Jerusalem should be safe, as there is peace between our pharaoh and King Solomon of Israel. At first I considered waiting for the Council's regular courier, who is scheduled to arrive in thirty days, but I worry the matter cannot wait.

Today I gave some food to the deformed beggar who is sitting in the street outside the house. I did this for the health of the Vessel. Am I losing my faith in the power of the Blessing, that I try to sustain it with the power of charity?

The twenty-ninth day of the month of Kahrka

Keeper Nedjem must already be on his way back to Thebes. I pray that the Council did not delay. What are we to do should the Vessel Intef die? It cannot be possible that the Blessing of Levi's line could end with him. No line has ever died. Yet one cannot deny what is before one's eyes.

The first day of the month of Ta'b

None of the Vessel's children carry the Blessing. Nor has he fathered another child. I have been his servant since he was a boy. He has rarely been out of my sight. And our town is not so large that a girl can be with child and go unnoticed. None have left our town without me observing whether they carry Intef's child. But these cautions have been needless: How could another possess the Blessing when it is plain to both Keeper Nedjem and me that Vessel Intef himself still has it? No, no mistake has been made. Intef is dying and he has not passed on the gift.

Two more deformed beggars sit outside the house. They sit there all day as if knowing that something is to happen. I give them a piece of bread every morning as an offering for the Vessel's health. I approach these nauseating wretches willfully, as an act of purification or self-castigation.

The third day of the month of Ta'b

The physician treats Intef but nothing helps. He has not told the children or me, but I can feel that he believes Intef will die soon. The children go to the temples and give money to the priests to pray to Amun and Osiris and Ra. I accompany them, although I pray only to our one Father. Tiaa, the oldest, thanks me for my prayers. My faith gives her faith, she tells me with tears in her eyes. I wish I could tell her the source of my strength and share it with her.

The sixth day of the month of Ta'b

Vessel Intef is being eaten alive by something in his body. His once-powerful arms and hands now lie on the bed without life, the bones jutting against the skin. His neck is only sinews and skin draped over the spine. He is more like a skeleton each day. Though none have told him, I can see he believes he will die. Earlier this evening he took my hand, the two of us alone, and told me he was releasing me. I have told Kyenebu of this, he said. Upon my death, you are free. He managed a smile and then added, but you know you have been free to leave whenever you wished.

I know that, Intef. My place has always been by your side.

I hope, though I cannot ask, that you will stay and watch over the children. You are an uncle to them. Just as you have been a brother to me.

My eyes began to tear. Intef, I said, you cannot die, not yet. God—the gods— would not permit this.

I am ready, he murmurs.

But not you, not yet.

The children are grown, he has seen grandchildren born, he has buried his wife. I fear he has accepted that he will die and no longer fights. If I told him who he truly was would he so willingly surrender? When will Nedjem return with news from the Council? I know Intef would fight to live if he knew who he was, what he was, what he meant not just to his family but to the entire world. Soon I will have to decide.

The seventh day of the month of Ta'b

Vessel Intef spent the morning saying goodbye to his children and grandchildren. At times he made all but me leave the room. The pain was awful and he did not wish his family to witness this, though the sound of his screams could not be hidden. His cheerful acceptance of what fate has placed upon him has always been most admirable. But now it does him harm. It does the world harm.

The ninth day of the month of Ta'b

Nedjem returned this afternoon. He was delayed because the Council deliberated long over what to do. Their message reads:

"A Vessel cannot die without first passing on the Blessing to a son or daughter. This has never happened for a thousand years since the twelve sons of Jacob, and we trust will never happen. Do not leave the bed of Intef. You or Nedjem must watch him every moment. You must observe carefully the moment of death and where the Blessing goes as it leaves his body. Watch carefully Tiaa, Kyenebu, Meketaten, and Mentuhotep. One of them, or their children, may be the next Vessel. Do not despair."

The letter continues to say that it is a mystery how the Blessing is passed from parent to child, and then raises some speculations. But these speculations are of little interest to me. My fingers take some courage from the sight and feel of the red stamp of the Council. But what if they are wrong?

The eleventh day of the month of Ta'b

Vessel Intef, son of Tiy, died this morning a short time after sunrise. Kyenebu, Nedjem, and I watched as his last breath left him. The Blessing was present as it had been his entire life, and as I watched him breathe his last till the Blessing was no more. It departed him as did his breath, which slowly left his chest. It was present for a long moment, then it was not. Both Nedjem and I looked about the room for It as one does for the soul of the one who has just died. And while I could still feel Intef's Ka, the presence of his soul, It was no more. It was heartbreaking to feel the essence of Intef without the Blessing.

Frantically Nedjem and I examined the children and the grandchildren. But it was plain that none of them received the Blessing after It departed Intef. How could that possibly be? My heart bleeds and I cannot write anymore.

The thirteenth day of the month of Ta'b

I spend many hours on the roof of the house, watching the sky. The Blessing in the air is pale as it never has been. And the world reacts to the dwindling Blessing. Fire broke out in the governor's palace, not three blocks from here, and destroyed a dozen houses. The horses in the king's stables broke loose and are trotting in the streets. Part of the bank of the Nile River has collapsed into the river, and scores of people drowned. The beggars have left the gate of the house and disappeared.

I have no doubt that all this is the result of Intef's death and the death of his Blessing. How will humanity continue to live with only eleven Vessels to protect them? What is the meaning of my being a Keeper, and of my life, now that Intef is dead and his Blessing with him?

13

Jerusalem, Israel

Professor Eliezer had four hours of sleep on his flight from Switzerland to Israel, which was all he needed per night. At nine in the morning he exited the international terminal of Ben Gurion Airport outside Tel Aviv. On the drive to Jerusalem, he decided to go straight to his office.

The semester at the Hebrew University of Jerusalem was about to begin, and he made his way to the Biblical Studies Department through clogs of students. The moment he opened the door to his office, the phone rang.

"Eli, you're not answering your phone. Erna sounded uncommonly agitated.

"Julia, hello. I apologize for not seeing you yesterday. Classes are starting and I'm behind…"

"It's not that. Something terrible happened last night. I can't talk, this isn't a protected line. Listen to your messages. I wanted you to know before the rest." She hung up.

Eliezer reached for his cellular. The message he retrieved was brief: "Eli, Vessel Mark Gregor has terminated. We will meet here as soon as the Council can assemble. May the Blessing be with us now more than ever."

Eliezer replayed the message, staring at his hands. "It's a different world now," he finally whispered. He gazed intently through the window. The Blessing was still full and pleasantly vibrant, but he knew this state would not last for long.

Not thirty steps away a young woman entered the Biblical Studies Department. The other students gathered in the hallway paid her special attention. She was slim and her hair a dark gold, and her face was certainly pretty. But it was not her beauty that attracted those around her, men and women alike. It was a vibrancy of a sort they couldn't have described. Several pairs of eyes followed her into the Department office.

"My name is Osnat Aviv," she said to the secretary. "I'd like to take some Bible courses this semester."

"You are not a Biblical Studies major, are you?"

"No. I'm afraid I haven't yet registered this semester."

Until today Osnat had little interest in college. Since finishing her mandatory military service seven years ago, at the age of twenty, she had been drifting. She had traveled to India, like many young Israelis, and then to Brazil. Several odd jobs had passed the time upon her return to Israel. Her father, a prominent businessman and widower living in an affluent neighborhood in Mevaseret-Zion, just outside Jerusalem, had pressured her to enroll. "Anything, just pick something," he begged her. "It's time, Osnat, to do something serious with your life." But she kept replying she was not ready. She would not go to university or embark on any project without first knowing this was her vocation. "Self-indulgent nonsense," he answered. "If I'd done that I would still be living in the slums of Katamonim."

But this morning she had awakened with a painful anxiety as if something terrible had happened. As she lay in bed wondering, she was engulfed by a sense of urgency she had never experienced. Her father was right: It was time to get serious. The time had come to study, to find a vocation.

She did not understand this conviction that now filled her, nor the sense of earnestness that accompanied it, but she complied and took a bus to the Mount Scopus campus of Hebrew University. There she wandered the corridors of the gigantic Humanities Building until she saw the words "Biblical Studies Department." She followed the sign upstairs. Why she did all this she couldn't have explained.

The secretary shook her head. "I'm sorry, Miss, but it's much too late to apply for this program."

"But I must."

After many years the secretary was immune to students' pitiful pleas, but the purpose in this young woman's eyes was different. "Then you take the courses you want as an outside student. But I can't guarantee this would count towards your degree. This will depend…"

"Fine."

"You will have to pay as an outside student…"

"I'll pay. Can you sign me up, then?"

"First, you'll need the professor's written permission. Which courses were you thinking of taking?"

"I haven't really thought about it yet. Which ones are you offering?"

The woman looked at the line of students trailing into the corridor and found her patience wearing. "Professor Eliezer is in his office. The second one down and to the left." She pointed over Osnat's shoulder. "Why don't you start with him? He is giving 'The Family in the Ancient World.' Ask him to sign this form then bring it back to me."

"Come in," Professor Eliezer said, not looking up from his work.

Osnat opened the door, and with the sight of Eliezer her feeling of anxious urgency began to subside as if she had arrived at her destination.

"I'd like permission to enroll in your course, please?" Somehow she knew his would be the only class she would need to take.

He signed the form and waited for her to leave.

14

Oleander—or Brother William as everyone in the monastery called him—entered his cell, placed a small "Let there be peace" cardboard sign on his door, and bolted it behind him. The monks who passed softened their steps but barely glanced at the sign. They were accustomed to Brother Oleander's regular retreats. Every Tuesday evening he would disappear into his room, see no one and eat nothing, until emerging the next day for the community's Morning Prayer. This was unusual. The St. Raphael monastery belonged to a strict contemplative order. Monks were expected to participate in all communal activities. But the monks knew that Brother Oleander's retreats had received the abbot's blessing, which meant there had to be very good reason.

No one complained. He had made the monastery's chocolate factory successful. He had turned their products into a coveted delicacy in now thirty-seven countries, transforming a hapless monastery into an affluent monastic center. The new central heating system, the large modernized kitchen, the new roof, the air-conditioned library and lounge, as well as the visitors' guest cottages, all were a consequence of the monastery's business success. They saw his retreats as necessary, given his work as the monastery's business manager. After the daily distractions of his managerial work Oleander needed time to regain his inner silence. Of course, Oleander couldn't reveal that discernment was the reason for his solitude. None knew he was a Keeper. They didn't know Keepers existed.

Oleander was grateful to them too. It was with this community that he could satisfy his religious needs and lead a life of prayer, something not found in his life as a Keeper.

Since having become a Keeper fifteen years ago at the age of twenty-three, he never missed his weekly discernment session. His ardent devotion to Keeperdom hadn't diminished since that day. He never forgot it was Eliezer who had rescued him from the purposeless life he had been leading, recognizing his gift. Having been born to a poor, hard-working single mother on Chicago's Southside, and having grown up on the edge of the world of crime and gangs, he didn't take for granted the sanctuary his life as a Keeper offered.

In fact, Oleander believed the path that had led him to Keeperdom was no coincidence. At twenty-one, he happened upon a robbery in his neighborhood. An urge to rescue the old man landed him in a fight. He won, but his attacker lost an eye from the beating Oleander gave him. This shook his soul and led him to God. His parish priest took him to a Trappist monastery where the young candidate became enamored with the monastic life. The abbot, however, disliked him—young Oleander seemed too aloof and self-sufficient, and too handsome—and sent him away. Oleander tried again at St. Raphael, his current monastery. And strangely, a few months later the abbot suggested he take a leave of absence and attend theology classes at Cornell University. Professor Eliezer happened to be there on sabbatical from the Hebrew University. He recognized Oleander's gift and convinced him that the monastic life and Keeperdom did not conflict. All these events, Oleander believed, had been too improbable. Divine providence had led him to the Keepers, and he was determined to fulfill his responsibility. He regarded discernment as his foremost duty.

Oleander sat in a straight-backed wooden chair. He breathed deeply, calming his mind. He was an experienced Keeper but even he couldn't plunge into discernment directly from the day's turmoil. The past few days had been especially tumultuous, and not only because of his meeting with Eliezer in London. He had been working day and night to establish a chocolate factory in Western Africa—as much to benefit the local community as the monastery. Yet the question of postponing his discernment never arose in his mind.

He closed his eyes and allowed his mind and body to uncoil. Gradually the clamor of his thoughts subsided, replaced by a deep stillness. And then, finally, the strange sensation he knew so well—a sinking feeling as if the elevator began falling, the descent to his own Inner Depths.

His body remained still but spiritually he was moving elsewhere. Slowly he descended until he reached the bottom of his Inner Depths. A familiar space opened around him. He was now hovering like a fish in a dark aquarium. A narrow, featureless tunnel opened before him. This was the entryway leading to the realm of Depths that underlay the world of everyday appearances.

He shuffled his mental weight, improving his balance, and was now ready to move from the corridor to the edge of the Void, that empty vastness which the first chapter of the Genesis calls "Tohu va-Vohu" and which separated the Earth from the Bible World. He formed in his imagination a crucifix and said the short prayer he always spoke before continuing. It was not part of the standard Keeper's preparation for discernment. Keepers came in all kinds of creeds and were not committed to any religious ritual or prayer.

He started gliding through the narrow entryway. It opened and he emerged on the beach-like stretch of a featureless plain. Beyond it loomed darkness, an ocean of nothingness: the Great Void. He stopped at the edge. As a Keeper, he could go no further. None but a Vessel could enter this emptiness and survive. The vast expanse seemed empty and foreboding as always, and the Bible World appeared no larger than a small moon far away.

His mind returned to the Bible—he was ready to discern one of God's twelve blessings to humanity described in the Book of Genesis, or what Keepers called "the Twelve Gates of the Blessing." He recalled Eliezer's words to him many years ago: *"The Keepers' task is to discern these twelve Gates. This is the main reason we Keepers exist. In some way we no longer understand, our discerning keeps them functioning. We don't know many things our ancestors knew, but this is certain: It is thanks to our discernment that the Vessels can cross the Great Void and bring the Blessing from the Bible to the world. Do you understand the magnitude of our responsibility? And the honor?"*

Oleander turned his mind to the Book of Genesis, Chapter 22, to God's fourth Blessing to Abraham's family. It was his custom to discern a different Gate every week in a fixed twelve-week cycle from the first and easiest Gate to the last and most difficult. Other Keepers preferred alternating easy and difficult Gates, or picking a different one each time to fit their moods. Some burnt-out Keepers always found excuses to avoid difficult Gates, exploiting the Council's instruction to remain within the boundaries of their capacities. Discernment, after all, was a dangerous business, and deaths had occurred. But Oleander cherished systematic order and put duty above his moods.

He started each cycle with the first Gate, God's blessing to Abraham in Genesis, Chapter 12. The following Tuesday he would discern Gate Two: God's covenant with Abraham in Chapter 15, which all novices were required to master in order to pass their first year and be sent for internship somewhere around the globe. In the next three weeks, he would discern Abraham's third, fourth and fifth Blessings. For most Keepers, this was the limit. But Oleander's extraordinary gifts allowed him to go through these gates with relative ease.

In the following four weeks, he would discern God's four Blessings to Isaac. Gates Six to Nine were difficult for all Keepers. Master-Keepers, such as Crumb and Pem, were able to discern them only with great effort. Oleander, too, found them challenging and draining.

The last three weeks of his cycle would be God's three Blessings to Jacob. Those very few who discerned Gate Twelve were made members of the Council. The Council was thus made up of those remarkably talented Keepers who had reached Gate Twelve at least once in their lifetime. Oleander was among those who regularly made it to the twelfth, but even he occasionally failed. And though such failures were only to be expected, he nonetheless blamed himself.

This evening, however, his task was easy—merely Gate Four. He began by splitting his attention into two, creating the two-pronged focus which novices found so difficult to master: He turned his mind to the first words of Genesis 22 while at the same time directing his gaze across the Void and toward the Bible World that loomed far in the darkness like a small moon.

He was in no hurry. Unlike many beginning Keepers who dreaded floating at the edge of this nothingness, or more advanced Keepers who felt overburdened by spiritual labor, Oleander was elated performing his discerning duties. For him, the vision was awe inspiring. It made him feel closer to the Bible and free from all Earthly burdens.

The first verse appeared in his mind:

And after these things, God tried Abraham, saying to him: "Abraham," and he said: "Here I am." And He said: Take now your son, your only one, whom you love, Isaac, and go to the land of Moriah, and offer him there as a burnt offering on one of the mountains which I will tell you."

Oleander's gaze reached into the Bible World like a telescope's lens. Soon his vision stabilized and he could see clearly the familiar figure of Abraham. Abraham appeared stunned, his face turned upward to heaven. Slowly he returned to his tent, agonizing over God's command.

And Abraham rose early in the morning, and saddled his ass, and took with him his two servants, and he split wood for the burnt offering, and he rose up and went to the place which God told him.

This was not yet the Blessing episode—the Blessing itself was still several verses away—and the discernment was almost effortless. Every beginning Keeper could get glimpses of non-Blessing passages. The challenge was discerning the Gate itself, where the Blessing's intensity was high. Oleander watched Abraham taking Isaac with him, the two servants walking behind them.

And they came to the place which God told him, and Abraham built the altar there, and laid the wood in order, and bound Isaac his son, and laid him on the altar on the wood.

This scene never failed to touch Oleander's soul. The vision was more real, more magnificent than anything he had experienced on Earth.

And Abraham stretched forth his hand and took the knife to slay his son.

He saw Abraham getting ready to commit the unthinkable act, and though he already knew the outcome, he gasped.

And the angel of God called out to him and said: "Abraham, Abraham," and he said: "Here I am." And he said: "Do not lay your hand on the boy and do not do anything to him, for now I know that you fear God and that you did not withhold your son, the only one, from me."

Immensely relieved, tears rolling down his cheeks, Abraham untied his son from the altar. Wordlessly he hugged Isaac, who was pale and unresponsive.

Soon God would bless Abraham—Oleander started feeling the approaching Blessing. The Void before him felt denser and discernment was no longer effortless. He watched Abraham find a ram in the thicket, slay it and place it on the altar where Isaac had been minutes earlier. As the fire dwindled Abraham knelt and prayed to God.

God's Blessing was very close now and Oleander awaited it. Then something took hold and shook him as if he had been pushed into a violent river. Instantly he lost control. He was being sucked into the Void. If he could not regain control he would die. He knew that many had drifted into the Void—drowned, as the Keepers call it, and were lost forever. His mind scattered as he struggled against panic. He fought to focus his gaze on Abraham.

He had managed to balance himself. Again he was hovering at the edge of the Void. Questions rushed into his mind and he held them back. God's words continued to resound:

I will bless you, and I will multiply your seed as the stars of the sky and as the sand on the seashore…

Oleander was now in the midst of Gate Four, feeling the outflow of the Blessing. It was distinctly more turbulent and difficult to navigate than in the past. For the first time in many years, he was not absorbed in the Biblical scene, instead waiting for it to end.

After what seemed a long time, the Blessing ended and Oleander could feel its intensity dissipating.

…and through you shall all the peoples of the Earth be blessed, for you have obeyed my voice.

He was in quiet water again.

And Abraham returned to his servants and they rose up and went together to Beer-Sheva, and Abraham dwelled in Beer-Sheva.

Oleander rose to the surface of his consciousness and emerged from his Inner Depths into his body. Back in his cell, he opened his eyes and remained seated. For a time he stared through the tiny window into the darkness outside.

Was it possible that Gate Four had changed? Keepers had always assumed the Bible World was eternal and unchanging. It was the very essence of reality, the ground of all existence. How could it possibly change? And what would happen if the foundations started shifting?

His first instinct was to repeat the discernment. But no one could discern twice in one day. Keepers who tried discerning before recovering risked disappearing into the Void, their minds and souls lost.

He went to his desk and took the cellphone he used exclusively for Keeper matters and called his mentor.

"Eliezer? Something strange just happened…"

"Oh, Oleander, we've been trying to get hold of you all night. We even talked with your abbot. He absolutely refused to interrupt you."

"What happened?"

"Vessel Gregor. An accident."

"*Another?*"

"No, William. Vessel Mark Gregor is dead. Terminated."

There was a long silence.

"William?"

"I wanted to tell you," the monk finally said, "something has changed in Gate Four. Now I understand why."

"There is a Council meeting, William. A day after tomorrow, Thursday night, Switzerland time."

"Tell Julia I'm on my way. Eliezer…"

"You are wondering whether this has something to do with us."

"We discern the Book of Creation, try to open the Primordial Gate, and Gregor terminates days later?"

"We need to talk. In person."

"Before the Council meeting.

"Café Seva at three o'clock, Thursday afternoon?"

"I'll see you there."

Oleander packed and informed the abbot of a sudden but necessary meeting. He had never outright lied to the abbot, but this didn't assuage his guilt over misleading him. As always, the older man wished his diligent manager a safe journey.

It was past midnight when they started driving downstate to the airport; he could tell that the young monk at the wheel wished to talk. But Oleander closed his eyes and allowed him to think his passenger was asleep. He had felt a decline in energy in the past few hours, more than could be accounted for by the normal fatigue following discernment. He knew from his historical research this was to be expected. Keepers were more sensitive to the Blessing than were ordinary people, and their energies more dependent on the Blessing; he wondered what further loss of vitality he could expect.

The road was familiar and thoughts drifted through his mind. Gregor had died with the Blessing. Another channel of God's Blessing to humankind had disappeared from the Earth. He wasn't surprised the words elicited no emotion in him; he was still numb. Gregor, 2015. Every Keeper knew by heart the years of "The Seven Tragedies." Now every Keeper would know this date too.

The plane was almost full. After takeoff, most of his fellow passengers engaged themselves in reading or prepared for sleep. This was Oleander's first opportunity to be alone since the phone call. He now faced his worry.

Can there be any connection between our discernment of the Book of Creation and Gregor's death? No, impossible. To think so would be megalomania. Eliezer and I don't have the power to shake the foundation of the world. Besides, Vessel Wyatt's accident proves that something was wrong even *before* our session in London, before we started doing what was forbidden. But that was a mere injury and could be unrelated to Gregor's death.

Seven Vessels have died over the ages, centuries before either Eliezer or I were born. Ergo, Gregor's death can't have anything to do with two Keepers discerning the Book of Creation. Unless… unless we were not the first.

15

The late September sun was rising as Gregor's Keepers climbed from the vans in the Abbey courtyard. The group was escorted into the north rectory. As the group passed, other Keepers eyed them with varying degrees of fear and judgment, as if they carried an unknown disease; but also with sympathy, wonder, and even envy for the historic nature of what they had been a part. LaPointe and Cordon tried to hold their heads high, though the others bowed theirs.

Peprini was standing in the rectory by the window with his friend Councilor Albrecht Sionn, watching the arrival. Peprini broke the silence. "The Blessing is weakening. This is unmistakable."

Sionn, tall and thickset, pensively rubbed the short beard on his chin. "Rudolf said it is just a local trough; like the lacuna of 1992 over the Balkans."

Peprini snorted. "Councilor Antioch is old. All our *residences* around the world report the same thing: a clear diminishment in the Blessing."

"We could hope it's but a temporary ebbing. Like the one that hit the entire world in 1929."

"An idle hope, Albrecht. I can recall wonderful waves and terrible depressions, but nothing like this: sudden, sustained, and everywhere." Peprini turned away from the window. "They will be here any moment. I will interview Cordon and you LaPointe."

Sionn was almost six-and-a-half feet tall, and standing next to Peprini he towered over the five-ten man. "Menach? Did you imagine when we were boys we would be presiding over the termination of a Vessel?" He shook his head. "I can't quite believe it."

Peprini was lost in thought. Only with Albrecht Sionn was he comfortable enough to do this. Sionn's father, Gunther, had also been a Councilor, and the two boys had attended the same private school in Lucerne. They had known they were very special, two of a kind, and this had formed a bond between them.

There was a knock. A monk opened the door and Gregor's ten Keepers entered the room.

"At the moment we wish to speak with just the two of you," Peprini said, motioning to LaPointe and Cordon. "Please take the others to the dining hall. I'm sure you're hungry after your journey. Thank you, Brother Thomas."

He waited until the door was closed and turned to the two young men. "You've had much time to think and, no doubt, discuss events. That will help us this morning. Because as tired as you are and as... dispiriting as Gregor's death has been, I'm afraid we must ask more of you. We would like you each to recount in as much detail everything that happened. Both yesterday, the day of Gregor's death, and the day before."

"But why, why Sunday?" Cordon asked, turning to LaPointe in confusion. His partner was too shaken to notice.

"Yes, Emil. I want you to begin with the first thing you did Sunday morning. Take your time, leave out nothing."

Sionn placed his hand on LaPointe's shoulder and the much smaller man flinched. He gently walked LaPointe into the rectory study. "Why don't we talk in here?"

He shut the door behind them.

Everyone in the Abbey and the Book Company buildings knew what was happening in the rectory. All voices were subdued. Though some believed Gregor might have passed on the Blessing ("We are not beyond making mistakes, nor lying to protect ourselves"), most could feel the dullness of the Blessing in the air and a vague heaviness seeping into their beings.

Two hours after they entered the study, Sionn opened the door and waited. A weary LaPointe stepped from the room, his head hanging. He looked for Cordon. Peprini was pacing in front of the chair holding the older Keeper. Cordon heard the door open, saw Peprini's eyes, but didn't turn.

"I think we are finished," Peprini said. "It's been a long morning for all of us, no?" Cordon slowly raised his head. His cheeks were marked with tears. "Brother Thomas is waiting outside the door. He will show you to your cells." He saw their shock. "Monks' cells. And gentlemen, it would be best if you did not speak of this to anyone. Though I think you will be asked few questions."

After the door closed the two Councilors were alone. Peprini opened a window, the cool mountain breeze pushing into the room, thick with the smell of dying roses.

"LaPointe is telling the truth. I've no doubt." Sionn said.

Peprini nodded, gazing at the shriveling blossoms on the rose bushes just beneath the window.

"Those poor bastards. For the rest of their days they'll be asking themselves what they did wrong, why Gregor, why them. I had Brother Thomas put them in the same room. Best they not be left alone, just in case."

"One might hope they would be mindful of not being any more of a problem."

"Menach, let me ask you this. Did your father ever tell you why he thought the Vessel lines had ended?"

Peprini turned from the window. "He believed it had to be our failure."

"How was it—how *is* it—our failure?"

Peprini stared at his friend and came to a decision. "What did *your* father tell you of the Montfortists?"

Sionn took his time considering his answer, as Peprini expected. "I've only heard that word once before. The day I got my first posting, and so would be among other Keepers for the first time, my father said if I ever heard the name 'de Montfort' I was to walk away."

"Yes," Peprini said, "I was given the same warning."

"But you know something about it, don't you?"

Peprini hesitated. "Something. In the 1240's, around the time the number of Vessels had fallen to six, an Englishman named Simon de Montfort, a Councilor, claimed it was now undeniable the Blessing was dying out. Vessels, he believed, could no longer play the role they had been entrusted with. The world could not afford to rely on them. We Keepers, he claimed, must attempt to find new ways of preserving, even increasing the Blessing on Earth."

"How exactly did he think Keepers could do that?"

Peprini shrugged. "I have been reading the Keepers' Chronicles since I was a child, as have you. The few references to Montfortism I found— disguised references—are all very vague." He examined his friend's face and then added in a low voice, "Maybe he wanted Keepers to replace Vessels; to find a way to go to the Bible World themselves."

"Instead of Vessels? That's unprecedented heresy. As well as impossible."

"Heresy—yes; but not exactly unprecedented, Albrecht. De Monfort apparently thought he was only reviving an ancient doctrine."

"That's fantasy. If that knowledge ever existed, it's surely been lost. If it's not in the Chronicles, if no Councilor knows of it, who else would?"

"Nothing about Keepers that important is lost." Peprini looked squarely at his friend. "Remember who we are."

At noon Cordon and LaPointe entered the dining hall. Scattered about the room of large tables were clusters of people. Conversations sputtered as they were noticed. After getting their trays, they turned to find seats. The groups at the tables, in movements they were mostly unaware of themselves, turned shoulders or heads slightly such that they turned their backs to Gregor's Two, as they were now called. Cordon and LaPointe saw their eight colleagues at a table and started towards them, but stopped as they recognized their plea. The Abbey hadn't yet decided how to regard these eight, and they knew the presence of the infamous Two would certainly tip the scales against them. As they would for a long time to come, the two friends found seats by themselves.

16

Something was wrong at the Keepers' *residence* in Alexandria, Egypt. Master-Keeper Ramona Amar sensed it the moment she entered the room. It was Wednesday—the day of the weekly briefings. But her seven Keepers around the conference table looked at her with apathetic eyes. They seemed gloomy and distracted, and the ambient Blessing around them was oddly pale. Two others were on duty, following Vessel Alifa Hadid, and Amar hoped they were more alert.

She looked disapprovingly at Schmidt. "What's wrong with you?"

"I don't know. I slept eight hours, but..."

"Eight hours?" She was indignant. For Keepers, who were vitalized by the Blessing, four hours of sleep was more than sufficient. It was enough to make them sharper and more vigilant than ordinary people who—she thought contemptuously—needed seven or eight or even nine hours.

"Maybe it's a virus," Walid said. "All of us are under the weather."

"Are you saying the gift no longer protects you from such nonsense?" She scanned their faces one by one. "In two hours the second shift is on watch. Is anyone here focused enough to keep an eye on our Vessel?"

There was no use asking if they were capable of discerning today. She sat down and deliberated. And now that she reflected, she too felt an unusual fatigue. No, *fatigue* was not the right word—she felt empty and debilitated. This alarmed her. As a Keeper, she was unfamiliar with the bouts of weakness and sickness that common people suffer.

"Alright," she said more tenderly but maintaining her commanding voice, "rest now."

She entered her office and closed the door. Then she called Lucerne to speak with her old friend Joanna Crumb.

After listening to Amar, Crumb sighed. "You should report this to your Councilor."

"What's happening, Joanna?"

Crumb hesitated.

"Is anything wrong? What's going on?"

"I really shouldn't say this," Crumb murmured, "but Peprini says we're experiencing a decrease in the Blessing."

"Where? Just here?"

"All over the world. But I really can't talk. There will be a Council meeting in a day or two, and then everybody will know what there is to know."

"No, Joanna, you can't leave me like this. Finish what you were going to say. Joanna?"

"You'll know soon anyway. Vessel Gregor terminated." She heard the stunned silence at the other end of the line.

"*Mark Gregor?*"

"Vessel Gregor, yes."

"I understand the words, but..." Ramona whispered.

"I know."

"Remember when we were at the Novitiate and Councilor Battsen, may he rest in peace, spoke of the protective powers of the Blessing? At first, we thought it was a myth. In time I saw we Keepers were healthier and aged more slowly. But now..."

"Everything is different."

"So what does it mean? We're not going to live to be a hundred?"

"Ramona, don't you listen to the news there?"

"I haven't had a chance yet today."

"Three jetliner crashes, the massive earthquake in Manchuria, another in Ecuador. At least a million dead. Not to mention a slew of minor catastrophes in just the last twenty-four hours. Are you forgetting the Blessing protects not just Keepers?"

"Oh, my God... yes, yes, of course. The protective power of the Blessing. The world now has less of it... So... does this mean..."?

"We still have four Vessels, and Peprini is saying that's quite enough to keep the world going. But from now on we'll have to do with less Blessing. And with less protection."

Channel Two News in Springfield was in chaos—like most other news stations around the world. At five in the afternoon, thirty minutes before airtime, anchorman Steve Nesbitt and the editors were still divided. The problem was which of the day's stories should lead the broadcast.

Early that morning a gas pipe had exploded in a residential area, setting off a fire that devoured twenty-one houses and an apartment building. Eleven were dead and three still missing and presumed dead. Many others were hospitalized. It was the worst fire in the city in one hundred years. At three that afternoon a shopper in Westmark Mall suffered a nervous breakdown while waiting in line at a cookie shop. He went to his car and returned with a gun, then sprayed the bakery with bullets, injuring five shoppers and killing the teenage girl behind the counter. The police and ambulance were delayed by traffic accidents blocking both major routes to the mall. In one, a car carrier dropped its load of nine new minivans along a mile stretch of Highway 23; in another, a tractor trailer jackknifed on Plymouth Road and prevented any vehicle from getting through.

Trance Cement Inc., whose chimney dominated the city's skyline, began emitting clouds of black smoke smelling of rotting eggs, and rumors were circulating that the smoke was poisonous. Meanwhile, inside City Hall two city council members came to blows over the issue of garbage collection. The rest of the council had to pull them apart. And across town, the roof of the largest church in the city, the Faithful Shepherd Baptist Church, collapsed without warning, injuring the minister and a secretary.

Ed Pinter, editor-in-chief, shook his head when Carrie Megaard, a staffer, asked if there would be time for a segment on the Church.

"We're like kids with too much Halloween candy. We'll need to shorten the national and international segment to three minutes."

"But we're talking about hundreds of thousands of lives," protested the assistant editor Jack Finklestein.

"I know but the networks will have to handle the quakes and the plane crashes and the rest. We've got too much around here today."

"We ignore the cement factory?" Finklestein said.

"It looks nasty but... If we get evidence the clouds are toxic, we'll look at it again."

"So the gas pipe explosion and then the gunman?" asked Finklestein.

Pinter nodded. "We just heard one of the customers died along with the girl."

"We've got tape with the police chief?"

"He said twenty minutes for emergency services to respond is understandable," Carrie said. "Considering the traffic jams."

"We lead with the fire. Any objections?"

Finklestein looked at his clipboard. "The brawl at City Hall?"

"Just an old man losing his temper," Pinter shrugged. "But, yeah, the election's in six weeks and Alderman Kinsey was hospitalized. One minute on that. Then we wrap up with footage of the two traffic accidents and the follow-up."

"And the church?" Carrie asked.

"Nobody's seriously hurt," Finklestein said.

"Still, it's a church." She was a devout Baptist.

"Alright," Pinter said magnanimously. "Thirty seconds at the end. Maybe a little religion to end the show might be a good idea."

He had meant it as a joke but found even he couldn't laugh.

17

Dina had been exuberant following the initiation ceremony. That night the nine novices gathered outside the Novitiate to celebrate. Dina felt a growing bond. At last, after many aimless and lonely years, she had a destination.

But the following day this feeling changed. The others began complaining of a strange heaviness. Some felt tired, others edgy or queasy. Dina was the only one who was unaffected, and peculiarly she felt ostracized. While the other novices exchanged experiences and speculations, she found herself with nothing to contribute.

Pem was concerned how they would adjust to the new levels of Blessing. It was unfortunate as they might always associate joining Keeperdom with this malaise. He held a staff meeting with Crumb and Garcia, who had come with the novices from the Frostburg Institute to serve under him as Novice Trainers. Although technically the two were his subordinates, he felt uncomfortable in authority and was grateful they ignored his title and treated him as an equal.

The three Master-Keepers noted that Dina was again an oddity. "It's as if her vitality doesn't depend at all on the Blessing, as strange as that sounds," Garcia remarked.

"Her aura is unchanged," Crumb replied, shaking her head. "Each of the others shows the expected diminishment." Her eyes took in Pem and Garcia, noting the distinct change in their Keeper essence, and grimaced as she knew her own must appear changed.

Pem informed his two colleagues that Peprini had ordered they were to carry on as usual with the training. They were to tell them nothing about Vessel Gregor's termination.

Two days after the candidates' arrival, Pem gathered the nine young men and women, welcomed them again to the Novitiate, and announced the beginning of their year-long novitiate program. Afterwards, he explained, they would be sent for internships around the world.

"During the upcoming year," he explained, his voice dry and monotonous compared to Crumb's and Garcia's engaging speech, "you will take two academic courses: 'History of Keeperdom' and 'Genesis Studies.' You will also have two practicums: 'Meditation'—to improve your powers of concentration and inner balance, and 'Aura Viewing.' But your most important class will be 'Discernment.' Your ability to discern will determine where we will send you for internship, what posts you will be given, how quickly you will advance—but most importantly, how much you will contribute to our cause. And to humanity's cause. It will determine your future. Because this is the most important thing Keepers do: discern. So summon your best so we know what you are truly capable of."

They looked at him anxiously, except for Tiplady, who grinned unconcerned. Pem wished that Peprini would take him away soon.

Pem's words touched Dina. She determined in her heart to do her utmost. The special attention given to her by the instructors encouraged her. She could envision her life spent in the service of Keeperdom. She could even see herself someday serving as a Councilor in Lucerne.

Discernment class occupied the rest of the morning. It was given by Garcia who was known for his virtually magical capacity to explain the unexplainable art of discerning.

"Your first task is to find your *Inner Depths*. Each of you possesses this dimension that extends down to the bottom of your being, and then further below it. *We* know you possess this because we detect your gift, but *you* don't know it yet. In the next several days you will get the first glimpse of it, and I have no doubt you will be astounded. This is one of the true gifts to Keepers."

The candidates were sprawled in especially comfortable, so-called discernment chairs dispersed throughout the room. Garcia explained only that they were to gaze into themselves with as much concentration as they could muster.

"Look very carefully, search every corner of yourself, and sooner or later you will find the opening."

He then asked them to close their eyes and to peer inside themselves. He, Crumb and Pem walked among them, occasionally giving advice. By inspecting their auras the Master-Keepers could tell quite accurately what they were doing internally.

After some twenty minutes, Garcia called for attention. "We will take a break now, everyone. You are doing well, but you must focus still more intently. You have something extraordinary inside you: an inner space like a shaft that leads down to unimaginable Depths. Ordinary people have nothing like it. But you alone must find it. No one can show you the way into yourself—you alone have the eyes to see this. Once you've located it, we will teach you how to enter this astonishing inner space, to descend through it to the Depths underneath your being. These Depths are no longer inside you but below you, where all the individual Inner Depths merge.

"A question, Amira?"

"Do you mean to say, Mr. Garcia, if we go deep enough inside ourselves, down to the point below ourselves, we will be able to see each other, to touch each other?"

"As strange as it may sound, the answer is yes. The chances are not great, considering the vastness of this place and the question of timing. Realize we are speaking of another dimension. But it happens. Only a month ago I happened to see Miss Crumb from a distance."

"And…?" Nalini asked eagerly.

"We acknowledged each other," Garcia said, "and went on to do our duty: to discern."

"What did she look like, in the Depths, I mean?" Lev asked mystified, "With her clothes on, and her watch and everything?"

The three Master-Keepers smiled. "Not with her clothes, of course," Garcia said, amused, and waited a few seconds to arouse their imagination. "Not with anything physical in the way we understand 'physical.' But neither was she naked. It's her spiritual presence that I saw."

The novices were enthralled. Even Tiplady seemed impressed.

"Alright now," said Pem who was keeping time. "Close your eyes and start searching again."

The door opened and Menach Peprini stepped in. The three Master-Keepers turned but he motioned to continue. The Councilor stood ramrod straight with his hands clasped behind his back. Pem followed his gaze— it was directed at Dina, then at Maria.

Peprini walked over to Dina and watched her efforts. Her aura was as glorious as ever but showed none of the fluctuations that could be seen in the others as their inner gaze happened to rest momentarily on the right place. She looked distressed.

"Relax, Dina," he whispered to her, "try to move your inner gaze in different directions."

Then he went over to Maria. He was impressed to see her aura showing a radiant line, indicating she was looking in the right direction. "Keep going, Maria," he whispered, "you are getting warmer."

When a second break was announced and the candidates opened their eyes, Peprini's eyes met Maria's. He nodded to her appreciatively, and she returned a smile. Pem felt of pinch of jealousy.

"I think I detected something," Maria announced excitedly.

"I believe you have," Garcia said. "And that's almost a record for quickness. When you do it again, Maria, try looking straight into it."

"I think I am getting an inkling of something," Alexi said, "but I still can't grasp it."

"Me too," Natalie agreed. "I feel something is there."

"As if someone is standing behind your back, and you can feel her but not see her," Amira added.

"Excellent," Mr. Garcia said enthusiastically. "In fact, Amira has just given you an important hint: try to direct your inner gaze not forward, but backwards, as it were, as if you have a sixth sense at the back of your head."

"I don't understand what you mean, Mr. Garcia," Dina complained.

"Don't use your logic, Dina, use your imagination. When you get there, you'll see what I mean. Now, everyone, we'll make one last attempt for today. Afterwards we will take luncheon, and then you will enjoy your first History of Keeperdom class with Miss Crumb."

As eyes closed and the inner searches renewed, Peprini again approached Dina and observed her. He was surprised at her lack of progress. He whispered a few hints that would usually work with difficult cases, but to no avail. He saw that she was disappointed in herself.

"I've no idea what I am doing, Councilor Peprini."

"It's important you keep a calm mind, Dina. Emotions, particularly frustration, are detrimental in this. You have excellent capacities. I can see them."

By the end of the session, Maria had observed the entrance to her Inner Depths. Alexi got a glimpse. Lev, Natalie, and Amira were getting closer.

The others, Peprini was certain, would no doubt soon succeed. He motioned to Eric Tiplady to wait for him by the door. All eyes followed Tiplady as he stood and nonchalantly walked across the room.

Peprini approached the three Master-Keepers. "Mr. Tiplady will be assisting me for the time being."

Although the announcement was hardly surprising, they had not expected it so soon.

"Will he be back, Menach?" Crumb did not hide her disapproval.

Peprini made no effort to lower his voice. "I hardly need mention he will never be a skilled discerner. He will be more helpful in other capacities."

Osnat sat on the lawn at the center of the circular Humanities Building. The mountain weather of Jerusalem was getting cool and she pulled her sweater more tightly around her neck. She had come to campus to buy the textbooks for her class. She felt unusually tired and sad, sitting alone on the grass. Perhaps it was the disappointment at seeing the note on the department's bulletin board: "Professor Eliezer will be absent from Tuesday to the end of this week. His classes will be given by his teaching assistant. Please read Chapter 2 in your textbook."

Maybe that was the reason. But hadn't she felt this uneasiness earlier this morning, at home?

Then she noticed Professor Eliezer standing at the edge of the courtyard. She jumped to her feet. His face was turned towards the sky. She took a few steps towards him. For days she had wanted to speak with him, she didn't care about what, just to hear his voice. She had no doubt he would say things that would be important for her to hear, important for her life. Now was her chance.

But when she approached him he was absorbed in his thoughts and seemed worried. She stopped. He was scanning the sky. Then he nodded sadly and turned away.

She watched him enter the Humanities Building and mingle in the crowd. And it struck her that he was far more important than all those people around him; not just important *for her*, but important period.

Despite the strange weight on her soul, she felt happy that only she knew this, she and Professor Eliezer.

18

Peprini locked his door, lifted the receiver and phoned.

"Anwar's Rare Coins."

"I wish to speak to Anwar's uncle, please. This is Mr. Peprini."

There was no immediate response. "One moment, please." Peprini could hear quiet voices in the background.

"This is Anwar. How may we help Mr. Peprini?"

"I wish to speak to Prince Kedma, soon if it can be arranged."

"I'm afraid that's not possible."

Of course not, Peprini thought. Even if it was something very much desired by them, Ishmaelites always said "no" the first time.

"This concerns a death that occurred in Paris four days ago."

Silence. "In that case, the Prince can see Mr. Peprini tomorrow morning at ten."

Peprini worried that the wave of accidents might delay his trip back from Geneva to Lucerne and make him miss the Council meeting tomorrow evening. But he knew there would be no negotiation on the time, just as he had known the meeting would take place. The Prince had owed a special debt to Alberto Peprini, Peprini's grandfather, one not collected before his grandfather died. With the Ishmaelites, an obligation passed down the generations, and so it was to Menach Peprini that the Ishmaelite Prince now was indebted.

"Very good. Ten, then."

The early morning train from Lucerne was full, even though the global calamities of the past several days had not skipped Europe's railway systems. Two major accidents, one in Spain and one in Belgium, as well as a proliferation of minor problems, had deterred relatively few—a decline of about 6 to 7 percent of the normal volume of passengers, according to railways officials. Most people treated The Wave, as it came to be called in the media, as just that: a temporary rise in unlikely coincidences which would soon subside.

The train was stuffy and noisy, and Peprini found even his first-class seat uncomfortable. The cab from the station was hot and smelled of stale incense. Peprini wondered if the driver was an Ishmaelite. He knew from his grandfather and father that the Ishmaelites took advantage of every opportunity to collect information. They regarded themselves as Knowers. If a negotiation was to occur, and if they could gain some glimpse of the opponent's demeanor or eavesdrop on a conversation in the backseat of a cab prior to the meeting, they would.

The cab traveled through a jumble of cobblestone streets. On Rue de l'Hotel-de-Ville the cab pulled up to an 18th Century building housing Anwar's Rare Coins on the street level. Peprini paid the driver and got out.

Waiting in the doorway was a broad young man wearing jeans and a bulky sweater, his black hair brushed straight and held in place by some cream, his face clean shaven. The man bowed his head slightly and held the door. The shop appeared to be closed for the morning, the cases holding the ancient Greek, Roman, and European coins were dimly lit. Through a door at the rear of the shop, Peprini followed him through a labyrinth of hallways and doors and staircases smelling of old sweat, stale cigarettes, and pungent food. They went down a flight of stairs and then down several more until a door appeared. The young man opened it and stood aside for Peprini to enter.

He gestured at Peprini's feet. "If the Councilor wouldn't mind, please."

Peprini removed his shoes and the man set them to the side.

His grandfather had described this room, but Peprini was still stunned. It was actually a hall, easily 120 feet long and 80 feet wide. The ceiling was painted a light blue with streaks of white that made it difficult to judge the height. The impression was of being outdoors under a sky layered with cirrus clouds; the design made the clouds appear as if possibly moving. The walls were sand color as was the rug that seemed to be of a single piece, arabesques of gold and crimson giving it body.

An old man, no doubt Prince Kedma, sat cross-legged on a slight dais with another man beside him. This would be Chief Masa, he thought. Both wore white robes. The young man motioned for Peprini to step forward and follow him. They walked towards the dais until the young man stopped, nodding to several pillows on the floor.

"Please."

The Keeper sat on the pillows with as much dignity and grace as he could.

"How may I help you?" The Prince said.

"As you know, a Vessel has died. Terminated. I wish to know the cause of his death."

"You must be more specific. To receive the right answer, you must ask the right question." The Prince observed him closely. "You have a suspicion about the cause... *the root?*"

Peprini deliberated again how much to reveal. He wanted to know whether it was he himself, through his clandestine experiments with the Void, who had contributed to the Vessel's death. But of course, he could not mention this to the Ishmaelite. He had no particular reason to blame himself but knew that any violation of the old laws could reverberate in unexpected ways. The Vessel's death had unnerved him, and he had to make sure.

"Has any Keeper," he finally asked, "done something that caused the Vessel's death?"

He didn't expect an immediate answer. Even if the Prince knew, he would make the visitor wait—as a demonstration of power, to conceal how readily the Ishmaelites possessed this knowledge, and to amplify the weight of the favor he was granting.

The Chief rose. "The Prince must contemplate on your question."

The young man motioned for the Keeper to follow him to a door that melded into the beige wall. He pushed and it opened to another room, much smaller, with a single leather armchair arranged at the end of an embroidered rug.

"I will come when the Prince has finished."

Almost two hours passed before the door opened. When Peprini was again seated on the pillows, the Prince began speaking.

"This is the answer that has been given to me: 'Illicit doings among the Keepers contradict the ancient laws and endanger the Vessels' lives.' After additional probing, a second answer was given: 'Penetrating the Void invites dangers.'"

"Penetrating the Void? What does this mean?"

The Ishmaelite appeared deeply fatigued. "I do not know. Perhaps it means cutting a new path through the Void. Or an attempt to open an old Gate."

"*Someone is discerning an uncharted path*—but for what purpose? In order to create a new Gate? Or to open a Gate that is closed—the Primordial Gate?"

The old man looked very troubled by the suggestion. "Possibly. But this is human speculation."

"Do you know who that Keeper is?"

The Prince slowly shook his head.

"Did anything else contribute to the Vessel's death?"

"It is possible. Most events have several roots."

Chief Masa rose, obviously concerned for the old man who sat with a bowed back and closed eyes. "That is all."

The young man appeared at Peprini's side.

On the street again, Peprini sighed and unbuttoned his collar, loosening his tie. The Prince said nothing about my experiment, my work in the Void. Penetrating the Void—I could be accused of doing that, but certainly not of opening a new Gate. So while the Prince's warning might refer to me, it is best to assume it means another Keeper is trying to open the Primordial Gate. *But who would have such audacity?* Even Grandfather rejected that avenue, believing it suicide. And yet, someone has attempted to open the Primordial Gate, shaking the foundations of the world enough to kill Gregor. *But who?*

Only one name came to mind, only one person would have such power and boldness: Eliezer.

19

It was Thursday morning in Washington D.C., some 60 hours after "The Wave" had begun. The eight visitors to the Pentagon were seated around a conference table. They included university professors and experts in fields as diverse as statistics, psychology, physics, and insurance. With them sat five representatives of several intelligence agencies, who identified themselves only by first names.

"I can tell you this," said the one called Jerry. "To the best of our knowledge terrorism wasn't involved in the plane crash in Africa or the two in Asia. The same with the train derailments in Europe and Central America. The power grid failures were strictly mechanical. But: our people have no reasonable explanation for the cascade of traffic accidents, fires, murders, you name it. That's why you are here."

"The President said the current events are tragic but that we're resilient as a nation," said Professor Tim Talin, a physicist. "Then he called for calm. That's how you're dealing with this?"

"I know what he said, Professor. Did you expect him to say: *We don't have a goddamn clue why all this is happening*? And you agree things have quieted down in the last twenty-four hours."

Professor Meredith White, a psychologist, cleared her throat. Her expertise was the psychology of panic and crises. "Given time, most people adapt to high levels of discomfort or danger—within certain limits, of course, and a new equilibrium is established. Look at how people continued their everyday life in London during the Nazi bombings, in Iraq during the American invasion."

Jerry stopped her. "Let's put aside the issue of people's reactions. We'll get to that later. First, I'd like us to try and understand the cause or causes of these events. As you can see," he turned to the Powerpoint screen on the wall, "incidents in all these categories—each represented in a different color on the graph—suddenly rose five-fold, roughly, in some categories six-fold, about two days ago. This line here represents vehicle collisions as reported by the Insurance Institute of America, this one reported fires, here is traffic deaths, murders, deaths by any cause, hospital emergency room admissions, and so on. I don't need to note the spike in airplane crashes. Beyond this, we have the collection of power outages, utility breakdowns, the earthquakes obviously, and the like. And I can tell you that pretty much the same has occurred in other developed nations. What you see here is probably the best summary of the sudden change. Fortunately," he added, "it seems the wave has stalled. It may even be trending back to normal."

"So if everything is going back to normal," Professor White asked, "why is the Pentagon so interested?"

"Because," the insurance expert Dr. Aaron Grey offered, "things are not returning to normal. There have always been anomalies. But no across-the-board sustained change in the probabilities of events. Not until this week. Nothing like it."

"What are you talking about?" The statistician, Professor Erin Salem protested. "How can probabilities change? The probability of getting a six in one roll of a die is one-in-six, and will continue to be one-in-six forever as long as there are dice."

"I'm basing this on the evidence of how things *are,* not on how they are supposed to be. I've studied the data. After the initial five-to-six-fold jump, the rate seems—seems, I emphasize—to be stabilizing at about triple. For the individual person, this makes essentially no difference. A train crash somewhere in the nation once a month or three times a month feels virtually the same. But from the larger perspective—think of the criminal courts, jails, hospitals, mortuaries, insurance agencies, physicians' offices—we have a very serious problem."

Professor Julius Smith, the white-haired historian, nodded. "Very interesting. A similar thing seems to have happened around the middle of the thirteenth century—my professional focus—and again in the sixteenth. Of course, there were no statistics and no real data collection, but the anecdotal evidence from written reports is suggestive. People witnessed significant changes in accident rates."

"If there is a protracted change in the likelihood of these events, it's not due to a change in the underlying probabilities." The statistician was annoyed. "There must be some human influence, a psychological change at work here."

Jerry held up his hands. "Please, everyone, the President wants a report by tomorrow night."

20

Oleander arrived at the train station in Lucerne two hours before his appointment with Eliezer. He took a cab to the Café Seva, then chose a remote seat and ordered a cup of tea.

Six months earlier, in this same café, Eliezer had revealed his theory about the Book of Creation. The book, he had explained, is a mystery. Scholars conjecture that it was written almost two thousand years ago in the ancient land of Israel, and they view it as an enigma because it resembles no other text of that world. It seems to have suddenly sprung into existence in the ancient Middle East, utterly different from any previously known teaching, laying out strange ideas in an authoritative tone, without any attempt to justify or argue. It is as if the Book had been dropped on Earth by an alien civilization, or born from the mind of a mad, solitary genius.

But Eliezer believed it was in truth a Keepers' book lost in the seventh century when Muslim armies invaded Jerusalem. Two-thirds of the Council perished and the Keepers' center burnt to the ground. Those who remained fled to Constantinople in the so-called "Great Diaspora."

Fortunately, some looted copies of the Book found their way to collectors. This was how the Book had been preserved, he believed, though no longer as a Keepers' document but as an allegedly Jewish text, and later as just another ancient spiritual manuscript that interests only scholars and mystics. In time the Council was reconstituted and Keeperdom flourished again. But the meaning of the Book had been forgotten, though not completely erased. For the Book of Creation is, Eliezer suggested, no other than the enigmatic SFR—pronounced as SEFER, the Hebrew word for "book"—mentioned several times in the earliest parts of the Keepers' Chronicles.

Oleander's reaction had been cautious. The young monk wanted good evidence for Eliezer's theory.

In response, Eliezer placed on the table a batch of photocopies which he had prepared. "Look here," he said, pointing to the texts. "These passages are from the Keepers' Chronicles. There are fifteen references here to 'the Sefer.' And the interesting thing is, all date before the seventh century AD. In other words, before the Muslim invasion of the Middle East. I couldn't find any reference afterwards."

Initially, Oleander wasn't impressed. If SFR meant Sefer, which meant book, then there was no reason why the word wouldn't be mentioned in the Chronicles numerous times. But after he examined the photocopies carefully, he had to admit that the word was evidently used to refer to some particular, unspecified book, and it would seem strange for the word to disappear from the Chronicles following the Great Diaspora.

"Alright," he finally said. "Your theory is fascinating. But why is it important? Why have you asked me to come halfway around the world? Why all this secrecy?"

"Because I believe I have discovered the powers of the Book of Creation. What's more, I think I know how to use them for a very important goal. The most important."

"The Blessing."

"We can use the Book to replenish the Blessing for the sake of the entire world. William, it has taken me forty years to realize this is my mission. I want to use the Book to replenish the Blessing on Earth, just as I believe our ancestors did. But I need your help."

"You're saying that in ancient times Keepers used the Book?"

"Exactly."

"That doesn't make sense. If the Book had an important purpose, then surely this would have been mentioned in the Chronicles over and over again."

"I suspect that Keepers used the Book only to enhance their personal Blessing for a few minutes, long enough to help them in their need. If you recite the Book you'll know what I mean: It gives you an infusion of Blessing."

Eliezer turned the book so Oleander could read it. After a brief meditative exercise, he recited the first sentence of the Book. He felt the sweet, wondrous caress of Blessing. For several minutes he savored the sensation.

"I hadn't expected that," Oleander said at last. "Will anyone who recites these passages feel this?"

Eliezer laughed. "Of course not, Old Monk. Only Keepers. I gave it to one of my classes as an exercise. None of them felt a thing."

"Alright, so what does all this mean?"

Eliezer leaned towards him and whispered, "My theory is that the Book of Creation was given to Keepers to allow them to discern God's Blessing at the end of the creation story—and survive."

"God's Blessing to Adam and Eve? I didn't know you'd become a Creationist."

"Oleander, I am not talking Creationism, and I have no opinion on how to understand those Biblical stories before Abraham. As far as I am concerned they can be symbols for whatever you'd like. However you interpret these passages, one thing is clear: they contain a powerful Blessing. They are an opening to a Blessing. They are a Gate: *the Primordial Gate.*"

"No one discerns the Primordial Gate and survives. This is the first thing novices are taught. It cannot be discerned."

"Except through the Book of Creation."

"All the Gates before Abraham have been closed forever. What purpose can the Book possibly have then?"

Eliezer breathed deeply. "To pry open the Primordial Gate. And I want us to do it."

Oleander shook his head. "What you are suggesting goes against four thousand years of Keeper tradition."

They had reached a dead end. In subsequent conversations, Eliezer kept trying to convince Oleander to join his endeavor, but in vain.

And then, less than a month ago, something unexpected happened: Vessel's Wyatt's injury. Oleander was shaken by the realization that a Vessel is not completely protected by the Blessing from accidents, and that the few remaining Vessels might die just as seven of them had died in previous centuries. It took Eliezer only one conversation to convince Oleander to join him. Two weeks later they had met in London—halfway between New York and Jerusalem—and had launched their endeavor.

William Oleander pushed these memories from his mind as he saw Eliezer enter the café. After ordering teas, Oleander watched the waiter walk away.

"Eliezer, I can feel the diminishment in the Blessing. Christ, I can see it." He looked over Eliezer's shoulder at the street beyond the windows as if confirming this.

The older man nodded reluctantly.

"Do you think we should continue our…undertaking?"

Eliezer tried to hide his doubts. "I think it is now more important than ever. Don't forget that our aim is to open an additional Gate, the Primordial Gate. The more Gates are open, the more Blessing flows into the world."

"All I've been thinking about since Gregor's death is whether your… *our* idea of discerning the Book of Creation isn't completely insane, even sacrilegious. Keeper law says very explicitly Keepers discern nothing but the Abrahamic Gates. We broke that law, and then—Gregor's death."

"No, William. The law says Keepers discern nothing *in the Bible* but the Abrahamic Gates. This is to stop Keepers from discerning dangerous passages in Genesis. It says nothing about Book of Creation."

"That's only because nobody knew it's possible to discern it."

"I don't know, Eliezer... I've been thinking about our session in London. I'm not sure I understand what happened to us there."

"Well, this much is clear: We discerned the Book of Creation and experienced immense intensities of the Blessing. Which proves that the Book contains, like *Genesis*, a Gate—the Primordial Gate."

"It proves only that *something* happened. Normally when we discern we visualize the Biblical episode we focus on. How come this time we didn't visualize the Primordial Gate? God blessing Adam and Eve at the end of Creation—I saw nothing of that. In fact, I saw nothing but a storm of incoherent darkness."

"That only shows that the Gate is still closed. We have not opened it yet."

"The formula we discerned is about circumcision: WITH THE CIRCUMCISION OF NAKEDNESS. What could that have to do with the Primordial Gate? In fact, the Book of Creation makes no mention of God's blessing to Adam and Eve."

"Who knows what 'Adam and Eve' means in the Bible? It's called 'The Book of Creation,' isn't it? It clearly talks of creating the world, which is what Genesis Chapter One is all about. If not the Primordial Gate, what other Gate could it possibly be?"

"Who knows? Maybe the Hidden Gate."

"Come, William, the Hidden Gate is a legend, one of how many in Keeper lore. But the Book of Creation, the Primordial Gate, these are real."

They sipped their tea in silence.

"Come," Eliezer finally said as he stood. "The Council meeting begins in less than an hour."

21

St. Ignacio Abbey, the Keepers' headquarters, was located on a mountainside above Lucerne. During the Middle Ages, the Abbey was a notable producer of Bibles and prayer books. Because they had to be self-sustaining, most abbeys operated businesses. The copying of books, in particular the Bible, was a common enterprise. Of course, before machine printing all books were copied by hand, and this work was done almost exclusively by monks. When the Keepers took over the Abbey in the 13th century, they also took over the Abbey's book production.

When the St. Ignacio Abbey broke from the Church, in 1893, the Council decided to take advantage of the reputation the Abbey had long established. The Keepers' Council began a rare book consulting firm on the grounds of the Abbey, called the *Lucerne Rare Book Company*. Its purpose was to hide the real nature of the place; the income would be incidental. Soon the Council decided to make it the headquarters of the Keepers. The St. Scholastica convent, one mile away, became the Novice Training School.

No group on Earth is more knowledgeable in ancient manuscripts than Keepers, and from the start the Lucerne Rare Book Company was lucrative. In fact, they had to be careful not to appear too knowledgeable. Aside from the accumulated expertise of four thousand years, in addition to the vast library of Keepers' Chronicles and personal diaries of Keepers which gave detailed accounts of events in history the equal of which scholars could only dream, the group had also accumulated the greatest collection of ecclesiastical manuscripts in existence. In the Keepers' library were also many literary and political artifacts unknown to the world. These were kept hidden because of the impossibility of explaining how one group came to possess them. But this didn't stop fortunate Keepers from sitting by lamplight in the vault and enjoying the secret pleasure of reading a book by Plato or a play of Shakespeare or Sophocles unknown to the outside world.

The vault had changed much since the 13th Century. The technology of the Abbey Archives rivaled the rare book collection rooms in the finest libraries; even the computer industry had nothing better. The rooms were controlled for exact temperature and humidity; the ventilation system was constructed so there was a slight but constant positive air pressure, preventing any dust or fumes from getting in, while expelling any contaminants that human beings bring. Should an arm brush a table and skin-dust fly off, it was carried away before landing.

In order to enter one had to open the outer door and step inside an airlock. The atmosphere in the airlock was then made sterile and the inner door opened. Only the Director of Archives—now Councilor Annette Goldman—or her assistants entered this room. If a Councilor wanted a volume, a request was made and the book retrieved from the vault. When the book was brought, so was a pair of cotton gloves for the reader.

Several stories below the Abbey, the vault was the repository of The Keepers' Chronicles, the collection of millions of pages describing the lives of all Vessels over the past four millennia. Most importantly, recorded here were the passing of the Blessing from parent to child. There were seven tragedies also recorded, the termination of seven Vessels while still possessing the blessing. And now another would be written.

Councilor Julia Erna could have ordered typed copies of the texts and read them in her office, but she wanted to touch the pages her ancestors had written upon. Hoping for... what? Inspiration? Courage?

Such an intensive library search was not a common practice for her. Not an especially bookish person, she was at her best when tackling problems. Yet her Viennese upbringing had given her a deep appreciation for thoughtfulness and prudence, and an equally deep dislike for rash behavior. Gregor's death had thrown the Keepers' world into turmoil. If wisdom existed that might help her understand the death of Gregor, Erna believed it would be found here.

A thick batch of papers had been growing on the table since the morning. The next document turned out to be minutes of a Council meeting. The date of August 5th, 1241 suggested it was one that followed the termination of Vessel Jason of Padua.

The minutes were tedious but as she raised the document to place it on the pile, a scrap of paper fell. Torn along the edges, it was the size of a postcard, undated and barely legible. It was written in Hebrew. Hebrew had been the Keepers' universal language in ancient times, but by the 13th century it had long been replaced by Latin (only to be replaced a few centuries later by French, and again by English). Someone had apparently tried to protect the content of the note from curious eyes, and that someone had been learned enough to know Hebrew. Deciphering the text she felt grateful to her mentor, Master-Keeper Roxana Ayana, for having forced her to study the original language of the Old Testament.

The writing was masculine and strangely irregular. The writer could have been sick or injured, or he might have written the note in the dark. With great difficulty Erna managed to make out the words, which she then easily translated:

Please, Isabel. You say the tragedy was the consequence of my transgression against the sacred laws. Allow me to send you these words from where you buried me: A higher death must have a higher reason, even if that reason has chosen a miserable man like me as its tool. Recall the poem we sang together at the novitiate: "When the flowers in the Lord's garden begin to die, a much greater life starts budding elsewhere." This ancient verse must surely mean something! Remember me, S.

Was this note addressed to the celebrated One-Eyed Isabel? She had been head of the Council in the 1230's, and maybe later too; she could not remember the exact dates. "A higher death." The death of someone of special importance? A Vessel? Could the writer be speaking of Vessel Jason? Was the writer implying that his "transgression" had been the cause of a "higher death"—of Vessel Jason's termination? *How could that be possible?* Jason died of typhus. Thousands had died in the epidemic.

An anxious excitement grew in her. The letter implied that the *tragedy* was a consequence of the writer's *transgression* against the sacred laws— obviously the laws of the Keepers. Had Mark Gregor's termination, two days ago, resulted from a similar transgression? The thought arrested her breath for a moment. Who could have transgressed against the Keepers' laws? *And what laws—if violated—could possibly lead to the termination of a Vessel?* The members of the Council were dedicated servants of Keeperdom, as were all the Master-Keepers. Erna couldn't imagine any of them having malicious intentions where the Blessing was concerned.

What kind of Keeper law could possibly affect a Vessel's life—or his death? It could only be tied directly to the Blessing. And Keepers affected the Blessing in only one way: discernment. A law of discernment, if violated, leading to the termination of a Vessel? But discernment had only positive effects on the Blessing, and so on Vessels.

Her mind ran over the Councilors and Master-Keepers one after another. She had to learn more about the meaning of the mysterious note. Whom could she consult? Menach Peprini might have some clue—he possessed three generations of Keepers history. But could she be certain he wasn't the offender? *Dammit, she had no evidence any law had been violated at all.* Annette Goldman was trustworthy, and a good friend, but… No, it would have to be Eliezer and Oleander. Of all the members of the Council, Erna felt the greatest affinity to the old professor and the monk. She glanced to make sure the librarian's assistant wasn't looking, then slipped the note into her breast pocket.

Erna took the elevator to the main floor and left the Abbey, crossing the cobblestones to the Rare Book Company. She stopped, and checking her watch she realized the Council meeting would soon start. Walking back to the Abbey, she barely noticed her surroundings. She felt rattled by the idea that Gregor's death might have been caused by the actions of a Keeper. She felt comforted, strangely. Then she realized why. This made the catastrophe more understandable, and perhaps she could do something about it.

Outside the Council Chambers, she noticed Eliezer and William Oleander speaking in a corner. Her anxiety eased at the sight of her old friends. But as she approached they got quiet and their eyes flashed wariness.

She had known Eliezer intimately for forty years and could tell he was hiding something. It was even more obvious that Oleander was.

"Hello, Eli. William."

Eliezer smiled broadly. "Hello, Julia!"

Nevertheless, she saw that part of him held back, and she decided not to confide in them right then.

"You two look conspiratorial." She kissed him on both cheeks, the same with Oleander.

She noticed Oleander make an effort to look blasé and fail. "I'm afraid I get that look when I'm worried," he said.

She glanced through the door. "We might as well begin."

22

Present were Julia Erna, President; Rudolf Antioch, Security Chief; Menach Peprini, Director of Training; Albrecht Sionn, Oversight of Vessels' Affairs; Annette Goldman, Director of Archives; Jeremiah Eliezer, Middle-Eastern Chapter; Theresa Fournier, Latin American Chapter; Sandrine Krystofski, Asian and Pacific Chapters; William Oleander, North American and African Chapters; and Margaret Connor, European Chapter. These ten made up the Council of Keepers.

As President, Erna sat at one end of the oval table. Peprini sat at the other in the chair his father once occupied. She examined the faces of her colleagues. They had overcome the shock but hadn't recovered their equilibrium. As Rudolf Antioch had said—she had overheard him this morning whispering to Fournier—"The only thing I understand is the mathematics of all this: Five Vessels minus one is four. Other than that, it is absolutely incomprehensible." The old Russian didn't deserve such a shock after a century of faithful service.

"Since the moment I called this meeting," Erna started quietly, "I have tried to compose an appropriate opening statement. Forgive me, but I have not the words for the magnitude of our loss... of the world's loss. Perhaps a prayer can be of some comfort."

She bowed her head and the others did the same. "You are our life, Oh Blessing," she quoted an ancient verse. "Give us strength so that we may breathe your breath, give us your wisdom so that we may be your Keepers."

The past two days had been tumultuous, and there had been little time for sleep, let alone reflection. Now, when she had a moment, these words nearly moved her to tears.

She looked at her fellow Councilors, wondering who—if any—had defied the rules of the Blessing. "Let us begin, my friends. Most of us have been traveling and may not have the most current information. Menach? Albrecht?"

Menach Peprini, after a nod to Rudolf Antioch, recounted the details of Gregor's death and the fruitless search for a possible child. It was undeniable that Gregor's Blessing was lost. Albrecht Sionn reported on the Keepers' *residencies* around the world and the status of the four remaining Vessels. "All seems to be stable, as best as we can determine."

Sandrine Kystofski, in her heavy Slovak accent, then gave an account of the rise in accidents and general misfortune triggered by the loss of the Blessing. No corner of Earth escaped the effects. "I think we all have felt a diminishment in vitality these last several days. I suspect this is permanent, if the Chronicles are an indication."

She did not appear in the least fatigued by her twenty-hour trip from her post in New Zealand. Her natural white-blond hair was striking against her tanned skin.

Eliezer's mind returned to his conversation with Oleander. Two weeks after our undertaking—our trespass?—a Vessel dies with the Blessing. This, when no Vessel has terminated in over four hundred years? What are the odds of these two events being unrelated?

For a moment Eliezer felt the urge to confess all, to relieve Oleander and himself of sole responsibility as well as to recruit the wisdom of those around the table. But then he imagined the punishment for attempting to use the Book of Creation. Even if technically the two had not violated any law, surely many around this table would seize on the possibility that they had somehow caused Gregor's death. What is the punishment for causing a Vessel to die with the Blessing? He shuddered.

"Eliezer?" Erna stared at him. "Are you with us?"

"I'm sorry, I was just wondering how previous Councils proceeded after a Vessel termination." Looking at Erna and then Oleander he saw that at least two people knew he had lied.

"I see. I would think the first thing they would have done, as we should now, is to make certain that none in this room—that no Keeper—has acted in any way that might have contributed to Gregor's death."

Erna had not intended to mention her suspicion—it still had no firm foundation, but the words somehow escaped her mouth. She saw Oleander shift uneasily in his chair and again wondered what he and Eliezer had been discussing before the meeting. Something other than Gregor's death had them worried. She found it hard to suspect them of tampering with the Blessing—Eliezer, because she had always loved him; Oleander, because he was simply too good, too obedient. But the more she stared, the more she believed she detected something wrong. Oleander looked especially nervous. He would be a bad poker player, she thought, unlike Peprini.

But as she looked at the Swiss she saw that he was holding his breath, so tense was his body. His head turned and as they made eye contact he exhaled sharply and looked away. He, too? It was no surprise that Peprini might be hiding something. She always assumed he was; it was the man's nature. What surprised her was the flicker of anxiety as his eyes had darted away.

She knew she should drop the topic—there was no point in continuing, but her sense of betrayal at the sight of the three Councilors compelled her to press the point.

"Anyone?"

Her eyes moved from Oleander to Peprini and lastly to Eliezer. He was stone-faced, and unexpectedly she felt deeply hurt

"What are you talking about, Julia?" Sandrine Krystofski exclaimed, taking offense.

"What could any of us have done?" Sionn said vehemently. "As far as I know, no one has ever suggested that Keepers can contribute to a Vessel's termination."

"Still," Erna insisted, "there are ways of meddling with the Blessing, and we simply don't know the consequences..."

"What do you mean 'meddling with the Blessing,' Julia?" Margaret Connor, the slight, red-headed young Irish nun interrupted. "The only way a Keeper can affect the Blessing is by discernment, and the consequences are always positive." She turned to the others for acknowledgment and got several nods in answer.

Erna opened her mouth to answer, but Annette Goldman was quicker. "Unless the discernment is done in some manner forbidden." The librarian leaned forward and looked about the table at her colleagues.

There was silence as the Councilors pondered the new idea.

Theresa Fournier was the first to speak. "It would have to mean discernment of a Biblical text other than the twelve Abrahamic Gates. But what would be the point?"

"Are we talking about the Primordial Gate? Noah's Gate?" Sionn said. "The Blessing in these Gates is much too intense, we all know this. It would be suicide."

"Unless one of us has found a special means of protection," Peprini said.

Sandrine shook her head. "That's absurd, Menach."

Peprini shrugged. He turned to Eliezer. "Who knows what is possible and what is impossible?"

The old man was expressionless. "Is someone discerning the Hidden Gate? Perhaps there is some truth in this legend. Or using the Psalms to discern the heavens?" It was hard to tell whether Eliezer was serious or mocking.

Annette shook her head. "Discernment doesn't work on anything but Genesis."

"Exactly, none of us is responsible for Gregor's termination." Oleander hadn't spoken during the meeting and felt the need to say something. His silence seemed to him to suggest subterfuge.

"All this is pure speculation," Sionn said, irritated. "Keepers have been wondering, agonizing about it since Vessel Intef's death 3000 years ago. We will never know why."

"What is the point in this?" Rudolf Antioch was unable to contain himself. "We will never fathom the whys of this. He giveth and He taketh away. What more can we know?" He was crumpled in his chair. His outburst had started with anger but ended in pleading.

Peprini sat up in his chair. "In any case, we must be certain that all Keepers meet their responsibility to discern. We know of at least one instance in our past when Keepers failed in this duty with horrific consequences."

Erna was relieved that the topic of transgressions was finally exhausted. "The Black Plague in the fourteenth century."

He nodded. "If our failure to discern could bring on that catastrophe, perhaps it could cause the termination of a Vessel. I propose we instruct the Master-Keepers to strictly supervise the discernments of their people. No laxity, no deviation from tradition will be tolerated. Punishment must be dealt for the smallest violation."

"Can we agree on this?" Erna asked.

There was no dissent.

"Theresa, would you undertake this task?"

"Certainly."

"Lastly," she added, "there is the submission to the Chronicles. If there are no objections I will compose a draft of both the account of Gregor's death as well as this meeting." Seeing no disagreement, she nodded. "Alright, we are all tired and I suggest we adjourn."

She stood, signaling the end of the meeting. There was silence as the fact of their impotence struck them. Was this all? Silently they left the room, realizing that while their meeting had been necessary—you can't ignore a Vessel's death as if nothing had happened—it did not and could not have achieved anything of value.

23

Erna decided to ask Eliezer and Oleander what they were hiding. But Margaret Connor blocked her path with a question, and by the time she was free the hallway was empty.

Returning to her office she noticed the door to the Blue Hall half open. She peeked in and saw Eliezer and Oleander in worried discussion. It appeared that Eliezer was trying to calm the monk. Peprini and Sionn might be secretive as a matter of course, but Eliezer and Oleander were another matter. What could be happening that must be kept from her?

Since the time they had been lovers, almost fifty years ago, Erna felt deep trust in Eliezer. They had met at a book auction in Lucerne. She had just ended her novitiate and, having been a most promising novice, was posted at the Rare Book Company. The Company sponsored an auction of several European family collections in the fall of 1959, and she was present as a representative. Eliezer attended as a private buyer. He was a successful merchant interested in a broad range of ancient manuscripts. His teaching position at the Hebrew University added to his reputation. Despite the wealth he had accumulated in his successful trade, he did not take his profession too seriously. At thirty-six years old he was still restlessly searching for his vocation.

Born in the Ukrainian village of Boyarka, now a suburb of the city of Kiev, where he experienced two anti-Semitic pogroms and where later he saw from his hiding place the Nazi SS execute his family, he had always felt he had a special mission: to help relieve the suffering of the world. This belief helped him survive the Nazi death camps and sent him afterward in search of his calling. Eventually, he found himself a professor of Biblical Studies at the Hebrew University of Jerusalem, as well as a wealthy businessman. But he knew these occupations were only temporary.

When they met at the auction house, they quickly realized their lives would be entwined. A few weeks later she introduced him to Roxana Ayana, an Argentinean Master-Keeper, her mentor. The old woman immediately recognized him as an extraordinary prospect as a Keeper.

And thus it was through Julia Erna that he finally came to understand his mission: to work for the sake of the Blessing, which meant to be a Keeper.

Soon the two lovers decided they could not devote themselves completely to both Keeperdom and marriage. Although marriage between Keepers was generally encouraged, Eliezer and Erna decided to forgo their love for the sake of their calling. But the intimate affection remained between them. She couldn't recall Eliezer ever hiding anything from her. In their frequent conversations throughout the years, they had always shared their most personal feelings and thoughts. She felt he was betraying their trust and this hurt her deeply.

As they were leaving the conference room Eliezer took Oleander's elbow and hurried him along. He nodded at the monk's quizzical look.

When he could speak freely he said, "Julia. We have to be more careful."

"What do you mean?"

"She knows we are keeping something from her."

"How do…"

"She was not subtle about it. Be prepared. If she contacts you we must have a story prepared."

"A story?"

"You have met someone on one of your business trips. A woman in the cocoa business. William, you think you might be falling in love."

"But she'll think I'm…"

"Human? She will not think less of you." Eliezer grinned. "I am confident that in the end, you will triumph over this temptation. I will then mention to Julia that you passed this test. I am already proud of you, my boy."

He grinned again and patted Oleander on the back.

24

Despite the late hour, Peprini returned to his office at the Book Company. He picked up the phone and dialed from memory. "I should have done this long ago," he said aloud.

"You are to assemble nine teams of three each." He listened. "Yes, I realize this may take several days to organize."

The actions of Councilors were traditionally above scrutiny. What he had in mind was an insult and a serious breach. But the Council meeting showed that his colleagues weren't without suspicions of their own. He had underestimated Erna. She had gotten too close in her speculation, however offhand it might have been. He had to know what the others were doing, what they were thinking.

One worry had to be dealt with tonight. He dialed another number. "You are to monitor Councilor Eliezer's movements... You heard me correctly. He is at the Abbey currently, but he's returning to Israel tomorrow. Get to Jerusalem as soon as you can. No, you'll be on your own for the time being. Soon I will send you help. I want reports each morning."

Neither Eliezer nor Oleander wanted to hold their next Book of Creation session in Lucerne, so near the heart of Keeperdom. Other Councilors might perceive an alteration in the Blessing, and there was no sense in taking that risk.

The next day Eliezer arrived in Zurich and made his way to the Swissôtel Zürich in the city's *Oerlikon* business district. He sank into the softness of a sofa in the lobby and waited. In less than an hour they would begin their second session with the Book of Creation. The first, two weeks earlier, had been glorious; or so it had seemed at the time. Now, after Vessel Gregor's death, things looked less clear.

Eliezer felt guilty for not sharing his doubts with Oleander. Was he not misleading him with a theory really little more than speculation? What if they were leading the world to disaster? Once again he reminded himself that the world was already headed towards disaster, towards the loss of all the Vessels, as Gregor's death should have reminded them all. To do nothing was to bequeath disaster, and the responsibility for dealing with this, to future Keepers.

He opened his briefcase and touched his copy of the Book of Creation. As a professor of Biblical Studies and ancient Jewish thought he had known about this shadowy book for many years, and was familiar with the scholarly understanding—or lack of understanding. But it was only three years ago that he had sensed the Book's special powers.

It happened in Jerusalem when he found a copy of the Book in a used bookstore. He had read it numerous times and lectured about it, but this time something different happened. While glancing at the text one day he had slipped into a meditative mode, and found himself caressed by a wave of gentle Blessing. He realized that his meditative reading of the Book had somehow activated the power of the Blessing.

A few minutes later, after the influence dissipated, he was struck by an idea: to use this new source to replenish the dwindling Blessing in the world. Replenishing the Blessing—this had been his dream for at least thirty years. He had seen too much evil and suffering to believe the world could be improved by the minds and hearts of human beings alone.

He had stepped from the bookstore with a new aim in life. Since then the Book had occupied most of his time. Putting this idea into practice was risky. It was nothing less than interfering with the Bible World—the foundation of all reality. It also involved a more mundane danger: If the Council found out... well, he tried not to think of that.

Eliezer stood with some effort, looked around, and walked to the hotel's restaurant. No Oleander. He returned to the lobby and slumped again on the sofa. He took out a book from his briefcase and opened it to the first page.

BOOK OF CREATION

WITH THIRTY-TWO MYSTERIOUS PATHS OF WISDOM ENGRAVED GOD, THE LORD OF HOSTS, GOD OF ISRAEL, THE LIVING GOD, GOD ALMIGHTY, HIGH AND EXALTED, DWELLING IN ETERNITY ON HIGH, AND HIS NAME IS HOLY, AND HE CREATED HIS WORLD WITH THREE SFR'S: WITH SFR AND SFR AND SFR.

TEN SEFIROT OF BELIMAH, TWENTY-TWO FUNDAMENTAL LETTERS, TEN SEFIROT LIKE THE NUMBER OF TEN FINGERS, FIVE OPPOSITE FIVE, AND THE COVENANT OF THE ONE SET IN THE CENTER, WITH THE WORD OF THE

TONGUE IN THE MOUTH AND WITH THE CIRCUMCISION OF NAKEDNESS.

TEN SEFIROT OF BELIMAH, TEN AND NOT NINE, TEN AND NOT ELEVEN, UNDERSTAND WITH WISDOM AND EXPLORE WITH UNDERSTANDING, EXAMINE WITH THEM, INVESTIGATE FROM THEM, KNOW AND THINK AND CREATE AND RETURN THE CREATOR TO HIS PLACE, BECAUSE HE FORMS AND CREATES BY HIMSELF, AND THERE IS NO ONE BUT HIM, AND HIS ATTRIBUTE IS TEN THAT HAVE NO END.

TEN SEFIROT OF BELIMAH, BRIDLE YOUR HEART FROM THINKING, BRIDLE YOUR MOUTH FROM SPEAKING, AND IF YOUR HEART RUNS, RETURN TO THE PLACE, FOR IT IS SAID: "AND THE CREATURES RUN AND RETURN." AND ON THIS A COVENANT HAS BEEN MADE.

TEN SEFIROT OF BELIMAH, THEIR END IS LINKED TO THEIR BEGINNINGS AND THEIR BEGINNING TO THEIR ENDS LIKE A FLAME CONNECTED TO A BURNING COAL. KNOW, CALCULATE, AND FORM, FOR THE LORD IS SINGULAR, AND THE CREATOR IS ONE, AND HE HAS NO SECOND, AND IN THE FACE OF ONE HOW CAN YOU COUNT?

TEN SEFIROT OF BELIMAH, THEIR MEASURE IS TEN WITHOUT END: DEPTHS OF BEGINNING AND DEPTHS OF END, DEPTHS OF ABOVE AND DEPTHS OF BELOW, DEPTHS OF EAST AND DEPTHS OF WEST, DEPTHS OF GOOD AND DEPTHS OF BAD, DEPTHS OF SOUTH AND DEPTHS OF NORTH, AND A SINGULAR LORD, GOD, FAITHFUL KING, RULES OVER ALL OF THEM FROM HIS HOLY ABODE UNTO ETERNITY.

TEN SEFIROT OF BELIMAH, THEIR VISION IS LIKE THE APPEARANCE OF LIGHTNING AND THEIR LIMIT HAS NO END, AND HIS WORD IN THEM IS TO-AND-FRO, AND TO HIS SPEECH THEY RUSH LIKE A WHIRLWIND, AND BEFORE HIS THRONE THEY BOW DOWN.

TEN SEFIROT OF BELIMAH AND TWENTY-TWO FOUNDATION LETTERS: THREE ARE MOTHERS, SEVEN ARE DOUBLES, AND TWELVE ARE SIMPLE, AND THERE IS SPIRIT IN EACH ONE OF THEM.

Eliezer recalled how he had first explained to Oleander the details of his plan.

"Do you want us to discern the entire book?" Oleander had asked.

"The Book of Creation is really no more than a thin booklet. It is made of six chapters, but I believe that only the first chapter is important. Look at it." Eliezer handed him the booklet. "As you can see here, the first chapter starts with a brief introductory sentence: WITH THIRTY-TWO MYSTERIOUS PATHS OF WISDOM…"

"I know. After our last conversation I spent some time in St. Raphael's library. I found out we have a decent collection of Jewish books."

"Good. So you must have noticed that after the introductory sentence, the book continues with a list of formulas that begin with the words TEN SEFIROT OF BELIMAH."

"Yes. Very enigmatic. Sefirot—are these the ten spheres of the Kabbalah mysticism?"

"Clearly not. The Kabbalah borrowed the expression from this book and provided its own interpretation. The Kabbalah, after all, is from the Middle Ages. This book was written at least a thousand years earlier."

"So what does 'Ten Sefirot of Belimah' mean?"

"Scholars would tell you that no one knows for sure. But I believe I do. You have studied Hebrew. What can 'Sefirot' mean? Which three-letter root does this word come from?"

"Obviously from the Hebrew root S,F,R, which is related to writing, or counting, or numbering. So 'Ten Sefirot' might mean ten numbers, or ten levels, or degrees."

"Excellent! Now, what about Belimah?"

"The word is mentioned once in the Bible, in the Book of Job." His capacity to memorize texts amazed Eliezer. "God is said to 'hang the Earth on Belimah,' which is usually interpreted as made of two words: 'Beli-Mah,' which means 'no-thing', or Void. Of course…"

"William, I'm not talking about Biblical interpretation. My question is: Which Hebrew root does the word 'Belimah' come from?"

"Well, then probably B,L,M. It means stopping or blocking."

"Excellent again. So 'Ten Sefirot of Belimah' might mean ten levels of blocking or closing." Eliezer's voice dropped into a dramatic whisper, "Which means that something has been closed—ten times, like ten turns of a key. Now, why would the Book of Creation talk about something having been *closed?*"

Oleander's eyes narrowed in thought but he did not answer.

"Because that which had been closed can be *opened* again. And because the Book contains the secret of opening."

"Opening what?"

"A Gate," the old man replied. "A Gate that has been closed and can be opened again."

"The Primordial Gate?"

"Of course. Ten Sefirot of Belimah means ten levels of closing—and opening again—of the Primordial Gate! If we are right, then these formulas are designed to produce ten pulses of Blessing. Each pulse opens the Primordial Gate wider, allowing more Blessing to flow from the Bible World."

"Let me think," Oleander said impatiently, clearly not liking where this was going, but intrigued nonetheless. "And the rest of the Book—the pages that come after the ten formulas?"

"There are five more chapters that seem to me like later additions. I don't really understand what they mean and I don't think they are important for us. Perhaps they were put there to disguise the Book's real purpose. Only the last few sentences of the book, at the end of Chapter Six, are interesting. They tell how God revealed to Abraham the secrets of creation."

"So what you are telling me is that you want us to discern the ten formulas one after the other, and in this way to open the Primordial Gate."

"Precisely."

"It won't work."

"Why not?"

"Because there aren't ten formulas in the Book. The copy in St. Raphael's library has only seven. And a monograph I got from the Columbia University library lists three different versions of the Book of Creation. None has ten formulas. Only seven or eight."

Eliezer smiled. "Because all the versions known to scholars today are later copies. The original text has exactly ten formulas. That's why the Book says: 'Ten Sefirot of Belimah.'"

"This theory of yours is just speculations built upon speculations!"

"Oh, no, William, because I found the original text. After all, I've been an ancient book dealer for 60 years, and a very good one. For three years I have been looking for the original. And two months ago I discovered it in a library in India. How it got there..." he shrugged. "Perhaps during the conquests of Alexander the Great. I paid a fortune for it, but I'll spare you the details of that little adventure. Once home with this treasure, I tested the paper—or, rather, the parchment. It has been confirmed to be at least two thousand years old."

Oleander seemed exasperated. "Fine. But what makes you think we can use it to open the Primordial Gate?"

"Because I went down to the edge of the Void and discerned it."

The monk inhaled. "Go on."

"At first, I discerned the introductory sentence. The result was a wonderful swell of Blessing, much greater than what you feel when you simply read it quietly. But I would think clearly not enough to open a Gate, if our discernments of Abrahamic Gates are any comparison. Then I tried going on to the first 'Ten Sefirot of Belimah' formula. Nothing happened."

"So..."

"I didn't give up so easily. And after a few days I got curious. When I examined the original document with a magnifying glass, I found that the Ten Sefirot formulas were numbered from one to ten—but not according to their order in the book. You see, the list of formulas was jumbled up."

"That's hardly surprising, Eliezer. Different manuscripts that exist today list those passages in different orders. What is the first in one manuscript may be the third formula in another."

"Yes, yes, William, but in my manuscript, right next to formula number one, it also said: 'The beginning.' These words confirmed my suspicion that the Book was used in ancient times for some kind of meditation. For some... practical purpose."

"Fine. But you don't know what kind of meditation."

"But I do. Because there was another handwritten note alongside the first formula. It was barely visible, maybe because someone attempted to erase it, maybe because of the ravages of time, I don't know. But I managed to decipher what it said. It gave me the clue."

"And?"

"It was written in Hebrew. It said: 'Ha-Hotam Hu Mila.'"

"The seal is a word," Oleander translated.

"A better translation is: The seal is 'Word.' A seal, in ancient Jewish mysticism, means password, or codeword. So what this handwritten message told me was that the codeword for using the Book of Creation is the Hebrew word 'Mila.'"

"Mila?"

He nodded. "Remember the first Sefirah formula: TEN SEFIROT OF BELIMAH, TEN SEFIROT LIKE THE NUMBER OF TEN FINGERS, FIVE OPPOSITE FIVE, AND THE COVENANT OF THE ONE SET IN THE CENTER WITH THE WORD OF THE TONGUE IN THE MOUTH AND WITH THE CIRCUMCISION OF NAKEDNESS. Now, in Hebrew, as you know..."

"The word for 'circumcision' and the word for 'word' are the same: 'Mila.' So WITH THE TONGUE IN THE MOUTH AND WITH THE CIRCUMCISION OF NAKEDNESS is a pun that hints at the word 'Mila.' Very clever. But every scholar knows it. Where is the great discovery?"

"The discovery is that a codeword is needed in order to discern the Book of Creation. You see, the first Sefirah formula is actually a riddle that tells you the codeword you need to discern the Book."

Eliezer chuckled when he saw his friend's skeptical face. "Now, do not tell me this is just another speculation, William. Because I tried it."

"What do you mean 'you tried it'?"

"Oh, yes. I went down to the Void again, discerned the introductory sentence, then the first Sefirah formula. Nothing happened. But then I said the password, 'Mila.' And the moment after I spoke it—incredible!"

Oleander's face screwed up in curiosity.

"The storm of Blessing was absolutely stunning. I have never experienced anything as powerful, as sweet, as wonderful. I was almost knocked unconscious. I could hardly keep my focus. I tried to continue but my discernment beam was too weak to penetrate this storm. That's why I need someone to discern with me. Our combined beam would be much stronger. That's why I need your help."

Oleander deliberated. "Who do you think wrote the codeword on the parchment?"

"I believe it was an Ishmaelite. An Ishmaelite prince."

"What makes you think that?"

"I found one more thing on the parchment: At the top of the first page a name was written: Prince Mivsam. It's an Ishmaelite name. In the Bible, Mivsam was one of the twelve sons of Ishmael."

It was unclear whether Oleander heard these words. For almost two minutes he continued to deliberate silently. Then he raised his face, looked into Eliezer's eyes, and said, "Alright, Eliezer, I am with you."

Recalling that moment, Eliezer smiled.

25

Eliezer heard steps approaching. Oleander, precisely on time. He rose and followed Oleander to his room. Oleander put out the "Do not disturb" sign and locked the door.

"The second *Sefirah*?"

"The second rung, William, the second pulse of Blessing that will push open the Primordial Gate."

They spoke no more. Eliezer removed the thin volume of the Book of Creation from his briefcase and placed it on the table. Not that he needed it during discernment, but it gave him a sense of security. He turned on a small lamp and closed the curtains, leaving the room in a mid-day twilight. They gave a last glance at the passages to be discerned and then closed their eyes.

Minutes passed as they found their inner stillness. In their minds they sensed each other's aura, and each coordinated his own with the other's—an ancient technique to ensure that the two discerners would emerge together at the same location in the Depths.

Eliezer hummed to give the cue, and this unexpectedly bolstered the younger man's resolve. Oleander started sinking to his Inner Depths. After a time he found himself at the entryway—that tunnel-like passageway that connected his own Inner Depths to the open Depths and the Void. He said his prayer and then proceeded to the brink of the Void. There he waited.

Eliezer descended to his own entryway. They found themselves at some distance from each other, and Eliezer signaled to Oleander to get closer.

He focused his mind on the overture now so familiar. Oleander did the same.

WITH THIRTY-TWO MYSTERIOUS PATHS OF WISDOM…

If his conjecture was correct, this sentence referred to God's creation of the world in the book of Genesis, and the "Ten Sefirot of Belimah" referred to the ten times the creation story says: "And God said." As a famous ancient Talmudic sage—and Keeper—put it: "The world was created with ten statements." These statements were composed, of course, of thirty-two basic elements: the twenty-two letters of the Hebrew alphabet, and the ten numbers from one to ten.

...ENGRAVED GOD, THE LORD OF HOSTS, THE GOD OF ISRAEL, THE LIVING GOD AND KING OF THE UNIVERSE...

A deep silence surrounded them. As in their first session, they were engulfed by intense yet tender Blessing energies. The Void before them was a veil of impenetrable darkness.

...AND HE CREATED HIS WORLD WITH THREE SFR'S: WITH SFR AND SFR AND SFR.

Now that the Book's introductory passage was completed, Eliezer prepared for the main text: the second formula. He wondered whether this time he would be able to visualize the Primordial Gate and what they might see.

He lost his balance and immediately brushed the thought aside. He knew that losing focus in discernment, especially in this uncertain territory, could be fatal. He started reciting the second Sefirah. Oleander spoke the same words:

TEN *SEFIROT* OF *BELIMAH*, TEN AND NOT NINE, TEN AND NOT ELEVEN,

As if floating in the eye of a hurricane being born, they felt the forces of the Blessing building and circling, binding them from a distance.

UNDERSTAND WITH WISDOM AND EXPLORE WITH UNDERSTANDING, EXAMINE WITH THEM, INVESTIGATE FROM THEM, KNOW AND THINK AND CREATE...

This hurricane of energies swelled around them, held back by something they could not see. They felt dwarfed by its magnitude. Suppressing their anxiety, they both plunged into the final passage of the second Sefirah:

...AND RETURN THE CREATOR TO HIS PLACE, BECAUSE HE FORMS AND CREATES BY HIMSELF, AND THERE IS NO

ONE BUT HIM, AND HIS ATTRIBUTE IS TEN THAT HAVE NO END.

The tension was at its peak now. The reservoir of Blessing was waiting for the codeword to unleash it. Oleander looked at Eliezer, who then nodded.

Oleander braced himself, then spoke: "Mila."

Nothing happened.

He exchanged glances with his older companion, and then uttered again, this time more forcefully: "*Mila!*"

This time, the Void rumbled and shook. A few seconds later, when the quake subsided, they exchanged glances. What was happening?

Eliezer signaled to Oleander that he wanted to try it himself. Slowly and forcefully he spoke the Hebrew word. Again the Void rumbled as if in anger. The two men felt its tremors in their bodies.

Something was definitely wrong, Eliezer thought. In a flash he understood: "*Mila*" was the codeword for the first Sefirah only! In order to activate the second Sefirah, they needed a different codeword.

Thoughts raced through Eliezer's mind. If the first formula contained a hint of the first codeword, then this second formula must contain a hint of the second: UNDERSTAND WITH WISDOM AND EXPLORE WITH UNDERSTANDING, EXAMINE WITH THEM, INVESTIGATE FROM THEM, KNOW AND THINK...

The codeword must be connected to wisdom, learning, knowing, calculating. "Understanding!"

An ominous quake answered him from the belly of the Void.

"Knowledge!" he tried again.

Another quake, deeper and more powerful, shook them both. They struggled to maintain their balance.

"Discovery!" cried Eliezer.

The angry rumbling was growing, shaking the two Keepers fiercely, roaring and growling, threatening to carry them across the brink into the Void.

Oleander turned to Eliezer and wondered whether they should stop. But the tremors had become too violent to move without losing balance. If they couldn't find the codeword very quickly, they would never get out of here.

"Truth!"

Eliezer was tossed sideways by a wild wave of energy, and then by another. From the corner of his eye he saw that Oleander was precariously close to the edge of the Void.

He forced himself to calm down and think. TEN AND NOT NINE, TEN AND NOT ELEVEN—this points at truth, exactness. EXAMINE, INVESTIGATE, KNOW, THINK—this suggests a search for truth but one that is not straightforward. The truth may be hidden and the search may require a resourcefulness or special eye. AND CREATE—the creator FORMS AND CREATES BY HIMSELF. *Create the truth?* A truth that is hidden and requires resourcefulness, a creativity to detect...

Could it be? The word sounded wrong in his mind but it persisted and in desperation he shouted. *"Cunning!"*

The rumbling stopped and the Void became silent.

They had regained their balance when an explosion of Blessing threatened to tear them apart. A vortex swirled them around with a combination of agony and sweetness almost impossible to bear. Then a bolt of Blessing shot through them, *from them*, into the Void. They watched it receding into the distance like a meteor, becoming smaller and still smaller until disappearing in the darkness.

The energies surrounding them subsided, the echoes of what they had heard, seen, and felt receded. Gradually they ascended from their Inner Depths to themselves, to their bodies, to their normal consciousness.

Oleander opened his eyes and saw Eliezer struggle against his exhaustion to sit straighter in his chair. The monk was also deeply fatigued yet felt purified. For the second time they had discerned the Primordial Gate—something no Keeper in recorded history had done—and withstood the violent forces of the Blessing. More importantly, if Eliezer's theory was right, then the Primordial Gate was now even more ajar.

26

Eliezer spent the afternoon and night sleeping on the bed in Oleander's hotel room, while Oleander took the sofa. The monk wanted to keep an eye on him to make sure he was alright. All evening a thought kept nagging him. Why "Cunning"? Why this word and not a thousand others? Eliezer himself did not know the answer, nor could he explain why this word had come to his mind at the very moment it was needed.

In the morning, after Eliezer said goodbye to Oleander, he sat at a sidewalk café by the hotel and called Julia.

"Eli, where are you? You disappeared so quickly yesterday." Erna sounded relieved.

"Zurich. I leave for Israel in a few hours. Can you come over from Lucerne? Let's take a walk before I go."

"Good, I've got a couple of questions for you. And for William."

"No, let us only enjoy each other's presence, like in the old days. No business talk, nothing about the Blessing, just you and I together. I'm worn out. I wish for only your company."

She detected the genuine fatigue in his voice. "Okay."

For an hour they strolled in the old section of the city, holding hands, and then sat in a small municipal garden. Erna kept her word and did not press him about her suspicions, and Eliezer volunteered nothing. Unexpected by either, their thoughts had turned to the question whether they had done the right thing years ago, when they had decided to forgo their romance in order to devote themselves to Keeperdom. But they pushed it from their minds, satisfied to savor the present and happy their love had survived. Aside from being Keepers, their love for each other had been the one constant in their lives over almost 50 years.

It took great discipline on Erna's part not to inquire what he and Oleander were involved in. Once she was on the verge of asking but saw in his face a deep worry, one he was not ready to share. She would wait.

Eliezer slept through the flight. When he landed at Ben Gurion Airport outside Tel Aviv it was already late afternoon. He pulled the car out of long-term parking and started driving along Highway 1 to Jerusalem, wondering how to find the codeword of the third Sefirah. The second Sefirah's codeword had been a lucky guess. It could not be left to chance again; they might not survive the next time. If they were to continue, he had to crack the secret of the codewords. But how?

He would search the Keepers' Chronicles again. Also, scholars and rabbis had published articles about the Book of Creation, and even though they were not Keepers, they might have had insights. He decided to go straight to the university's Jewish Studies Library. At the entrance to Jerusalem, he did not turn left onto the bypass that led to the Mount Scopus campus. Instead, he went straight and then turned right towards the Givat Ram campus.

Osnat felt restless all morning. For several days she had been on the border of depression and had hardly left her apartment. But this morning she felt the urge to go out into the world. She decided to go to the university.

She went down to the street and waited at the bus stop. The number 9 bus was approaching but it was going in the opposite direction, returning from Mount Scopus. It stopped and disgorged its passengers—and something made her sprint across the street and jump onboard before the door closed.

"What's going on with you?" she chided herself as she sat down by a window. "Where do you think you are going?" There was only one significant place on the bus' route: the Givat Ram campus—which had no interest for her since it housed the natural science departments and the National Library.

She got off at Givat Ram. She had never been to this campus, dominated by the National Library. "I might as well see what's here." She walked on the lawn towards the large structure that housed a number of libraries. There was nothing interesting on the first floor, so she climbed to the second. Noticing the sign "The Jewish Studies Library" she opened the heavy door.

Crossing the threshold, she stopped. Eliezer was at a nearby table, immersed in a journal, a pile of books to one side. There was an imposing air around him, and unconsciously or not the other patrons kept a distance. She wanted to speak to him but did not find the courage to interrupt his work.

Eliezer raised his head and saw a young woman pushing open the main door. For some reason he focused his gaze not on her appearance, not on any visible shape, but on the Blessing around her. Against the dark background of the door he saw an impressive aura surrounding the young figure, not yet sharpened and intensified by experience and training but promisingly rich and vibrant. For several moments he was captivated by the unusual sight. To his knowledge, he was the only Keeper in Israel at this time. He stood and hurried to the door, but when he stepped outside she was gone.

27

Erna drove back to the Abbey, her heart full of emotion. The meeting with Eliezer had been like finding a forgotten photograph of a joyful time. Pulling into the courtyard of the Abbey she sighed seeing Peprini's car approaching and slowing. He rolled down the window. Unwillingly she did too.

"So there you are. Did you have an enjoyable time in the city?"

Erna wondered whether he knew or was guessing. There was no point in lying. "I saw Eliezer off to Israel."

"I'll speak to you tomorrow, then," he said and drove away.

Peprini looked in the rearview mirror and watched her car receding. That morning he had examined the credit card records of Eliezer. The old man had flown to London two weeks ago and left on a flight later that day. On impulse he looked at Oleander's accounts. He had arrived in London on that same day, taken a hotel room, then left also that afternoon.

In the past six months they had met four times, but never for more than a day. Why would they travel such distances to meet? Further, neither had notified him—as de facto Director of Security—of leaving the country, as was their responsibility as Councilors. It seemed the two were joined in some clandestine business. Were they the Keepers the Ishmaelite Prince had spoken of? Was Erna a part of it? The question disturbed him all the way to the Frostburg Institute. Only when he parked his car did he dismiss the idea. No. If she were, she wouldn't have spoken at the Council meeting about unauthorized actions. Eliezer and Oleander were on their own.

The next morning Eric Tiplady was the first thing on Peprini's mind. His personnel would soon be stretched very thin and the boy might be needed. He summoned Tiplady to his office at the Frostburg House.

Peprini gestured to a chair in front of his desk. "Your past experience is showing itself."

Tiplady examined him. "I'm not sure what you mean."

Peprini noted there was no honorific, no "Sir" or "Director" or "Mr. Peprini." This wouldn't do.

"I'm speaking of deception, Mr. Tiplady. Pretending to be what you are not. You must realize you cannot fake talent as a Keeper. Mimicking what your classmates describe in their experiences is pointless. We can see the truth… at all times."

"Alright."

"In fact, you're a thief." The boy had a juvenile police record Peprini had managed to have unsealed. Nothing violent, just a pure disregard for others. Fear seemed to be the only bridle on him. The Councilor was pleased he made no attempt to deny it. "You have a penchant for breaking and entering. It seems you enjoy invading the privacy of others."

Tiplady shrugged as if such a tendency was natural. "What's this got to do with me being here?"

"With you being here *Sir*."

Immediately Tiplady grasped his situation. He had been reveling in the new autonomy and aristocracy of Keeperdom, finding a justification for feeling himself above society and its rules. But in this fiefdom *other laws* applied. Looking at the severity of the Councilor's face he realized Peprini was the sole judge and jury, and no lawyer, not even the police could protect him.

"Yes, Sir."

"Unfortunately, Tiplady, in your case we will have to cut short the training normally given to novices. I have a special task for you."

Tiplady's natural defiance surfaced again. "I'm actually enjoying myself here, Councilor. I'm ready to apply myself."

"You have not yet proven yourself worthy of our hospices. This is your chance. Tomorrow you will go abroad."

"To do what, Sir?"

"I am sending you to New York. In due time you will learn more."

Peprini waited for his response. Tiplady examined his face and then smirked.

"You find something funny?"

"You need me for something. Something personal, don't you? Sir."

The Councilor was impressed. The boy managed to unbalance him. He is irritating, he thought, but daring, mean, and observant.

"I need to know what I'm getting into, Mr. Peprini, before I agree."

"Your impertinence will lead you nowhere," Peprini said coldly, "except back to your pathetic little common life. Or worse."

They stared at each other.

"I'll take your offer, Sir."

"Of course you will. You will be ready to travel tomorrow morning at eight-thirty."

"To New York?"

"Madrid. A week of training, then New York." His eyes kept returning to a small tattoo on the boy's neck. It was a Chinese character. Tiplady was wearing a tee-shirt and this was the first time the tattoo had been visible.

"That is a curious mark you have," he said, placing his finger on his own neck. "What does it mean?"

"'Freedom.' Sir."

Peprini had a working knowledge of Mandarin through his family's history with the Rare Book Company. He smiled, aware the characters did not mean "freedom" but instead "small annoying dog."

"The artist. A friend of yours?"

The boy shook his head.

"Though the outside world doesn't know of us, you still represent us in a fashion. As such you will wear proper dress."

"So hide the tattoo."

Peprini nodded. "When you arrive in Madrid you are to purchase suitable clothing. What you need will be provided."

28

The Frostburg House, Lucerne, December 1952

"Who am I? We all ask that question. But where can we look for answers?" The old man came around his desk and sat in a chair across from his grandson. He saw that the boy was thinking and was pleased.

"Who are we Keepers? Ah, now this question we can answer. Our story, as found in the Keepers' Chronicles, defines us. Or does it? Remember, what is written in those documents is nothing that cannot be taught to anyone willing to listen. One can choose to be a historian, yet one cannot choose to be a Keeper. Many have Esau's blood, but very few are Keepers. How it is determined who receives this gift from his ancestors, we do not know. Sometimes it passes from a parent to a certain child, but usually it skips a few generations, sometimes it never appears again in that family's line." He shrugged. "Some are chosen, that is enough. We are given, as a gift from God, the ability of discernment. It is this ability that makes us who we are.

"Yes, Menach, we also have the special capacity to sense the Blessing. But in my opinion, this is simply another side of our ability to discern, another side of our openness to the Blessing. All other people are blind to it. Of course, the Blessing is always present—the world could not have existed without it—but only Keepers can sense it. When you start learning to discern, you will see what it is like. You will see its magnificent radiance."

"The Blessing is always in the air?"

"Oh, yes, but it changes all the time. Like the weather: there are prevailing currents, overcast days and brilliant days, even storms. Even dead zones where, for reasons we do not understand, the Blessing is extremely faint. Sometimes it swells and intensifies—like a ridge of high pressure—and then there is nothing more wondrous. Yes, it changes constantly. How else would people have good luck one day and bad on another? Why would an artist suddenly have an inspiration, or an entire country be steeped in war? Why do misfortunes come in clusters?"

He stared at the boy as if he had no place to go and nothing to do but sit with him. The office had been the drawing room of the original Frostburg House. The room had no windows and the lighting hadn't been fully modernized, and so it always seemed on the verge of darkness, the chandelier more decorative than practical.

"You have a question, yes?"

"Why do we discern?"

"Excellent. It is the question all Keepers ask. Oh, discernment of the Bible world is a marvel, to be sure. But what purpose does it serve? We discern, Menach, in order that the Blessing may be renewed. The Vessels cannot do this without us. Why we are needed for the renewal of the Blessing—this, however, is not known."

"Why not?"

"Unfortunately, Esau our forefather and his descendants, for some hundreds of years, wrote nothing of this, nothing that survived. Perhaps they kept these secrets as an oral history. I imagine it never occurred to them such knowledge could be lost. That was a mistake we decided three thousand years ago we would never make again. Yes, Menach, and so we store copies of the Chronicles in several different locations."

"How could something so important end up lost?"

"Wars, famines, plagues, disasters—natural and human. Our own Great Diaspora. By the time we have a written record there is little mention of discernment beyond its unexplained necessity."

"Didn't Keepers try to find out how discernment works?"

"Did they make guesses? Of course. The first guess we find in our records suggests that God, through Isaac, gave his son Esau the gift of discernment as compensation for *not* receiving the Blessing. A consolation prize of sorts. As the eldest son, Esau should have received this birthright, and would have, but for Isaac's trickery. An interesting idea, but it fails to explain what discernment does and why it is necessary.

"Others believed that discernment serves to cleanse the Vessels' path to the Bible World; to sweep from the Void the flotsam that blocks the Vessels' way. No, I don't like that conjecture either. There is no evidence of any kind of debris hovering in the Void or that we sweep it away.

"Another guess, rather popular since the Middle Ages, says we discern in order to know the Bible World. The idea is that Isaac's gift was split into two equal parts: Esau received the knowledge of the Bible World, and Jacob received the capacity to travel to the Bible world. Together we are a team.

"Oh you like that one, do you? I'll tell you a secret I have never told anyone, even your father. So do I. But, sadly, in the end I think no. The essence of what we gain *in knowledge* from discerning—from peering into the Bible World—is written in the Bible for anyone to know.

"We know *that* we must discern, without knowing exactly *why*. It does sound confusing, yes. I said the meaning of discernment was lost. Our ancestors for thousands of years practiced discernment because it was what Keepers did. And discernment is a reward in itself. But it requires great discipline. Further, though the experience of discernment is rewarding, after a difficult discernment session a Keeper's own Blessing is weakened for several days. When you learn to perceive the aura surrounding a Keeper you will see for yourself. So it is not surprising that over time Keepers discerned less and less. When a practice is hard but we do not understand the reason for it, why we are suffering, it is very difficult to maintain. This is what happened in the middle of the 14th Century. Looking back at the Chronicles we can see the Council in those years was weak. Novices still underwent the training but it was mainly an initiation ritual. They all but ceased discernment. What happened? Do you recall your history?"

"The Black Plague?"

"Yes. 'The Great Mortality,' as it was called then. One of every three people in Europe and Western Asia died. I'm sure it looked as if the world was ending. The Council, out of fear, and no doubt some resurrection of duty, began in earnest discerning once again. And within months the Plague largely subsided. Yes, Menach, it might have been coincidence, but I doubt it—there have been other similar instances. In any event, this was frightening enough to motivate Keepers to continue discerning. Even though the exact… mechanism by which discernment works to renew the Blessing is still unknown to Keepers."

The elder Peprini appraised his grandson and decided to continue.

"At some point in your discernments, you might encounter a Vessel at the edge of the Void preparing to enter it. Vessels can enter the Void and return unharmed. The Blessing which they carry in their soul protects them, we assume. *We cannot enter the Void.*" He had spoken sternly and the boy was startled. "Never forget that. No matter how enticing, no matter how much you would like to go nearer the Bible World, you must not enter the Void. Those who enter never return. They are lost forever."

"Do they die?"

The old man nodded. "We find them in their chair as if still discerning. Others are alive but their minds are gone. Some remain in a coma, perhaps for years, before their bodies die. A few awaken, yes, Menach. But they never leave the hospital. Yes, we have a special place where we take care of them… You are frightened? Good, one would be foolish not to be.

"Just one moment." He walked across the expanse of Persian carpet and left the room. He returned with a plate of ginger cookies that he set on the edge of the desk. "Mrs. Schonstein will bring us some hot chocolate." He rubbed his hands together. "It has started to snow."

The boy took a cookie from the plate. A woman entered the room carrying a tray with two steaming cups.

"Ah, thank you very much, Mrs. Schonstein. Please set the tray on the desk. I think we will let them cool." He waited until she closed the door.

"Mmm, especially tasty on a snowy day, yes? Well. We might just ask the Vessels what it is like to travel through the Void. That would be most simple. But that is forbidden."

"*Why?*"

"The answer to that question is the answer to why we do most of what we do. The reasons have been lost. All we have is tradition and it tells us that Keepers are *never* to reveal themselves to a Vessel. Why not? Would anything terrible happen? Or is it simply some pride in knowing what they do not?" He shrugged.

"Well, to return to the question of what Vessels experience in the Void—we have clues. As you know, throughout our history we have often been friends and advisors of Vessels. It would happen that Vessels would tell our ancestor about a dream they had. In fact, 'dream' is the wrong word, because it is not dreaming in the normal sense. It feels quite real—which it is. Often they remember their visions only vaguely, as happens with ordinary dreams. But we have been able to reconstruct their experience. It seems that every week or so they dream, feeling a deep need to go to some faraway place. Some feel they are being called, they don't know by whom or to where. They find themselves at the edge of the Void. When they enter, they float in the darkness for a long time. Sometimes this is all there is to their vision, and they awaken with a disquieting feeling. But sometimes they see a disk of light which we know is the Bible World. They start moving towards it."

"*How do they find their way, I mean—before they see the light?*"

"We are not sure. Perhaps they have an instinct like migrating birds. Some Vessels report that they follow a faint glow. We are not sure. But when they do reach the Bible World they are drawn to one of the twelve Gates of the Blessing. And then something extraordinary happens. They find themselves in the midst of a Biblical episode, right next to Abraham or Isaac or Jacob as God gives His Blessing. They kneel beside their ancestor, feeling the bond of family, and are then filled with the Blessing. Afterwards, they return from the Void, full of Blessing, and awaken in our world. They feel graced, overflowing with purity and divine beneficence.

And the entire world is Blessed through them again." He stared at the boy. "We can only imagine what this would feel like."

He gripped the armrests of the chair so hard his old hands strained, and he appeared to change his mind. "It is *not true* that we can only imagine this."

An old ache, or an old excitement, seemed to return to him.

"When I was much younger, and an assistant to the Director of Archives, I was sent to investigate a journal that had come up for sale at Christie's Auction House in London. This was 1899. It has long been our practice to examine any document that might contain information about us. This diary of a seventeenth-century monk interested us because the abbot during that time was a Keeper. We needed to be sure there was nothing revealing. The diary turned out to be quite dull. But as I was leaving they began preparing for the next day. It was an estate sale: everything from carpets to dinner silver to various statues to suits of armor. It included the owner's library. There was a very long list of the library's contents, among them an early description of religious sects in the Middle East. It was written by an Arab historian named ibn-Khaldun in about 1370, and printed in the mid-1800's. Though in old Arabic, and difficult to follow, I was fascinated. I spoke with the son of the deceased owner of the estate—he thought little of this torn book and agreed to give it to me for a symbolic price, instead of waiting for the auction.

"On the train to Lucerne I read; all through the night I read. It was during that night that I found it. One chapter talked of a sect of Jews who believed in regeneration; not of life, but of God's presence. These Jews had an incantation."

He saw the boy's confusion.

"A magical sequence of words that one chants. They believed that it protected them. Perhaps it did. Ibn-Kahldun says their village was untouched the whole of the Crusades."

The old man was no longer looking at his grandson but through him.

"He transcribed the sounds in Arabic letters. The incantation looked like a meaningless sequence of some twenty-four words in Hebrew, though the tribe no longer spoke this language and didn't understand what it meant: *Eser, eser, eser, hamisha ke-neged hamisha ve-shtayim, esrim otiot, etsbaot ve-brit, lashon mehuvenet ba-emtsa, Sefirot Sefirot yesod, milat ha-maor, ve-ba-pe mispar yihud, be-milat Belimah.*"

"What does it say, Grandfather?"

The old man smiled kindly. "I translated it once into English—which is really next to impossible, since many sounds can stand for different Hebrew words, just like 'two' and 'too' and 'to' in English. Besides, some words are too ancient and rare to understand nowadays. 'Belimah,' for example. In any case, my translation went something like: *Ten, ten, ten, five opposite five and two, twenty letters, fingers and covenant, tongue set in the center, countings, fundamental countings, circumcision of nakedness, and in the mouth a number of the one, in the word of station.*

"Puzzling, yes? Maddening. These Jews agreed to share this incantation because the words were not in the right order. They knew nobody could find the right order, because the number of possible permutations—combinations—of the twenty-four words is stupendous. You can spend ten lifetimes combining these words without going over even one percent of the possibilities. Ibn-Khaldun says that they chant for an hour or so in a kind of trance, changing the order of the words each time. When at last their leader decides the time is right, they chant the words in the correct order, and God's presence is renewed among them. They describe it as a wave of infinite joy that radiates goodness all around them."

"The Blessing?"

"Yes, Menach. It was clear to me they had a way of calling forth the Blessing. This sent me into the Archives for the next several years. Some months I never saw daylight, in the library before dawn and returning home in the evening. I think I wear these glasses today because of what I did to my eyes in those years." He paused, taking off the wire-rimmed frames and rubbing his eyes. He didn't begin speaking until he placed the glasses back on his face. "I did not bother with the Chronicles. No, what I was looking for—if it existed—would be found in the personal documents of the old Keepers."

"Yes, Grandfather?"

"And I found it. A Keeper in Damascus, about 1450, wrote of a village of Jews he had encountered in his travels. He speculated they might have been a lost line of Keepers. A number of them had perceptible auras but unrefined, undeveloped by training. He said they had a very unusual prayer, a kind he had never heard of, a chant made of a chain of Hebrew words. One Sabbath they permitted him to worship with them. The eldest chanted a word, and everyone repeated this. To our Keeper it was an endless string of gibberish. But, soon after they stopped, he began to feel what he described as 'the essence of God's grace flushing through me, like the pure air after a thunderstorm.' The Jews smiled knowingly. He knew better than to ask them for the true sequence. And it would be impossible to duplicate what they had done. They saw he was a true seeker of God and gave him a glimpse of their secret. They might have even felt the kinship all Keepers feel. The experience had a profound effect on him. He never felt that again, so his diary says. And he longed for it.

"You are thinking: What does this mean? I believe this small village of Jews was able to summon the Blessing of God, at least a hint of it."

"So the Keeper who chanted with them became a Vessel for a little while?"

"Yes, Menach. That is what I believe."

"Did you try and find these people?"

"Certainly. I searched for many years. But they had disappeared, like so many other peoples. They are gone."

He stood and looked as if there was some place he needed to go, but he seemed to remember he was an old man, and there were no longer places he needed to go. He sat down.

"Your twelfth birthday is in two months, Menach. I did not tell your father this story until he was nearly ready for university. I myself did not learn some of what I have told you until I had been a Councilor for some years. But each generation must reach further, and so you must start still earlier."

The boy nodded soberly.

"What I will now tell you none but the Peprinis and perhaps a few others know. During our history, a very small number of us refused to accept that we must blindly follow tradition. In Keeperdom, like in every religion, there are dogmas. Through the years they become sacred and petrified. Merely to question them is regarded as heretical. Heretics have been punished most severely, even by death. So if one had a mind to question, two roads existed. You stifle your thoughts and perform your duty, a duty we all agree is an honor. Or you learn to be very careful to whom you speak of your questions."

"Are we heretics?"

From long-honed instinct the old man examined the face to determine how well he could be trusted. But he saw a boy with a cookie in his hand, his own flesh and blood. The old man smiled.

"Yes. But that is because we recognize a higher duty than obedience to our Order. We serve the Blessing and so serve God before man. Do not confuse this purity of motive with naiveté, with being innocent. We must always hide this part of ourselves. We must be more intelligent and more cunning than others. The first rule is to confide in no one except myself and your father. This will guide you until you are on the Council. Yes, you will join your father when it is time. We will see to it, and you will be more than prepared.

"For those engaged in heresy, the written record is more dangerous than a whisper in the wrong ear. That is your second rule. All must be kept in your memory. What does not exist cannot betray you. It is not surprising that virtually no records exist of such activities within our Order. There are hints and allusions, but one exception occurred in the thirteenth century. An English Keeper, a Councilor named Simon de Montfort proposed the worst treason: to forsake the old ways of discerning and to search for new ways to renew the Blessing—without Vessels. He had a plan, it seems, and revealed this to the Council. As a Councilor, and one with many friends, he could not be silently dispatched. Killed. The event is described in the Chronicles. But we know from other sources that much was left out and the rest was misrepresented."

"*Lies?*"

"Lies. I learned of it through a conversation I had with Councilor Battsen just before he died. He was a friend despite... well, he was my friend. When he knew he was dying and punishment no longer scared him, he told me of Simon de Montfort. He had learned in much the same way. Of course, I would not have betrayed him, and he should have known this. But...

"De Montfort believed we had become caretakers of a growing cemetery. By the thirteenth century, six Vessel lines had ended. He looked into the future and saw that in fifteen hundred years the Blessing would disappear from Earth. It was necessary, he reasoned, to find new ways to bring Blessing to the Earth—without the Vessels. He was a visionary and was regarded as are all visionaries: as a dangerous provocateur. He threatened Keeperdom.

"Was he truly dangerous? As you read the Chronicles you will see that, above all, stability is valued. Even after the death of a Vessel, especially so, our ancestors held tightly and counted on the fact that Vessel deaths are exceedingly rare. But de Montfort realized this attitude was like a child pulling the blanket over his head." The old man paused, smiling at his grandson. "Like an ostrich sticking his head in the sand. The Vessels were dying and we could no longer hide from the fact.

"Since de Montfort's time, another Vessel line has ended, leaving only the five. What he feared has occurred. We have held to our traditions, stood our post like good soldiers, while the battle is being lost. The present Council is no different.

"*The Peprini family is special.* You are the first third-generation Keeper in the history of Keeperdom, and you will be the first third-generation Councilor. Having this continuous line will allow us to search for what de Montfort believed he understood. In the past a Keeper might come to understand one piece of the puzzle, but whom could he tell? Excommunication is a serious enough matter in the Catholic Church, but Keepers do not merely excommunicate. We cannot take the chance. The rare Keeper who gains a piece of the de Montfort puzzle will take the secret into death. The next person must start from nil.

"Our family line will enable us to assemble the pieces, the clues. There is a reason God has graced our three generations with the gift of discernment. And I believe that reason is our destiny."

Lucerne, March 1956, the Peprini family home

As some children learn rhymes or songs and absent-mindedly repeat them as they play or walk to school, Menach had the habit of stringing together those Hebrew words in whatever order they popped into his mind, whispering or singing them to the tune that happened to be in his ear. Perhaps in the beginning he had some childish hope of striking upon the right combination, though even then he knew it was pointless. But the repetition was comforting. Eventually, it became unconscious.

He was sixteen and studying for an exam in ancient Greek. He had closed his book and was gathering his notes when his skin began to tingle. The letters and numbers he was whispering now became audible. His heart began to well up with a profound compassion. This feeling grew far past anything he had known until his heart burst and it seemed his skin shattered and showered everything around him in a tender love he hadn't known existed. He cried tears of joy and devotion. The feeling passed but left behind a quiet, divine presence that lasted until he fell asleep.

He told no one, not even his grandfather. It would be impossible to duplicate. He was certain it had been the Blessing which the desert tribe possessed but he had no idea of the string of Hebrew words he had chanted to invoke it. His grandfather's respect meant too much to be thought of as a pretender. But that taste of the Blessing remained the most powerful experience of his life. Nothing else, not the birth of his children or the deaths of his grandfather, father, and mother touched him as deeply.

29

Menach Peprini sat behind the immense walnut desk that had been his father's and before that his grandfather's. With his father's death in 1990 he had assumed the post of Director of Keepers' Training and now occupied the office in the former drawing room of the Frostburg House. Marcus Peprini had modernized the lighting, everywhere replacing the traditional twelve candle holders—representing the twelve Vessels—with twelve bulbs. His son Menach had done the same for the electrical to accommodate the computer and fax and other requirements of the contemporary office. Otherwise, nothing in the room had been changed.

There was a knock on the door.

"Come."

A groundskeeper entered with an armful of firewood. He knelt by the large fireplace and went to work. Peprini turned away and picked up the file of a young Keeper. For the past year he had been personally training this young woman for her internship and for his *project*. She was indeed special, and he had become quite fond of her. She had been a good choice. It was unfortunate, he thought, that her life must be put at such risk, but there was no practical replacement for her. He realized he was procrastinating and put down the file.

The groundskeeper finished and a fire began crackling and popping. On the drive from home that morning there had been just a smattering of snow flurries. Peprini always waited until the first snowflakes in autumn before permitting himself a fire. He moved to the fireplace and felt the smoky warmth push into the room. He turned and assessed the ambient Blessing in the room. A month ago this would have been a bleak day, but in today's world, the morning was as blessed as could be hoped. It occurred to him that the new novices might never experience the glory of the Blessing as it had been just weeks ago. He shook his head. "Again I am delaying."

Returning to the desk he picked up the phone. "Have Pilar Diaz come to my office in one hour."

With the death of Mark Gregor, he felt an uncomfortable urgency. But his project to this point had gone very well, and this gave him reason to be confident. And his visit to the Ishmaelite Prince had alleviated most of the worry that he had somehow caused the Vessel's death. More importantly, he was convinced it was no accident that he was a third-generation Keeper—a third-generation Councilor. God must have had reason to grace the Peprini family in this unique way. And so he believed it was he who was destined to reap the fruit of the hard and dangerous research of his three predecessors: the medieval de Montfort, Alberto Peprini, and Marcus Peprini.

Alberto Peprini, an exceedingly ambitious man who kept this hidden behind a mantle of propriety, had deeply envied the Vessels. He harbored a secret humiliation at being a mere Keeper, while the chosen ones walked in the Bible World. After finishing the Novitiate with distinction, he petitioned to be posted as an assistant librarian at the Keepers' Archives. His request was granted, and he began using all his free time to search this vast collection for clues of forgotten knowledge about the powers of Vessels and Keepers.

Years later he came across a batch of anonymous letters from the 13th century mentioning a shadowy figure, an English Keeper named Simon de Montfort. He came to believe that de Montfort had made a revolutionary discovery, and consequently had been silenced and his writings destroyed. He then committed himself to unearthing de Montfort's discovery, searching in the diaries and letters of the endless Keepers' Archives, as well as in documents he had privately purchased from collections across Europe. Eventually, he pieced together an intriguing picture.

De Montfort's starting point was the well-known fact that Vessels only occasionally traveled all the way through the Void to the Bible World. During most nights they would have normal dreams, and only once a week or so they would experience a journey to a Biblical scene—which, of course, they would mistake for a mere vivid dream. It was Keepers' dogma that such trips were enabled by Keepers' discernment, although it was unknown exactly how this worked. What de Montfort realized was that Vessels' successful journeys occurred most often when, or shortly after, two particular Keepers happened to be discerning. The Keepers were himself and another Councilor, Isabel Camille Gistreau, or so-called One-Eyed Isabel, soon to become the head of the Council. They had in common an exceptional capacity for discernment, as well as the self-discipline to practice regularly, unlike the majority of Keepers, even senior officials, who did little more than the minimum discernment their position required and sometimes not even that. De Montfort concluded that these powerful Keepers—in contrast to ordinary ones—*did* something that helped Vessels find their way.

And here de Montfort took a second step, simple but brilliant. It was Keepers' common knowledge that those with greater ability to discern could see the Bible World more brightly and clearly than could those with lesser ability. Keepers had taken for granted that this special power meant a keener perception. But what if, he reasoned, this power works the other way? What if certain Keepers were powerful because they could better *illuminate* the Bible world, not because they had keener vision? This explained why Vessels might reach the Bible world when powerful Keepers were discerning but seldom when they weren't. These Keepers provided a powerful beacon, so to speak, for Vessels to follow through the Void. When such a beacon was present, the Vessel's chance of reaching the Bible World, though still uncertain, was significantly higher.

Now, it was known that when Keepers discerned they produced a discernment beam, though it was not grasped that the beam indeed illuminated the Bible World. Nor did Keepers realize that the Vessels followed these beams, for the twin reasons that Vessels reached the Bible World even when no Keepers were discerning, and that even when Keepers were discerning Vessels often failed to reach the Bible World. These facts made Keepers conclude the discernment beams were coincidental, not causal. But what Keepers did not realize was that these discernment beams functioned in an unexpected fashion. For some time after a Keeper has finished discernment, traces of the beam continued to linger in the Void, enabling the Vessel to sense the path, even if Keepers could no longer see these traces. The stronger the discernment beam, the longer those traces lingered.

De Montfort's writings suggest he was wary of revealing these heretical ideas to the head of the Council, Nicholas of Genoa, a rigid man locked in tradition. But when Nicolas died and was replaced by Isabel—whom de Montfort considered his friend—he felt that the time was ripe. De Montfort convened a special meeting of the Council.

Here the record becomes murky. The elder Peprini learned that de Montfort was going to present his case that Vessels were able to find their way to the Bible World not because of an inborn compass, as was commonly believed, but because their way was marked by Keepers' discernment beacons. Based on this discovery, he then planned to make a proposal to the Council, one that evidently had Isabel deeply worried. The Chronicles report only that in this meeting de Montfort proposed heresy. The Council's reaction—including that of Isabel—was outrage, and he was arrested on the charge of contempt for the sacred traditions. He was imprisoned in an undisclosed location and disappeared.

There appeared no further record of him. What exactly had he suggested to the Council? The elder Peprini believed that de Montfort had proposed one of two things: either that Keepers should begin to cooperate with Vessels in renewing the Blessing, which meant revealing themselves to these Vessels—a very serious violation of tradition. The second possibility was even more blasphemous: assuming all Vessel lines would eventually die out, Keepers should learn how to enter the Void and follow the discernment beacons to the Bible world. These Keepers would then receive the Blessing, in essence becoming new Vessels.

Alberto Peprini passed all this to his son. Marcus Peprini lacked his father's ambition but he was an energetic man with a bold spirit. He had no interest in continuing his father's tedious research but was intrigued by the idea of venturing into forbidden territory. Finding a way to the Bible World was for him the greatest adventure, and preserving the Blessing the noblest one. The great problem, of course, was crossing the Void. While Vessels regularly plunged into the Void and returned unharmed, it was well known that no Keeper had survived more than moments in the Void. And so, Marcus began experimenting with this obstacle.

He carried out many tests, yet gained no better understanding of the powers enabling Vessels to negotiate the Void. But after several years he achieved a breakthrough. Using discernment in a novel way, he managed to dip briefly into the Void and return unharmed.

His idea was perfectly logical. Keepers had assumed that discernment worked under one condition only: when directed to the Bible World. But, Marcus reasoned, if discernment functioned as a guiding beacon, why couldn't it be used to guide travelers not all the way across the Void, but rather to a point *in the Void?* The Void was indeed very dangerous, but it did not kill instantly. Sometimes Keepers became lost only because they were too disoriented and blinded by the darkness to find their way back quickly enough. But if a beacon was sent to the Void—not *through* the Void but to the Void itself, it would be visible there, and could show the way out. Indeed, a beacon *through* the Void dilutes across the great distances to the Bible World, but a beacon sent to illuminate the Void itself would be direct enough and concentrated enough to be detected by a capable Keeper. Using the discernment beacon as a guide—as a safety line, Marcus would travel only a short distance from the edge, then immediately return. If he could do this and return safely, it would allow him to learn about the Void firsthand.

Accordingly, Marcus decided to discern a Biblical passage dealing with the Void. He tried the creation story of Genesis 1—*In the beginning God created the Heavens and the Earth, and the Earth was chaos, and darkness was upon the face of the Void*—only just managing to abort his experiment when he realized the forces he was encountering were much too powerful for him to withstand. As with all Keepers, he had been warned about this, but he had to know the prohibition was justified. There is no other passage in Genesis that explicitly mentions the Void, but he believed one passage does so implicitly: the story of Cain and Abel. After Cain murders his brother Abel, God punishes him by cursing the ground under his feet. Cain can no longer find a place of rest on the Earth, and he becomes a fugitive and a wanderer. God gives him a protective mark to ward off potential enemies, and then we are told: *And Cain went out from the presence of God, and lived in the land of Nod…*

Marcus knew that in Hebrew, the original language of the Bible, 'Nod' means wandering. The land of Nod was not a place on Earth—God had after all banished Cain from Earth. Rather, Nod was no place at all, a realm of eternal wandering, which is to say the Void.

He was right. When he discerned the Nod passage he found himself visualizing Cain traveling into the Void. He also visualized how, as the Bible says, *Cain built a city, and named the city Enoch, after the name of his son, Enoch.* Marcus Peprini's experience might not have been unique. Though Keepers' tradition forbade discernment of anything but the twelve Blessing episodes, it was probable that during the Keepers' long history a few unruly souls had tried that same experiment. But Marcus made an additional, crucial step. He found a helper, a young Keeper completely faithful to him, and had her discern that Nod passage. While she was discerning, he entered the Void. Since her beacon was directed to a point in the Void (rather than to the Bible World beyond, which required projecting the beacon over a greater distance thus diluting its intensity and protection), he could follow it into the blackness and immediately back to safety. He emerged from the Void exhausted but enthralled.

One evening he summoned Menach—the young Peprini was himself a Master-Keeper by this time—and revealed his triumph. Marcus explained to his shocked son that he had traveled four times into the Void. Although his travels had been limited to less than a minute, this was the first step, he declared, eventually to traveling all the way across the Void to the Bible World and becoming a Vessel. They celebrated with a toast to Menach's grandfather.

Unfortunately, Marcus Peprini underestimated the destructive powers of the Void. In his fifth experiment, he stayed too long in the Void. Menach discovered the lifeless body, still sitting as though discerning, in the cottage his father kept outside of town. The young female Keeper had phoned Menach in her panic. He had no difficulty swearing her to secrecy. All were stunned that a Councilor had died while discerning, something unheard of in the history of Keeperdom. This was doubly disconcerting since he was sixty-six, a very young age by Keepers' standards. There were murmurs of nefarious causes, but most preferred to regard it as a terrible accident.

This was eighteen years ago. Menach lacked his father's adventurous spirit but inherited his grandfather's driving ambition. He took his father's death as a sign that the final step in the centuries-long effort was his to make. It was he, Menach Peprini, who was destined to open new horizons for Keeperdom, to reach the Bible World and replenish the Blessing, and liberate the world from its dependence on a dwindling handful of unknowing Vessels. Lifetimes of work built upon centuries of contemplation were to reach their fruition through him.

He began his own research, though for fifteen years he avoided repeating his father's excursions into the Void. Such experiments seemed to him not only unnecessarily dangerous but pointless: a few moments in the Void were hardly promising. He preferred continuing his grandfather's careful and thorough study of ancient documents, combing through the Archives from among the thousands of diaries and letters of former Keepers. Yet he failed to learn more about de Montfort's ideas or the Vessels' special immunity to the Void.

Then two years ago, somewhat discouraged, he was lingering at the edge of the Void after finishing his normal discernment. He moved along the edge, away from his customary place, idly exploring. Keepers rarely did this as it achieved nothing and the danger of the Void loomed near. Immediately an intriguing incident happened. He saw from a distance a Vessel—he was not entirely sure who—dreaming his or her way into the Void. Rarely were such Keeper-Vessel encounters mentioned in the Chronicles as they were considered insignificant coincidences.

Peprini kept returning to that spot. Several weeks later he saw him again. It was David Wyatt, the New York businessman. He established a pattern: David Wyatt passed this location on the way into the Void every six to ten days, always at about the same time: at about 2 to 3 AM Eastern Time. For many months he kept observing David Wyatt, hoping to gain some insight into the Vessel's ability to enter the Void, but he learned nothing new.

Weary and becoming disillusioned, a new inspiration came. As a Keeper, Peprini had no protection against the Void. *But could he exploit David Wyatt's protective powers?* The idea so captivated him that he dropped his grandfather's careful library investigation and renewed his father's daring experiments. He started discerning the Land of Nod passage and envisioning Cain entering the Void. He then selected the ablest young female novice for the test, Pilar Diaz. He trained her to discern the Cain passages. With the help of her guiding beacon he entered the Void and returned safely; he had to make at least one trip himself.

Then he sent her for brief excursions into the emptiness while he was discerning. As expected she was terrified. But it was necessary that she know that she could survive and return safely in order to persuade her to accompany the Vessel. As a Councilor, his beacon was much stronger than hers and so provided much better guidance and protection—an error his father had made. In the past month, she had seen David Wyatt four times. On her last journey not only did she remain in the Void more than two minutes, the Vessel brushed past her on his way into the darkness, so close that their eyes met.

That night the Councilor stood in front of the mirror and looked at his image. "Menach Peprini," he said, "you will become a Vessel, the only soul ever to be both Keeper and Vessel. Just as the Blessing was rightly Esau's, so it rightly belongs to the Peprinis, to you."

30

Peprini recognized her soft knock. He called and a young woman entered. Pilar Diaz was of mixed Portuguese and Spanish descent. At thirteen she told her priest she had witnessed events as they were happening in the Bible. Somehow the story made its way to the local bishop who, being a Keeper, kept watch over her. Several years later she was invited to study at the Frostburg Institute. She was thrilled to learn who she was and devote herself to the great cause. But she was even more elated to learn that Councilor Peprini found special interest in her and her capacities.

The young woman walked towards Peprini with a smile. This was not the shy and uncertain girl who had first entered the room a year ago. She wore a white blouse and beige skirt a little long to be fashionable. She had a beautiful smile. When she was close he noted, as he had before, the small smile lines to either side of her mouth. A happy girl, he thought. He half-stood and adjusted his suit coat and tie, looking away from her. She reached the desk and he continued looking at the wall.

At that moment he understood his anxiety and hesitation: He was not worried about this woman's life—a great mission may demand sacrifices—but about the prospect of failure. The failure of three generations of dedication. The loss of three generations of hope.

"Sit. Did you sleep well?"

"Yes, thank you." She pushed her dark hair back behind her ear and sat down, leaning back comfortably in the chair. It had taken many visits before she began to relax in his company.

"Very good. The Blessing today is as strong as can be hoped. I have seen much better days, but that was before the… tragedy. We will make our first attempt today." She tensed. "Only if you feel ready," he added, knowing she trusted him.

"I do."

"Good." He picked up the phone. "Have my car brought around."

They got in the large silver Mercedes with Peprini driving, turning south as they exited the gates of the Frostburg House. The mountain sky was low and a cool mist coated the windshield. They drove slowly through town but the car picked up speed down the valley. Neither felt the desire to speak. Twenty minutes later the car wound through a stand of pines that hid the property from the main road, opening to a small stone house. Smoke rose from the chimney.

The cottage had been used by his father chiefly for his trysts. It was also where he had died while discerning the Void. He opened the door and was met with a rush of warmth and the smell of burning wood. The housekeeper had arrived earlier and made preparations. They took off their coats and he looked at his watch.

"It's just before two in New York. We are right on schedule."

They settled in the main room, just the right distance from the fire for comfort.

"I'll say once more, though I'm sure it's unnecessary, that when you emerge from your Inner Depths you are to wait for David Wyatt at the edge of the Void. Do not attempt to discern or look into the Void—both will sap your energies."

"We have practiced this for two months now, Councilor. I'm ready."

"But now the part we have never practiced. When Vessel Wyatt appears at the Void's edge you are to reach for him." She nodded. "He is no longer surprised to see you during his dream. He should accept you."

"Last week he looked at me and smiled."

He nodded. "If he turns away don't pursue him. We will try another time. But if he accepts your embrace, cling to him. I'll begin discerning the Bible World. Gate One. He should instinctively want to go along my discernment beacon deeper into the Void. Don't let anxiety overcome you—you will experience the protection of his Blessing while holding him. How long this will take for you, I can't say. With Gate One I can maintain discernment for a long time. If he travels all the way to the Bible world, remain close to him. Once he receives the Blessing he might leave quite suddenly. Again, hold close and he will bring you back."

She nodded. She knew these instructions as she did the Lord's Prayer. Peprini wished he were as confident as he knew he sounded.

"I feel like the first astronaut," she said. He realized she grasped the danger better than he did. "Thank you for your faith in me."

He was moved as he hadn't been for many years and could only nod. He had proceeded very slowly with Pilar. Keepers were trained to think in terms of centuries. But then Gregor terminated. He could wait no longer.

They now prepared to descend. They narrowed their eyes to slits, slowed their breathing and heartbeat, and coordinated their auras so they would emerge in the same location in the Depths. They closed their eyes and entered the discerning mode. Peprini emerged first in the corridor at the bottom of his own Inner Depths. With confident, experienced movements he moved towards the boundary of the Void. Minutes later Pilar appeared.

They stood side-by-side. The thought passed through Peprini's mind that if he had to paint this scene—to translate this spiritual scenery into ordinary physical shapes—he would portray it as two figures standing on the shore of a gigantic, dark ocean where the black of the water and the black of the sky were indistinguishable.

He signaled and they began moving along the edge of the Void. They arrived at the location.

Now they waited. Vessel Wyatt had proven very predictable, and they didn't have to wait long. He appeared and, as seemed to be his routine, stood at the Void's edge for a time, like a cliff-diver readying himself for the plunge.

Pilar turned to Peprini, a questioning look on her face. He breathed deeply—*now was the moment*—and suppressing a surge of anxiety, nodded. She turned and moved towards the Vessel. When just a few feet away she held out her hand. Wyatt hesitated and then took it.

Peprini now turned to the Bible World and illuminated the scene of God's first blessing to Abraham. Pilar stepped closer and the Vessel took her in his arms. And then they were gone.

31

David Wyatt made sure the doors to the townhouse were locked and turned on the alarm system. As he prepared for bed he thought of the woman he had dreamed of several times in the past few weeks. She was now familiar enough he could picture her. Young, slender, with dark hair and… green eyes? That's odd, he thought, do I normally dream in color? It was strange he should keep dreaming of her. He could not recall having seen her in his waking life. She was pretty in an unremarkable way, except for eyes that radiated intelligence, as if she knew something he did not.

He climbed into bed, set the alarm and picked up his book. The day had worn him out and he put down the book even before opening it. Soon he was asleep.

Wyatt found himself moving towards the familiar cliff overlooking the emptiness. As a boy, this part of the dream left him soaking in sweat when he awoke. But after years of dreaming this same scene, he was no longer scared. He stood at the edge and felt the accumulated memory of all the times he had been here. He wasn't alone. The dark-haired woman was again waiting for him.

She was coming towards him and he examined her. Behind her he saw an older man, staring into the blackness. She was very near, closer than she had been before. She smiled in a reassuring way and gave him her hand. Unthinkingly he took it. Now he felt the indescribable need to leap into the blackness.

"I have to go," he said.

She smiled and stood toe to toe with him, wrapping her arms around him tightly. He did the same to her.

They fell into the emptiness. Immediately it felt as if gravity changed randomly in power and reference like a plane in rough turbulence. Like an experienced air traveler, this no longer scared him. But the young woman was petrified. Her face was buried in his neck, her fingertips dug into his back and her entire body was rigid with terror. She lifted her head and squinted, but then hid her face again. He took a hand off her back to stroke her head to tell her she would be alright, but she spasmed in alarm.

They were flying smoothly now, yet her embrace tightened. He started feeling her clutch as an irritation, and he pushed her away—more forcefully than he intended; he only wanted a bit of distance between their bodies.

There was a terrible scream and suddenly she was no longer with him. He then saw her tumbling into the dark space, and what was most terrifying—she was silent now.

"It's just a dream," he told himself, watching her fading in the distance. But her inhuman silence horrified him. He plunged after her and grabbed her arm. With a jolt, her body woke from its stupor.

There was a bump in his sense of time as if he had dozed for a moment, and he realized his hands were over his ears. He remembered a shriek, painfully loud, and knew this was the sound he had been blocking. Now he recalled carrying her back to the cliff. She was clutched to him, hiding her face in his chest. "You're safe, you're safe. It's fine." She was sobbing and still clung tightly. He remained there until she calmed. She released her hold and raised her head. "You're okay, we're back." She was better now and nodded. He smiled at her, and with no conscious decision he withdrew. He was wondering whether he would see her again when he became aware of the *beep-beep-beep* of his alarm clock.

Peprini waited anxiously holding his discernment. Minutes passed. He glanced at his hand as if looking at his watch—which, of course, remained in the superficial world. "She can't still be alive," he said, trying to convince himself he was wrong. "If she dies before I get a chance to hear from her what happened, then all this will have been in vain."

He saw a speck in the distance. It grew larger, and soon he could see it was David Wyatt carrying Pilar, her body limp in his arms. Wyatt left the Void and carefully set her down. He appeared to speak to her, then giving her one last look, he disappeared.

Peprini moved as fast as he could. But before he reached her she started floating backwards into her corridor. Evidently, she had enough strength to return to her Inner Depths. Moments later he followed.

He opened his eyes. Pilar was sitting tall in the chair. Thank God, she was breathing. Her eyes were closed, and her hair was damp with sweat, as was her blouse around the neck and armpits.

"Pilar," he whispered. He touched her arm and she opened her eyes. "How do you feel?"

"I'mmm..." She was very pale. She took a deep breath, feeling the hollowness and constriction in her core.

He went to the kitchen and returned with a glass of water. She took a sip, then moaned lightly and greedily drank the rest. He waited.

"Better, yes? Now tell me what happened."

"It was," she finally mumbled weakly, "like nothing else."

He waited for her.

"From the moment he took us deeper… nothing could prepare a person for this. The short trips into the Void we took?" She shook her head wearily. "It was nothing… nothing like that. This was… chaos. I speak five languages… there aren't words in any to describe it." She closed her eyes.

He sighed. "You did very well. I'm proud of you." She smiled wanly. "Are you strong enough to return to the Institute?"

"That would be…," she swallowed with difficulty. "I'm sorry…" She groaned, twitched, and her head fell on her chest.

Peprini stooped over her and put his ear to her heart. She was unconscious.

The rain had ended and the sun pushed through the overcast sky. He carried her to the car and set her down across the backseat. Taking a blanket from the trunk he spread it over her. He got behind the wheel and realized how tired he was. He had refused to acknowledge any loss of vitality as a consequence of Gregor's death, but now it was undeniable. Turning, he examined her face. Dark circles had already formed under her eyes and she continued to perspire.

They arrived at the Frostburg House and one of the maids helped carry Pilar up the stairs to her room. Seeing her wilting body, he came to a decision. The idea of clinging to David Wyatt and being carried by him to the Bible World was too risky. The behavior of the Vessel was too unpredictable. Success would only come with David Wyatt's cooperation. But how to manage that?

32

Dr. Peter Loyev withdrew from Pilar's bed. Peprini waited for his verdict with a deference rare for him. With no sense of hurry, Loyev put his stethoscope in his doctor's bag, and a pensive melancholy took over his tanned and craggy face, his mustache maintaining a red hue despite a thick head of unruly gray hair. The doctor was not much of a Keeper—he himself was well aware of that. His discernments were awkward and he had never gone beyond Gate Two. On the other hand, he was a superb physician, as he himself very well knew. Peprini's grandfather had told young Menach how, as the Novitiate's Director, he had allowed the doctor to pass the Verification exams which by all standards he should have failed. But the Peprinis had gained a physician who owed allegiance to the family.

Dr. Loyev shook his head. "Nothing to be done," he said in his Russian accent. "She's been in the Void for, I'd guess—perhaps thirty seconds. Surprising she survived at all."

Peprini stopped himself from saying "much longer than that." He just nodded, and the doctor continued. "A discernment accident, you say?"

"As I said."

"Hmm. Human beings, we are not meant to crawl about without the Blessing for too long. The machine starts crumbling very quickly. First the brain goes, then…"

"Is there no way to treat the injury?"

The doctor looked at him with something between curiosity and concern, glanced at the sleeping Pilar, and again at Peprini. He opened his mouth to ask but something hard on the Councilor's face told him he shouldn't. Instead, he said flatly, "It's like a brain that suffered oxygen shortage for too long. The damage is permanent."

Peprini's eyes caressed her placid face, her body appearing fragile even beneath the bedcovers. What a pity; all that time training her. His thoughts now turned to Dina Carlini. With her exceptional aura, she might be more resistant to the Void than Pilar. But it would take some time to gain her confidence and train her for his purpose.

"Will she be able to discern?"

"If you don't mind her fainting all of a sudden into the Void."

Peprini winced. He turned to Pilar. He wouldn't try entering the Void again without David Wyatt's cooperation. The Vessel would have to agree to help Carlini or Jongsma—he still needed to decide which of the two he would use. This would mean that Peprini would have to speak to him, convince him of the need for his help, and gain his trust. And it would mean violating another important law of Keeperdom.

He walked to the door, showing the doctor out. "None of this need go beyond this room. You understand, yes?"

The doctor winked. "Of course, Councilor. I understand perfectly well."

Peprini returned to the Rare Book Company. Shortly after four in the afternoon he left his office and went to the courtyard. He was hoping the air might renew him.

He spotted Dina Carlini sitting alone on the stone bench beside the flower beds. Even at this distance he felt an unusual presence about her, and he walked across the cobblestones which were drying in the afternoon sun.

"It's a shame," he said.

"I'm sorry, sir?"

He nodded at the roses. "The gardener failed to cover them. I should have liked their pleasure a little longer."

"Yes, it looks like someone was taking good care of them."

"How are you enjoying our School?" He asked her.

"It's not what I expected, sir."

"Oh?"

"Well, it's amazing, of course." She glanced around the grounds of the Abbey. "But… It's the Inner Depths exercises. I'm afraid I'm having some trouble with them."

"Everyone finds it exhausting at first to descend to the Inner Depths." He realized that for the past two days he had not checked on her progress, and added consolingly, "Soon it will become second nature to you."

She hesitated. "The truth is I haven't been able to descend. Not even once."

"Really?" Peprini was surprised. He did not expect her to be still struggling with the most elementary task every Keeper, even the poorest discerner, soon learned. He appraised her closely and was momentarily captivated by the deep aura surrounding her. "I'm sure it's only nerves. Believe me when I say I have special justification in my optimism about your future."

The Director's words hung in the air as he left her sitting again by herself. Obviously, he expected her to do well. Then why was she having such trouble? The other novices had been talking about their travels to their Inner Depths, while she was still groping for the entrance. What was her problem?

33

The following evening Peprini arrived at the Novitiate School. The moment he entered the old convent he sensed the dark atmosphere. The mood was as solemn as during the Black Plague, he thought, recalling what he had read from the abbesses' diaries during those years: something fundamental to God's relationship with the Earth had changed for the worse.

Pem interrupted his musings. "Menach, I'm glad you're here."

"Yes?"

"The novices. I've maintained the typical schedule, despite... the fact is none of us are ourselves since the tragedy. And they, too, sense something's wrong."

"We would have been mistaken in choosing them if they did not. I take it you would like me to tell them."

"I would undertake the task, but news of such importance, I was thinking, ought to come from one such as yourself."

"Fine. Have them assemble in Founder's Hall. But first I'd like to have a look at the progress reports of our novices. Do you have their files?"

Pem handed him the eight files, struggling to rid his face of any trace of jealousy or disapproval. Peprini picked two and sat down at Pem's desk. Dina Carlini's report was as bad as could be. Except for her aura, there was absolutely nothing to suggest she was a Keeper. He opened Maria Jongsma's and read it carefully. Very good, he said to himself. Jongsma would do.

Minutes later Peprini stood in front of the eight novices just as he had the previous week. "Several days ago Councilor Fournier gave you the first glimpse of our history. She explained that of the original twelve Vessel lineages but five remain. In four thousand years only seven times did a Vessel terminate—that is, die before passing on the Blessing. The death of a Vessel under these circumstances is extraordinarily rare, as you see."

He paced for several moments before turning to them. "One of the remaining five Vessels, a man named Mark Gregor, he of Naphtali's lineage, died in Paris fourteen days ago, the same day you arrived at the Frostburg House." He read their faces. "Yes, I'm saying he died before passing on the Blessing. There are only four Vessels now."

The novices sat stunned. He waited until he had their full attention again.

"This is the cause of the exhaustion and anxiety you have been feeling. Keepers are acutely sensitive to the Blessing, much more than common human beings. Naturally, you are wondering about the broader impact of this tragedy. Vessels carry the Blessing to the Earth. If their number is reduced, this means the Blessing is reduced. So if the Blessing is reduced, what are the consequences for the Earth? This is what you wish to know?"

Several nodded.

"When you learn to sense the Blessing around us, you will know exactly what less Blessing feels like. On those days and in those places where there is a temporary depression, you will feel gloominess, emptiness, vulnerability. But the Blessing is more than a feeling. It is flourishing and order, the essence of life itself."

He smiled wryly. "You are wondering how the Blessing is expressed concretely in the world. Keepers have always known that the Earth is protected from what might otherwise befall it, though they were not always clear how this protection works. In ancient times Keepers believed the Blessing was a kind of magic talisman, giving protection from whatever might cause harm. But today, to our scientific minds, a better description might be that of an immune system. Think of the Earth as if it were a human body. Many viruses and bacteria are constantly entering our bodies, but if our immune system is sufficiently strong, then usually our bodies will be protected. The Blessing provides such protection to the Earth. But protection against what, you are wondering?

"How often," he continued after a pause, "are people struck by a passing car?"

"I've read somewhere," Natalie Norisot said, "that there is one accident for every million times someone tries to cross the street."

"Good. Now, why don't these accidents happen more frequently? Why not one accident for every half-million attempts to cross the street? Or for every ten thousand attempts? Or even one hundred?"

Silence.

"Most of you," he continued, "take a shower once or twice a day. How often do you slip and fall while in there?"

"To most of us it never happens," said Alexi Samsov.

"Which in the general population means one fall for every, let's say, 300,000 showers. Why not once for every thousand?

"Think of the possibility of hitting your head against a sharp corner, of cutting your fingers when you prepare a meal, of tripping and falling down the stairs, of squeezing your fingers in the door jamb, of choking on a piece of bread, of being struck by a lightning or by falling branches, of catching those myriad germs that hover about in the air and in food. Think of the possibility of cigarettes starting a fire, malfunctions in air-traffic computers, airplanes hitting birds, trains slipping off the rails, cars sliding into the opposite lane, earthquakes, floods, and the like. Think of the confluence of events that lead a person to commit murder, or heads of state to start a war. Do you realize how many potential dangers we face every moment of our lives? Given all this, it is amazing that any of us, let alone most of us, should survive into old age."

Peprini waited for them to mull over this. "Now, why don't these things happen to us more often than they actually do? Considering the virtually infinite number of opportunities, they hardly happen at all. Why not?"

He waved off their thinking. "The answer is: the Blessing. It is the power of health, of growth, of order. Your science education might have included the 'principle of entropy,' meaning that the natural tendency of the universe is to move towards disorder. Chaos. It takes energy, to put it one way, to maintain order or growth. But order does not happen by accident. The Blessing provides a barrier against chaos. It provides for the world to flourish, it provides for *life.* Indeed, *life is order.* One of the more palpable effects of the Blessing is to reduce the probability of misfortunes, preventing them from happening more often. It acts as the Earth's immune system. When Vessels travel to the Biblical sites and connect to God's blessing of Abraham our father and his family, they thereby supply humanity with this invaluable immunizing substance: the Blessing. *In you will all the families of the Earth be blessed.*"

He decided to indulge their curiosity. "Have you questions?"

"Councilor Peprini," Maria asked, "has the state of the world gotten steadily worse over the centuries as the Vessels have died out?"

"Very good, Miss Jongsma. Yes, in fact, this has been happening. The chance of a given type of accident today is much greater than its chance four thousand years ago. A greater portion of the population today is struck by lightning than two thousand years ago, for example, once you factor in changes in technology and lifestyles. Fortunately, humanity's scientific development has provided us with the means to minimize and avert many dangers. Our buildings are more resistant to the elements and collapse less easily, our ships vastly more seaworthy; advances in medicine alone have done much to make up for this increased vulnerability. So far, these technologies have been making up for the loss of Blessing. I say 'so far'—because mere science has limits. If there are further decreases in

Blessing… well, no science can replace God's Blessing."

Lev Bolski, hardly able to contain himself, burst out as soon as Peprini acknowledged him. "And we Keepers, can't do anything about it?"

"We discern. Our discernment somehow enables Vessels to bring the Blessing to the Earth."

"Yes," Bolski continued, "we've already been told that much. But does this mean, Councilor Peprini, that the more Keepers discern, the more Blessing the Vessels bring to the world?"

"Up to a point. Vessels cannot carry more Blessing than their personal capacity, just as you cannot carry more weight on your shoulders beyond a certain limit." Peprini glanced at his watch. "The point here is the immense responsibility each of us has to the welfare of the world. There are just over four-hundred Keepers in the world. With Gregor's death, it will be necessary that we all discern to the best of our ability. Very soon this will include you."

As Pem escorted him from the hall, Peprini said, "Tomorrow afternoon at three please have the top student report to my office at the Book Company."

The little man quietly sighed and nodded.

Maria Jongsma arrived at his office the following day. Peprini asked her to search a batch of photocopies of ancient Keepers' documents and look for certain keywords. For the next two hours, until she went back, they browsed those 13th-century letters, conversing pleasantly.

Julia Erna sat at a table in the Keepers' Archives below the Abbey. She examined her hands beneath the circle of light cast by the lamp. Eliezer's touch was so familiar she could still feel his warmth. He hadn't lied to her, not with words at least, she reminded herself. Just as she wasn't being disloyal in trying to satisfy her curiosity and genuine worry for Eliezer, and perhaps for Keeperdom. She realized she was cold; the Archives were always cold.

Annette Goldman, the librarian, appeared beside her.

"Here is a printout of everything sent to Eliezer in the last twelve months. Nine pages. It's quite a list."

Erna glanced at the entries. She debated but believed she could trust Goldman. She was the closest to what could be called her best friend in Lucerne. "Is there any… common theme?"

"Theme?"

She exhaled. "What do you think he is looking for?"

Rather than answer, Goldman handed her another document. "William's requests. Starting about six months back, the two are nearly identical."

Erna set the documents side-by-side on the table.

"I got curious." The librarian pulled out a chair and sat. "I ran a search on all the Council members, as well as Master-Keepers. None have anything like the number of requests Eliezer and William have made. There is nothing I'd regard as unusual. Except for one person."

"Menach."

"What's unusual is the *absence* of a record. All entries for him prior to two months ago have been deleted. Deliberately. Too many distinct steps have to be taken to accomplish this."

"Your people?"

"I approached the matter simply as a procedural issue. None admitted to it."

"Do you believe them?"

"I wish I could say I do, but… Menach, of course, makes all the posting assignments of novices. He chose my assistants."

The same power had been in the Peprini family now for almost eighty years. She wondered just where their tentacles reached.

"Back to Eliezer and William," she finally said. "You have no suspicions what they are looking for?"

Goldman stared at her. "Let me take a closer look."

She nodded. "Annette…"

"You needn't say it."

34

It was the semester's second week at the Hebrew University of Jerusalem. Fifty students waited in the classroom for Eliezer's course, "The Family in the Ancient World." The commotion settled when Professor Eliezer entered. He was a very popular lecturer and his students were pleased to see he had returned from his trip and would be teaching them himself—rather than his dull teaching assistant. Osnat was excited to hear him for the first time, even if she had to sit among a roomful of others.

"Last week," the Professor started, "my assistant talked with you about brotherhood in the Biblical world. She asked you to read about two pairs of brothers in the book of Genesis: Abraham's sons—Ishmael and Isaac; and Isaac's sons—Esau and Jacob. Has anyone found parallels between these stories?"

"Obviously," said a young man in a military uniform, "in both cases there's competition between the two brothers."

Eliezer nodded. "Over what?"

"Well, Ishmael is disinherited by his father Abraham in favor of Isaac, his younger brother—half-brother. And Esau loses his inheritance to his younger brother, Jacob."

"In both cases," said a plump woman in glasses, "the brothers compete for their father's inheritance."

"Right," the soldier agreed, "they fight over birthrights."

"Fight?" asked Eliezer. "Does the Bible actually say so?"

The soldier shrugged.

Osnat found herself saying, "Yes, fistfights."

Eliezer saw an attractive woman sitting at the far left. He recalled her visit to his office last week for permission to join his course. Did she say "fistfights"? No such thing is mentioned in the Biblical text. Only those who actually *saw* the Biblical events—only those who *discerned* them— could know that both pairs of brothers actually came to blows over their birthrights.

A student interrupted his thoughts. "In both cases, the older brother gets a raw deal."

"Good. In the ancient Middle East, the older brother's priority over his younger siblings was a near-inviolate tradition. Twice the Bible challenges this conception. Why? What does the Bible want to tell us?"

"That the Patriarchs of the Jewish nation were more virtuous than those of any other nation. That's why we are God's chosen people," declared a burly man with a yarmulke on his head.

"Enough of this fanatic nationalism," came from an irritated voice in the back.

Angry voices drowned him.

Eliezer raised his hands. "Hold it, hold it," he said sternly but obviously amused. The arguers simmered down. "No contemporary politics, please. Let me remind you that we are talking about four thousand years ago."

A tense silence reverberated in the classroom.

Osnat's voice sounded oblivious to the tension. "The Bible tells us that something very important passes from father to son—to one son only. And that it's something worth fighting over: God's blessing."

Eliezer stared at her. "How… what makes you think so?"

"That's what God said to Abraham, didn't He? After Abraham drove away Ishmael and his mother, God told Abraham that the Blessing would pass to his son Isaac, and that it would continue to pass on from generation to generation until the end of days."

"The Biblical text says nothing about this. Where did you get this from?"

His harshness surprised her.

"Did you read the chapters I assigned?"

"Not completely, no. I thought I already knew the storyline fairly well. My memory…"

"Your memory obviously doesn't come from the text."

She felt her composure shaken.

"Where, then, do these memories come from?" Eliezer insisted.

"I don't know, I'm sorry. I guess I no longer remember what comes from the text and what comes from my imagination."

He scrutinized her face. Imagination—could these be pre-discernment experiences? He contracted his eyelids and focused his discerning powers—and now he could see: An aura hovered around her head, colorful and rich. A potential Keeper?

"Daydreams…" he said vaguely. Her aura seemed familiar. Now, where had he seen it? Not when she came to his office. No, he had been too distracted. Ah, yes, at the library on the Givat Ram campus. "Daydreams..." he repeated.

Several students grimaced, thinking the professor was now being too hard on her.

She moved uncomfortably in her chair. "Yes. My imagination," she said defiantly.

Eliezer stared at her, lost in thought.

"Your name?" he finally said.

"Osnat Aviv."

"Osnat," he repeated absently. "The wife of Abraham's great-grandson. It's all in the family."

He then gathered himself. "Come to my office hour, Osnat, if you will. We will discuss this some more."

35

Later that day Eliezer sat in his office, staring out the window at the ancient walls of Jerusalem below. The Blessing in the air was pitiful, as it had been for the past two weeks. Accidents continued to occur with disturbing frequency, though the situation seemed to have stabilized. But more people were suffering and dying every day. He wished his experiment with Oleander could be accelerated.

He opened the Book of Creation and again examined the formula of the second Sefirah, trying to understand how the codeword "Cunning" might be detected in it.

TEN SEFIROT OF BELIMAH, TEN AND NOT NINE, TEN AND NOT ELEVEN, UNDERSTAND WITH WISDOM AND EXPLORE WITH UNDERSTANDING, EXAMINE WITH THEM, INVESTIGATE FROM THEM, KNOW AND THINK AND CREATE AND RETURN THE CREATOR TO HIS PLACE, BECAUSE HE FORMS AND CREATES BY HIMSELF, AND THERE IS NO ONE BUT HIM, AND HIS ATTRIBUTE IS TEN THAT HAVE NO END.

He shook his head. Without the codewords, he and Oleander could not continue.

Now he looked at the formula of the next Sefirah, the third:

TEN *SEFIROT* OF *BELIMAH*, BRIDLE YOUR HEART FROM THINKING, BRIDLE YOUR MOUTH FROM SPEAKING, AND IF YOUR HEART RUNS, RETURN TO THE PLACE, FOR IT IS SAID: "AND THE CREATURES RUN AND RETURN." AND ON THIS A COVENANT HAS BEEN MADE.

The expression "and the creatures run and return" was obviously from the Book of Ezekiel, from the mystical vision of the prophet. But *bridle your heart?*

A knock woke him from his thoughts.

"Yes?"

The door opened. "You asked me to come?" the student said.

Her eyes were lively, an unusual shade of blue, and her dark-gold hair fell about her shoulders in a carefree way. He could sense a tender but pronounced aura. It was substantial, indicating a potential Keeper, but there was something odd about it, he could not say exactly what.

"Osnat. Yes, come in. Sit down please." He motioned to a chair beside his desk.

"Was there anything wrong with what I said in class, Professor?"

"What? No, no, on the contrary. It was... intriguing. Tell me about yourself, please."

"Well, what exactly would you like to know? I'm twenty-seven—a bit old for an undergraduate, isn't it? That's because after my mandatory military service I didn't go straight to university, as my dad wanted me to. I traveled abroad for a couple of years."

She paused. His silence felt attentive and reassuring. "My dad wants me to take over his business after I finish my education. He's an industrialist, self-made, wealthy actually. But I have no interest in playing that game."

There was something about the old professor that encouraged her to reveal herself.

"What will you do instead?"

"I don't know yet, something more important than making money. I'm waiting."

Her entire presence—not just her aura, but her voice and demeanor too—manifested spiritual depths probably unknown to herself. But such potential needed careful nurturing. Spiritual depth was no more than a first step towards the gift of discernment.

"I see," he said. "Now, tell me again your daydream."

"Well, after your teaching assistant told us to read the two stories of the disowned brothers, somehow Isaac and Ishmael stuck in my mind."

"Stuck in your mind?"

"Especially that evening. When I got home and sat down to relax, the scene came back before my eyes. I felt..." She hesitated.

"Yes?"

"I felt... an energy... a gentle kind of energy."

"Go on."

"I understood... I saw..."

Eliezer nodded but she fell silent.

"You saw," he said softly, "God telling Abraham that he did right by driving his son Ishmael out of his home."

"Yes."

"Abraham was sitting by a well," Eliezer whispered, his eyes closed, recalling the scene he had witnessed so many times, "shaken by the experience. He loved Ishmael dearly, even though his mother was only Hagar, the maid. He did it only to appease his wife Sarah. He was wrapped in white with a black shawl on his head. The dog at his side began barking. Then Abraham heard a voice from above. He jumped to his feet…"

She looked at him, stunned. "How can you know this, Professor?"

He opened his eyes.

"This isn't in the Bible. After class this morning I read the passages carefully. How could you know what I saw?"

"I know because this scene did not happen in your mind. It is a reality, and I have seen it too. Many times. We call it Gate Four."

"We?"

"Osnat, have you had similar experiences with scenes from other parts of Genesis? Have you envisioned in this way God's covenant with Abraham?"

"No, Professor. But sometimes I've noticed a sort of… a pulse of energy… when I read the passages in Genesis where God blesses someone; especially when He blesses Abraham. Ishmael too."

How strange. She could discern the vicinity of Gate Four, but could only vaguely feel earlier—and easier—Gates. And how odd that she visualized God's Blessing to Ishmael. He had never heard of this before. Perhaps she was indeed simply imagining that passage.

"The power of the Blessing is a marvel. Once you experience it you cannot help wanting to understand it."

"Are you saying the Blessing of the Bible is real, Professor?"

"Absolutely. I know it well."

Osnat raised a skeptical eyebrow. "Don't you think it's just a fable, like the myth of Adam and Eve, or the parting of the Red Sea?"

Eliezer reached a decision. She was too promising to pass on to Frostburg. He would somehow find the time to train her.

"Oh no, Osnat, the Blessing is not at all a myth. I can perceive it just as I can perceive you; in fact, even more clearly, more convincingly."

He looked at her doubtful expression and smiled. "There is no reason for you to believe me. I would like to convince you, but not in words. If you allow me, let us do a… little demonstration."

"Wait a minute, Professor. Let's say it's true. Why are you telling me all this?"

"I will give you an answer, but after our demonstration. How about right after our next class?"

The lunchtime crowd was noisy in the cafeteria of the School of the Humanities. Eliezer's hand froze in mid-air, holding the cup of tea he was about to bring to his lips. The face staring at him from across the room looked like none he had ever seen. The man, with his long disheveled hair, unshaven face, vacant eyes, and ragged shirt seemed a spiritless body. His head wobbled slightly as if balanced by some hidden mechanism. His arms rested on the table with the palms of his hands upwards. He looked like he had been sleeping outside for weeks.

Unfamiliar nausea rose in Eliezer's consciousness like a sickening fog, a quality the exact opposite of the Blessing: a stench of the spirit.

No one around him took notice, but this was hardly telling. Most people couldn't see beyond the visible surface, or at most the psychological layer and no further.

His eyes narrowed for a better viewing of the Blessing, a reflex he had acquired in his search for potential Keepers. But instead of an aura what appeared around the vagabond's head was a sphere of darkness, queerly of emptiness, barely visible but definite. Eliezer was almost overwhelmed by the spiritual stench. He closed his eyes and breathed deeply. When he looked again a group of students blocked the view. As they passed, Eliezer saw him shuffling out of the cafeteria.

Who was this person? He stood, already feeling better now that the man was gone.

36

Two days later the old professor and the young student were sitting in what appeared to be a library. The ceiling was unusually high, the walls covered by glass-enclosed shelves stacked with old books and decaying manuscripts. Twelve tall, narrow windows opened the room, three on each side, but they were too slim to permit much light. The shadows made the large table look like a granite slab. This odd-looking room was on the third floor of an imposing house in Jerusalem, one of many hundreds the Keepers owned around the world.

"This book," Eliezer touched the Bible that lay on the table, "unlike any other, is the visible aspect of an unseen reality. It is like the tip of an iceberg mostly hidden from view. Most people can see only the book, the text, the Biblical story, not the reality behind it."

"I don't understand, Professor. What kind of hidden reality?"

"We call it the Bible World."

"Who is this 'we' you keep mentioning?"

"Later. The point is there is much more to the world than the eye can see."

Osnat felt uncomfortable sitting with him in this eerie room. She started to doubt her initial trust in him. Jerusalem was full of self-proclaimed messiahs, prophets, and visionaries who flocked to the Holy City. Psychiatrists even have a name for this mental state: the Jerusalem Syndrome.

"The Bible," she said dryly, "is an ancient document written by human beings, isn't it? A piece of literature, a historical artifact."

Eliezer smiled patiently. "So you think it is mere coincidence that more than a billion people regard it as a holy book? People of all religions, even atheists, can sense something undeniably unique about it."

She shrugged.

"Let me give you the demonstration I promised. I will show you something of the reality that is hidden behind the visible surface."

"Fine, okay."

He grinned at the hint of youthful sarcasm in her voice. "Good. Now, I want you just to sit and relax for ten minutes or so. Pretend I'm not here."

Divining her discomfort, he withdrew to a corner of the room and sat down. Osnat closed her eyes and tried to relax.

Some time later, Eliezer stood beside her. "Alright, Osnat. Now, if you allow me, I would like to place my hands on your head."

"What?"

"Just on your temples. Lightly."

She nodded.

"Good. See? You can hardly feel my touch."

He turned to the window, searched the sky, and noted a surprisingly intense spot of Blessing. For a few seconds he marveled at it—such a concentration of Blessing was rare even before Gregor's death, but now, when the sky had become so bleak... Like the old days, he thought sadly.

"We have a special treat for you." He pointed. "Look through this window and focus just above the tip of the juniper tree over there."

The moment her eyes looked in the indicated direction she was flooded by a tremendous wave. She felt her entire being swell with a glorious energy. Eliezer was astonished to see the magnitude of her aura's reaction.

He quickly removed his hands, afraid the intensity would prove too much for her. The sensation slowly dissipated. When she regained her breath, she turned to look at his face.

"What was that?" she gasped.

"What you experienced was a wisp of the Blessing. The Biblical Blessing."

"That was amazing!"

"Alright. Now look through *this* window. And focus your gaze just above the horizon. Near the bottom right corner of the window."

She turned her eyes to where he pointed, focusing her attention, but nothing happened. Her aura was unchanged. "I don't feel it this time," she said, disappointed. "Have I lost it?"

"Oh no," he chuckled. "There was simply very little Blessing in that place."

"Then why did you tell me to look there?"

"To make sure you could distinguish between Blessing and no Blessing."

"You mean, Professor, there are people who... react even if there is nothing there?"

Eliezer did not answer immediately. "Yes," he said at last, reminiscing. "In fact, I met a young woman like that just last week."

Osnat opened her mouth to ask further but he interrupted her. "Let's continue. Now, relax again. When I tell you, turn your eyes to this window over there."

For some two hours they continued viewing the Blessing, Osnat savoring every moment. When Eliezer finally called it a day she was not ready to quit.

"Professor, let me at least experience the first spot once more. Compared to the first, all the rest were so weak."

He smiled sadly at her eagerness. "That spot of Blessing is gone now. Dissipated in the sky."

"But how can you tell, Professor?"

"Because I can see the Blessing."

"You can actually *see* it?

"Quite easily, if I only concentrate for a couple of seconds. 'See,' of course, is only a figure of speech."

He led her downstairs to the more inviting living room. They took seats across from each other. He needed to rest even if she did not.

"So. Have I convinced you the Biblical Blessing is real?"

"More real than anything."

"You are quite right. Now listen carefully. Many have a residual capacity for… 'seeing' in this way. You seem to have a great measure. Yet without training your gift is worthless. What you sensed today was thanks to me: I enhanced your sensitivity by placing my hand on your head. You must cultivate this if you want to use it. You will have to decide: Do you want to devote yourself to developing this gift, or forget all about it and return to the normal course of your life?"

"I want it."

"I must warn you this isn't something you do for personal enjoyment. It is for *all the families of the Earth,* as the Bible puts it."

"All the better."

"Then here is my offer, Osnat. I can take you as… an apprentice. I will teach you to sense the Blessing and to 'see' where it is coming from: the Bible world. But that will require much from you. Indeed, it will require everything. You will have to devote your life to one cause—an immensely rich, satisfying cause, but terribly demanding. You will have to forsake most of what you consider your present life."

She started to speak but he stopped her. "Don't answer now. Think about it. We will talk again soon."

She nodded. "Alright, Professor. But I already know the answer. This is what I've always been waiting for."

Back home, Professor Eliezer parked his car, got out and locked it. For a moment he stood still in the quiet street of the *Bak'a* neighborhood. He had work to do, but he needed to think, which meant he needed to walk. He turned away from his house and started walking.

The streets were busy with people returning home from work. A small crowd stood in front of a restaurant talking cheerfully. Instead of crossing the street Eliezer deliberately walked through the group, slowly making his way between the friendly conversations.

The people seemed happy, enjoying the Blessing of life. He narrowed his eyes and saw a current of Blessing moving through this area, accounting for the buoyant mood of the group. Unexpectedly this saddened him. None of them knew the Blessing they were enjoying was in grave danger; that the few Vessels who were responsible for it were dwindling; that human life as they understood it was not something guaranteed by the universe but a profound improbability, a true miracle, a Blessing, a Blessing that might very well not last.

But Eliezer knew. Like all other Keepers, he knew the Vessels were dying out and with them the channels of the Blessing. But unlike the many Keepers who knew and preferred not to think about it, he knew what he could do—or rather was obligated to do, together with Oleander. The thought of Oleander, his young friend and comrade, warmed his heart.

The street around him had grown quiet. He entered the municipal Promenade Park. Across the valley, the walls of old Jerusalem rose on Temple Mount. He stood in the darkness and looked at what was the largest concentration of holy sites to more than two billion people of three religions and countless denominations. According to tradition, on this mountain Abraham bound his son Isaac on the altar and stood, knife in hand, ready to sacrifice him to God. It was probably near here that God gave Abraham the Blessing.

He heard footsteps. A Palestinian neighborhood was just ahead and he realized he shouldn't be here at this time of the day. It would be stupid, he thought, if something happened to our mission just because of a nightly stroll.

A silhouette approached. Eliezer didn't move. The figure passed against the background of the city lights. Then the figure entered a circle of dim light and Eliezer's breath stopped. He had seen this man only two days earlier: *the vagabond from the cafeteria.* At the same moment he was struck by the foul odor.

An alarm went off in the Professor's mind. Had their previous encounter not been accidental? The man limped awkwardly up the path, his hands secreted in the pockets of his coat. He still wore the same shabby clothes and had the same unkempt hair. He looked to be middle aged but the poor light made it hard to tell. He now passed in front of Eliezer. Their eyes met. The man stared and Eliezer felt he was looking into the Void. The sickening nausea welled up inside him.

The old Keeper gasped. For a brief moment he struggled to regain his composure. A second later he turned to look at the man but he had already disappeared into the darkness.

Slowly Eliezer walked home, pondering. *Who was this man?*

37

Amira Tarik, the young Turkish novice, finally had found the entrance to her Inner Depths. Dina was now the only novice yet to succeed. After dinner, when the others congratulated Amira, Dina excused herself and left the building without even bothering to pretend she was happy for Amira's success.

Dina walked aimlessly on the lawn surrounding the old convent, hugging herself against the cold, biting her lip to keep back the tears. Master-Keeper Pem had not kicked her out of the Novitiate yet, but she felt it would come soon; it was clearly on his face. Miss Crumb and Mr. Garcia had begun avoiding her looks. And then? All her hopes to devote herself to this great cause would be gone. What was she going to do then? How could she return to her old life?

It was in this state that Peprini found her. He had stopped by the Novitiate before flying to New York. He first noticed her aura hovering in the dark, and when he got closer he could make out her silhouette. She was shaking her head in apparent frustration.

"Miss Carlini? Is anything wrong?"

"It's no use, Councilor. I've tried and tried to find my Inner Depths but… I simply don't have Esau's gift."

Peprini observed the rich aura that glowed around her. This aura, he admitted, as splendid as it was, was different from those he had seen around any other Keeper. Its streaks were too pronounced, too steady, unaffected by the fluctuations of the ambient Blessing in the air or her own changes in strength.

She could be right. But if not a Keeper, who was she?

He glanced at his watch. "Come, Dina. Let's try once more. I can spare thirty minutes before I must leave for the airport."

He led the way to his office. Her hopes were somewhat revived. He was a Councilor after all, and must know the ways of the Blessing better than her teachers.

He motioned to her to sit. "Let me tell you a little trick, a secret I sometimes used many years ago when I was too anxious to discern." He smiled. "It will remain between us, yes?"

She nodded eagerly.

"Good. You are nervous because you are afraid of failing. And every failure makes you more pressured, more self-controlled. Now you cannot let go of your self. You cannot let the Blessing take over and do its job. So let's get this obnoxious self out of the way. Let's make it faint."

"Faint?"

"Almost. I want you to breathe very hard and very fast until you become lightheaded. And when you feel you are almost ready to faint, then look for the entrance to your Inner Depths."

If this would not work, he thought, nothing would.

Obediently Dina followed his instructions. She found herself hyperventilating but kept breathing hard. This was her last chance. At last, just before fainting, she stopped and started meditating. Her head whirled, but she fought to keep her focus.

Peprini watched her aura, waiting for the familiar flash that would announce success. He could tell that her inner efforts were great and found himself admiring her willpower. The minutes passed, but the telltale flash did not come.

Some ten minutes later she opened her eyes. She shook her head. "It just won't work. I'm sorry."

"You are very close," he told her, but his voice betrayed his words. "Don't give up. When I return from New York I want to see you descending."

At the airport, Peprini's cellphone rang.

"Reza here, Councilor, from Electronics, Madrid. We've just escorted Tiplady to the plane. He is on his way now."

"Any problems?"

"Nada, Sir. We crammed into his brain everything we could in a week. He isn't a genius, but he'll do fine operating the basic equipment." He chuckled. "He was dying to leave us. He thinks he'll have an easier time in New York."

"Very good."

Eric Tiplady slept through the transatlantic flight from Madrid to the USA. After some twelve hours and a change of planes, he found himself walking down the steps from the plane onto the tarmac in Utica, New York, greeted by a cold rain. He entered the terminal and found the baggage area. He was irritated. When Councilor Peprini had told him

New York, he assumed New York City. It wasn't until he checked in at Barajas airport that he learned his true destination.

He was waiting for his luggage to come around on the carousel when he felt a tap on his shoulder.

"Tiplady?"

He turned and looked into the brown eyes of an attractive woman.

"I'm Monica Berg," she said with a Scandinavian accent. "Councilor Peprini asked that I retrieve you."

He guessed she was in her mid-thirties, with short blonde hair, taller than his five-feet-seven-inches. She wore a leather coat over a heavy turtleneck sweater and jeans. Although she could afford to lose a few pounds, he thought, she was pretty.

"I'm Eric Tiplady, yeah."

"You checked your luggage?" The insinuation was this had been foolish or inconsiderate.

He spotted his bag on the carousel. "Relax, it's just this one." He picked it up as it moved past.

"Follow me."

She turned and began walking in long, quick strides. He struggled to keep up. Her black BMW was parked only twenty feet away next to the curb. She pulled past the terminal and he swiveled in his seat.

"Okay, what am I doing here? What's special about this place?"

She smiled, not surprised that Peprini had said nothing, even though a few sentences of explanation would have prevented much anxiety on the boy's part. "This town is special to us only because it is near St. Raphael monastery. And St. Raphael is special only because William Oleander lives there."

"This is all about a priest?"

"A monk. And he happens to be a Councilor."

"All right. So?"

His heavy, lower-class Australian accent grated on her. She turned the car onto the highway entrance ramp and the powerful motor in the BMW surged forward. There was a surprising amount of traffic but she smoothly threaded the car into the flow.

Now she turned to him. "Watch your tone. He is a Councilor. Do you understand what that means?"

"He discerns really well, I know. What's this got to do with me?"

"Councilor Peprini said I might find you a chore."

"Look, I'm tired, I'm hungry, and I'm in some place called *Utica*. Just tell me why I'm here."

"Most importantly you're here because Councilor Peprini—for reasons he hasn't chosen to share with me—thinks you can be of some use. Why *I am* here, and not in Geneva where I had been, is that you will need to continue your novice training. Part of my job is to instruct you."

Tiplady frowned; he thought he had escaped the dull labor the others in Lucerne were going through.

"So that's why you're here." Outside the window was the landscape of a once-thriving factory town, now suffering a slow if dignified decline. "Why am I here?"

"We—myself, Krueger, Velasquez, and it seems you—have been assigned to monitor Councilor Oleander."

"Monitor?"

"Keep track of his movements."

Tiplady smirked. "That doesn't seem quite kosher, does it?"

"What would you know?" She changed lanes and sped up. "Did they tell you Vessel Gregor died?"

"Yeah."

"Then you should grasp that everything has changed. If Councilor Peprini decided it's important that the Councilors be watched, then that's what we do. What we don't do is ask foolish questions."

"Alright, take it easy, I just asked." She was quick to become emotional and a true believer in this Keeper business. He allowed himself a little smile. "Were you a borderline case too?"

"What? No. I've discerned Gate Five several times." She spoke as if this made her better than him.

"That's impressive."

She gave a sidelong glance, uncertain if he was mocking her. "That's the main reason I'm here. To train you." Her face tightened. "I thought you said you were tired. We've got another half-hour in the car. Let's try some quiet."

"Fine with me." He closed his eyes. "Wake me when we're there."

38

Peprini sat uneasily in the leather chair. He was unaccustomed to waiting for anyone. He wished he had scheduled this meeting for the next day. The night flight from Lucerne had left him unusually fatigued. The blond receptionist smiled at him.

He set his briefcase on his knees and opened it. He felt the weight—surprisingly heavy—of the old document. Even Councilors were forbidden to remove this from the Archives, but he needed something *substantial* in his hands. When the time came, he wasn't sure his voice and presence would be enough. This lack of confidence took him by surprise. But the feel of the ancient document gave him courage as well as a feeling of entitlement, just as it had when he first touched it as a boy.

The intercom buzzed. "You may go in now," the receptionist said. "Good luck."

The oversized office door was solid walnut yet moved weightlessly on its hinges. Peprini entered the room and recognized Vessel David Wyatt behind the desk. The cast from his recent accident was off his arm and he appeared healthy. He was slightly taller than Peprini, with dark hair showing the beginnings of gray around the temples. An athletic man, Peprini knew, and somewhat vain about his weight. He was 43-years-old, still a bachelor. Once he had come close to marrying, but that had been ten years ago. That he was still unmarried and childless caused anxiety among some Keepers.

"So you're Menach Peprini and you... how did you put it on the phone? You have information about an inheritance in my name. Is that right?"

"Yes." He had decided to use his real name. If Wyatt investigated him, as he was certain to do, and found Peprini had lied about his identity, that falseness might taint everything he would say.

Wyatt extended his hand and the two shook. "Have a seat, please." Peprini sat in one of the burgundy wing chairs that faced the desk. "This kind of news usually comes from a lawyer."

How many times had Peprini imagined this conversation? Again the awful nature of his decision made itself felt. He surveyed the office. Thick walnut paneling on the walls, rich Berber carpet, an antique desk and companion sideboard with crystal decanters and glasses. The Gauguin on the wall above the sofa. It was no doubt an original, Peprini thought. The man had excellent taste. The luxurious yet efficient office of a self-indulgent yet hardworking man. Contradictions.

"As I said on the telephone, I have news of a bequest you received."

"From whom?"

"Your ancestors."

"My ancestors," David Wyatt said. "And what is this bequest?"

"I cannot tell you that without telling you who I am."

They looked across the desk at each other. David Wyatt, normally a quick judge of people, had to admit he was mystified. Hundreds of men had sat in that chair but there was a seriousness about this one he had never encountered. Though it was David's office, this Peprini had an authority that made the office seem *his*. Despite his affluent appearance, he realized this meeting wasn't about money.

"Go ahead."

"I am chairman of the Lucerne Rare Book Company. We are located at the St. Ignacio Abbey in Lucerne, Switzerland."

"So we're both businessmen."

The visitor couldn't hide his distaste for the term. "Actually, no."

"You don't look like a monk."

"Our order is no longer exclusively a religious one."

The businessman prided himself on rarely being surprised by the world, certainly never by anything in his own office. But he was today.

"Allow me to ask you this, Mr. Wyatt. Do you consider yourself a lucky person?"

"I don't know what people mean when they use the word."

"Fine. To what do you owe your success in the world? Why have you prospered, why you—when so many other intelligent, hardworking people do not? Why is it that when you put your hands to something it always turns out well?"

"I work hard. I trust my judgment. I'm able to act when the time is right."

Peprini nodded knowingly. This irritated Wyatt for a reason he couldn't say.

"I am sure. But consider this: People in your work, on Wall Street, often make enemies, yes?" Wyatt gave a small nod. "It seems natural when so much money is at stake. Why is it that you, alone among all those at the peak of your profession, have no enemies? No one has a sour word to say about you. Why is this?"

"I'm not granting that's true, but if it is, I'd say it's because I'm fair, I keep my word. If you're going to last in this business, you'll see those people again. It's only wise."

Again the visitor nodded. "But I would think many of your competitors are equally fair and prudent in that way, yet they have accumulated quite a war-chest of bitterness and envy. How do you account for this? Yes, I can see you have noticed this. Nor, by the way, do your employees resent you, the very wealthy boss. This is nearly unheard of."

"What makes you think you know what my employees and my competitors think of me?"

"But is it true?" He waited for the businessman. "I'll take your silence as assent." Peprini leaned forward in his chair. "When we first spoke I said I had news of a bequest you had received," Peprini continued. "I chose those words carefully. I meant that you have already received this inheritance. You have had it since your birth. It is nothing less than your birthright."

"My *birthright?* This isn't feudal Europe. There is no title to inherit. What does birthright mean today?"

"What it has always meant. By virtue of your blood, you have a right. We can call it a gift."

"Again, what gift?"

"Tell me about your ancestry, if you will. What do you know?"

The businessman began talking against his will. "My father's family came to America from Poland and Russia around the turn of the 20th century. My mother's from England and Scotland a little earlier. I've never investigated my genealogy." He shrugged.

"The ancestry I have in mind goes back thousands of years. Four thousand to be exact."

"Nonsense. I doubt there's anyone in the world who can claim that with any legitimacy."

"Not quite. It is my belief there are only..." he hesitated, still uncomfortable with the change "...four people among the billions on Earth today who have a complete record of their family line going back four thousand years. Even that's not exactly true. Because while these lineages are known, the four individuals themselves do not know."

David Wyatt grinned, realizing he was not in control of this meeting. "And who are these four people? The Queen of England? The Emperor of Japan?"

"Few have heard of them; certainly they are not famous. They are ordinary people." He smiled at his last comment.

"What?"

"It was incorrect to call them ordinary. Whatever else is true of them they are not ordinary." He stood and began pacing. "Do you know who Abraham was?"

"From the Bible? The patriarch of the Jews?"

"Very good." Peprini went on to outline, as he would to a novice, the origins of Vessels and Keepers, the passing of the Blessing over the forty centuries and the work of Keepers. David Wyatt said nothing, revealed nothing in his manner or expression. "Think of it. Four thousand years of history. The Babylonian empire; the birth of the Greeks; Homer, Plato, Aristotle... Alexander the Great, the demise of Egypt... the Roman Empire comes into being and passes away. Families separated by war, children sold into slavery, plagues and famines, migrations of whole peoples. In the midst of all this, a sacred duty continued, known only to those charged with that duty."

Wyatt doubted what the man was saying was true, but he was convinced his visitor believed.

"And this duty continues today?"

"Yes."

"Would it be your Order that carries out this record-keeping of descendants?"

"It is."

Peprini opened his briefcase, taking out a thin sheaf of papers. He handed the document to Wyatt. On the top of the first page was typed "The Line of Simeon." He leafed through the pages.

"Okay. It's a genealogy of some sort."

"Not of some sort. Yours."

Below "The Line of Simeon" was the single name "Abraham."

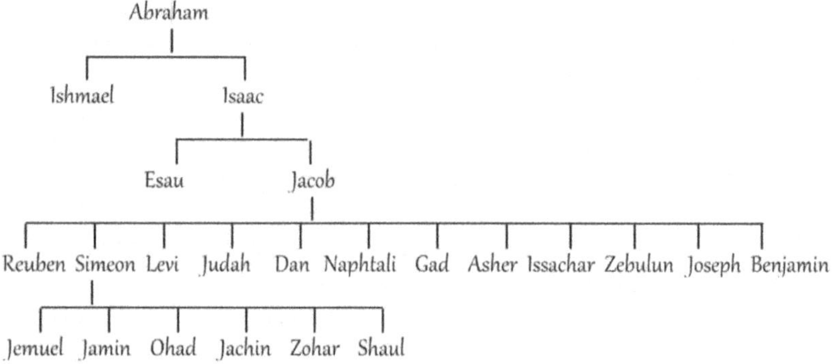

He turned to the last page. The very last name listed was his own. Moving backwards he saw his father's, then a line from him to his paternal grandmother, then great-grandmother Rachel Dabin Horenberg (whose name he now recalled, though the middle name "Dabin" he had not heard before). Beyond hers, he ceased to recognize names. Yet without a gap, the line moved up the page.

Is it possible? Why would the man lie to him about this? Caught off balance, the natural suspicion of all successful businessmen took over.

"What is it you want from me?"

The visitor reached again into the briefcase and pulled out an odd object. It looked to be a piece of parchment paper encased in a thick, uneven, yellowish but transparent resin. He passed the object to Wyatt. It was a single sheet, the paper very thick, obviously very old. He had to tip the document to find an angle that would let him see through the resin. On the top was written a word in a language he couldn't read. Hebrew, he guessed. But the language aside, it appeared nearly identical to the first page of the typed document he had just examined. He looked at Peprini.

"I have no words to describe the value of what you hold in your hands. Next to it, the Declaration of Independence, the Magna Carta, the Dead Sea Scrolls, are nothing." Being in the presence of the ancient document inspired him. "Do you remember me mentioning Esau?"

"One of Isaac's sons?"

"The document you are holding was started by him."

"Started?" He looked and saw that even in Hebrew it was clear the handwriting changed.

"The first three lines are in the hand of Esau. Then his son, Timna, makes a single entry. And so on."

"You must realize you're asking me to believe the unbelievable. This word here," and his finger traced over the word he now knew said 'Abraham,' "was written by *the* Abraham's grandson, the actual flesh-and-blood man, this Esau mentioned in the Old Testament?"

"Yes."

"And what's this covering the document?"

"At some point, our brethren decided to protect the original paper of Esau. That thick shell is pine resin. Essentially they varnished the parchment."

"Look, I can see you believe this, but…" He exhaled sharply, sensing for the first time that to believe this meant his life would drastically change in an unknown way.

"Do you consider yourself a man of science?" Peprini asked.

"I'm a well-educated person who understands we live in a technological world. So, yes, I'm a man of science."

"If what I've told you is true that paper must be at least four thousand years old."

David nodded.

"Then you know that the age of this paper, as an organic compound, can be accurately measured using radiocarbon or Carbon-14 dating.

True?"

Again David nodded.

"If you need proof, I am permitted to allow you to remove a small piece of the document and submit it to the lab of your choice for testing."

"You'd let me do this? After you've told me how valuable it is?"

"That we would allow this is a measure of how important it is that you believe me, believe us."

"You're that confident it's four thousand years old?"

"We have already checked it. The laboratory confirmed the age of the parchment. Furthermore, the other documents dated appropriately. The ones listing earlier stages in the genealogy are older, the later ones newer."

"But that only means the parchment is that old, not that this word at the top was written by Esau."

"True."

"So you're asking me to accept this on faith?"

Menach Peprini smiled. "That is just the beginning of what I am going to ask you to accept."

The traffic noise drifted up from the street below. The everydayness of the horns and sirens made what had just happened in the office seem even more fantastic. Wyatt walked to the window overlooking Fifth Avenue. Without turning around, he spoke.

"You mentioned others have this birthright. Have you told them?"

"No. It is my belief none since Jacob's sons have known they possessed this gift."

"Then why in the hell have you told me? Why after four thousand years have you... *Keepers* decided to break the rule?"

"It was not done lightly."

Wyatt walked over to the sideboard and poured a drink from one of the crystal decanters. "I'm having a scotch. Do you want one?"

"Yes. Single malt, please."

They each settled back in their chairs, facing each other across the desk, and sipped their drinks. With the darkness outside, the window now reflected the light from the office. Peprini glanced at his image.

Now, more quietly than before, Wyatt said, "You said there were three other Vessels beside me, of the original twelve." Immediately he was aware he had referred to himself as a Vessel. "How do you know there are not more of us? And how do you know which son or daughter received a parent's Blessing?"

"We have been following you through the ages. Keepers have a power, though nothing like that of Vessels. Ours is a power to discern the source of the Blessing. And a feature of this knowing is the ability to recognize a Vessel."

"How? Do they glow in the dark?"

The Keeper smiled. "Vessels possess what we can call an aura, if it helps you to visualize it. An aura that none but Keepers can see. This is how we knew when a lineage died out."

"So lineages die out. If that's true, how could four of twelve survive? I'm no expert, but even that high of a success rate seems very improbable."

"I would agree, except for two points. First, this inheritance is very much heartier than others. Those who possess it will almost always survive at least long enough to pass it on. You see, the Blessing is a protective power."

"And the second reason?"

"After the first line ended, a number of us decided that we had not fully understood our mission. So we began a more active role. This was in about 1000 BC. We started to protect the Vessels as much as possible. Often this meant befriending them and their families. Sometimes it meant having money for a physician when a child was ill, or accompanying a friend to war. In more than one instance the Vessel's parent died and left a Keeper to raise the child-Vessel. Vessels have had help in surviving."

Wyatt sat down at his desk. He picked up the document of his lineage. "I don't imagine I can keep this for a while?"

"I'm afraid not. You are the only person outside our Order who has ever seen it."

He turned to the last page. There, one row above his grandmother's name was "Rachel Dabin Horenberg, died November 15, 1893. Buried in the town of Cransk, Poland." He jotted this down. Then he looked above and wrote down "Marion Lipinska Ossing, died December 10, 1879. Buried in the town of Lancut, Poland."

Peprini watched without expression.

Wyatt leaned back in his chair. "What now? You've told me of my birthright, though I haven't forgotten you still haven't told me exactly what it is. You've broken the sacred rule that abided for four thousand years. What has changed?"

"That I cannot tell you. Not yet."

"This is like telling someone he has a terrible disease but not what it will do to him."

"Whatever comfort this may bring you, remember you have always had this power. I would think you could wait a little longer to understand. But to be as forthcoming as I am permitted—something has indeed changed, as you put it. We had worried this time would come. The worry began when the first line died out. That was our first sign that this story," he raised his arm and made a sweeping gesture, "our human story, has an uncertain ending."

For the first time, David glimpsed the weight of the man's burden. They sat, both suddenly tired, and surveyed the other's eyes.

"You're speaking of saving the world, aren't you?"

"Yes, David."

After several moments of silence, Peprini stood. "I must be going."

"And?"

"I will wait for you to digest what I have told you. Here." Peprini took a card from his suit coat pocket. "This is a telephone number to contact me. I will not answer, but leave your name and I will return the call shortly."

Wyatt examined the card. It was blank except for a telephone number in the lower right corner. The visitor turned and left.

39

Wyatt got up and walked out to the reception area of Wyatt Inc. Everyone had gone home. He wandered through the empty offices, stopping now and then and peering at one of his assistants' desks. All of them busy in the pursuit of… what? Money? To what end? He had more than enough money to retire for several lifetimes and live like a king. Why was he doing this? Had it become a mere habit? A pang of envy gripped him as he thought of Menach Peprini's devotion to a noble cause. Could his own life be described as noble? It could not. He gave a great deal of money to charity; indeed, his philanthropic activities took up an increasing amount of his time. He was wealthy, successful by most standards, and had a certain power. But standing in the dusk of the empty offices all this seemed little consolation.

He then sat at his secretary's desk and thumbed through her dog-eared Rolodex. Ronald Creighton had been in the FBI for twenty-one years. He and several other ex-Bureau, former CIA and NSA agents, and a collection of foreign counterparts had formed their own investigative agency. He dialed the home number and waited.

"Ron, this is an odd request. I want you to find out where my great-grandmother is buried. My father told me that no one knows what happened to her. At a point she disappeared. Her name was Rachel Dabin—D-A-B-I-N—Horenburg—H-O-R-E-N-B-U-R-G."

"We're talking about Europe?"

"Poland, I'm pretty sure. This would have been in the mid-to-late 1800's. More than that I don't know. I don't even know if she was Christian or Jewish. Is this something you can do?"

"We've got an ex-CIA station chief for Eastern Europe heading our London office. We should be able to tell you something."

"Ron, I need this fast."

"But David, I gotta tell you, 19th Century, possibly Poland… it could take some time."

"Whatever it takes. And thanks, Ron."

He stared at the phone and wondered whether or not he wanted what

Peprini had told him to be true.

At that moment Peprini walked through the doors of the discrete, elegant hotel. It was located on Sixth Avenue and would be unrecognizable were it not for the small plaque outside reading "The Heights Hotel." He took the elevator to the third floor.

Once in his room he took off his suit coat and loosened his tie, then turned the heavy chair to the window. For several minutes he took slow, deep breaths. His calmness surprised him. Having the audacity to break a four-thousand-year-old rule should cause more disquiet.

He checked his cellphone for messages, one from the Book Company, confirming his travel arrangements, and one from Sionn. He had told Erna and Sionn he was going to New York to appraise David Wyatt in light of the recent death. A meeting would be arranged with Peprini representing himself as the head of a European charity seeking a donation. Peprini had to undertake this ruse because the Vessel's Keepers would surely note that the Councilor was visiting their charge.

A momentary panic gripped him, but he reasoned his way out of it, reminding himself that even if Wyatt believed him, the knowledge he had was useless. He could always deny what had been said to Wyatt.

"Nothing has been done that can't be undone. Not yet."

40

Throughout his flight home, Peprini felt a growing impatience. He was anxious to begin training the girl who would replace Pilar. She would need no more than basic discerning capacities, but he would have to prepare her to plunge into the Void. He had been lucky with Pilar. She was not so terrified by her first trip into the blackness that she refused to continue. He wasn't certain his next choice would have the same courage.

Arriving at the Abbey, he was not surprised to learn that Dina still had not passed the examination. Neither was he disconcerted. His mind was already set on Maria Jongsma.

The following morning Pem, Crumb, and Garcia joined the Director in his office at the Novitiate.

"Let us begin," Peprini said.

Pem motioned to Crumb to start. "Of the eight, seven are doing well," she said, "that is, not counting Tiplady," she looked at Peprini, not covering her dissatisfaction with Peprini's habit of taking novices out of the program. Even Tarik and Pinedo are showing progress, slowly but surely. Maria Jongsma is the jewel of…"

"Tell me about Dina Carlini," Peprini interrupted.

The three had been aware of the Director's interest in the American and looked at each other uncomfortably.

Pem's eyes locked on the floor, and Garcia leafed through some papers. Crumb saw the task would be hers. "Her performance shows no indication of Esau's blood. None at all. It's not that she has only minor ability, or that she's clumsy in the use of it. It just isn't there."

To their surprise and relief, Peprini seemed calmly to accept this. Garcia found his voice. "Judging by her halo of Blessing, she seems to have the gift, but I suppose it's possible to have a developed halo without the gift."

"Perhaps," Peprini said doubtfully, "although I know of no historical record of such."

"If she isn't a Keeper," Garcia replied, "and of course she isn't a Vessel either, then this still leaves the possibility that she has Abraham's blood through another lineage; we know there are several. Through Ishmael perhaps."

Pem moved forward in his chair. "Who knows? Ishmaelites have been sighted only rarely. Perhaps they have an aura too."

Peprini shook his head. "The records say that Ishmaelites' aura is almost colorless, barely visible. After all, Ishmael received only a secondary Blessing."

"What about the famous Genesis Chapter 25," Crumb asked, "that has intrigued quite a few Keepers? Abraham, after the death of his wife Sarah, marries a woman called Keturah, and they have six children. Could Dina be a descendant of one of them?"

"Nowhere in the Bible," Peprini dismissed her, "does it say that these children received any kind of Blessing. Besides, if they had a significant halo, our ancestors would have noted and recorded this."

"Binino recognized *something* in Dina," Crumb thought aloud. "In his report he says she visualized several Biblical scenes in great detail – the rape of Jacob's daughter, Dinah, and the revenge of Dinah's brothers on the city of Shechem. He regarded her as a great find."

"That is enough speculation," Peprini said with finality. "Pem, please write the usual dismissal letter to Miss Carlini."

"Are you sure, Menach?" Garcia pleaded. "There is something very special about this woman. I don't know how to describe it. It's something… precious."

Crumb nodded. "She seems extraordinary in some way I can't put my finger on. I can't help feeling she still belongs among us."

Peprini stood. "It was wrong that she was sent here. Let's not make it worse by allowing her to remain." He started collecting his papers, signaling the meeting had ended.

The three, however, remained seated.

"Could she remain here in some other capacity, Councilor? You always need good people. Like Tiplady."

"You know very well, Garcia, that no one devoid of Esau's blood is admitted into Keeperdom even as a driver, even as a maid. Even people like Eric Tiplady have *some* discerning capacity. Good day, Master-Keepers."

And with that, he left the room.

An hour later Miss Crumb sat with Dina in the library at the Novitiate.

"I'm sorry, Dina, but we must ask that you leave. We are truly sorry to have caused you to come all this way."

Dina had known this moment would come, but now that it had she broke down. "Please, Miss Crumb. What is it I've failed? That meditation exercise? I have a degree from Columbia University. I've always been a good student. I know I can do well here if you give me a chance."

"I'm sorry. A car is waiting outside for you. We've arranged your transportation back to New York."

Dina could see that Miss Crumb was upset. "Director Peprini said something our first night, and I've thought about it every day since. He said if we left this place we would never know who we really are. Was he telling the truth? I just want to understand. Please." Dina felt her eyes well up but stiffened against it. "Was Father Binino wrong?"

Joanna Crumb put her hand on Dina's. "Once in a great while we are mistaken about those we invite. I'm afraid you will have to learn your answers on your own. I'm sorry. And… there is one last matter." She held out her hand. "I must ask for the ring back."

Dina pulled it from her finger and put it in Crumb's hand. Crumb stood and left the room.

Dina couldn't make herself move. Her will was defeated and she no longer fought the tears. In these two weeks, she had come to understand the depth of her hope and need, the need to know who she truly was, all made harder by the look on the faces of the people here. They had expected so much from her, promised so much to her. Then to see their disappointment, to be told she was a mistake…

Klaus, the same man who had driven her from the train station upon her arrival, stood in the doorway.

"I'm to wait while you pack your things, Miss Carlini. We must leave within the hour."

Nineteen days after she had arrived, Dina Carlini left the Keepers.

41

It did not surprise Eliezer when Osnat said she wanted to join the Keepers, yes, emphatically yes. He took her to the Keepers' *residence* in the Jerusalem suburb of Ein Karem. To celebrate he gave her two wrapped packages. One contained a short book on the history of Keeperdom. The other contained a cellular phone.

"It has an encryption," the professor explained. "No one will be able to listen to our conversations."

They met three times that week. Osnat found the historical material fascinating. She took home any book Eliezer would let her borrow. But her adventurous spirit was especially thrilled by the discernment exercises. To Eliezer's great delight, in her second session she found the entrance to her Inner Depths. He had no doubt now: She had the Keeper's blood.

When they met for her third training session, both felt that a new bond had already been established between them. Sitting in the passenger seat beside the professor, she felt at home as she had never felt before. They chatted about the last book she had just finished reading, *From Jerusalem to Constantinople*, written some four hundred years ago by a Councilor who tracked Keeperdom after the Muslim invasion of the Holy Land.

When they arrived at the *residence* Eliezer's phone rang. It was Oleander. He asked Osnat to wait for him and stepped into the hallway.

"Eliezer, listen, I've got an idea. You said you could find only the first codeword written in the margins of the original Book."

"Even with a magnifying glass I could see no traces of any others."

"There are better technologies today, aren't there? You are the book-dealer so you should know. I heard they use laser or infrared or whatever to detect what the eye can't see."

"*Why didn't I think of that, yes.* I know someone who specializes precisely in this. In fact, I may just be able to catch him before he leaves for the day."

While the two were talking, Osnat sat down at the large mahogany desk in the study and looked at the book lying open on the desk. "TEN SEFIROT OF BELIMAH..." This didn't sound like the Keeper books

Eliezer had let her read. "...BRIDLE YOUR MOUTH FROM SPEAKING..."

Ten minutes later Eliezer found Osnat leaning over the Book of Creation.

"Well, Osnat," he said smiling at her youthful enthusiasm, "have you deciphered the riddle?"

She was startled as if waking up. "Riddle? I don't know. I read this first one and I had a strange experience, a little like what I felt when I read about Abraham in the Bible. Then..."

He glanced at his watch. "And?"

"Something spoke to me."

"Hearing voices, are you?" He opened a cabinet door and carefully took out an ancient-looking book and placed it in a box. "I have something urgent in town. We'll have to postpone today's session. Can you take a bus this time? I am not going your way."

Three hours later Eliezer left his colleague's lab, his face flushed with excitement. He sat in his car and called Oleander.

"William, your idea? Ingenuous! The infrared detected two more handwritten notes, both in Hebrew of course. My friend said he could tell by the smears they had been erased intentionally. One was next to the second formula. It said '*Orma*'—cunning in Hebrew; which we already know is the codeword for the second Sefirah. The other note was next to the third formula: *Eherish*."

"Is that Hebrew?"

"Yes, a Biblical word. Four letters were visible: *H,H,R,Sh*. Of course, there were no vowel signs. This could be '*haharash*'—the blacksmith, or '*hahoresh*'—the forest. But looking at the text, more likely it is '*haharesh*' or '*heherish*'—keep silent or kept silent. That's the obvious meaning of BRIDLE YOUR HEART FROM THINKING, BRIDLE YOUR MOUTH FROM SPEAKING. AND IF YOUR HEART RUNS, RETURN TO THE PLACE. I guess that can mean don't chase your thoughts and emotions and stay in the place of silence. I am not sure what the end of the formula means. Anyway, we will try these two possibilities. One of them should work."

"Is that all?" Oleander sounded disappointed. "What about the other seven Sefirot?"

"We found some additional traces, but none could be reconstructed. My friend will keep working, but he's not optimistic."

"So what do we do when we get to the fourth and the fifth and all the rest?"

"We may learn more from our third session."

"Let's hope you're right. But this codeword business is odd. Why is the third formula connected to 'keeping silent' rather than to 'silence' or 'meditation' or 'listen' or a hundred other possibilities? Or for that matter, how is the second formula connected to 'cunning'?"

"That I don't know, William, but fortunately, we don't really need to know. What we do know allows us to go to the next Sefirah. Can you come to Jerusalem in the next few days?"

"I'll let you know after I book a flight."

Peprini opened his private, encrypted email e-mail account. Monica Berg reported that Oleander had not left the grounds of the St. Raphael monastery and had no visitors. Tiplady had arrived. He moved down the list to the Jerusalem report. His two men newly posted in Israel had been sending detailed daily reports about Eliezer's movements.

"What's this?" he muttered. *"The professor took a young woman, Osnat Aviv, to the Keepers' residence in the Ein Karem neighborhood. They stayed for fifteen minutes. Afterwards she left by bus. He went to the office of AncientWorks Inc. He…"*

Eliezer was the only Keeper in Jerusalem, other than Peprini's men. He picked up the phone and dialed the number in Israel.

"Yes, sir."

"Has Eliezer been with this young woman at other times?"

"Twice, sir. Also at the Ein Karem *residence.*"

"Did you report that?"

"Yes, sir, but at the time I was by myself and wasn't aware it was a Keeper *residence.*"

"They've had how many meetings?"

"Away from campus, four. We keep a record of all his meetings at the University, but not with students in his classes."

"She is a student?"

"Yes, sir."

Why would he take her to a Keeper *residence?* This was strictly forbidden. He felt both a burgeoning curiosity and power over the old man. "Get me a photo as soon as possible. If they meet on campus I want to know. If he should take her off campus again, learn what they are doing."

A picture was beginning to form. One: Someone was attempting to open the Primordial Gate as the Ishmaelite Prince had said. It had to be a Councilor—he accepted it was very unlikely that even a Master-Keeper would have the discernment power to accomplish this. Two: Eliezer and Oleander had been having peculiar meetings, judging by the locations and durations, and the fact they did not notify the Security Office of these trips.

Three: Eliezer must have a strong reason to violate Keeper law by taking an external to a Keeper *residence*. Four: he had learned that this morning Erna had been to the Archives asking for a record of everything Eliezer had sought in the past year. Why not simply ask him? If she had to go behind the old man's back, she must suspect he is hiding something from her. And if he had to hide it from his oldest friend…

42

The sudden light in the room woke him. Tiplady tried to focus.

"Get up." Monica Berg clapped her hands harshly. "*Now!*"

"What?" He looked at the clock. It said 5:30 am.

"Councilor Oleander is leaving the monastery at this moment." She picked up his suitcase which had been prepared for a sudden departure. "Put something on. You can clean up at the airport. Move. Velasquez is waiting."

"Alright, alright." He had still not adjusted to the time change, having arrived at the farmhouse only two days earlier and had slept little in that time. The bed sagged almost to the floor and some small animal had clattered across the floor in the attic above his room each night. He hated the musty odor of the old house and the sickly-sweet smell of the rotting pears from the abandoned orchard higher on the hillside.

On his way to the front door, Tiplady tucked in his shirt and saw Krueger, the terse Swede, sitting in front of a spotting scope trained out the farmhouse window at the dark monastery. Without moving from the eyepiece he said, "He put luggage in the car. A young monk drives him. I'm certain to the airport."

"We can make up time on the highway," Velasquez answered.

"Do you have your passport and the rest?" Berg frowned at Tiplady.

"I think so..." he patted his jacket and took out his wallet and passport. "Yeah."

"For some reason, Councilor Peprini wants you on this task. Try not to muck it up." Berg put a cellphone into Tiplady's hand.

"What's the number?"

"You won't need to know that. Call Councilor Peprini when you arrive at the airport and know where you're going. Now get moving."

She took the thick, bearded Spaniard by the arm. "The Councilor, God only knows why, has a special interest in this kid. Keep him out of trouble."

"Councilor? This is Eric Tiplady."

"Yes?"

"I'm at the airport in Utica. Velasquez and me. Oleander—Councilor Oleander—just checked in. I overheard him talking with the ticket agent. He's on his way to JFK, then to Tel Aviv. Then Nairobi the next day."

"Well done. Follow him." Peprini had been monitoring Oleander's credit cards and already knew of his ticket purchase and destination.

"To JFK?"

"Tel Aviv."

"Israel? But..." Tiplady hesitated.

"What is the problem?"

"I didn't know I'd be going overseas. I just woke up an hour ago."

"We'll try in the future to take into account your sleep schedule. Buy your tickets and whatever else is necessary. Once in Tel Aviv, you are to follow him. Be discrete. Is there anything else?"

"I don't think so."

"Good," Peprini said. "Call me when there is news."

Tiplady stepped up to the ticket counter. "We need two seats on the next flight to New York, then to Tel Aviv. El Al flight 008."

"First class, business, or coach?"

He slapped the American Express card on the counter, grinning at Velasquez. "First class, all the way."

Twelve hours later, on the other side of the ocean, Eliezer drove from Jerusalem to Ben Gurion airport to pick up Oleander. The monk emerged into the reception hall, and Eliezer led him outside to the short-term parking lot. Neither noticed Tiplady and Velasquez getting into a taxi, or the two men in the tan Subaru waiting in the parking area several spots from Eliezer's Volvo.

"How did you explain your trip to your abbot this time?" Eliezer smiled. "Did you tell him you are thinking of starting a Holy City chocolate factory?"

"I'm officially on the way to Kenya. I told him I wanted to stop in Israel to pray at the Church of the Nativity."

"And I suppose you'll want me to take you there, so you will not turn out to be lying to your abbot."

"You know me too well."

"It's about a half-hour from my home. It should be a nice evening for a walk, and you can unwind after your flight. Tomorrow morning we'll hold our session. You can then rest on the way to Nairobi."

That evening they did not mention the questions heavy on their minds. Instead, after visiting the Church of the Nativity, Eliezer took his friend to an Arab restaurant in East Jerusalem, where they passed the evening in pleasant conversation, for a time able to set aside their responsibilities.

Early the next morning they left Eliezer's home and drove across town to the Jerusalem *residence*. The car slowed as it rolled up to the wrought-iron entrance gate. They stopped talking and their mood turned somber.

They climbed the stairs to the second floor. Wordlessly, like actors in a well-rehearsed play, they arranged two chairs at the dining table, took their seats, loosened clothing, took one last look at each other, and sank into silence.

Soon they found themselves in their Inner Depths. Minutes later they were hovering at the periphery of the Void.

Eliezer began reciting the already-familiar introductory passage of the Book, Oleander immediately joining in—WITH THIRTY-TWO MYSTERIOUS PATHS OF WISDOM ENGRAVED GOD—and they felt the odd stillness descend on them, and then the velvet darkness.

They continued into the third Sefirah passage:

TEN *SEFIROT* OF *BELIMAH*, BRIDLE YOUR HEART FROM THINKING, BRIDLE YOUR MOUTH FROM SPEAKING...

Great energies appeared in the distance, silent and dark, announcing themselves to the two Keepers by a sudden change in the pressure of the atmosphere surrounding them.

...AND IF YOUR HEART RUNS, RETURN TO THE PLACE, FOR IT IS SAID: "AND THE CREATURES RUN AND RETURN." AND ON THIS A COVENANT HAS BEEN MADE.

The pressure rose higher and then still higher, now not far from them in the darkness, still constrained by some invisible dam, alive, tense and eager to explode. In the face of this immensity, they felt absurdly minuscule, grains of dust facing a coming sandstorm. Though they sensed it was the Blessing behind the dam, the sheer enormity of it was at the same time awful.

They held their breath, bracing themselves. And now the codeword...

Eliezer inhaled deeply then spoke: "*Heherish*..."

They waited...

A *pop* rang in their bodies as the pressure suddenly gave way and an immense wave of glorious energy exploded forth, sweeping by them and onward into the Void. They were spun around and fought to keep from being dragged over the edge into the nothingness. Cast aside like driftwood, they were floating now in a momentary eddy, struggling to keep their balance against the pull of the current. Eliezer sensed he was slipping, a deep fatigue coaxing him to yield to the divine sweetness pulling at him. Moment by moment he held, forcing himself not to think beyond the next moment, knowing that if he faced the uncertainty of how long this trial might last he would quit and let go.

The tumult subsided, leaving them near the edge but safe. They looked at one another, relieved to see the other safe.

Gradually the two Keepers ascended to their bodies. They lay quietly in their chairs for some time, recuperating, as the atmosphere in the room discharged. Oleander was the first to open his eyes.

"Eliezer," he said quietly. "I don't understand."

The old man slowly righted himself in his chair, opening his eyes. "Yes, William."

"The codeword '*Heherish*.' I assume it comes from "BRIDLE YOUR MOUTH FROM SPEAKING. But the last words of the text: AND ON THIS A COVENANT HAS BEEN MADE. What covenant can this possibly be? We are assuming the text is about the Primordial Gate, but in the story of God's blessing to Adam and Eve there is no covenant—no agreement or contract of any sort."

The old man closed his eyes, then spoke slowly. "Could this refer to some covenant in some other place in Genesis, for example Jacob's agreement with Hamor, in the story of Dinah?"

"But there's no blessing in that story. And again, just like the first two sessions, if the text is about the Primordial Gate, then why didn't we see this Gate? Why didn't we see Adam or Eve or some picture of God's first Blessing of humanity?"

"It was hard to see anything at all. Perhaps we will learn more in the next session."

"Let's be honest, Eliezer. Do we know now any more than we knew after the first or second session? These strange codewords—Circumcision, Cunning, Keeping Silent—do you have any idea what they mean?"

There was a long silence.

"I want to ask you a question I've already asked a dozen times. Do we have the right to continue when we are uncertain what is happening?"

For the first time, Eliezer wavered. "We are certainly doing something very powerful. The problem is we are not sure what it is." He looked at his young friend. "What do you think we should do?" Then he added quietly, "If you decide to quit, I will understand."

Oleander's chest rose and fell, his eyes moving about the ceiling. "The safe course is to stop. We both know this."

He grasped the armrests and pulled himself upright, looking squarely at the old man, taking a deep breath and exhaling sharply. "But no. *No.* If we quit we'll never understand what we've done, what might have been achieved."

"And the risk?"

"Whatever else is happening, it's undeniable we are activating the Blessing. We both feel it. And how can that be bad?"

Eliezer felt his courage revived. "Thank you, William. Thank you. So we continue. Ten days, then? I am assuming we'll both have sufficiently recovered by then."

The monk stood up with difficulty. "Oh Lord, my body feels like a train hit me."

"Councilor Peprini? It's Eric Tiplady."

"Where are you?"

"Tel Aviv airport. The Councilor is checking in. To Nairobi. I thought I'd…"

"Don't bother." Peprini had learned Oleander had legitimate business in Kenya and was booked on a return flight to New York. "What has Councilor Oleander done in Jerusalem?"

"Nothing much, as far as I could tell. They went to the Church of the Nativity, then a restaurant, and then stayed at the Professor's apartment last night. Then they went to another house in…" Peprini heard the rustle of paper "…Ein Karem?" Peprini grimaced at the boy's ineptitude with the pronunciation of any non-English word. "It's an expensive-looking place."

"Just the two?"

"Yeah. It doesn't look like anyone lives there. Anyway, they stayed about three hours."

Peprini sighed. "That's all you have to report?"

"Well, I'm not sure…"

"You are not sure what?"

"I think Eliezer and Oleander were being followed."

"*Councilors* Eliezer and Oleander. And followed by whom?" This was not good news. If Tiplady had seen Peprini's men, perhaps Eliezer or Oleander had too.

"I don't know, Councilor, I thought it might be one of your men. I'm guessing you've got somebody following Councilor Eliezer. So I didn't look too hard."

"Describe him."

"Like a beggar. Dirty clothes. He smelled…"

Peprini sighed again. "Never mind. There is no point staying in Jerusalem. Return immediately to Utica."

<h1 style="text-align:center">43</h1>

Dina woke with a start. The room was dark. Once again the same strange dream.

She threw off the covers, walked over to the window and pulled the curtain aside. A dark Manhattan street. When had she checked into this miserable hotel? Two days ago? Three? She could no longer remember and could hardly care. After being expelled from the Novitiate she had been escorted to the Lucerne airport. Hours later she had landed at JFK, taken a taxi into the city and found this cheap hotel, and locked herself in this room. So much had changed so fast. None of it had seemed real. For several days now she had been staying in bed until late, wandering the streets until sundown.

The shock of the expulsion had been unexpectedly painful. She still did not understand what test she had failed, what quality she was lacking, and this frustration magnified the hurt. But this she did know: At Frostburg she had been promised something extraordinary: *to know who she was.* Councilor Peprini had promised this and she knew it was true, despite their claim that she was a mistake. Before leaving for Frostburg she had quit her job at Social Services, sublet her apartment and put her things in storage, saying goodbye to her mother, sister, and few close friends. There had been no man in her life for over a year. Looking back, it seemed she understood her departure would change her life permanently, and had gradually but surely begun distancing herself from other people.

She had spoken to no one since returning. Shame kept her from calling friends or even her sister in Albany. It had been difficult enough telling them she was entering an institute for the study of the Bible. They had respected her decision, though understandably were surprised by it. But then to be expelled, and for a reason she herself still didn't exactly understand… It was too soon to explain this to anyone.

Dina went back to bed and deliberated. What an eerie dream—so vivid, as if not a dream at all. What happened in that strange land? She vaguely remembered seeing a young woman—called "Dinah" by the others, though the name sounded somewhat different from her own. And there was a young man, a local prince. The prince wanted to marry Dina but her brothers wouldn't allow it. What happened next? There was violence, a terrible slaughter....

I have to talk to Father Binino, she thought. I have to know what this dream means. Dina cringed at the idea of talking to the priest and describing her failure. For days she had resisted calling him. But the utter reality of the dream gave her a new determination.

It was four in the morning, but she picked up the phone. A sleepy voice on the other end answered.

"Father Binino? It's Dina. Carlini."

"Dina, yes." A pause. "Are you here in New York?"

"How did you know?"

"Director Peprini called me. He said... he said your test hadn't gone well."

"They expelled me."

"I still can't believe it, Dina. And I told the Director exactly that."

"How could you have been so wrong about me? You said I was the most gifted person you'd ever known." It embarrassed her to repeat his words.

She heard him search for consoling words. "I'm sorry, this was all my fault. Dina, for your own sake, try not to think about it anymore. Don't torture yourself. Go back to your life."

"But I had one of the dreams again. Just now. Father..." and now she felt on the verge of tears but stifled them. "Father, it was so *real*. I was there, I mean really there, like I'm here now. Even more real than this," she said, looking at the anonymous hotel room. "Why did you send me to Lucerne? What did you see in me that the people at Frostburg didn't?"

She could hear his voice becoming distant. "Listen, Dina, the Lucerne episode is behind us now. We will never talk about it again. You must not talk of it to anyone."

She said nothing.

"Dina? Are you there?" He could hear her breathing. "Why don't you come to the church tomorrow morning at eleven. *Today* at eleven. We will talk about your plans."

Dina quietly hung up and started sobbing.

44

The weekend passed slowly for David Wyatt. He watched more football on television than he had in years. He tried to avoid thinking about Peprini's visit.

Monday came and he went to the office. He had placed Peprini's card in his wallet just to remove it from his sight. And he had always possessed a strong ability to put areas of his life into boxes until he was ready to attend usefully to them. As well, the visit had begun to seem unreal.

He was just ready to leave the office on Thursday when Barbara buzzed him.

"Mr. Wyatt, Ron Creighton is on the phone."

"Ron, good to hear from you. Any news?"

"We've been through every database in Poland. We also checked Slovakia and the Czech Republic on the chance your great-grandmother didn't die in Poland. Our people contacted every church and synagogue in virtually every town. I say 'virtually' because some of the hamlets don't have phone service, believe it or not. We've had priests and rabbis and who-knows-who digging through their records and going through graveyards all over the country looking at headstones. So far nothing. Sorry, David."

"I know you did all that could be done."

"Do you want us to keep looking?"

"No. Actually, yes. I want you to check just one town. Check the town of Cransk in Poland."

"Will do."

When he arrived the following morning, Barbara handed him his messages. One was from Creighton. He dialed the number.

"Cransk. You were holding out on me."

"Tell me."

"Well, there is no town called Cransk. Not anymore. It always was tiny, and apparently the Germans bombed it out of existence. It's just some rubble in the weeds now. We found an old man on a nearby farm and he showed us where the cemetery and church used to be. In the weeds, among the trees, we found headstones. Barry—our man there—told me not many are still upright. Some just fell over, others were upended by trees pushing up through the ground. And yes, we found your great-grandmother's headstone. Rachel Dabin Horenburg, born August 30, 1863, laid to rest November 15, 1893. I've got to ask. How did you know to look in Cransk?"

"The name was stuck in my mind."

"Well, I'm glad we could confirm your suspicion."

"You did much more than that. I want to ask one more thing. Would you send somebody to Lancut in Poland and check for the grave of Marion Lipinska Ossing? If you don't find her there then forget it. If you do, see if they have any record of her having had children."

"M-A-R-I-O-N, alright. Now, L-Y?'

"L-I-P-I-N-S-K-A, O-S-S-I-N-G."

"That's easy enough. I should know something tomorrow."

He knew what Creighton would say even before he received the call the next day. Yes, Marion Ossing was buried in Lancut. And the headstone also listed the names of her three children. A "Kurt," a "Sebastian," and "Rachel."

After the call, he realized his limbo was over. He had to face the truth. There was simply no way the Keepers could know where his great-grandmother had been buried. No one in his own family had known. Beyond that, no one in his family had even known the name of Rachel's mother, let alone where she had died. And he knew that as far back as records would permit confirmation, the lineage recorded by the Keepers would prove accurate. And this could not be, unless what Peprini had told him was true.

45

Maria Jongsma made her way down the narrow corridor of the Novitiate School, stopping at the steep staircase. She took a breath and began climbing. The old convent had three floors. On the first were the general offices of the Novitiate, the students' rooms (formerly the nuns' cells), dining room, and Founder's Hall. The second floor held the reference library, once the "scriptorium" where books were copied, and the instructors' private offices. The third floor was strictly out of bounds for students. The message Mr. Masking had given her this morning instructed her to go to the third floor at this time. There was no mention of why.

The stone steps ended. There was no door. The archway and corridor beyond were dimly lit. A shadow detached itself from the wall and she almost jumped. She recognized Tennier, the watchman. Maria opened her mouth to explain, but he gestured wordlessly towards the end of the passageway where light poured from a room. She did not see him shaking his head behind her, half in disapproval, half in amusement as his eyes glided up and down her slender body.

"Enjoy, Director," he muttered. "You definitely have good taste. Just as last time."

Menach Peprini liked his assistants to be beautiful young women; women—because he found them easier than men to manage and charm; and beautiful—because his exacting aesthetic taste demanded a pleasing environment even when beauty was beside the point. He had allowed certain rumors to circulate in the Novitiate although they were untrue.

They sat opposite each other. Maria sipped the tea which Peprini had offered. A fire popped and crackled in the hearth, making the stone room especially cozy. He was unusually amiable and she started to relax. They talked of her childhood in Holland. He seemed to know a great deal about her.

He smiled, knowing how to create the right combination of charm and authority. Yes, he thought, Pem's reports were accurate. She is a perfect candidate for the experiment: smart, devoted, a potentially superb discerner, and quite lovely. He was pleased. It was a pity about Pilar; he had spent so much time training her. But now that he would have the Vessel's cooperation, Maria would manage with what training he could give her in the next few weeks. Would that be sufficient? It would have to be.

His first task was to gain her trust. She must be devoted to him, more loyal to him than to Keeperdom, fully convinced of the absolute importance of his confidential mission. Only then could he trust her to protect his secret from other Keepers and to plunge willingly into the dangers of the Void.

"Maria," he said, almost intimately. "I invited you here because I want you to accompany me on a little journey. To the edge of the Void."

"But sir… I am only a novice…"

"Nothing too challenging," he interrupted. "No discernment, just a pleasant stroll really. Unless, of course, you don't feel up to it."

"No, Sir, I'd like to."

He smiled. "Come then, Maria."

They descended to the Depths and held briefly at the edge of the Void. Her agility at the Depths was excellent. Peprini was pleased with her performance.

The following three days Maria came to his office again, and they repeated the exercise, each time remaining longer at the boundary of the Void. On the fourth day, he sensed she was ready.

"Today I would like us to try something a bit unusual. Obviously, I cannot force you to participate." He waited for her, but she sat still. "Are you interested, Maria?"

"What would this be, Councilor?"

"Again we'll go to the edge of the Void. You will not discern, so you need not fear any kind of strain or fatigue. Once we are there, I would like you to step into the Void for a few seconds."

She looked him in the eye a long moment. "We were warned…"

Peprini nodded reassuringly. "A few seconds, that is all. I discovered a method to move in and out of the Void unharmed." His expression became stern. "But this must remain strictly between you and me. What you are about to learn is something no other Keeper knows. *No one.* And that is the way it must remain for the time being. Can I trust you, Maria?"

She hesitated. "Yes, Councilor, you have my word. But why…"

"I told you and your fellow novices about the death of Vessel Mark Gregor. You have been feeling the diminishment of the Blessing, yes?" Peprini now leaned towards her and whispered conspiratorially. "I have discovered a way to remedy this tragedy and replenish the Blessing on Earth. I have chosen you, among all Keepers, to help me in this mission."

Behind her green eyes he could see her mind work. For a moment he worried she would decline. But then she nodded. "I'd be honored, Sir."

Peprini sat back. "You are welcome, Maria. You will learn about our enterprise as we go along. Today I will tell you one of my discoveries: If I discern the Void in a certain way, you will be able to float along my discernment beacon into the Void and back to the edge—with no harm."

"No one can discern the Void. That's what our instructors told us."

"Ah!" he smiled. "They do not know what I—what *we* know."

They were seated in Peprini's office at the Novitiate. He was careful to attune himself to her, to make sure they would emerge in the same place. When Maria appeared from her Inner Depths, she saw Peprini waiting for her at the boundary of the Void. A few minutes later they were hovering side by side.

She signaled that everything was fine, and he started to discern. She waited as he had instructed, and watched his discernment beam growing in intensity and focus. The Bible World was hovering in the distance like a moon in the dark sky, but she was not surprised to see that the beam was directed away from it, towards the darkness itself.

Peprini discerned those passages in *Genesis 4* in which Cain is exiled from the Earth as a punishment for the murder of his brother. Very slowly the words passed in his mind: *And Cain went out from God and settled in the land of Nod...*

He nodded to Maria. And she, her trust only barely defeating her dread, moved into the Void.

In the combined terror and wonder of the experience, she almost forgot his instructions. Then Peprini signaled to return. He was relieved to see her taking control of herself and floating back to the edge.

Minutes later she rose from her Inner Depths. When she opened her eyes she turned to him.

"So it is possible."

"As I said, yes." He had expected more reaction from her. And indeed, her posture and her eyes reflected the strain of the Void. "How do you feel?"

His question seemed to interrupt her thinking. "And what else is possible?" she asked.

46

At the same time Peprini was directing Maria into the Void, Erna was engaged in her weekly discernment. She had completed Gate 2—effortless for a Councilor. Far from being exhausted, she lingered at the border of the Void, staring vacantly into the nothingness, contemplating its unique silence.

Something caught her attention: a faint beam spearing into the blackness and disappearing. Noticing another Keeper's discernment beam was unusual but not unheard of. Yet this time there was something odd. She squinted, trying to make out the muted line in the distance. Then she grasped why it was peculiar. How could that be? The beacon was not directed towards the Bible World. *It was directed away from the Bible World—at the Void itself.*

She first concluded that some novice had become confused while discerning. Immediately she dismissed the idea. You simply *can't* discern the Void itself, because there is no Gate there. There is no Biblical passage that refers to the Void, other than at the very beginning of Genesis, a gate far too powerful for a Keeper to discern.

The beacon was remarkably steady and focused. It clearly belonged to an especially powerful discerner, a Master-Keeper or more likely a Councilor. A Councilor discerning the Void! Was that possible? Evidently, it was. The beam slowly dissipated and vanished. The steady diminishing proved again that this was a superbly experienced discerner.

Erna rose from her Inner Depths. She opened her eyes, and then the meaning of her observation struck her: *Someone was violating a fundamental law of the world of Keepers and the Blessing.* How long had this breach of law been taking place? And now another idea shook her. Could this have any connection to the termination of Vessel Gregor?

She had to talk to someone about this. But she could not go straight to the Council—it was likely one of them was guilty. She pictured her colleagues around the table and wondered who it was.

Two decisions formed in her mind: First, to search the Archives for previous instances of such forbidden (though presumably not impossible) discernment. If she was right, these would have occurred just prior to each of the Seven Tragedies. And second, to descend to the Void as often as she could and hopefully detect the bizarre beacon again. If she remained in the Depths without wasting energy on discerning, she could do this several times a day. Now that she was looking for it, the faint beacon in such an unexpected direction would not escape her notice.

Eliezer was at home that evening, sifting through a pile of articles on the topic of the Book of Creation when his cellphone rang. He pressed the "speaker on" button and continued to work.

"Professor Eliezer, guess what? I just discerned."

"Osnat." He looked at the disarray of his office, surrendered, and sat down, picking up the phone. "Tell me what happened."

"I discerned. At least that's what I think I did."

"It happens that some novices descend to the Inner Depths and then start imagining Biblical scenes. It's to be expected, but this is not discerning."

"No, no. After I reached the Inner Depths I started chanting some Biblical verses I had just finished reading. Then I drifted through the corridor, and I found myself at the edge of this huge emptiness..."

"The Void. Osnat, you must be more careful, for heaven's sake. Thank goodness you didn't fall into it. How did you get back from the Depths?"

"I just turned around and ascended."

"Amazing," he murmured. "Do you realize you could have gotten lost forever? You simply must be more careful, Osnat. This is not a game."

"It didn't feel dangerous. It was exciting."

"Exciting? The first time I came out of my Inner Depths through the corridor to the edge, I floated about helplessly, terrified. And mind you, all my teachers agreed that I was an exceptional student."

"The truth is, Professor, it was a little confusing at first. But when I got used to it, I moved to the edge of the Void and looked."

"At what?"

"The Bible World—the bright moon in the Void is the Bible World, isn't it?"

"It is."

"And then my vision zoomed in—do you know what I mean? And then I could really see."

"What did you see?"

"The verses I spoke talked about Gate Four and that's exactly what I saw: Abraham goes to sacrifice his son, Isaac; then God blesses Abraham and his seed; then God promises to bless Ishmael..."

"You must be mistaken, Osnat. No one can discern even Gate One with only two weeks of exercises, let alone Gate Four."

"But I saw things that aren't in the Bible."

"Again, your imagination." Eliezer grew impatient. He felt the strain of being solely responsible for her safety and wondered whether it wouldn't be better, after all, to send her to Frostburg. "Okay then. When Abraham received God's Blessing, how was he dressed?"

"In black, a black robe. He was walking in a grove of trees when…"

"Was he alone?"

"A servant walked behind him. A boy, in a sort of loose tunic, not really a robe. It was white."

Thoughts raced in Eliezer mind. How could that be? And why Gate Four of all Gates?

"What did Abraham wear around his neck?"

"A pendant. Silver, I think. It looked like a ram… yes, a ram."

There was a long silence.

"Professor Eliezer?"

"Osnat, I will meet you tomorrow afternoon at four in the usual place. *Do not attempt to discern again, please.*"

47

Alifa Hadid had her own opinions about her country, Egypt. She had seen her brothers inherit the opinions and prejudices of their grandfather and father. This seemed inevitable, though she had somehow escaped this cycle, as had her mother. She saw that people rarely change past a certain age. The effort to change the world must begin with young children who can be taught to see with open eyes. Of course, this she kept to herself. When asked why she chose to be a schoolteacher she simply answered, "Because I love children." This was the kind of answer expected from a woman in Arab society, and so she avoided the disapproval and tedious lectures on the role of the sexes that men often gave women.

That morning her father suggested that she would be more comfortable wearing her *Hijab* over her head and face. "The wind is quite strong this morning."

She and her new husband smiled conspiratorially; her father was a traditionalist who was struggling to change with the times. "That's a good idea, father." And she put on the scarf because she liked it.

She finished preparing lunches for her husband and herself to take to work. The two of them were alone in the kitchen and they sneaked a kiss. She thought of finding a house of their own, but generations of a family living together was a tradition she appreciated. Her husband didn't mind. If she was happy he was happy, though at times she did wish they could be completely alone. Sound traveled in the old house particularly in the dead of night.

Her life had been successful and remarkably devoid of the small and larger misfortunes that befall most other people. She had the Blessing which she had inherited from her mother, although of course, neither of them knew this. She was a Vessel.

She and her husband, Sa'id, climbed into his blue Volvo and turned out of the drive. Neither noticed the scruffy woman standing across the street, her jaw dropping half-open and her empty eyes following them. Nor was the vagabond given attention by the man in a house down the block, looking through the spotting scope.

As they made their way through the busy streets, Sa'id explained to his wife that the excavation on his office building project had been delayed for at least thirty days, possibly much longer. During the digging they had unearthed ancient ruins. This was common in Alexandria and newfound remnants of the ancient city plagued the builders.

Alifa paid little attention to the details. She was still enamored of listening to her husband's mind work, the hard reasoning tempered by a soft heart.

"So I will be late tonight and won't be able to take you home. You don't mind riding the bus?"

"Whether you drive me home or the handsome bus driver, why should I care?" She laughed at the moment of worry on his face then squeezed his hand, all the affection the drive of the school would allow.

That afternoon at three, Alifa walked her children to the drive where some were scooped up in cars and the rest boarded the school bus. She waved goodbye and got a smile from even the tired and cranky ones. Then she gathered her things and walked out into the late afternoon sun.

The bus stop was down the block and the sun felt intimidating. She paid no attention to the unkempt man squatting on his heels against the wall of the school gaping at her. Suddenly she became lightheaded as if she had stood too quickly. She took a few more steps, passing by the vagabond, and then stopped to collect herself. It was a strange mixture of dizziness, anxiety, and vulnerability.

"Mrs. Hadid, how are you?"

She turned and saw a fellow teacher standing by the open trunk of his car. With some strain, she put on a polite smile.

"*Marhaba,* Mr. Rifaat. How was your day?"

"*Marhabtein.* Each year the kids seem to take from me my last bit of patience. Then I find by the start of the next term it has returned, thank Allah."

She was aware of the perspiration on her face and the effort it took her to push aside her wooziness and continue with the forced friendliness, and she hoped he didn't notice this.

"Say, are you feeling well? Do you by chance need a lift?"

It was less than proper for a woman to ride alone in a car with a man not a relation. Normally she would thank him and refuse without a second thought. But in her weakened condition, thoughts she seldom entertained came to mind: Why should she stand in the heat and wait for a bus certain to be late, then travel needlessly more than an hour to reach her home only twenty minutes away? A man would not have to endure that. A man could simply accept a ride from a colleague. She had worked alongside him for two years and he was politely offering to do her a favor.

Her skin was hot and clammy, her legs unsteady. She needed to sit down.

"Yes, thank you, that would be very nice, Mr. Rifaat. Saad Zaghloul Street is not too far out of your way?"

"Not at all."

She forced another smile and opened the passenger door and got in. The old, tiny sedan sputtered as it joined the traffic.

It was a relief to sit and the air flooding through the window cooled her. She began to feel better. They talked of the politics at the school.

"But you seem content, Mrs. Hadid."

"Oh, I think it's just my nature."

"You are still young, that's the main thing. No children yet, is that correct?"

"Soon, we hope." The thought of motherhood made her smile.

"Of course, you just recently married. My advice is to enjoy your youth, Mrs. Hadid. Aging is hard on a woman in our culture. My wife, she is already old. I am only forty-two, in the prime of life, and I now have an old woman for a wife. Does this happen everywhere or only in the Arab world?"

Alifa could think of nothing to say. She hadn't met his wife but knew what he was talking about.

"It must be very difficult for her too."

He nodded with no smile, and shifted the car into a higher gear, pressing harder on the gas. "I wish she was more like you, Alifa."

He had never used her first name and this made her uneasy. He drove with purpose, manhandling the little car through a turn.

The car was traveling fast and she realized she didn't know where they were.

"Mr. Rifaat, I believe the turn was…"

"She is like an old date left in the sun." He stared straight ahead as he spoke as if she was not present. "Dried, wrinkled. There is nothing alive in her… nothing soft or juicy anymore."

He made a quick left turn and then another, and she was thrown hard against the door in two quick jerks. When she recovered, she found they were traveling as fast as the little car could go down a dirt road, gravel and rocks pinging loudly against the car's undercarriage. Dust flew in the open window and she waved it from her face. Through the dust and the dirty windshield she could see the road ended up ahead. She saw huge columns supporting a bridge under construction over the Nile River.

"Where are we going? Where are you taking me?" she demanded above the noise.

The bald tires slid on the dirt as he fought to keep the car on the road. She reached for the door handle and couldn't find it. She clawed at the metal on the inside of the door and a hand clamped brutally hard on her left wrist. He snickered loud enough to be heard over the roar of the engine and the rocks pinging.

"On these little pieces of *Hara*? These are too cheap to have handles on both the inside and out, not like your prick husband's new Volvo."

She reached with her right arm out the window but he jerked her back.

"This will do," he said over the clatter.

On the hill two hundred yards away a car holding the two Keepers idled in the sun. The men looked questioningly at each other. Since the death of the fifth Vessel everyone at the Alexandria *residence* had been edgy. Alifa had never presented them with this type of situation. They knew Rifaat; he was a harmless sort. Everything in their training told them to stay back. The older man in the passenger seat handed his partner the video camera he was using and took a pair of binoculars from a duffle.

"What's happening?" the driver said, looking through the lens. "She isn't going to… I don't believe it.

"Quiet." It wasn't their job to keep the Vessel faithful. No Keeper could know if the path of the Blessing was for a child to be fathered by a man other than Alifa Hadid's husband. They watched.

The car braked hard and Alifa lurched against the seatbelt in pain. She turned to him angry as well as scared. Her breathing stopped when she looked at his eyes. Now she understood. Of course. *How could you have been so stupid*, Alifa, she said to herself.

"If you're smart and don't make me hurt you, no one need know. You can go home and no shame will be on you. You will not have shamed your husband, nor your father and brothers. This doesn't have to be unpleasant for you. I bet you'll enjoy it, you modern little slut."

With that, he reached over and began pulling up her *Jilbab*. She tried to push his hand away but he was unstoppable. At that moment she realized how gentle her husband had always been with her, how much strength he held back out of respect or love or fear of hurting her.

"What did I just tell you?" He slapped her hard.

This enraged her and she raked her fingernails across his face. She shot her arm out the window and felt for the door handle. She had it! She pulled and the door began opening and she jumped out only to be tugged harshly back by the seatbelt. Frantically she tried to release the restraint when the world turned black and then filled with stars. A deep ache exploded from her face and she started to cry. She couldn't stop the crying; he had broken her nose and in reflex her eyes teared. She touched her nose and her hand came away bloody. Again he clamped his hand around her wrist and looked at his face in the car mirror.

"*Look what you did.*" Starting at the bridge of his nose and traveling down across his cheek were three deep and bloody scratch marks. He turned to her now with his eyes burning.

"What's happening?" Hassan asked.

"I can't tell," Aziz said. "But it can't be good. Let's…"

Then the binocular image showed a commotion in the car and her arm shoot out the open window searching for the door handle, the door opening, and her leg appearing only to jerk suddenly and start flailing.

"Go!"

The driver put the car in gear and accelerated. Aziz saw Rifaat's arm swing and Alifa's head snap backwards.

"Go, go, go!"

The driver stomped on the gas pedal and the Citroen shot forward in a billow of dust. Through the bouncing glasses, the Keeper saw Alifa's head shove the car door open. Rifaat was stretched over her. The Citroen reached fifty miles an hour when the driver jumped on the brake pedal with both feet, the car sliding sideways to a stop. They scrambled out and ran to the little car. The older Keeper reached the passenger side in time to see the man's hands let go of her throat. Rifaat backed out the driver's door and fell backwards into the dust. He looked up as Hassan rounded the rear of the car. Rifaat looked into the car and saw Alifa's still body in the front seat.

"Oh no!" Rifaat cried.

Aziz put his fingers lightly on her neck, looking for a pulse, still searching long after he knew. Hassan and Rifaat waited in silence.

"No, I couldn't have done this. It's not possible!" Rifaat was crying now.

"Aziz, I don't see it!"

"He crushed her windpipe. She's gone." Aziz looked at Hassan. "*It's* gone." His face turned hard. "Don't let him move."

The order wasn't necessary. The murderer was frozen. Aziz went to the Citroen's trunk and returned with a length of twine. "This will have to do. I'm going to make the call."

He checked for a pulse once more, though the unnatural depression across her throat and look in her still-open eyes told him it was futile. Then he moved into the shade of the giant bridge column. He punched in the code on the secure phone and waited.

"This is Communications."

"This is Aziz in Alexandria."
"Go ahead."
"I need to speak to a Councilor. It's an emergency."

48

"Councilor Sionn, you'd better take this."

Albrecht Sionn had taken to spending most of his day at the Abbey since the death of Vessel Gregor. He found the atmosphere more comforting than that of the Book Company offices.

"What is it?"

"It's our team in Alexandria. I think something has happened."

"Put it through." He waited. "This is Councilor Sionn."

"Vessel Alifa Hadid was just murdered." Aziz rapidly continued with the details, Sionn not interrupting, his heart already falling.

"And the Blessing?"

"It's gone, Councilor. She terminated. I'm afraid there's no doubt."

"*Are you certain the Blessing is gone?*" Even as he spoke the words Sionn knew the question was pointless. If she had passed the Blessing, it would be to her unborn child. And with Alifa dead, so would be the child.

"Sir, *she is dead.* It's gone. Sir?"

"Have you called the police?"

"No. It just happened minutes ago. Nobody knows about it but us. We're beneath a bridge viaduct and…"

"This is what you do: You have the man who did this, correct?"

"Yes, sir."

"Tie him, gag him and put him in the trunk of your car. I'll arrange a private plane for you at the Alexandria Airport. You will be able to drive right up to the plane. You and—who's with you?"

"Hassan."

"You two get him on that plane. Stop at the *residence* first and retrieve the memory disks…"

"We have the video camera with us."

"I want all the files from the last two weeks, since we started. Then go straight to the airport, the private terminal. I'll text you with the details"

Sionn leaned back in his chair. Nothing made sense anymore. The death of another Vessel on the heels of Gregor's termination? *Was it possible?* Without consulting the Chronicles, he knew that no Vessel line had ended through murder. He reached for the telephone, knowing he was about to cause a panic.

Annette Goldman ran down three staircases to the library's lower stacks, unable to wait for the elevator. Erna, who had been absorbed in a diary of One-Eyed Isabel, turned to the librarian questioningly. Goldman opened her mouth but couldn't find her voice.

"What is it, Annette?"

"I can't… it's happened again."

Erna felt the anxiety rush into her veins.

Goldman shook her head. Then she placed a note in front of the Head Councilor.

Erna read the note—it was in Sionn's handwriting—and her face turned ashen. She read it again. The death of the fifth Vessel, Gregor, had been shocking but not out of pattern. Now Alifa Hadid only two weeks later? The world she believed she understood was no longer.

Slowly Erna climbed the stairs. Instead of going to the conference room, as Sionn had requested, she walked out to the garden. She turned and looked down at the city. The ambient Blessing in the sky over Lucerne seemed thinner already. Could the effect of Hadid's death be so quick?

There must be another Council meeting—though to what purpose she didn't know. Best to postpone it as long as possible, she thought. Let the skies and roads stabilize before asking five Councilors to travel to Lucerne.

"What am I doing?" she said aloud, knowing this attention to administrative tasks was a sign of her numbness.

Then she recalled the strange discernment beacon she had encountered two days ago. Someone had discerned the Void and only 48 hours later another Vessel terminates? A fundamental transgression of Keeper Law, of the Laws of the Blessing—could this have caused the death? She *had* to find out who the violator was, and soon. But how?

49

The "Wave" of three weeks earlier, as it had been called in the press, had died down. The newspapers and evening television news appeared, once again, much the same as always. In fact, the occurrence of accidents, illness, and calamities of various kinds was still roughly triple what it had been a month ago, but this escaped the attention of the great majority of people. How many among us keep track of the number of earthquakes that occur in any given month? Of how many buildings collapse, boats capsize, water mains or gas lines break? Of how many jars fall and shatter in the aisles of supermarkets? Of how many industrial accidents occur, how many children miss school because of illness, or how many shoelaces break? And yet, here and there one could see that all was not normal. Hospitals no longer permitted private rooms, and it was common to see doctors' waiting rooms overflowing into the hallways. Most police and fire departments were on mandatory overtime indefinitely; utility companies canceled vacations. But this had receded into the background for most of the population, and to a remarkable extent the patina of normality had returned.

Now this calm was shattered. The earthquakes were extraordinary because they occurred on all continents and along both active fault-lines as well as ones dormant for centuries. Several were in areas with no previous history of seismic activity. Geologists were in a frenzy to collect data in order to meet the demand for predictions of aftershocks and new quakes. Casualties had topped six million. The quakes gave birth to tsunamis that hit Japan, Okinawa and Guam, killing at least another million. Massive power outages compounded the disasters. Air travel was curtailed due to the unrelated crashes of four commercial aircraft. More or less the same headline was on all newspapers: *The Wave is Back*!

The President's Chief Scientific Advisor sat on one of the two couches in the Oval Office, the Vice-President and National Security Advisor on the other. They stood as President Prevost entered.

"Jeremy, what the hell is going on?" The President had visibly aged in the last month. The man's face showed a fixed tension unusual for him, his normal easy smile absent. "Why didn't we have any notice with these quakes?" The worst of the quakes in the U.S. had been focused around Boise, Idaho, and had killed more than 20,000. "Don't you people keep track of these damn things?"

"We do, Sir," Jerome Hunnicutt, the Science Advisor, said. "These were unexpected."

"That's my point. Why didn't you know about them?"

All four were standing. Only when the President took a seat beside Jerome Hunnicutt did the others joined him.

"We are constantly learning about the geological matrix and the interplay between the continental plates, Mr. President." The President glared. "Sir... Given the pervasiveness of the quakes... It's as if the entire geological underpinnings of the Earth have been subjected to a tremendous force, at least one unknown for the last several hundred years, since modern science was born."

"And what could be this tremendous force, Jeremy?"

Hunnicutt turned to answer the Vice-President.

"There are a few possibilities, Mr. Vice-President. One, the polarity of the Earth is in the process of changing. About every 250,000 years or so the polarity of the Earth—the North and South Poles—switches. Somewhat more often the magnetic field starts to weaken, as if beginning to change, then returns."

"*Good God.*" The president seemed exasperated and the Science Advisor regretted mentioning this. "Compasses would point south? And how the hell would that cause Earthquakes?"

"It would cause the planet to move, slightly, on its axis. We doubt this is occurring, Sir. But we would need an event of such magnitude to account for the quakes."

"The planet is wobbling? Jesus Christ."

"As I said, it's unlikely. But we have noted significant changes in the Earth's magnetic field. And no, we don't understand the cause or causes. There are a couple scenarios involving geological events at the Earth's core. As you know, the core is largely liquid, and if this liquid begins to shift then it could cause quite dramatic..."

"No lectures today, Jeremy."

The President turned to his National Security Advisor. "The Guard's on the ground in Idaho? Does FEMA have everything it needs? I want no doubt we're doing everything we can."

"The roads are impassable in many places and the helicopters... they've already had three crashes. Nineteen Guardsmen killed." He met the President's look. No one had an answer why flight had suddenly become so dangerous. "We're moving in aid as fast as we can. Boise's in the worst shape but we've got other problems. Missouri was hit hard, but luckily the quakes were centered in the rural areas. But power's out in most of the Ozark states. And there's looting, it's gotten very bad." He met the President's look with a nod. "Other places too."

"I want the military to cancel all leaves," the President said. "All Guardsmen and Reservists are to be called up."

Less than forty-eight hours had passed since Alifa Hadid's termination. Sionn battled a lethargy unknown to him. He thought of the haggard and frightened faces of Aziz and Hassan, the same look that had been on LaPointe and Cordon, and of the murderer Rifaat now locked in a room below the Abbey. He stood and left his office in the Abbey and went outside, hoping this would invigorate him.

He inhaled the crisp mountain air, redolent with the last days of autumn. The sun was bright and warm on his face. But this contrasted with the dismal weakness of the ambient Blessing across the sky.

Brother Flavius approached, holding a note. The monk's aura, so familiar to Sionn, was fainter than he had ever seen it. The Councilor assumed his own had diminished as well.

"Councilor, a message."

Sionn opened the note. "*Keepers Rosemary Khalil Halil and Betina Morrison were seriously injured in an auto accident in Addis Ababa at 10 am today while following Vessel Anina Lenoma. The Vessel is unharmed. Both are at Black Lion Hospital in Addis Ababa.*"

In his lifetime as a Keeper, stretching back sixty years to his childhood, never could he recall a Keeper suffering such an accident, never mind two at the same time. He shuddered even in the sun's warmth at the vulnerability he assumed would be his companion from now on, his and all other Keepers.' Was this what ordinary human beings live with their entire lives? Such people who had always seemed to him lesser beings— with justification, he believed—now appeared more courageous than Keepers would ever know. Or perhaps, he feared, we will come to know this all too soon.

Master-Keeper Ramona Amar of the Alexandria *residence* no longer had any doubt. Never in her experience had the Blessing behaved in this way. The malaise she and the Keepers in her charge felt had been constant since the death of Gregor two weeks earlier. Discreet phone calls to her Keeper friends revealed the same thing: an unfamiliar level of fatigue, as if gravity had increased and their muscles had not yet grown accustomed to the new effort. Even her thoughts seemed to be slower.

Then Alifa Hadid had terminated. Councilor Sionn had ordered only Hassan and Aziz to Lucerne. No one from Lucerne had contacted her. She believed it was only because there were more important matters demanding their attention. But this silence nevertheless ate at her. She was in charge of the Alexandria *residence*. Alifa had been her responsibility. She had watched her grow from a shy thirteen-year-old to a confident woman. Not only did Amar revere this Vessel of Blessing, but she had loved the child as a mother would her own.

The *residence* had felt unbearably empty. Never had all her Keepers been in the house at the same time, since two had always been watching the Vessel and others discerning or resting. Habit pushed her to the café across from the public library, a favorite place for her to retreat from Keeperdom.

The strong Turkish coffee tasted bitter this morning; she hadn't eaten in two days and the liquid burned in her stomach. She pushed the saucer to the middle of the table. Someone had left a local newspaper behind and she turned it to read the headlines. *The Asharq Alawsat* reported the new tide of accidents and natural disasters as unrelated—what else could they think? Had she not known of the Vessels' termination, she would have concluded the same. Tomorrow didn't promise to be better, as she was sure they believed, as she would have believed only a week earlier.

50

Professor Eliezer drove to the Cinematheque Café to meet Osnat. He looked at the car clock, beginning to worry he would be late. The traffic around the walls of old Jerusalem crept along because of a collision between a cement mixer and an ambulance, and another he had passed earlier involving a truck that was still blocking much of the road.

His thoughts turned to Osnat. She had been persevering in her spiritual exercises and had improved tremendously. Her capacity to endure spiritual stress without rest was unprecedented in his experience. He could no longer postpone the decision whether to send her to the Novitiate. He really didn't have the time or energy to train a novice—he was wrapped up with Oleander and the Book of Creation. And now with Hadid's death... all morning he had felt a pervasive melancholy, a new weakness.

Yet, her capacities were nothing less than astonishing. This combined with the thought of her vibrant youth made him sit up straighter as if gaining some of her strength. I will train her, he thought. As a Councilor he had this prerogative, although the practice was rare and the conditions for approval from the Council vaguely defined. After Hadid's death, it was certain the Council would object to him occupying his energies on a novice. Osnat would have to remain a secret.

But now he would have to suspend their meetings—indefinitely. Hadid's death changed his priorities. He must fly to New York to meet Oleander and discuss their work in light of this new death. Then a Council meeting in Lucerne—thankfully Julia was delaying it for several days. And he couldn't say what new tasks and responsibilities might result from that.

He regretted leaving Osnat, then scoffed at himself. He had become too fond of her.

Tomorrow he would meet Oleander in New York. *Was there any connection between their discernment of the Book of Creation and Hadid's death?* If so, then they must stop immediately. But if there was no connection, then their efforts were even more urgent. An additional gate might make up for the loss in Blessing.

He glanced at the clock and turned on the radio in the typical Israeli obsession with the news.

"…and more on the earthquakes in our special report at one o'clock. Again, this is Kol Israel from Jerusalem. The time is twelve thirty, and here is the summary of the main news: A Boeing 747 and an AirBus 88 collided over London today and crashed in the densely-populated area of Kensington. At least two thousand people are feared dead. Casualty figures from yesterday's four airliner crashes are still being compiled, but currently number over one thousand.

Locally, the entire Western Galilee is without power. Technicians are working to identify the cause. Preliminary reports suggest a coincidence of several independent local failures. It is unknown when service will be restored.

The police continue to report a surge in traffic incidents. Transportation experts estimate the number may exceed the rash of accidents of two weeks ago. Drivers are advised that Highway number 1 from Tel Aviv to Jerusalem is blocked in several places, and so is the Netivey Ayalon Highway in Tel Aviv, Highway number 2…"

Eliezer turned off the radio and steered into the parking lot. He spotted Osnat standing at the top of the stairs leading down to the café.

"Listen, Osnat," Eliezer said after they found a table on the balcony. "I will not be able to meet with you this coming week, and probably the following as well. I must go abroad."

"Something happened."

"It is Keeper business. I am sorry but I cannot say more."

"Professor, did something happen to the Blessing?" This took him by surprise. "All these accidents."

"What makes you think that?"

"And you're afraid something you did might have caused it."

His body jerked at this.

"Osnat," he said quietly, "you know things that a novice should not. Tell me how."

"All morning I've been feeling a heaviness, even before you called. As if there wasn't enough oxygen in the air."

"But that could have any number of causes."

"Wait. After you called, I started worrying why you wanted to meet with me. I was anxious so I did a basic Inner Descent exercise to calm down. And when I resurfaced, I felt—how can I describe it?—a new awareness, a kind of knowing inside me. Does that make any sense? I knew something very bad had happened, though I couldn't tell what it was. Then I noticed a thought reverberating in my mind. It was whispering inside me again and again."

"Go on."

"It said: 'The Blessing has fallen—are Keepers the cause?' The rest was guesswork."

Eliezer pondered. What would make her suspect this? *Of course she can see I am worried.*

"This gift of knowledge that you seem to have—we will have to look into it when I return."

"I don't suppose," Osnat finally said, "you know when you're coming back."

He shook his head. They looked silently at the ancient city and at the Arab village below.

"You do not need me for your Inner Descent exercises. And do not forget your homework. Every Keeper knows the entire book of Genesis by heart. When the time comes to discern, your mind will be too preoccupied to struggle with remembering the Biblical text."

She nodded.

"Tell me," he said to change the topic, "have you read the books I gave you?"

"Both."

"Any questions?"

"Actually, yes. Why do Keepers discern only the Twelve Gates? What about the other places in Genesis where God gives a Blessing?"

"Any Blessings in the first eleven chapters of Genesis, from the creation of the world until Abraham appears on the scene, are not discernible and are quite unknown to us. The Blessing there is much too powerful for human endurance. Under Keeper Law this is forbidden territory. For our own protection."

"No one has tried?"

"Well... who knows? Some may have."

"Is it dangerous, Professor?"

"It is always dangerous to attempt to discern a Gate beyond one's capacities. Remember that."

"I was mainly thinking about another Blessing."

"Let me guess: God's Blessing to Ishmael?"

"As a girl, I used to wonder why the Bible virtually ignores him and talks only about his brother Isaac."

"Half-brother. Ishmael was the son of Abraham, but his mother was Hagar, an Egyptian maid. For obvious reasons, Abraham's gift—his Blessing—passed only to Isaac. That is why we..."

"I know all this, but Ishmael received something too. Remember God's words to Abraham? *And as for Ishmael, I have heard you, I have blessed him and will make him fruitful.* What's the meaning of this Blessing?"

"Who knows? The important thing is what God says next: *but my covenant I will establish with Isaac.*"

"Still, Ishmael was blessed. And then God's angel tells Ishmael's mother that her son would be *a wild man, his hand will be against everybody and everybody's hand will be against him.*"

Eliezer smiled. "A real savage. Why so fascinated with him?"

"In some strange way, I feel for him."

Eliezer grinned. She was unique, no doubt. He glanced at his watch. "I must go. I'm leaving for New York in less than twenty hours. Do not worry about Ishmael." He winked at her. "And keep practicing."

Eliezer set a fifty-shekel bill under his teacup and stood.

"By the way, remember your meditative reading of the Ten Sefirot formulas, last week in Ein Karem? You told me a word spoke in your mind. What was it?"

"*Heherish.*"

"*What?*" Several people turned their direction. Now more quietly he said, "What did you say?"

"That the word was *Heherish*—kept silent. Why, what's wrong?"

Eliezer stared at her. "How could you possibly know? Obviously, BRIDLE YOUR HEART FROM THINKING is related to inner silence. But it could have been many other words—quiet, reticence, contemplation, calm, hush, perhaps a dozen more."

"I don't know, Professor. I told you. I was reading the lines, I had a sinking feeling, and then the word '*Heherish*' appeared in my mind."

"Tell me more."

"Well, I looked at the text, I saw it was talking about silence, and then the word was there. I don't know what more to say."

"You are trying to tell me," he spoke slowly, thinking as he went along, "that these formulas are not ordinary riddles. You are saying that you cannot solve them by logic alone. That you also need to... meditate or contemplate on them. Some intuition seems to be required."

Osnat shrugged. "I'm not giving you a theory. I'm just telling you what I experienced."

"Yes," the old professor murmured, hardly listening to her, "that's it: Logic alone can't give you the codeword. What you need is logic plus intuition. Yes... It certainly worked for you, but then, why not for me?"

He deliberated for a long moment, bent over the table. He had known there was something very strange about this young woman—her odd aura, her surprising discernment capacities. And now this. He turned away and looked out across the valley, feeling his heart thumping. Is it possible that she is able somehow to divine the codewords of the Sefirot formulas? If so, then her contribution to his efforts with Oleander could be crucial.

"Osnat, go back home now. I am going to call you in about an hour. Make sure you are at home."

She flinched at the commanding voice. "Alright."
But he had already turned away.

"Osnat?"
"Professor. Is everything alright?"
"Listen, can you come with me to the USA tonight?"
"Really? Absolutely! Can I still get a ticket?"
"I will take care of it. Do you have an American visa?"
"I'm an American citizen. I was born in California when my father worked in San Francisco." She paused. "But is it safe to fly now, with all those accidents?"
"I have no choice. If you are concerned..."
"No, it's okay, Professor, I want to come."
"And one more thing. Stop calling me 'Professor.' Everyone calls me 'Eliezer.'"

51

It was early afternoon when Eliezer and Osnat landed at JFK airport. The terminal was unusually empty. The string of air crashes had caused considerable fear and the airlines reported forty percent cancellations. Experts of all kinds appeared on television and tried to calm their audiences. Clusters of accidents were statistically likely over great numbers of events. A six-fold rise in air collisions and malfunctions, they explained, was significant only from the statistical perspective of large populations. One in a million instead of one in six million—this made a difference to hospitals, insurance agencies, highway crews, municipalities. But for the individual person, the chances of being involved in a car or plane accident were still minuscule.

As soon as Eliezer entered the baggage claim area he felt the familiar nausea. The vagabond? *But how?* He scanned the thin crowd. Those passengers who had braved the skies were huddled around the baggage carousel. It was difficult to pick out a face in those tight groups, even one as unusual as the vagabond's. Eliezer put down his briefcase and waited for Osnat. She got stuck behind an obnoxious passenger at the immigration counter.

The nausea was distinct. The vagabond had to be close. Had he followed them all the way from Israel? There had been no stench on the plane.

Osnat finally approached. "What's wrong, Professor?"

Now he saw him. "Oh, good. Over there," he whispered to her. "Under the 'Hertz' sign. See that man with the dirty orange shirt?"

"With the cap? That can't be Oleander."

"No, no. Don't stare. But let's have a closer look."

They started strolling toward the vagabond.

The man was now ten feet away. He was not the same vagabond Eliezer had encountered in Jerusalem, though there were similarities: the lifeless eyes, scruffy clothes, the same awkward posture as if he was unused to being in his body. He seemed to be taller, however, and chubbier than his Israeli counterpart. He was undoubtedly the source of the foul emanation.

Eliezer's eyes met the vagabond's. The man recoiled and his face contorted in childish embarrassment.

"Who is he?" Osnat whispered.

"That is exactly what I would like to know."

"What a stink!"

"You feel it?"

"It's not a smell, it's different. Worse."

"Good. I bet the others around here don't sense anything." The baggage carousel began ringing. "That should be us." He took one last look at the vagabond. "Tell me if you feel that stench again."

Oleander walked up and took the suitcase from his mentor's hand, hugging him. He then stepped back to appraise the young woman.

"William, this is Osnat."

"Pleased to meet you, Mr. Oleander."

"Call me 'William.'"

They shook hands. He examined her face, keeping her hand clasped. Her aura was distinctly powerful for a novice, he thought. His eyes penetrated her being just as Eliezer's had several weeks ago. She shuddered just as she had then. It was hard to tell whether he welcomed her. She was surprised at how young he looked. Eliezer had said he was thirty-nine but he didn't look any older than she was. He was quite handsome though did nothing to emphasize it; no doubt he didn't realize he was good looking.

"I hear from Eliezer," he finally said, "you are bringing with you some still-uncharted talents."

She smiled awkwardly. He let go of her hand.

It was a sunny day in New York, and against the visible smog the Blessing seemed to Eliezer thin and wan. Osnat sat between the two men in the cab's back seat. She could sense they were reluctant to speak in her presence. Half an hour later they reached the hotel downtown and went up to the tenth floor to the suite Eliezer had arranged.

When Osnat came out of the bathroom, her hair wet and her clothes fresh, Oleander walked over to the window, turned his back and looked outside. Eliezer smiled at her but she could sense he was preoccupied.

"Osnat, William and I have some matters to discuss. Why don't you go for a walk and do a little sightseeing? I hear there is a new exhibition at the Metropolitan."

52

The moment Osnat closed the suite door Oleander looked sternly at his old friend. His impassive mask vanished. "I really hope this Osnat of yours doesn't get in the way."

Eliezer smiled.

"She's attractive," Oleander continued. "In fact, beautiful. Not what I expected from your enthusiastic description of her talents."

"Did I tell you anything about her physique, William?"

"You never know about pretty girls. They grow up surrounded by too much attention."

"Her discernment capacities are quite extraordinary."

"Gate Four, so you said."

"She did discern Gate Four, I have no doubt. But never any of the lower Gates. Strange, isn't it?"

Oleander nodded in concession.

"But the important thing is she knew the codeword of the third Sefirah, I don't understand how. As I told you, she simply meditated, and the word appeared in her mind."

"A coincidence."

"We both know that is just too unlikely."

"Did you ask her about the codeword of the fourth Sefirah?"

"Not yet. But I will, Old Monk."

"A monk, you say. Yet here I am lounging in a Manhattan hotel. How much does this room cost? This suite of rooms. Two thousand a day? Three?" He cast his eyes about the luxurious surroundings. A continual friction between the two was Eliezer's habit of free spending. Eliezer was quite wealthy in his own right, beyond the enormous assets of Keeperdom which as a Councilor were always available to him without scrutiny. The old man liked his comfort. Knowing of his childhood and how hard he had worked in his life, Oleander couldn't judge him harshly. But it made the monk feel guilty enjoying this comfort alongside him.

"How much time can you spare with us here?"

"I took an indefinite leave from my monastery. My abbot thinks I'm coordinating distribution agreements for our chocolate. He gave me a free hand." He sat down. "What kind of a monk am I?"

"A devoted one, William." Eliezer patted his shoulder. "Devoted to Keeperdom, and devoted to the economic well-being of your monastery."

Oleander frowned in grudging acknowledgment. The real issue, still untouched, now had to be met.

"Two Vessels in the space of three weeks." Oleander shook his head.

"Indeed. But we must calm down and start thinking."

"Fine. Where do we begin?"

"The way I see it, William, four extraordinary things have happened recently. The question is whether they are related, and if so, how."

"Gregor's death and then Hadid's. That's one and two."

"Of course. Two Vessels have never terminated within one century, let alone one month. The third is our discernment of the Book of Creation, of the Primordial Gate."

"And the fourth? The vagabond you saw?"

"Not one, but two. At JFK I spotted a second. You haven't seen anyone like this? Or experienced sudden nausea?"

"St. Raphael is surrounded by woods, as you know. We don't get casual visitors. Anyway, why do you find these vagrants so remarkable? There are millions all over the planet."

"Not *this* kind. There is a very distinct stench around them that ..."

"Hardly unusual."

"*Spiritual* stench." Eliezer searched for words to describe the experience. "When you get close to them, they make you feel lightheaded, not physically, but... You feel hollow, as if... as if they are sucking the Blessing out of you." Eliezer noted Oleander's raised eyebrow. "You find it hard to believe?"

"On the contrary. It reminds me of Gregor's termination. The two Keepers who followed him, Emil Cordon and Martin LaPointe, said they felt a 'cloud' of emptiness just before he died."

"So what do you make of it?"

"I'm not sure," the monk admitted. "But I've kept Annette Goldman busy the past two days scanning and e-mailing me portions of the Chronicles that were stuck in my mind. I found two interesting reports. One from the year 748 and the other from the thirteenth century. In the year 748, a certain Master-Keeper—Basri—reported his Keepers sensed a 'spiritual disease' around the house of Bruno Mossen, the Vessel they were monitoring."

"748 was the year Vessel Sarah Saladin terminated," Eliezer said, knowing perfectly well that Oleander knew this.

"In fact, the Master-Keeper's report was made only a week before Saladin's termination. Which was followed by the so-called Plague of Constantinople."

"And you think there might be a connection?"

"The problem is that Saladin lived and died in Persia. Mossen, on the other hand, lived in what is now Germany."

"Spiritual queasiness in Germany, and a week later a Vessel terminates in Persia. Mmm... Maybe these vagabonds, or whatever they were, had been near Saladin too, without his Keepers noting it."

"Possibly, Eliezer. Now, the second case happened in the winter of 1239—about a month after Vessel Julius Jason's termination. The records say that one of the Councilors demanded a commission be created to investigate reports that a number of high-ranking Keepers had reacted to Jason's termination by an unusual *'coisier* to the spirit.' *'Coisier'* in old French was an early word for 'queasiness' and meant an injury or bruising. Curiously, this happened only when they were outside, among the general populace. The prescribed cure was to remain indoors at their homes or the monastery. This seems to have worked."

Eliezer pondered. "1239—that was when One-Eyed Isabel headed the Council. What did they find out?"

"Isabel dismissed the commission." He shrugged as if to say who knows why.

"She dominated the Council at that time, she was very powerful. If she quashed the investigation she must have had a special reason."

"Anyway, some three centuries later, the great historian of Keeperdom, Katherine Osvalt of Bavaria, is quoted as saying it is a fact that Keepers—especially high-ranking ones—feel bouts of 'sickness' around the time of a Vessel's termination."

"They feel it before or after the termination?"

Oleander shook his head.

"So we cannot know whether these spells of sickness were indications of the presence of vagabonds or just predictable reactions to the loss of the Blessing. Has anyone reported seeing vagabonds following Vessels or Keepers?"

"For four thousand years, Keepers have been filing routine reports about the everyday life of every Vessel. Obviously, some of them mention individuals habitually near Vessels' homes. There may have been vagabonds among them, though the words used to describe them have likely varied over the centuries and from one culture to another. For example, I seem to remember that 'outcasts' were seen around Vessel Intef's home in ancient Egypt just before he terminated three millennia ago. I'll do some more checking."

"This is a relief. It seems these vagabonds are not a new phenomenon. Which means that they are not here because of us."

"Even if they are not totally new," Oleander said sternly, "it's curious they appeared around the time we triggered the Book of Creation. I wouldn't be so quick to dismiss the possibility that we've had a hand in this."

"Vessels have been dying long before us."

"You really want to continue with the Book of Creation no matter what, don't you, Eliezer?" He had raised his voice but caught himself and continued. "I don't know about you, but I haven't been able to sleep peacefully since Gregor's termination. And now we're down to *three*."

Eliezer sighed. "Perhaps that's why we should do everything possible to replenish the Blessing."

"Or, it's time to start behaving more responsibly. We are *Keepers*, not damn adventurers. Where do you get your confidence we haven't caused all this?"

"You know of the rumors that other Keepers, too, have tried to discern the Primordial Gate. We are not the first."

"More than rumors," Oleander granted. "In the year 1306, an entire group of Montfortists—at least I'm fairly sure they were Montfortists if I'm reading the clues correctly—was caught red-handed performing some ritual around Genesis Chapter 1. This was strictly taboo, of course, and they were all put to death for attempting to open the Primordial Gate. Seventeen men and women burned at the stake. This was not in the Chronicles."

"I don't remember you mentioning this before we started our work with the Book."

"It was in a diary I came across in an ecclesiastical collection at NYU a few weeks ago." The monk looked embarrassed. "I did some looking on my own."

"I am grateful for your caution, William."

"Unless you are a Keeper, you wouldn't know how to interpret this particular diary. You'd think these seventeen were being executed as typical heretics."

"And the year 1306 is not even close to the termination of any Vessel. Which shows that discerning the Primordial Gate doesn't have to lead to a catastrophe."

"Maybe those thirteen were caught before they actually started doing anything significant. Besides, they were probably not the first to succumb to the temptation of the Primordial Gate. Every novice Keeper is aware of this Primordial Blessing. Who wouldn't be curious? The idea is so tempting: to tap into the reservoir of God's first Blessing on humanity."

Oleander stopped, seeing the lines of fatigue on his mentor's face, his rounded shoulders—an old man. "Tell me, Eliezer. Tell me what you truly think."

"The truth is… If we are right, we restore some of the Blessing lost to humanity. And Father Esau knows the world needs it. But if we are wrong…" His hands made a helpless gesture.

Neither spoke for a time as they felt the reverberations of their discussion, and realized their mission would have to be suspended until they learned more.

When Eliezer withdrew to take a shower, Oleander remained in his chair. Absently he turned on the television. The news channel replayed clips from the President's talk to the nation the previous evening.

"As we struggle to come to terms with these changes in our world," the President announced somberly, "we must all be doubly careful. I am not talking about panic and anxiety. On the contrary, we must keep our heads cool and our eyes open. If last month it was safe to look once before crossing the street, we must now look twice. If driving seventy miles per hour on the highway was once safe, we will now drive a maximum of fifty, as I've mandated. Our emergency services personnel are over-burdened, and we must each take responsibility for being safer…"

Oleander turned the channel and viewed excerpts from the same talk.

"…and yet," the President pleaded, "we must return to normal life. We must go about our lives with the faith that this Wave will soon be over. As the Bible says, 'this too shall pass.' I believe this is a test of who we are as a nation, as a people. I believe in the inherent strength and goodness of humanity. Let us return to our offices, our farms, our factories, and our schools. The well-being of our great nation depends on each of us continuing to do our duty. May God bless us all."

Oleander turned off the television. He was exhausted and felt a strong urge to sleep. Instead, he knelt and prayed.

53

Osnat wandered up 5th Avenue, still stiff from the flight. She wasn't in the mood for sightseeing, but soon began to find the walking pleasurable. The streets were surprisingly empty, as citizens stayed at home as much as possible. Mishaps had showered the city for the past two days, from common fender-benders to traffic light malfunctions, from waterlines breaking to neon signs bursting, to several satellite dishes falling from rooftops. An expression of worry was just below the surface on the faces she saw in the stores and on the sidewalks. Most drivers were careful to the point of distraction.

Osnat looked at several galleries and drifted through a bookstore, but she still had hours to kill. She decided to visit the Metropolitan as Eliezer had suggested.

Like every other public place, the Metropolitan was experiencing a sharp decline in visitors. Her footsteps echoed in the entryway. With no direction in mind, she moved through the rooms on the first floor. She had just entered an exhibition room of Gustav Klimt's drawings when her stomach convulsed and the taste of bile reached her mouth.

The vagabond…

There were six people in the small room but none resembled the man in the tattered orange shirt and dirty cap. She was about to look into the adjacent room when she realized she didn't know what to expect of an encounter with him. Should she be scared? Eliezer hadn't seemed frightened at the airport.

Hesitantly she approached a doorway, but before crossing the threshold she felt a tide of the sensation: a loathsome, putrid presence. The room felt too small for her. She turned to another doorway and moved quickly through a chain of rooms, following the signs. When she finally found the museum exit the nausea was gone, and the New York air felt fresh by comparison.

It was much too early to return to the hotel and she continued down the street. Besides, she didn't want to run back like a scared schoolgirl.

Eliezer had so much confidence in her and it would hardly make a good impression on Oleander, who she was sure didn't want her here.

The nausea returned. It seemed to be coming from behind her. She glimpsed over her shoulder. None of the ten or fifteen men she could spot resembled the vagabond. Hastening her steps, she weaved through the passersby, turning right at the intersection and then left onto a narrow street. The foul presence was still behind her.

She was hurrying by a tobacco store when she stepped on a sewer grate. It shifted and she felt her foot begin to slip into the hole. Lurching forward she fell onto her hands and knees, feeling her foot dangling over the opening.

Rubbing her bruised knees through her jeans she peered into the hole— she could have been killed had she fallen into it. At that instant an awareness struck her, a sense of knowledge still mute. She felt it coming into focus, and then something inside her said: "*An accident is not always an accident.*"

After a couple of blocks she stopped to rest and thought she managed to lose him, but a minute later the presence reappeared. Across the street was a run-down diner. With a slight limp she made her way to the other side. She needed a vantage point where she could watch for him.

A few customers occupied the booths of cracked red vinyl, chewing sandwiches or reading the newspaper. Osnat sat down facing the entrance. She could sense the nausea but no likely candidate was in sight. She looked down at her hands, at the street grime and roughed-up skin.

She walked to the back of the restaurant and pushed open the 'Ladies' door. The smell of urine hit her. The floor was filthy. She washed her hands, then ran the cold water over her palms, soothing the scrapes. One knee on her jeans was slightly torn, and poking her finger through she could feel the abrasion. She took a paper towel and wetted it. There were two toilet stalls and she stepped into the nearest and turned the latch behind her. She lowered the cover of the toilet seat and sat down.

She was about to lower her jeans and clean her knee when she felt the nausea. He was in the restaurant. Before she could unlock the stall she heard the restroom door opening. She froze, holding her breath against the stench, and listened to his footsteps on the tile floor.

The invisible man tried to open the door of her stall. Her heart leaped. When he found it locked he didn't insist. She heard him pacing in front of the stall.

What did he want?

She scanned the frame of the stall, but a six-inch gap between the floor and the door was all that afforded a view outside. She bent down, keeping her cheek at a safe distance from the disgusting tile. Inches away were the tips of a pair of scuffed shoes. But something about the picture was wrong. Suppressing her revulsion, she placed her cheek against the floor. She was gazing at what seemed to be a woman's calves and ankles below a soiled skirt. The skirt was of a rich fabric now torn in several places, and the shoes, scuffed to the point of shredding, had no doubt been very expensive when new.

Osnat smiled in relief. So that's why she hadn't noticed the pursuer—she had been looking for a man!

She was about to stand when she noticed on the woman's lower right calf a dark-red tattoo. No, not a tattoo. It looked like an engraving in the flesh or a birthmark the size of her palm: several red parallel stripes, about an inch long: one, two... she counted seven. Seven red stripes.

The strange woman apparently lost patience and shuffled out of the restroom. Osnat followed.

The woman-vagabond stood in the center of the restaurant. Her dark hair, faintly speckled with gray, looked as if it hadn't been washed or combed in weeks. It was difficult to tell how old she was under the grime. Her eyes were empty and her mouth slightly open. She had on a navy blazer over a white shirt, both the worse for wear.

Osnat walked over to her—the nausea became more intense, although no one else in the restaurant seemed to notice it. The woman stared emptily. Osnat shrugged, turned around and walked out of the store. Let the vagabond walk behind her if she wished.

54

The telephone rang in Peprini's office. He looked at the Caller ID, and then at Maria Jongsma who was sitting across the desk. "Maria, would you step outside for a moment, please?"

He waited until the door was closed.

"What is it, Eric?"

"Councilor Oleander went to JFK to pick up Councilor Eliezer."

"Who is with you?"

"Velasquez, Krueger, and Berg. All of us."

"Good."

"They're staying at the Sheraton. I'm calling from the lobby. And there's a third person with them—Eliezer brought the Aviv girl with him."

"What are they doing now?"

"The girl went out. The two Councilors are in the suite."

"I'd like you to find out whether they are discerning. Periodically walk by their room. Do you remember your test at Frostburg to determine if you can sense the Blessing?"

"They said I didn't do too good on that."

"You did well enough. If you attune yourself to the Blessing as taught, you should be able to tell if even one of the Councilors is discerning on the other side of the door. Better still, see if you can obtain a room on either side of theirs, or across the hall. For that, you may need to offer an inducement to a hotel employee. Be creative but don't draw attention to yourself."

"Right, Sir. Another thing. When Councilor Eliezer and the Aviv girl got out of the terminal, a man was following them. I don't think he was one of yours."

"What sort of man?"

"Homeless, he drooled, the whole bit."

"Alright, Eric. Keep your eyes open."

Peprini brought up Osnat's photo on his monitor. She was sitting in a café with Eliezer. She was quite lovely. Vital though the old man was, he doubted Eliezer was involved sexually with the girl. So why take her to the Keeper mansion? And why take her to New York?

He rose and opened the door. "Maria, are you ready? You did wonderfully well in the first two experiments. You are quite something."

He didn't receive the admiration and gratitude he expected. She merely returned to her chair in front of his desk.

"The same thing again?" she asked.

It was late in the afternoon and Annette Goldman had been working for more than twenty-four hours, finding sleep impossible unless she exhausted herself first. Erna was her best friend, so when the Councilor implored the librarian to come to her office in the Book Company, Goldman reluctantly agreed.

Erna handed her the note she had found in the Archive three weeks ago. "What do you make of this?"

"Please, Isabel. You say the tragedy was the consequence of my transgression against the sacred laws…"

The librarian took off her glasses and stared at Erna. "Where did this come from?

"It fell out of a 13th-century manuscript. Who is the writer, Annette? And does he mean what I think he means?"

"I hope you didn't remove this from the Archives."

"Not now, Annette."

Goldman again scanned the note. *"Allow me to send you these words from where you buried me…* 'Buried' could mean imprisoned, in the language of Medieval Keepership. *A higher death must have a higher reason, even if that reason has chosen a miserable man like me as its tool…* Mmm… *Remember me, S."* Goldman deliberated. "'A higher death'—the death of a Councilor perhaps."

"Or higher."

"Are you saying this…*S* is… what? Apologizing for causing the death of a Vessel?" Erna said nothing. "The timing might fit."

"That's what I'm thinking."

"But Julia, Jason of Padua died from typhoid. The epidemic in 1238 and 1239 killed tens of thousands."

Erna shook her head. "Who is the writer?"

"Let's see… someone imprisoned by an Isabel—this is likely One-Eyed Isabel."

"It was secreted in the minutes from a Council meeting shortly after Jason's death."

"So One-Eyed Isabel. *Remember me, S…* Ah, it has to be Simon de Montfort! He was Isabel's lover for a time. Then she accused him of treason and he disappeared. A bizarre episode."

"Do we know what he did?"

"Something so terrible, all records about it were destroyed. But why can't this wait until tomorrow?"

"De Montfort admits he was *the tool*—he thinks he was—that eventually brought about Jason's death. Isabel—and the Council— believed de Montfort did something to cause the death." She looked squarely at Goldman. "Isabel claimed he transgressed against the sacred laws."

"All right," Annette Goldman agreed. "But I still don't see how…"

"If Vessel Jason died because one of us transgressed, then perhaps Gregor and Hadid have died for the same reason. Annette, one of us may be violating the laws again."

"It's possible," Goldman said skeptically.

"I want you to do something with me. It won't take too long. I want us to go to the edge of the Void."

"I'm in no state to discern, Julia."

"No discernment, just standing at the edge. I want to show you something. If I'm right," she looked at her watch, "we might be able to see it now."

Quickly the two Councilors coordinated their auras to ensure they would emerge in the same location in the Depths. Minutes later the two stood side by side, the emptiness before them.

Goldman, frustrated, looked at Erna who only nodded, imploring patience. They waited.

Then Erna signaled with great urgency. Far in the distance, she could make out a discernment beam. It was focused and concentrated, very likely a Councilor's. Few Master-Keepers could discern in such a fine beam.

At first she did not understand Erna's excitement; that someone was discerning was unremarkable. Only a moment later, when she noticed the beam was not pointing at the Bible World as it should, but rather off into the Void, in a different direction, she gasped. *Someone was discerning the Void.*

An idea struck Erna. She signaled to Goldman and hurried back to her Inner Depths. She quickly ascended, much faster than was advisable. Goldman stayed by the Void and continued watching the strange beam.

A sudden headache told Erna she had ascended too quickly. Nevertheless, she got to her feet. She glanced at Goldman's body still sitting motionless with eyes closed, and made her way to the door.

Leaning against the door jamb, she called out to her secretary. "Quickly, Ingrid, call every Councilor…"

She closed her eyes and slid to the floor.

"Councilor!" Ingrid held Erna's hand.

"*Right now*, call all Councilors on their private phones! All except Goldman. I want to know who may be discerning at this very moment."

"I can't ask Councilors if they are discerning. It's…"

"If they answer the phone they can't be discerning. The moment you hear their voice, hang up and call the next. We'll do the explaining later."

Erna felt her head whirling and spinning, and she sank into a peaceful blackout. Some time later she opened her eyes to find Ingrid trying to revive her. Erna sipped the cup of water she handed her.

"What did you find?"

"We were lucky and got a good connection to everyone. I got hold of Councilors Sionn, Connor, Krystofski, and Fournier. Councilor Antioch didn't answer, but his assistant checked and said he was asleep in bed. Councilors Peprini, Eliezer, and Oleander were nowhere to be found. I left messages to call back as soon as possible."

The telephone rang and a moment later a second joined in. Ingrid smiled mischievously. "And now they probably want to know why I hung up on them. What shall I tell them?"

Erna made up her mind instantly. "That there is a Council meeting in three days."

55

A disturbing report came from Edinburgh, Scotland from the squad sent by Peprini to reinforce the Keepers of Vessel Soren Lessing. They described a man, several in fact, haunting Lessing's home and movements.

"What do you mean 'haunting'?" Sionn asked the Keeper who had phoned in the report.

"They look like ghosts, Sir. I mean they're spooky."

Sionn was not fond of American slang. "What is this 'spooky'? Tell me exactly what you saw."

"I don't know how long it's been going on exactly. At least two weeks. None of us took it as noteworthy that these people were hanging around. Edinburgh has street people, but these are like…"

"Like what, for God's sake?"

"Their clothes are normal, if grubby. But when you get close to them the smell is absolutely awful. It's not exactly their smell, it's something else."

"So what does this have to do with ghosts?"

"Their eyes are glassy, their arms dangle from their shoulders like dead branches. They just look very strange."

"Again. Other than their stench and their odd appearance, what called them to your attention?"

"One sits outside Lessing's home now and then, Councilor. There's a lot of pedestrian traffic on the street. Had it been out in the suburbs we would have tipped to it right away."

"Are there more?"

"Another will show up outside Mrs. Fielding's—his mistress'— apartment building. We never see these people anywhere except for where Lessing is, or usually is. Whatever they're doing here, there's no doubt it's got something to do with the Vessel. And with Gregor and Hadid terminating, well… "

"Of course. You were correct in reporting this." Sionn could hear the relief on the other end of the call. "I want you to photograph them and e-mail me immediately."

"But I don't know if we can find one…"

Sionn put down the phone only to pick it up again to call the Novitiate School.

As Peprini left his office, one of the secretaries, Miss Davois, stopped him. "Mr. Sionn asked that you call him. It's urgent."

"Now when we want one, they disappear." Krantz wiped the foggy windshield with his bare hand. His two associates did the same to the glass blocking their view. The midday sky was leaden and almost down on top of the buildings in Edinburgh and spit a sharp rain. Even through clear glass it was hard to make out the people on the street. Everything was a shade of gray in the late afternoon. "How long has he been in there now?" English was spoken as it was the only language the three men had in common.

"Two hours. He should be out anytime if the *residence* team is right."

Mrs. Fielding's flat was on the third floor of a nineteenth-century building. There were two entrances, one facing the street and one to the side, both visible from the parked car.

"I need to take a piss."

Two buildings down from the apartment house was an ancient drinking establishment. The young man stepped from the car and ran in athletic strides to the door of the pub, his right arm across his chest as if hugging himself.

"Let's get a little heat in here. And get the windscreen."

The driver turned over the engine and put on the defroster and the wipers.

Several minutes later the pub door opened and a man stepped out. "Is that Gus? Turn off the wipers, I can't see shit."

They peered through the cloudy glass and the rain.

"Oui. That's him."

They both sat back. But as their comrade came closer, the angle between him and the car widened and something appeared behind him.

"What's that guy doing?"

Again they leaned forward and strained to see. In frustration Krantz rolled down the window and stuck his head out. The barrier of the wet glass was gone but the windblown rain stung his face. Still, he could see a little better, and now he could tell a person was following behind, gaining on him.

Gus cupped his hand around his ear and threw out his arm in a gesture of questioning. He and the person behind him were now coming up on the apartment house.

"What's he wearing?" asked the driver.

Krantz realized that was part of what was bothering him here. "A damn T-shirt and shorts."

The driver stepped from the car.

"What's wrong?" Gus yelled, confusion growing on his face.

Now he became aware that someone was behind him. At that moment the door to the apartment house opened and Lessing stepped out. Gus came up short to keep from bumping into the Vessel. He turned and saw the vagabond, their faces no more than two feet apart. The man's stench struck the Keeper like a punch in the stomach. A visceral revulsion filled him, and in the next moment Gus drew the pistol from underneath his left arm and shot the vagabond in the chest. The man crumpled before him.

"*My God,*" Lessing gasped. The Vessel felt woozy and leaned against the building, managing to stay on his feet. Then he looked in terror at Gus, who put away his pistol.

"Don't worry, Doctor. It's alright."

Lessing, his horned-rim glasses crooked on his broad nose, pulled his overcoat tightly around himself in a futile effort at defense. The other Keepers sprinted up to the scene.

"Pick him up. I'll get the trunk. Doctor, it's best you forget this and go home."

Lessing, numb and confused, watched as the three men in a matter of moments lifted the body and put it in the trunk. The car sped off.

The adrenaline was coursing through them. "Turn here," Krantz ordered. The car tore down the street. "Slow down, we look like we just killed somebody. Turn right up here." The car made the corner a little too fast, skidding on the wet pavement. "Pull over. Busco, you stay with Lessing. We can't leave him alone, even with the *residence* team around. We don't know how many more of these there are."

Busco jumped from the backseat and dashed down the street. Gus and Krantz opened the trunk and examined the body. Krantz checked for a pulse on the neck. "He's dead, no question."

"Shit, that happened fast but he came out of nowhere. It was just instinct. It was like he hit me and with the Vessel right there... Strange, he doesn't smell very bad anymore. You'd think he'd still smell, whether alive *or* dead, but..."

"Shut up, Gus. Just calm down." He dialed from memory the number Councilor Sionn had given him."

"This is Sionn."

"Councilor, this is Krantz in Edinburgh. We've got one."

"You've *got* one?"

"He's dead. It couldn't be avoided. Before..."

"Is Lessing unhurt?"

"He's fine, Sir. Scared and confused as hell, I'm sure, but otherwise fine."

"Are the police involved?"

"I don't think anyone but Lessing knows it even happened."

"Go straight to the airport. I'll call in a few minutes with details."

56

Sionn paced in front of the bank of windows facing the apple orchard on the southern slope of the monastery's hill. The Blessing in the air was painfully thin—as it had been since Hadid's death—but today it was sprinkled with agitated wavelets of energy. He liked this kind of ambient Blessing, although most of his colleagues preferred a softer, steadier kind. It usually gave him a feeling of expectancy. But it was unpleasant this day and made him anxious.

An effort of reason was required to remind himself of what was at stake, and that one man's life—a man who might be causing harm to God's own Vessels—was a price that must be paid. This calculation of the cost and worth of lives was not natural to him. Keepers protected the Blessing. Their duties left them outside the typical human conflicts that resulted in deaths and the justifications for those deaths. What had he begun?

A dark tarp was draped over the body resting on a table. The room, one of many beneath the Abbey, had been used for centuries to prepare deceased monks' bodies for burial, but hadn't served this function for seventy years. Nevertheless, the room smelled of the bowels of the Earth. Two physicians were present along with Albrecht Sionn, Menach Peprini, and Annette Goldman.

"Let's see," Peprini said.

Julia Erna and Sandrine Krystofski entered the room and joined them. The tarp was pulled away and the physicians began removing the clothing.

Goldman inhaled deeply. "I can't detect anything exceptionally unpleasant. Just the ordinary smell of unwashed flesh and soiled clothing. I wonder what our Edinburgh people were talking about."

Sandrine Krystofski picked up the well-worn sneakers. "When these were new they were expensive. Easily a hundred Euros."

"This T-shirt," Goldman remarked, checking the label. "A nice Pierre Cardin."

"He doesn't appear a man who could afford such things." Peprini inspected the unshaven grimy face. "But his teeth are in excellent condition, he's well muscled, well fed and fit. He hasn't been living rough for long."

"What is this mark?" Erna pointed to the man's thigh. There were seven parallel dark-red lines, the whole design half the size of a postcard.

"I've never seen anything like it," said Krystofsky.

It was almost midnight and the five Councilors—all those who were still at the Abbey—were seated in the Abbey's conference room. Through their networks the Council had access to every significant computer database in the world, including those containing criminal, military, and civilian records.

The fingerprints turned out to be those of Jerry Kindle, a forty-two-year-old London businessman who had disappeared ten days earlier while on a picnic with his wife on England's eastern seashore. A little mystery shrouded the incident. Mr. Kindle apparently had a heart attack while jogging with his wife and collapsed. His wife wasn't able to resuscitate him. She had to leave him in order to get back to the car and phone for help. When she returned, his body was nowhere to be found. A police leaflet and a few announcements on the media produced no clue to his disappearance.

"What I don't understand," Erna said pensively, "is how a successful man suffering an apparently severe heart attack in eastern England would turn up as a vagrant in Edinburgh. It's what, 250, 300 kilometers away?"

"Yes," Goldman murmured, "at least 200 miles." The daughter of Belgian parents, she had grown up in London and had never fully adjusted to the European metric system.

Sionn nodded. "And why Edinburgh? Our search shows no connection between Mr. Kindle and that city."

"Judging by the state of his shoes, he must have walked all the way," Goldman mused. "200 miles in ten days. In short-sleeves and shorts."

"Any history of mental illness?"

Sionn turned to Krystofski and shook his head.

"Perhaps he faked his heart attack. People run away to start new lives every day." Krystofski stared at the man's face.

"A new life as a vagrant?" Peprini screwed up his mouth. "Too unbelievable."

"I have a suspicion," Erna said quietly, "the facts will be even harder to believe."

57

The four Councilors in permanent *residence* in Lucerne, Julia Erna, Menach Peprini, Albrecht Sionn, and Annette Goldman, as well as Sandrine Krystofksi who had remained in Lucerne since the last Council meeting, met the following morning.

"Is there anything new, Albrecht?"

"Nothing yet on the autopsy. I've been assured we'll have the report soon. But there is more, yes."

Sionn pressed a button on the telephone console. Moments later there was a knock on the door and a young monk entered.

"Flavius, please ready the video."

Flavius used a remote and turned on the television on the wall, then placed a disc in the DVD player.

"After Gregor's death," Peprini said, "I ordered the remaining four *residences* to begin video recording the Vessels at all moments when in public, to the degree possible. Last night I had Aziz examine the videos." He inhaled and paused. "Better from the source. Flavius?"

The monk placed the remote control in front of Sionn before leaving the chamber. No one spoke as they waited. The door opened and a Middle Eastern man entered.

"This is Keeper Aziz of the Alexandria *residence*. The recordings have been edited to show only the relevant portions."

Sionn picked up the remote and the screen flickered, settling to show a mosque on a busy street. People began streaming from its entrance into the sunlight, the camera image a little unsteady. Alifa Hadid, the Vessel who had lived in Alexandria, Egypt, appeared beside her husband, covered from head to toe in a black *Jilbab* except for hands and face. The image froze.

"Do you see anything out of the ordinary?"

All peered at the screen. Annette Goldman put on the glasses that hung on a chain around her neck.

"What are we looking for, Albrecht?" she said.

He didn't answer. The screen jumped to another street scene showing a royal blue Volvo coming towards the camera and turning left into a notch in the wall bordering the street.

"Now what do you see?" Again they peered, and the frustration began to show on their faces.

"Albrecht, please. None of these games today, my nerves are bad enough as it is."

He made no indication of having heard Goldman. Again the image advanced, now to a crowded market of food stands: all varieties of vegetables, fruits, fish, nuts, and more, lining the pathway. The screen froze. Once again they could see Alifa Hadid, now with her mother.

"Albrecht," Erna said sternly, "what are we supposed to be seeing that we are not?"

"I didn't see it at first either." He turned to the Keeper standing at his side. "Tell us, Aziz, what we are missing."

The tall man approached the television, reached out and put his finger beside a woman's face. The woman was several paces behind, watching Alifa and her mother. "She is what we didn't see."

Sionn reversed the images, stopping again at the point the Volvo turned into the drive. Aziz pointed at a man squatting against the wall near the Hadids' drive. It again reversed, now stopping at the mosque scene.

"And here," again the finger pointing to a woman walking several steps behind Alifa.

"Is that the same woman?" Krystofski asked. "Can we enlarge that?"

"It's being done as we speak," Peprini said.

"Councilor, it's the same woman, if you'll permit me." Aziz turned and looked at Sionn who nodded.

"Her clothing is the same in each frame, down to every detail visible. And she is holding her head in this strange manner, tilted to the right." He pointed to her face. "Look at her eyelids, they are almost shut. Now that I've looked at her as I have most of the night, I am certain I saw her several times; or some woman looking much like her. Always near the Vessel."

The occupants of the room stared at the screen.

"What this tape cannot show is that this mosque and market are a great distance apart, at opposite ends of Alexandria. Beggars do not commonly roam such distances," Aziz said. "She must have been following Mrs. Hadid."

"Before we go into speculations, why have you included the scene showing the homeless man?"

"Yes, Julia, why the man?" Sionn picked up the phone. "Are they ready? No, bring the ones you've completed." He put down the phone.

"We'll learn momentarily if I was right to include the man in this presentation. Thank you, Aziz, you may go."

Flavius opened the door and handed a file to Sionn, just as swiftly leaving the room.

Sionn opened the file and examined several photographs. They all waited. He raised his eyes and handed one stack to Peprini on his left. Then he passed another stack to the three women.

"You will see it is the same woman in both photographs. Enlargements of the scenes we just saw. The face is the same in each."

Again he passed a stack of pictures around the table. "This is the man sitting outside the Hadid house. Look at his left ankle, just above the foot."

"Is that a birthmark?" Erna put on her reading glasses. "No, the edges are too straight. It's a rectangle."

Peprini switched to another picture. "This is a close up."

"My God, they are the same."

"Indeed," said Peprini. "I find it unacceptably coincidental that both this man and our friend laid out on the table below us have identical tattoos on their legs. I wouldn't be surprised to see the same mark on that woman's leg, had she been less modestly dressed."

There was a shuffling of the photographs as the Council members examined them silently.

Flavius knocked and then entered, bending to whisper something in Peprini's ear.

Peprini nodded. "I propose we adjourn for half an hour as we absorb this considerable news."

Once they returned, Erna began. "Who the devil are these people?" She could not remain sitting and began pacing. "And what do they want from our Vessels?"

"The mark on the leg," Goldman added. "Have we ever run across such a thing before?"

"The questions on all our minds," Peprini said. "But I have another bit of news. During our interlude I had these photos e-mailed to other *residences*. These—what shall we call them?—these vagrants have been seen in two more places, near Vessel David Wyatt and Vessel Anina Lenoma."

"The same kind of people?"

"Unclean, disheveled clothing, sleepy facial expressions, awkward bodily movements. But most importantly the telltale mark, at least on those where it might be visible."

"Who *are* they?"

"I share your frustration, Annette. But first things first. Can we agree that these vagrants were somehow involved in the Vessels' deaths?"

"Involved in what way?" Erna asked. "Gregor was hit by a negligent driver, and Hadid was murdered by a fellow teacher."

"The vagrants were present in both deaths."

Erna shook her head. "Do we have any reason to believe that the mystery of these people and the mystery of the Vessels' death are connected?"

"We have some circumstantial evidence," Peprini replied. "On two occasions our people reported that a similar-looking man was seen following a Keeper. Mind you, not a Vessel but a Keeper. This strongly suggests to me that these vagrants are not after Vessels in particular. They are after something that both Vessels and Keepers share."

"The Blessing," Krystofski said.

"Exactly, Sandrine. It would seem these creatures are attracted to the Blessing. And since there is much more Blessing around Vessels than Keepers, they are attracted mainly to Vessels."

"Still," Erna said, "all you are telling us is *why*—perhaps—the vagrants are following the Vessels. Maybe you are right: they feel the Blessing and are attracted to it. Maybe. But do we have any reason to believe that this should cause death?"

"Who knows? Speculation at this point is an indulgence we cannot afford. Only one thing matters: to protect the remaining Vessels. Can we then agree that the vagrants were involved in the Vessels' deaths?"

"I grant you it is a possibility," Erna offered.

"More resolve is needed for what I have in mind."

"And what is that?"

"I propose these vagrants be shot on sight. Or, considering the police attention that might cause, that we remove them and dispatch them elsewhere."

"We murder them, Menach?"

"Yes." His sober matter-of-factness was a challenge. "You would have us do what, Julia? Wait until another Vessel has terminated? Or perhaps two?"

"We can't go about killing people just because this *might* solve the problem."

"Julia, if I may," Sionn said. "As you know, we brought Hadid's killer to the Abbey. I interrogated him. He claims that he had never felt any violent urge, nothing like what occurred, until the afternoon with our Alifa Hadid. On that day, a sudden impulse overpowered him—an unfamiliar urge, alien, uncontrollable, malevolent. That is what he claims."

"Are you suggesting," Goldman asked, "that the vagrants caused this impulse? That the presence of the vagrants encourages people to hurt our Vessels?"

Sionn remained uncommitted. "If their presence can cause spiritual nausea, as our people report, then it's possible it can cause changes of temper. Perhaps other changes as well."

Peprini nodded toward his friend.

"Murder, is this what we've come to?" Erna said quietly.

"If we are right, the lives of our three Vessels are in grave danger. Those three lives are all that prevent the end of the Blessing on Earth. Are we willing to risk that? Do you forget who you are? What right have you—have any of us—to gamble with the very existence of the Blessing? We cannot permit the self-indulgence, the timidity of conscience. If murder is necessary to secure the safety of the Vessels, so be it."

Erna noticed that all eyes were expectantly turned to her. "Given Albrecht's testimony," she conceded, "I agree we can't wait. But we should first try to determine definitely whether these people are responsible for the deaths before we set out killing them. I propose we kidnap and interrogate one of them."

"Kidnap if possible, yes, but our first priority must be to protect the Vessels," Goldman said.

"Precisely," Peprini said, acknowledging her. He turned back to Erna. "What if while we are undertaking this kidnapping and interrogation another Vessel dies? That is too great a risk."

There were several nods around the table. There was no point, Erna realized, in resisting Peprini.

"So it is agreed," she said reluctantly. "We try to kidnap some of these vagrants and interrogate them. In the meantime, we kill them if necessary."

Everyone left the room except for Erna. The image of Peprini holding court still burned. *He so naturally feels superior to the rest of us. He's an imperious bastard. But is he wrong? We have Peprini and Sionn to thank for those pictures of the vagrants, for even knowing there may be a plot to kill the Vessels. But more than knowing, what Peprini truly enjoyed was knowing what others did not. He revealed a great deal in the meeting. But all? Certainly not. What does he know about these recent events that he's not telling?*

58

Pilar was beneath the bedcovers. From her gaunt face it appeared she continued losing weight, though Peprini had been informed that she was eating the meals brought to her room. He waited until Dr. Loyev lifted the stethoscope from her chest.

"Your job now is to regain your strength." He turned to the doctor who only shrugged.

"I'm getting stronger. I am." She glanced at Dr. Loyev to see if he was listening. "Councilor… may I ask… is another novice helping you now? Another girl?"

He nodded. Answering the appeal in her eyes, he added, "Once you are well, you are back to business."

Dr. Loyev gathered his things and left.

"Councilor?"

"Yes?"

"I know another Vessel died."

Peprini had ordered this news be kept from her so as not to strain her further, but being a Keeper of her abilities, surely she noticed the change in the Blessing. "I knew something was wrong, then I asked Dr. Loyev." Tears appeared in her eyes.

"It happened eight days ago. Alifa Hadid."

"This makes the project—*your* project—even more important than before. I will be ready."

"I know you will," he said, smiling. "But now you must rest." He closed the door behind him.

He had hoped to see more improvement. That thought annoyed him as he walked down the hallway to his office. He detested hope and had little regard for those childish adults who lived by it. Hope implied and bred a lack of self-determination. His endeavor could not be left to such a vagary.

Approaching his office, he asked Miss Davois that a plane be readied for tomorrow morning. Enough of waiting for David Wyatt to make up his mind.

As de facto Director of Security, Peprini had a solemn duty to protect Keeperdom. That this duty coincided with his natural distrust was, to his mind, merely efficient. He looked again at the files on Eliezer and Oleander he had begun assembling. Why had they kept secret their meetings over the past several months? In particular those in London, Zurich, and then Jerusalem. And now the two were in New York, again without notifying the Security Office. Doing what? Even stranger was the fact this Osnat Aviv was with them.

Should he reveal this at the coming Council meeting? He pictured Eliezer playing the doddering old professor and Oleander the naïve monk, claiming they simply neglected to report their travels. Without firm evidence, Eliezer and Oleander would say it was preposterous, and Peprini would be left having to explain his relationship with the Ishmaelites. No, he needed more information on what the two Keepers were doing and why Eliezer had brought along this Aviv girl.

Since Hadid's death, communications across the world were periodically disrupted. Cable systems, telephone exchange stations, satellites, and computers were all inexplicably breaking down at a surprising rate. The earthquakes had disrupted the sea beds and severed trans-oceanic telephone and fiber-optic cables in many places. Cellphone calls overseas were somewhat more predictable.

Peprini had to dial three times on his cellular to get through. The message on the London exchange said only: "All right, I accept what you've told me. Now what?"

Getting through to New York was more difficult. Ten minutes he tried calling David Wyatt's home number, only to receive a busy tone or a recorded message from the phone company. Finally he heard the phone ringing.

"I'm pleased," he said in answer to Wyatt's greeting.

"Okay, Mr. Peprini. Now are you going to tell me what this is about?"

"I am coming to see you tomorrow. Your office at, say, three in the afternoon?"

"Fine. Just to let you know, I want answers this time."

"Answers I can promise."

A thought suddenly struck the businessman. "When we met last time you spoke of saving the world. Does your coming to see me have anything to do with all these… with the two Waves?" There was silence. "Are things going to get worse?"

"I do not imagine you have been harmed in any way. Rather, I suspect you have managed to capitalize on these events."

"You'll have to tell me how you know these things about me."

"Tomorrow at three, then."

As he hung up the phone, Wyatt noted with irritation that the man again managed to evade his questions.

Peprini boarded the Gulfstream jet at Terminal 2 at the Zurich Airport the following morning. The cabin was warm and the young assistant took his coat as he sat down.

"Good morning, Councilor," she said.

"Good morning, Patrice." Peprini knew all Keepers by name as all had to pass through the Novitiate. "How are your discernments?"

"Fine, sir. I managed to do Gate Four last week, at last. Master-Keeper Vajdak told us how important it is, especially now that..." she hesitated, and then the words spilled from her. "The Blessing, Sir. I've never seen it like this."

She blushed at her impudence in speaking to a Councilor in such a familiar way. Peprini understood she spoke from genuine anxiety. His eyes followed hers and both scanned the horizon through the small window. The presence of the Blessing was depressingly bleak, even having the quality of promising to diminish further, though this might have simply been brought on by the pessimism that accompanied an attunement to these conditions.

"I'm not worried about myself," she whispered apologetically, "even with the airplane accidents and me flying much of the time." Her eyes pleaded for reassurance.

"We are fortunate to live at such a momentous time."

She nodded, trying to understand and accept this. "Yes, sir."

He peered towards several baggage handlers standing on the tarmac, bundled against the cold wind. "They have no grasp of what is happening, nor have they anything to offer the world's salvation. It is a wondrous responsibility to be a Keeper."

"Thank you, sir."

He settled into the leather chair and closed his eyes as the plane taxied and lifted off. His thoughts turned to Tiplady and his report earlier that morning. A curious boy, this Australian, resourceful and without conscience. The others he had sent to follow Eliezer and Oleander were smart and competent, but none had the criminal mind of Tiplady. Even against orders, the boy had managed to secure a hotel passkey and had done a quick reconnaissance of the suite of Eliezer, Oleander, and Miss Aviv. According to the woman's journal, Eliezer was training her—without notifying the Council. If her accounts were true, she was already discerning Gate Four despite having trained less than one month. This was unparalleled. Why are they hiding her? Why not tell the Council of this extraordinary prospect?

I will meet with this Osnat, he thought, and appraise her myself. She will tell Eliezer, of course. Fine. This will rattle his cage and perhaps make him expose what they are hiding.

The New York he saw through the window of the Lincoln Town Car was different from the city he had seen only weeks earlier. The traffic from Kennedy was light. They passed a number of stalled cars pushed to the side of the road and abandoned, most stripped down to the shell, downed power lines, and several burned out buildings. The city, however, had received little damage from the quakes beyond a collapsed tunnel and several blocks of buildings now condemned as structurally unsafe.

He had time to check into his hotel, shower, shave and change his suit. At precisely three o'clock he entered the reception area of Wyatt Enterprises.

David Wyatt stood as the Keeper entered the office. Neither spoke as Peprini crossed the carpet to the desk. They both sat.

"So you have accepted who you are."

The other man hesitated. "I grant you know more about my family than anyone in all probability could know."

Peprini grimaced as if Wyatt was playing a game. "I thought we were beyond this."

Wyatt turned away as he began speaking. "It's possible you could know this about me without the rest being true. Without me being... a Vessel of God's Blessing to mankind, without you being a Keeper. But then, why would you go to all this trouble? The Lucerne Rare Book Company, and you personally, have very significant financial holdings, and I'm assuming a lot more hidden. I had someone do a little looking. Just about the finances, not the Keeper business. In other words, I doubt you're after my money."

Peprini deliberated for a few seconds. "David, this is not helpful. You can always find reasons to doubt, to want more proof. But at some point, you must decide. Now I ask you: Do you accept you are a Vessel of God's Blessing?"

David Wyatt stood and walked to the window.

"Very well. You saw me before our first meeting."

Wyatt turned and inspected his face, trying to remember.

"Several times. I can see you have wondered about this: Where did I see him, where...?"

Peprini smiled but there was nothing amused in his expression. Wyatt glimpsed the power, the severity the man hadn't previously revealed.

"I can see you do know where, David. You have seen me... what do you call that place in your dream?"

"I've always called it the cliff."

"I suppose that's as good a description as any."

"How can you possibly know my dreams? I've never told a soul about them." He closed his eyes and remembered. "In the dream, you are always some distance away. You never come closer. But the girl... she comes right to the edge."

"Her name is Pilar."

"Pilar. She is...?"

"A Keeper. Quite special."

Wyatt moved to his desk. They sat in silence for nearly a minute.

"You are working out how it is possible I know this; what this means. To begin, what you call a dream is not a dream. Your experiences at these times, the places you go, are very much real. They exist every bit as much as the everyday world, as this room. Think of these dreams as voyages to another world, another reality, another dimension. As Hamlet said, *there are more things in this heaven and Earth, Horatio, than are dreamt of in your philosophy.*

"That dark space that borders the cliff is called 'The Void.' As a Vessel, you are able to travel through the Void. And when you do pass through the Void and reach the Bible World, the world of Abraham and Isaac and Jacob, and renew the Blessing, you return as a Vessel carrying God's Blessing to Earth." Wyatt listened with calm resignation. "We sent the young woman with you hoping she might make it more likely that you would reach the Bible World and return with more Blessing. And you only need to look at what is happening in this city, around the world, to see how crucial it is."

"So that's why you decided to speak with me. You want me to take her with me. So she can guide me."

"Exactly. She cannot cross the Void by herself. She cannot even survive in the Void by herself—only Vessels can. So the next time you see her in your 'dream,' I want you to protect her. But it will be a different girl this time. Maria."

"Why a different one? And what do you mean the next time *protect her?*" The memory of her surfaced in his mind and he froze. "When she went with me the last time..." His recollection of the dream was disquieting. "If I was supposed to protect her, why the hell didn't you tell me before? Is she all right?"

"Calm yourself. She's fine. By 'protect' I mean only hold tightly to her, make her feel secure. Pilar is simply too weak at this time. It's nothing serious but we cannot wait. So it will be Maria."

"Okay. But from now on I want it all out in the open."

Peprini nodded but it appeared perfunctory.

"When do we do this?"

"You have the *dream* each week to ten days."

"So I'm due."

"I should think some night later this week, given that your last few attempts to cross the Void failed."

Wyatt winced at the word *failed.* Now that he grasped how profoundly important it was that he reach the Bible world and renew the Blessing, he would feel these dreams to be great tests. The thought of facing such a test nearly every week for the rest of his life hit him hard.

The years of his life he had spent making money. In the accumulation of *things.* He looked at his Vacheron Constantin watch, worth more than most automobiles. The Gauguin on the wall above the sofa. A crystal of understanding formed. The world he had created for himself was safe. He rarely failed in making money; the rewards were immediate and visible, and he enjoyed that others recognized his success. But it wasn't the life he was meant to live, and a part of him understood this, had always understood. *This* was why he never married, never had children, never rooted himself despite having friends and something of a home. He believed he must keep himself free so when he was called—by what he couldn't have said—he would be ready. A task worthy of life, of his existence.

Peprini watched him closely. "It is a remarkable feeling to have a divine purpose, yes, David?"

The Vessel slowly nodded.

Peprini stood. "Go about your routines. There is nothing else for you to do. When you have the dream, expect to see me."

59

In the three days since their arrival in New York City, Eliezer and Oleander had been working almost incessantly on the mysterious Sefirot formulas, trying to unearth their codewords.

True to his historical interest, the monk was searching the Chronicles in the hope that some ancient Keepers might have already investigated the Book. The professor preferred permuting words and letters of the Sefirot and reading academic treatises on the ancient Hebrew language in which the Book of Creation had been written. Although they had suspended their discernments on the Book, they wanted to be ready to continue, whenever they could, to the fourth Sefirah:

TEN SEFIROT OF BELIMAH, THEIR END IS LINKED TO THEIR BEGINNINGS AND THEIR BEGINNING TO THEIR ENDS LIKE A FLAME CONNECTED TO A BURNING COAL. KNOW, CALCULATE, AND FORM, FOR THE LORD IS SINGULAR, AND THE CREATOR IS ONE, AND HE HAS NO SECOND, AND IN THE FACE OF ONE HOW CAN YOU COUNT?

The text seemed impenetrable. Oleander pointed out that some of the words—"counting," "calculate," "one," "second"—clearly suggested numbers. Eliezer agreed that the wording suggested some kind of cycle where the end is connected to the beginning, like counting which goes from one to ten, and then starts again at one (eleven) to ten (twenty), and then again (twenty-one to thirty) and again and again.

They hoped Osnat would be able to help them—after all, she had guessed correctly the codeword for the third Sefirah. They gave her the text of the fourth Sefirah and asked her to meditate on it. She read and re-read the formula, trying to meditate on it in different ways but with no result.

"I'm sorry," she said in frustration, "it doesn't depend on me. It's like inspiration—either it comes or it doesn't."

"You're not trying hard enough," Oleander accused her.

"Maybe you should tell me why you are so interested in this book. You ask me to solve a puzzle that you can't. But you won't give me all the clues."

At last they gave up on her. Their best guess was that the fourth codeword was *"Counting."* But they couldn't continue with the attempt to open the Gate with only a guess.

Peprini stepped from his hotel and turned west. At the intersection the traffic signal was out. A police officer directed the streams of cars. A particularly thin veil of Blessing covered the area, and he was relieved to move beyond it, misfortune being more likely in such a place.

On instructions Tiplady had followed Osnat that afternoon, so Peprini had no difficulty locating her. She was in a café near her hotel.

The café was mostly empty. He bought a coffee and then sat at a table beside hers. She was absorbed in a book and he examined her face. There was a strength about her unusual in a young woman, but there was no denying her beauty even with only the barest makeup. He understood why Eliezer wouldn't want to share her.

He narrowed his eyes and examined her aura. It was rich and powerful for a novice, unique even. He watched her close the book and set it face down, quickly covering it with a newspaper. He glimpsed the book's spine and recognized it as the famous *Early History of the Keepers*. She sipped her coffee.

"Should you be doing that here?"

She turned to him. "Pardon me?"

"Are you sure this is the place to be doing that?"

He enjoyed the nervous look on her face. "I don't know what you mean."

"I would have thought Eliezer, certainly William Oleander, would have warned you about reading such a book in a public place. Despite your precautions."

He looked at the newspaper-covered book. Her body tightened, and in her confusion she was struck dumb.

"I'm sorry," he said smiling now, "I did not mean to alarm you."

"Who are you?"

"My name is Menach Peprini, Osnat. Yes, I know who you are."

"You are…"

He lowered his voice. "A Keeper, yes. And a Councilor. Has Eliezer explained to you about the Council?"

She shook her head. She was surprised by his appearance. Eliezer's clothes though expensive were a bit worn and out of date, and Oleander's suit clearly off the rack, this man could have been a stylish investment banker.

"I've known Eliezer most of my life, Osnat. My father and grandfather served on the Council with him before me."

Her shock was gone but she was guarded. "Why...? Were you looking for me?"

"Are you aware of the recent Vessel deaths? Of the unprecedented nature of these deaths?"

"What do you mean?"

"Eliezer didn't tell you?"

"I'm sorry, but I don't know what you're talking about."

He couldn't help but admire her loyalty. "Hmm. Well, if he has not told you there must be a good reason. Perhaps I'm not the one to say."

"Perhaps not."

He gave a small smile at her defiance despite what he was sure was a burning curiosity. "I have traveled from Switzerland—you do know that we Keepers have our home there—in order to see you."

"Why would you want to meet me, you a Councilor and me... a beginner?"

"Our word is 'novice,' since you have been in a fashion accepted as one of us. I am the Director of Novitiate Training. All those recruited as possible Keepers must attend my School and train under my direction. So you see why I would have an interest in you. And why it would be peculiar for Eliezer to deny you this training."

"He is training me himself." Something in her suppressed the impulse to say more despite the man's way of eliciting answers.

Peprini now had her admission. Eliezer had violated the rule in not disclosing the fact he was training her. Training meant disclosing the existence of Keepers. Even for a Councilor this was serious.

"Yes, of course. At the meeting, Eliezer insisted on keeping you at his side instead of giving you the advantage of the traditional training at the Novitiate. He thought you might experience some difficulties being among the other novices—some are frighteningly talented."

This had the desired effect.

"What did he say?"

"Nothing in words. But denying someone the formal Novitiate training typically means she needs... how shall we say, special attention. That the student is a marginal case. But talking with you now, and seeing your aura—it is clearly impressive—I don't know what could have made him think this way."

He observed as she weighed her sense of loyalty to Eliezer against the fact she now had to admit she knew nothing of the world of Keepers beyond what Eliezer and Oleander had told her.

"My reason for visiting you was only this: I wanted to assuage any fears you might have about your welcome at the Novitiate School. But now I see no need for worry on that account. The opposite indeed seems true."

"Well, thank you."

He stood. "We are a very small community. When some have secrets, especially at a time of great crisis, it is very troubling. Keeperdom has endured for four thousand years because of our sacred respect for traditions and duty. Forgive me if it seemed I was forward today in the fulfillment of *my* duty."

She watched him leave the restaurant. Why didn't Eliezer send her to the Novitiate? He and William said I have these special abilities. Are they trying to keep me away from other Keepers? Why?

Now it struck her: Are Eliezer and William doing something they shouldn't? Am I part of something they are hiding from the others like this Peprini? If so, I've been dragged into it. Would Eliezer do this to me?

This Peprini may have told me the truth, she thought, but he wants something more than to train me. And his interest isn't sexual; he wants something else.

She recalled his words, his calculated voice and gestures, his self-controlled demeanor. Then a small bubble of knowledge arose within her: *This Peprini needs me—to help him become more than he is.*

She had no idea what this meant but was certain it was true.

At the hotel, she told her companions of Peprini's visit.

"*Jesus*, Eliezer."

"Just wait, William, wait. Let me think." He stood and began pacing.

Oleander dropped onto the couch, his head in his hands.

"If Menach knew what we were doing," the old man said, "he would not have revealed himself to Osnat—and through her to us. He would have sprung it on us at the Council meeting in a few days. No, it is because he does *not* know that he is poking about in this way."

"If our work is exposed and the Council... God knows what will happen to us. Just because you brought her along. Dammit, Eliezer... I told you it was a bad idea."

"William, calm down."

Osnat's eyes moved from one Keeper to the other. "You two are doing something you shouldn't."

Oleander looked helplessly at Eliezer. The professor stared at her, then nodded.

"Then you are making me an accomplice. I don't even know what crime it is, or what the punishment might be! Don't you think I deserve to know about it?"

"You are a *novice!*" Oleander snapped.

Eliezer sighed. "Shhh, William. She is right."

"I've traveled halfway around the world. I've had crazy vagabonds chasing me. I was just interrogated by some enemy of yours, apparently. I think I deserve to know."

"Alright. Let us all sit down."

60

The next morning Eliezer gave Osnat a discernment exercise. He then took Oleander to a restaurant several blocks away. The episode with Peprini had unnerved the young monk and Eliezer hoped the walk and change of scenery would help.

For several hours Osnat toiled at the Inner Depths. By mid-morning, she was unaccountably restless and felt the need to get out of the hotel. Soon she was downstairs and out the door. Without a deliberate choice, she found herself walking north along the Hudson River.

The cool wind invigorated her and she walked in long and energetic strides, pushed along as if in a hurry to get to some appointment. She enjoyed the sensation of her muscles stretching and contracting and the perspiration beginning to form in her pores. She loosened the buttons on her coat as she warmed under the overcast sky.

A while later the urge to hurry vanished. She was in a small park. A clamor of shouts drew her attention. Some two hundred feet away were four wild-looking boys. One was tugging at a sign pole trying to pull it over; two others were upending a trash can. A young woman sat on a bench in the midst of all this. She seemed oblivious. The fourth boy now began advancing towards her. The woman didn't move. Was she frozen by fear? Mentally ill? The boy jumped onto the bench, stomping on it several times, trying to break it. She still didn't move. Now the three others arrived.

But then the kid on the bench pointed towards something and yelled to his friends. With a whoop of riot they moved towards their new object of vandalism, leaving the woman untouched.

Osnat sighed in relief. She felt a curious desire to speak to her. As she got closer, the woman seemed slightly older than herself, thirty perhaps. She wore a dark dress and a hip-length leather coat. Her brown hair was short and her face had a sad Mediterranean beauty.

"Are you alright? I thought those boys…" Osnat asked.

"Just kids. And it's daytime."

"Still." Osnat started to sit down. "Do you mind the company?"

"I'm not doing anything."

"I'm Osnat, by the way."

"I'm Dina. Your accent?"

"Israeli. I'm from Jerusalem."

The word 'Jerusalem' seemed to arouse Dina's interest for a moment. Osnat felt inexplicably drawn to this woman. Despite her sadness, there was something luminous about her.

"If you're from Jerusalem," Dina suddenly said, "you might know what Dinah felt."

"Dinah?"

"My namesake. From the Bible."

"You mean Jacob's daughter? From Genesis?"

"*And Dinah, the daughter of Leah, whom she bore to Jacob....*"

"Are you talking about the Biblical story of Dinah's rape?"

Dina shook her head. "No, no, it's not..."

Osnat started quoting (by now she knew most of Genesis by heart), hoping to penetrate her reticence: "*And when Shechem, the son of Hamor the Hivite, prince of the country, saw her, he took her, and lay with her, and defiled her. And his soul clung to Dinah the daughter of Jacob, and he loved the maiden....*"

"I meant that Jacob blessed his twelve sons. But his daughter was left out."

"Was she? Are you sorry for a woman who died four-thousand years ago?"

"Sounds strange, doesn't it? I've always felt a connection to her since I was a little girl. I would even dream about her. Maybe because I have her name." She smiled for just a moment.

"You know, I've always had the same feeling, but about Ishmael. The Biblical black sheep. I'm always attracted to the bad boy."

They both grinned.

"You dreamed about her?"

Dina nodded. This made her think of Frostburg and her expulsion. She stood, appearing embarrassed at revealing so much. "I have to go. It was nice meeting you."

She walked away. Now Osnat detected a distinct whiff of the vagabonds. She surveyed the park but saw no one.

On her way back to the hotel Osnat realized she should have asked for a phone number or at least for her last name. She felt a pang of regret. For a reason she couldn't understand she wanted very much to see this Dina again.

61

Peprini steered the car down the valley road more slowly than usual. The frost on the hillsides made him look closely for black ice on the pavement. All Keepers knew of the recent auto accident and serious injuries of two of their own in Addis Ababa. Councilor and novice were absorbed in their own thoughts.

"Do you think he'll be there?" Maria said.

"It's been ten days. He must be feeling the craving. That is what Vessels feel when they are depleted of Blessing: something like hunger."

The previous day Wyatt had approached the edge of the Void, unaware of their presence, only to withdraw. Later, over the phone, the Vessel had been defensive and apologetic. The Keeper assured him that by all accounts a Vessel does not have complete control over the "dream." It was no one's fault. They would simply keep trying.

The gravel road appeared, and the car wound through the pines until it reached the house. Smoke from the chimney signaled that the housekeeper had made preparations.

Soon they were seated in the wing chairs a comfortable distance from the fireplace.

"How do you feel?"

"I'm ready." She didn't sound enthusiastic. On her pale, slender neck he could see the artery pulse rapidly.

"Would you like to review?"

She shook her head. "I want to get on with it."

"Good."

She didn't take his cue but instead was still.

"I know Keepers have died in the Void." She looked into the fire. "Do we know what happens to their souls? Does the soul remain… trapped there? Forever?" She turned to him. She had asked him a question she knew he couldn't answer. "If I am unsuccessful, will you make the attempt yourself?"

"It will depend."

"If another Vessel dies?"

"Then I must, yes."

She considered this. "If that happens, then there isn't much hope for any of us, I suppose." She looked at her watch. "It's time."

They relaxed in their chairs. After some fifteen minutes of meditation, when their minds were sufficiently calm and focused, they sank to their Inner Depths. At length, they were hovering at the edge of the Void.

Maria scanned the emptiness. It was completely uniform without any visible feature, the dense blackness seeming to suck away the very possibility of seeing something. She recoiled from it. Though she hadn't told Peprini, each trip into the Void had been worse than the one before. She felt her anxiety swell and fought to keep it under control.

Peprini saw David Wyatt approaching from a distance. She was already moving towards him. Now Peprini turned to the Void, focused his gaze, and prepared to discern Gate One.

From the corner of his eye Peprini watched him—Wyatt was likely trying to penetrate the haze of his *dream* and recall what he was supposed to do.

"Come, David," he willed the Vessel, "come closer…"

The Vessel now moved straight towards Maria, his resoluteness indicating he remembered what to do. Maria stood in front of him. She touched his cheek and the Vessel took her in his arms. They moved closer to the edge, and the Void enveloped them.

The Councilor began his discernment on the first of God's Blessings to Abraham. He saw the familiar scene:

It is evening. The sun has gone down behind the dunes but it is still light. Abram—before God changed his name to Abraham—had buried his father Terah in a grove of date palms. Abram is already an old man of seventy-five; his wife Sarai (soon to be named Sarah) is there, as is his nephew Lot and his wife. Now God tells Abram to leave the land of his father and go forth to found a great nation. None hear the voice but Abram. Lot is crying and does not want to leave the grave of his grandfather. But Abram touches his shoulder and Lot agrees to follow his uncle.

Peprini had been absorbed in his effort when he became aware of his fatigue. The collective exhaustion of the previous discernments of the Void had caught up to him. Even Gate One was draining, and he worried how long he could continue.

An object appeared in the Void. It slowly grew larger. He quit discernment and struggled to see, but it was still too far away. *Was it one person or two?* He strained harder still. The wait was almost too much for him.

Now he could make out the Vessel... *and Maria was in his arms*. He strained to detect any change in Wyatt or Maria but the image was too vague. When they were almost to the edge Wyatt released her and disappeared.

Maria floated just inside the Void, her back to him.

Peprini stood at the murky boundary line. With no discernment beam to protect him, it was perilous to venture even that short distance. He inched forward but couldn't reach her, though he could begin to feel the chaos literally tugging on his toes. Unless he moved immediately he knew he never would. He focused as strongly as he could on Maria and stepped forward. Whatever was under his feet fell from beneath him, and continued to fall away, but he understood it was an illusion and maintained his focus. With great effort, he reached out and his fingers grasped her wrist. He carried her back and laid her down. She had no aura. Her eyes were open, the pupils eclipsing the iris, her face contorted in terror. He let go and watched her drift into the blackness.

Once again Peprini was in the chair in front of the fireplace. Maria's body sat upright, eyes closed, her head balanced on her slender neck, her face gripped in anguish. Touching her neck he found no pulse. She seemed quite cool to the touch as if she had been dead for many hours. Her hands were balled into tiny fists. With difficulty, he opened her fingers and saw four cuts across her palm. The same four cuts were on her other palm. Then he saw the blood on her fingernails.

He stood, still looking at Maria, and took his cellphone. He spoke briefly to his assistant, Miss Davois, requesting that Dr. Loyev come to the house with two men. There wouldn't be a problem. Loyev would sign the death certificate, the manner of death natural causes. A tragic discernment accident. Next, he phoned David Wyatt. Before the third ring the Vessel answered, surprisingly alert, given the Keeper had just awoken him.

"It didn't work, did it?"

Peprini hesitated. "No. Can you tell me what happened?"

"The moment we plunged into the Void she was shaking and groaning. And when the cliff was out of sight she started screaming. It was terrible. I've never heard anyone scream like that."

"And then?"

"I tried to hold her tight. I think she passed out. After that..."

"Yes?"

"I'm not sure. Already I'm having trouble remembering what happened. Is she alright? What does she say?"

"She is exhausted. It was a frightening experience for her, as you witnessed."

"She's fine, then."

"I don't think she will be capable again soon. The Void has an effect on Keepers you are unable to appreciate."

"What do we do now?"

"For the time being—nothing. You will 'dream' as you always have, and continue to renew the Blessing."

"So that's it? All of... *this*... is over?"

"No, David. But it won't be as simple as we might have wished. What happened was certainly not your fault. But I need time to rethink our strategy. I will be in touch soon."

Later that afternoon Peprini returned to his cottage. Thanks to Dr. Loyev's involvement, he had avoided the complications of an autopsy or inquest. Maria's body was already lying in a brass coffin. She was clothed in a white dress, her head uncovered, her feet bare. The wounds on her hands had been cleaned but were not bandaged. A van was waiting to take the coffin to the airport, to be flown to Holland, where her family would bury her. He had telephoned her father, saying it was tragic that one so young should die from heart failure, that she had been a joy to everyone at the Frostburg Institute. The death certificate would confirm the cause.

Peprini stood by the van and watched the driver and a helper load the coffin. He felt the bitter wind bite at his face. One anxious thought kept nagging him: What do I do now? Pilar is incapacitated, Maria is gone, and no one to replace them. Am I trying the impossible? Maybe the Void simply cannot be survived.

He returned to the Novitiate. No one would question Maria's absence. Privately, the other novices, as well as Master-Keepers, would gossip, of course, but they would assume she was given an assignment elsewhere. Pem might ask but would accept whatever he was told.

62

Dark thoughts raced in Peprini's mind all night. Had three generations of Peprinis wasted their effort? Had his father died for nothing? Is it *my* failure to complete what they began?

Sometime before dawn he managed to fall asleep, only to wake two hours later deeply fatigued and in the blackest of moods. More than the lack of sleep, he was humiliated by his inability to control the contents of his own mind.

After a cup of coffee, he managed to drive away most of the anxiety. He would persist to his last breath. Pilar and Maria and twenty others meant nothing in the face of the greatness of his mission. With that renewed conviction came a plan. After working out in his mind the details, he called New York. Eric Tiplady was unhappy at being awakened at three o'clock in the morning but listened to the order from Peprini.

"I can do that, Sir. No problem."

"I thought it would appeal to you, Eric."

Late the next morning, Eliezer, Oleander, and Osnat went for a walk in Central Park. The sun was shining, and though the Blessing was dismal, the warmth brightened their outlook.

"No business talk," Eliezer announced. "All of us need a little diversion."

It was Saturday and a crowd had gathered in the park to enjoy the sunshine. Increasingly people stayed close to home. The likelihood of accidents while traveling had become too high to risk unnecessary trips. Following two derailments of El-trains involving more than fifty fatalities, and the collapse of the A-train tunnel which had crushed just over three hundred passengers under thousands of tons of rock, the subways were used only when no alternative existed.

The three Keepers walked parallel to the sidewalk, enjoying the feeling of the grass beneath their feet. Oleander and Osnat kept a slow pace to accommodate Eliezer, whom they saw moved with what seemed unusual effort.

A group of three mimes, their faces covered with theater masks, approached the Keepers and started jesting goodheartedly. One bowed to Osnat in mock worship, as if she were a queen. She gave a small laugh. He reached out as if holding her hand in great reverence and led her ceremoniously along the path. The other two mimes walked behind her, holding the imaginary hem of her dress. She looked over her shoulder at Eliezer and Oleander and smiled, lifting her chin in a royal manner. The two Keepers, separated from her by the two men, walked some distance behind, amused at the unexpected entertainment as well as Osnat's joyfulness.

Unnoticed by the Keepers, a black BMW moved slowly up the drive and stopped by the sidewalk twenty yards away. The theatrical procession made its way up the sidewalk. As they neared the car, the man at Osnat's side leaned towards her.

"Osnat Aviv."

She stopped. "Councilor Peprini personally requests your presence in Lucerne." He took off his mask and opened the rear door of the sedan. "He asked me to bring you to him."

Osnat started backing up. "I don't think so."

"I know him," Eliezer murmured. "Oleander, that's Eric Tiplady!"

"Who?"

"A novice. What...?"

Tiplady took a step towards her. "It's not actually a request."

Osnat, still backing away, stopped as if yielding. He smiled wickedly and reached for her. A nauseating pain then exploded through him and he dropped to his knees, holding his groin.

Osnat turned and sprinted away, the two others on her heels.

Oleander and Eliezer started running towards them. "Stop!"

Eliezer stumbled and lost his footing, hitting the ground. Oleander helped him to his feet. They watched as Osnat quickly put distance between herself and the two men.

"Forget her! Get back here!" Tiplady yelled from his knees.

The men quit the chase and ran back. They helped Tiplady into the BMW, and the car sped away.

"Young lady," Eliezer said as Osnat walked up to them, "where did you learn to fight like that?"

She looked at them as if nothing had happened, though her face was flushed and her breathing fast. "The Army. And every woman knows where to kick a man."

"You're shaking. You're not hurt?" Oleander said.

She saw for the first time the Oleander that Eliezer knew. He was obviously deeply concerned about her.

"I'm fine, William. Thank you for worrying about me."

"Let's get out of here," said Eliezer.

They quickly found a taxi. A glass partition separated them from the driver.

"It must be Peprini," Eliezer whispered.

"I *know* it's him," Osnat told them about the invitation to Lucerne.

"But why would Menach take such a risk?" Oleander asked. "And what would he want with her?" Surely he knows that, successful or not, we'd reveal this at the Council meeting."

"He knows we do not dare speak of it. His meeting with Osnat at the café—it was to tell us he knows we have been working behind the Council's back."

The three sat in silence absorbing this.

"We have to assume we're being watched from now on," Oleander concluded.

"At all times. For whatever reason, Menach is becoming reckless. Even desperate. And that worries me as much as anything."

Peprini picked up the phone and listened to Tiplady's report. He said nothing and hung up. He would not get a second chance. His men might succeed in abducting her, but Eliezer and Oleander would have poisoned her against him. He paced in front of the fireplace. He stopped and looked at the ashes of the morning's fire. What now?

63

Eliezer's conversation with Julia Erna left him uneasy. She had called to report the findings regarding the vagabonds and to discuss the upcoming Council meeting; at least that is what she said. She sounded remote. She remarked that Annette Goldman had run across a letter in the Archives claiming an ancient Vessel had terminated because of some Keeper's violation of the law. What law did he think this could be? Erna then asked if he thought it possible that a Keeper could discern the Void. He had to fight the urge to answer defensively. Did she know that he and Oleander were experimenting with the Book? Unlikely, he thought. After all, it was not the Void they were discerning. Still...

The call ended awkwardly with Eliezer informing her, as if in passing, about his decision to train Osnat. At least Peprini couldn't spring that on a completely unknowing Council.

Erna's report about the vagabonds' attraction to Vessels alleviated much of Eliezer's and Oleander's fears. They were now convinced that it was these vagabonds, not their own work on the Book of Creation, who were responsible for the Vessels' deaths.

"If it is the vagabonds who are killing off our Vessels," Eliezer said, "then we *must* open a new gate for the Blessing, to make up for the damage they have done."

"Agreed. But, Eliezer, who the devil are these creatures?"

"I am confident they belong to some ancient lineage, some Biblical descent."

"You said that before. But which? Some split-off faction of Keepers?"

"No, William. These are not Keepers. Their presence alone..." and he recoiled at the memory of their rankness. "Could they be Ishmaelites? Ishmaelites are the only Biblical group we know for certain exists today, other than Keepers and Vessels. What do we know about them? You are the historian."

"Very little. They zealously guard their privacy. We know, obviously, they are descendants of Ishmael. Are they still resentful of us, of Keepers and Vessels? Do they think that our forefather Isaac received the blessing that should have gone to the elder brother, Ishmael?"

"Why should they feel resentful? After all, they have their own Blessing."

"A private Blessing—unique among all God's Blessings, isn't it? And then the enigmatic remarks that the angel of God made to Hagar, Ishmael's mother: *Behold, you are with child, and shall bear a son, and you shall call his name Ishmael, because God heard your affliction. And he shall be a wild man as the desert ass, his hand shall be against everybody and everybody's hand shall be against him...*"

"That's just the standard translation," interrupted Eliezer. "The original ancient Hebrew says: *His hand shall be in everybody and everybody's hand shall be in him.*"

"And what does *that* mean?"

"Perhaps we could ask the Ishmaelites. I was thinking we should try to contact them."

"Revealing ourselves as Keepers? Especially to the Ishmaelites? That would be an outright violation—another one—of the laws."

The Professor smiled inwardly at his protégé's ever-present concern at defying authority. "Tell me more about them. How are they organized, what is their agenda?"

"They are ruled by twelve princes. Twelve *Nessi'im*, or *Nassi* in the singular. They still use the original Biblical word. Each prince is supposedly descended from one of Ishmael's twelve sons. At least that's the legend."

"Ah, just as in Genesis 25: *These are the sons of Ishmael, and these are their names by their villages and by their encampments, twelve Nessi'im—princes— according to their nations.* And where do these twelve princes live?"

"All over the world. Each prince rules over one of twelve regions of the Earth. Their people are mingled in society but still manage to live separately. They are extraordinarily wealthy, even more than Keeperdom. But they too conceal this. And they are, well, 'nosy' probably says it best. They pride themselves on being knowers."

Eliezer grinned. "*His hand shall be in everybody.* The Arabs claim they are descendants of Ishmael. Are they?"

"Probably no more than any other modern nation. As things stand now the Ishmaelites are of all nationalities, just like Keepers."

"Alright, William, how do we contact them?"

"It's they who contact us. The last reported meeting with them was in 1936. They wanted to warn us of an upcoming 'worldwide war'—yes, that was their expression—and urged us to try and prevent it. Of course, we told them there were limits to what we could do."

"Come, William." Eliezer turned and moved towards the table. "We are procrastinating." He looked at his watch. "We have perhaps three hours before Osnat returns."

"You're confident enough the codeword is *counting*?"

"If that fails, then as we agreed we will try 'number' and then 'numbers.' If those do not work, we stop the session. I fear we cannot risk any more."

Eliezer scrutinized Oleander's face. The old man was deeply apprehensive but he put on a confident face.

"Cheer up, William! The Primordial Gate is reacting to our discernments. Sooner or later it will start opening, and then... can you imagine the wondrous Blessing that will pour out?"

Each read one last time the passage to be discerned upon and closed his eyes. Silently they descended to their Inner Depths and saw each other arriving at the same moment. For a while they stared at the Void. Then, at Eliezer's sign, they started speaking the words, very slowly, one syllable at a time:

WITH THIRTY-TWO MYSTERIOUS PATHS OF WISDOM...

Once again, as in previous sessions, great energies started accumulating around them, but they were now well-prepared. They finished the introductory sentence, and were now ready to plunge into the fourth Sefirah:

TEN *SEFIROT* OF *BELIMAH*, THEIR END IS LINKED TO THEIR BEGINNINGS AND THEIR BEGINNING TO THEIR ENDS...

Without warning, unseen forces started heaving on all sides. They could sense the terrifying torrents in the distance. Each fought a growing vulnerability. The recitation was becoming increasingly hard.

LIKE A FLAME CONNECTED TO A BURNING COAL...

The pressure was agonizing. They held their focus and lost all sense of time, feeling the terrible yet wondrous powers raging around them.

KNOW, CALCULATE, AND FORM. FOR THE LORD IS SINGULAR, AND THE CREATOR IS ONE, AND HE HAS NO SECOND, AND IN THE FACE OF ONE HOW CAN YOU COUNT?

The energies were at their peak now, ready to explode at the sound of the codeword.

"*Sefirah!*" Eliezer spoke the modern Hebrew word for 'counting' into the Void.

The ocean around them moaned and rumbled.

"*Mispar!*"—Number—Eliezer tried again.

The rumbling grew more menacing.

"*Misparim!*"—Numbers—spoke Oleander.

An awful tremor rose as the walls of energies got closer, now encircling them. Eliezer signaled to Oleander to stop. It was clear that with another failure the ocean of energies would crush them. They turned and saw that the way back to their Inner Depths was blocked by the storm. Both understood that their only chance was to wait and hope that the storm would dissipate before they lost the endurance to sustain themselves in the tumult.

When Osnat returned to the hotel suite she found Eliezer and Oleander seated at the table, their eyes closed. They were obviously discerning. Their faces were twisted in anxiety and glossy with sweat. Oleander's fingers clawed into his knees.

For a few seconds she watched them, wondering what to do. Then she knew. She sat down, attuned herself to their auras, and closed her eyes.

She had never descended so quickly and it made her lightheaded. She found herself emerging from her corridor at the edge of the Void. An immense storm of energy was blowing everywhere. Through it she could see Eliezer and Oleander looking at each other in alarm.

For a few seconds she hovered in place, gathering her wits. And then she felt a thought stirring inside her. Despite her fear of the threatening storm, she knew she mustn't hurry its maturation. She watched the thought, caressing it internally, protecting it, waiting.

The entire formula of the fourth Sefirah, word for word, sounded in her mind. A pause followed as if waiting for her to respond.

LINKED… FLAME… CONNECTED… ONE AND HE HAS NO SECOND—she could almost see the connecting theme. Then her attention rested on the word "flame"—*Shalhevet* in the Hebrew. The word is very rare in the Bible…

Shalhevet… A popular Israeli melody of a Biblical verse resounded in her mind: "For love is strong as death, its jealousy is cruel as the grave, its coals are coals of fire, a vehement *flame*."

"Love!" she shouted.

A deafening explosion froze everything. She was unable to breathe, unable to move. Unseen cracks opened; she could feel currents rush by her. Then the dam broke, the entire sea of energies was being sucked into the Void. She was carried along helplessly, her untrained motions useless against the pull. The Void was going to take her.

Something seized her arm. It was Eliezer! She fought to gain some purchase to lessen the strain on him but found she could do nothing. But his hold on her remained firm.

The currents subsided. The three Keepers collected themselves. Eliezer motioned for them to make their way back up.

A great time later—or so it seemed—they were back in their bodies, sitting at the table.

"I could suddenly see the word." She shook her head unable to say more.

"Perhaps the spiritual effort brought it forth. We need to understand more how this talent of yours works," said Eliezer.

Oleander returned from his room after having changed his shirt. He pulled a sweater over his head. "How is *love* linked to the formula? THE CREATOR IS ONE, AND HE HAS NO SECOND... what's the connection?"

"It's very simple," the old Councilor smiled. "Once you stop being such a romantic."

"Romantic?"

"Don't think about love to a woman, William. Remember the Biblical verse Jews are supposed to recite three times a day? *...the Lord is one. And you shall love the Lord your God with all your heart...*"

The monk blushed. "Of course, I see."

64

For three days Julia Erna and Annette Goldman kept descending to the Depths as often as their schedule and endurance allowed, trying to detect again the stray discernment beam. They were determined to find it and, by the simple method of immediately phoning all Councilors, determine the offender. Merely descending without discerning was not too demanding. They descended three or even four times a day, sometimes together and sometimes separately, but learned nothing more. During that time they sighted more than a dozen discernment beams—most of them weak, obviously of ordinary Keepers, one quite focused suggesting a Master-Keeper—but none directed at the Void. They were all appropriately shining towards the Bible World.

On the morning of the fourth day, they descended and immediately noted a beam in the distance. It was in a different place from where they were looking, and it seemed to be directed at the Bible World, and so at first they ignored it. It took them several moments to realize that there was something strange about it: Although the beam was pointing towards the Bible World, nevertheless it did not reach it! Oddly, it ended abruptly one-third of the way through the Void, as if blocked by an invisible wall.

How is it possible that a beam—especially one of such strength and vibrancy—could stop suddenly? *How could it not reach the Bible World?*

The two Councilors gazed at the sight. The thin line seemed strongly focused and stable, a Councilor's beam no doubt. Goldman thought that it might consist of two distinct beams—perhaps two Councilors discerning side by side—but it was too far away to be sure.

And then to their amazement, a surge of Blessing appeared at the beginning of the beam, at the edge of the Void, and started moving along its path towards the Bible World like a wave rushing through a canal. Spellbound, they watched as it moved farther and farther, receding into the distance, becoming smaller and fainter. It was approaching the point where the beam ended and they waited expectantly… A fireball exploded and glowed in a brilliant gold. At such a distance, it was only the size of a very large star in the sky, but out there, at the place where it happened, it must have been a tremendous explosion.

They gawked at the sight, hardly believing their eyes. The Blessing-ball now continued advancing into the darkness, beyond the tip of the beam, as if hewing a pathway—a new pathway—through the Void. It was quickly dissipating as it went along until nothing could be seen of it. The beam remained for a time, longer than before, for it now reached halfway to the Bible World. Then it too disappeared.

What had they seen? Could it be someone was carving through the Void a new pathway to the Bible World? To a place apart from the traditional Twelve Abrahamic Gates? But that was impossible!

Half an hour later, when Erna was convinced no more was to happen and started ascending back to her body, she realized it was too late to learn the identity of the mysterious discerner. By now he or she would be awake and would answer a phone call as if nothing had happened.

65

Eliezer asked Osnat to leave them alone for several hours. As had become her habit she went for an afternoon walk. The late October sky was sunny one moment and cloudy the next, a strong wind pushing heavy clouds across the sky.

She found herself saying "Times Square." The words came with an authority she could not deny. She walked in long strides. Now and then she thought she could detect a vagabond's presence behind her, but she was no longer anxious. The creature seemed content to stay a distance away.

When she reached Times Square, her eyes glazed over at the neon and degradation. Like so many other places it had suffered a sharp decline in the last month as the city had more important tasks than to pick up trash and remove graffiti.

A tap on her shoulder startled her.

"Dina! My God!"

"I thought it was you."

"If I believed in providence I'd say someone wants us to know each other. Oh, Dina, you look much better now."

"Our meeting helped a bit. It was my first real conversation in a couple weeks."

They walked together towards smaller streets.

"I've been thinking about you. Why were you so sad the other day, if I may ask?"

"Yes, I'm sorry about that. I... well, it's embarrassing, really. I just got kicked out of a school. Expelled, I suppose."

"Really? From where?"

"I'm sure you've never heard of it..." Dina hesitated; Frostburg was publicly known. "It's in Switzerland. The Frostburg Institute for Biblical Studies."

Osnat grabbed Dina's arm. "The Frostburg Institute in Lucerne?"

"You know it?"

"I was supposed to go there. My mentor, though, decided it would be better if I studied with him. He's a professor at the Hebrew University."

"When I was there we had a lecture by somebody from that place."

"Professor Jeremiah Eliezer?"

"He's your mentor?"

"Yes."

Each examined the other, wondering how much she knew, wanting to reveal more but wary of saying too much.

"Why did they expel you?"

Tears appeared in Dina's eyes, and with annoyance she wiped them away with her fingers. "I couldn't pass their entrance exams, the Verification."

"I never would have dreamed we had so much in common."

"We have nothing in common. You're so special you're above or beyond whatever they do at Frostburg. But me... When I got to the Institute... I can't tell you how important I felt it was for me to be there. And just when..."

Dina suddenly became agitated, her eyes darting away. "It's crazy talking this way to you. You're almost a stranger."

Already Dina was backing away, shaking her head.

"But how do I get in touch with you?"

"Why would you want to do that?"

"Dina..."

But she had already disappeared around a corner.

66

Osnat glanced at her watch and was glad it was time to return to the hotel. Her legs were heavy and she wanted to lie down. Waiting for the pedestrian light to signal "walk," she turned and saw the vagabond woman from the restaurant about thirty yards behind. She felt the woman even at this distance. The light changed but for the moment, at least, the woman wasn't following.

Ahead there was a construction site—a renovation of a third-floor apartment. Power tools hissed and a thin cloud of white dust hovered. Several levels of scaffolding had been erected above the sidewalk.

On the third floor, a group of men worked to maneuver a refrigerator, suspended from a pulley, through an open window.

"Look out!"

She looked up at the voice and realized that something was tumbling down, ricocheting and crashing through the scaffolding as it rushed towards her. Time stopped. Every detail in her field of vision was lucid and distinct, every kink in the scaffolding, every blotch of paint. At that moment she understood that the refrigerator from the third floor was falling and that in a moment it would crush her and there was no way to move her feet fast enough to avoid it.

Then, in the midst of this frozen clarity, her arm was taken and pulled back. A split second later a large refrigerator crashed to the ground right in front of her.

A young man was holding her arm and smiling.

"Careful there," he said.

She was feeling shaky, and he led her gently into a goldsmith shop two doors away.

He had a small, amused smile. His eyes were a deep brown, almost black, as was his hair. It was strange to see such a wise expression on so young a face. She sat on a stool by a jewelry case and composed herself.

"I'm Kedar."

"Osnat."

The man turned his face toward the door and motioned with his chin. Osnat looked. The vagabond was standing on the other side of the street, staring at them.

He moved to the doorway of the shop and waved his arms as if scaring away an animal. The woman moved down the street.

When he returned, Osnat looked at him astonished. "How did you… do you know her?"

"As the saying goes, our hand is in everybody."

A hand in everybody—Osnat was not familiar with what she assumed was an American expression. "What do you mean?"

"Think you'll be okay, or do I need to follow behind and keep you out of trouble?" He chuckled.

She felt herself blush. "I'll be fine. Thanks…?"

"Kedar. You're welcome, Osnat."

When Osnat returned to the hotel, she told the two men about her near accident and the man who had saved her.

"How is it these Ishmaelites can appear as if from nowhere?"

"Ishmaelites?" asked Osnat. "The vagabonds are Ishmaelites?"

"That is our best guess," replied Eliezer. "The descendants of Ishmael."

"Why are they following us?"

"I wish I knew, but I don't find it surprising. Their motto is: Everything is our business. Or, in Biblical terms: Our hand is in everybody."

The goldsmith, Osnat wondered… was he an Ishmaelite too? But then, who were the vagabonds? She thought to raise the question but both Keepers' faces were screwed up in worried thought.

67

The following morning Eliezer told Osnat that he and Oleander were going to leave for Lucerne that evening.

"The Council meeting," he explained. "We have some preparations still, Osnat. Would you mind leaving us for a little bit? By noon we will be finished."

Osnat took her walk again. She found herself heading towards the goldsmiths. From down the block, she saw Kedar standing by the doorway to his store. He left the doorway and approached her. They smiled at each other, and his eyes said he was happy to see her.

"How about a walk around the block?" he suggested.

They looked at the store windows and chatted, but did not ask each other any personal questions.

They returned to the goldsmiths.

"Will I see you again?" he asked.

Osnat looked at him solemnly. "Are you an Ishmaelite?"

He was knocked off balance for a moment.

"Are you, Kedar?"

He smiled. "What a strange question."

"Why did you tell me your hands are in everybody? I know my Bible. That's how Ishmael is described."

Kedar regained his poise. "Is it?"

"And your name—*Kedar*. That's the name of one of Ishmael's sons."

"So?"

"You knew something about the vagabond who followed me, that woman. Is she an Ishmaelite too?"

"I simply happened to see she was following you," he said and shrugged.

"Besides," persisted Osnat, "You... you are not just anyone."

"You are not just anyone either." His hand brushed against hers. "Come see me again."

Osnat did not withdraw her hand. "Assuming you are an Ishmaelite, we need to talk to you. Can you arrange a meeting for us?"

"Who is *us*?"

"A... a friend," she said. "A professor..." She hesitated, but then understood that if there was any chance of a meeting, there was no choice. "His name is Jeremiah Eliezer. A Keeper, if you know what I mean. He needs to meet your people. It's very important."

She realized the risk she was taking. She was not yet formally accepted as a Keeper and was already telling perfect strangers about them, acting as an official emissary.

He shrugged. "Don't forget to come again."

"Don't forget what I asked you to do."

When Osnat returned to the hotel suite, Eliezer and Oleander were immersed in a discussion. They were in Oleander's room but she overheard enough to know the topic was the upcoming Council meeting. She made herself a cup of coffee and waited.

When they came out of the room Eliezer only gave her a vague smile and Oleander merely nodded. She had never seen them so worried. She hesitated whether this was the right moment to tell them about Kedar. Now her confidence disappeared. He had not admitted to being an Ishmaelite. And she had revealed Eliezer as a Keeper. She imagined how upset Eliezer would be, Oleander no doubt furious, if she told them about her conversation with Kedar.

68

By mid-afternoon, the two Councilors were ready to leave for the airport. Their suitcases had already been taken down to the lobby and the taxi was waiting.

"Keep practicing, but no more discernments," Eliezer said to Osnat, his affectionate hand on her shoulder, "and be mindful when you go out. I doubt Peprini will try again, but still…"

Oleander gave her an awkward hug. "We'll probably be back in a few days. But we can't be sure just when."

Left in the suite by herself, Osnat paced back and forth. She had intended to finish *Early History of the Keepers*, a book by the 19th century Master-Keeper Eva Valeiro. But she was much too restless. She picked up her purse, put on her coat and went out the door.

The thought of Kedar kept crossing her mind as she made her way to the shop. Several blocks later she stood in front of the goldsmiths and peered through the plate glass. A young woman in a short leather skirt had her back turned to Kedar, holding up her auburn hair as he fastened a delicate gold necklace around her neck. A stab of jealousy surprised Osnat. But a moment later he noticed her and a delighted smile came to his face. He held up a finger as if to say "Just a minute."

The young woman left the store fingering her new necklace, Kedar holding the door for her.

"You can't imagine the trouble you got me into," he said.

"For saving my life?"

"I passed on your message about Eliezer wanting to meet us. The *Nassi*—the Prince—was livid I revealed myself as an Ishmaelite."

"And?"

"He has agreed to meet. He wants to see all three of you."

"Me too?"

Kedar nodded. "Tomorrow evening at eight. Meet me here and I'll take you to him."

"But Eliezer won't be in New York tomorrow night. He's leaving the U.S. in three hours."

"That's too bad. A Prince's word is final."

Osnat gazed at his face, her thoughts racing, then looked at her watch.

"Alright," she said in a sudden surge of determination. "How long do you think it should take me to get to JFK?"

"These days?"

"Okay, I'm off. We'll see you here tomorrow night at eight." Her eyes caught an approaching cab. "JFK," she barked at the driver.

At the airport, she leaped from the taxi and rushed into the terminal. There was a long line at the Swiss ticket counter, almost exclusively business people who had no choice despite the danger and anxiety surrounding air travel. She scanned the area and spotted them standing at the counter. She moved quickly through the winding, cordoned line. A blonde Swiss employee, screening passengers for violations of the carry-on rules, blocked her way. "Can I help you, miss?"

"I must talk with someone at the counter," she pointed to Eliezer. "My grandfather... it's very urgent..."

"I'm sorry, but you'll have to wait for him here."

Osnat quickly moved around the woman and dashed to the counter.

"Miss!" the woman called.

Osnat squeezed herself between Eliezer and Oleander.

"We've got an appointment," she whispered. "With the Ishmaelites. Tomorrow night. I couldn't postpone it. It's tomorrow or not at all."

"What are you talking about?" Oleander murmured.

Eliezer deliberated for a moment. "Let's step aside."

"Now. How did you arrange a meeting with the Ishmaelites?"

"It's a long story."

"This is a *Council* meeting we'll be missing, Eliezer."

"I'm telling you what he told me: tomorrow at eight pm. Take it or leave it."

From the corner of his eye, Eliezer saw a woman from the airline approaching.

"Alright," Eliezer said, "we will meet with them."

Oleander was still wavering. "Wait, who are we going to meet? Some frustrated Ishmaelite doorman?"

"A *Nassi*, a prince," Osnat said defiantly.

"A *Nassi*?" He looked at Osnat with a new seriousness.

Eliezer turned to the blue-uniformed Swiss representative. "Sorry for the trouble. We will not be flying tonight."

"I'm sorry, gentlemen," she said in a polite voice that hid irritation. "You must proceed to your gate. Your luggage is already on the way to the aircraft."

"We are truly sorry but we are unable to travel this evening."

"We are not allowed to take off with unaccompanied luggage."

"Sorry," said Eliezer calmly but firmly. "We cannot."

"Sir, your tickets might not be refunded and your luggage will be impounded."

"We will forgo the refund. I will phone later about our luggage."

69

Peprini had resigned himself to the fact that he wouldn't have Osnat Aviv for his project. He thought to find another novice to replace Maria, but a visit to the Novitiate proved disappointing. After reading the novices' files it was plain that the three remaining women, Amira, Nalini, and Natalie, all were mediocre. Their movement in the Depths was sluggish and awkward, and as Keepers they would never go beyond Gate Two or Three. Even the best male, Alexi Samsov, was not near the quality of Maria. There was no reason to put them at risk in a task they were certain to fail.

His project was at a standstill.

His frustration at being denied Osnat Aviv provoked the question: *What was she doing with Eliezer in New York?* Why at this time of crisis would the old man take his time and energy to train her? Finally, how did her presence figure in whatever Eliezer and Oleander were doing behind the Council's back? He issued an order to Monica Berg. They were to search the hotel suite, though this time the concern was not the girl.

Tiplady was glad for the opportunity to redeem himself after his failure with the kidnapping. Since Eliezer, Oleander, and Osnat now recognized Tiplady, it was Berg who took a room across the hall from the Councilors' suite.

Shortly after six-thirty in the evening, she phoned the hotel room of her three fellow Keepers to report that Eliezer and Oleander had just left their suite with the girl. Minutes later the three stepped from their hotel and into a taxi.

Krueger waited in a café across the street affording a good view of the hotel entrance. Jaime Velasquez sat in the lobby of the hotel, a final line of defense should the Keepers make it by the Swede unnoticed.

Berg was waiting by the elevators and they encountered no one as they walked down the hall to the door of the suite. Tiplady used the passkey he had stolen from a hotel maid a few days earlier and was relieved to find it still worked.

Even after the kidnapping attempt Eliezer and Oleander had left all their possessions out in the open behind only the one locked door. He had a thief's disdain for those he stole from, and it disgusted him to see Councilors—who were supposed to be the protectors of Keeperdom—so sloppy about security.

"Start in the bedrooms. Don't bother with the girl's. Let me know about anything odd," Berg ordered, though Tiplady was already searching.

Each Councilor had left behind one suitcase. The contents were carefully removed and examined, then the case itself, before they were returned to the original condition. The clothing in the closets was next, then a general search of the nooks and crannies of the closets and bedrooms.

Tiplady shook his head when he found an unlocked briefcase marked with the letters *JJE* in gold. He took it into the main room and sat down. The case held only a few Keeper reports, an old Bible, two pairs of reading glasses, and some travel documents. Most prominent among its contents was a thin volume wrapped in a ceremonial cloth. It was printed in a foreign script, which he guessed was Hebrew.

The first page contained a list of several short paragraphs. Next to one of them, in the margin, someone had written: "1." Additional portions of the text were numbered in the same handwriting from 2 to 10. Tiplady found the title, like the rest of the small book, indecipherable.

Berg was combing through Oleander's briefcase. "I've got a computer printout of an e-mail addressed to William Oleander plus a large attachment—photocopies of a variety of Chronicle entries. Some monastery business papers, it looks like. And there is… This is odd." She leafed through a small book.

"What?"

Berg held it up.

"Let me see that."

It was entitled "The Book of Creation" and was, as the front page stated, a Hebrew-English edition, Hebrew appearing on the right-hand page and the English translation on the left. Comparing the Hebrew script with that in Eliezer's little book, Tiplady realized it was the same.

She looked at him impatiently. "Just note what it is and let's finish up. We've been in here too long."

He sensed immediately it was not a common Keeper text. It was unlike anything he had seen in his training, full of incomprehensible incantations. The notes in the margins of each only deepened his suspicion.

Then it dawned on him. He turned to Berg. "I'm going to scan these."

The Australian began scanning the pages with his phone. "They're *using* these," Tiplady thought aloud, excited at being able to report something of value to Peprini.

Berg stood. "Just hurry up. I don't like being in here. I don't like anything about this."

She waited near the door. "Alright, let's go," she said, seeing him finish. "Put it back and take one last look. Make sure everything is the same."

Back in his own hotel, he phoned Peprini.

"I think I found something. I'm e-mailing it now."

"What is it?"

"It's called 'The Book of Creation.'" He waited as Peprini searched his memory, sensing when to continue. "It's in Hebrew and English. I'm sending both. Both Councilors had a copy in their briefcase. But it doesn't look like the books I saw in training. And sir?"

"Yes?"

"They're using it for something."

"What do you mean 'using it'? Using the book for what?"

"You'll see. It's full of, well, riddles or incantations, like they're using magic."

"Magic, Eric?" Peprini's budding anticipation shrank. Keeperdom obviously granted the existence of the supernatural, but magic to him was weak-minded fantasy.

"It's some kind of ritual. I don't know what it is. But Eliezer and Oleander seem to be moving in a certain order. They're not studying it, they're using it."

"Excellent work, Eric." And as was Peprini's unconscious practice, he ended the call without saying goodbye.

He waited anxiously at his desk, staring at his Inbox on the computer screen. The 'ping' of incoming mail sounded and he opened the attachment. As he surveyed the pages the words "*Sefirot*" and "*Belimah*" caught his eye, and an excitement grew in him even before he could have said why. He could feel his understanding forming and he tamped down the growing fever. He read the words aloud:

TEN *SEFIROT* OF *BELIMAH*, TWENTY-TWO FUNDAMENTAL LETTERS, TEN SEFIROT, LIKE THE NUMBER OF TEN FINGERS, FIVE OPPOSITE FIVE, AND THE COVENANT OF THE ONE SET IN THE CENTER, WITH THE WORD OF THE TONGUE IN THE MOUTH AND WITH THE CIRCUMCISION OF NAKEDNESS.

His mind went back to that day, nearly fifty years earlier, when his grandfather had told him of the strange invocation of the lost Jewish tribe. The invocation was supposed to arouse the Blessing, but only if the words were spoken in the right order. He recalled how as a child he was in the habit of trying all kinds of permutations, chanting them quietly in the hope of hitting upon the right combination. Then he remembered the divine joy he had experienced some four years later when he stumbled upon the improbable combination, never able to reproduce it.

He still remembered the meaningless string of Hebrew words:

Eser, eser eser, hamisha ke-neged hamisha ve-shtayim, esrim otiot, etsbaot ve-brit, lashon mechuvenet ba-emtsa, Sefirot Sefirot yesod, milat ha-maor, ve-ba-pe mispar yihud, be-milat Belimah.

He had no trouble remembering his grandfather's translation:

Ten, ten, ten, five opposite five and two, twenty letters, fingers and covenant, tongue set in the center, countings fundamental countings, circumcision of nakedness, and in the mouth a number of the one, in the word of station.

Now he realized that the enigmatic chant was none other this passage in front of his eyes which Eliezer had marked as "1." His grandfather's translation was not bad, given that he had to decode a meaningless list of isolated words with no context to help him.

For the first time since his loss of the Aviv girl, Peprini smiled. "Grandfather," he whispered, elated, "*I have found it. I have found the Book of Creation!*"

As he stared at the screen, focusing on the passage, he sensed a change taking place. As it had when he was a teenager that evening in his room studying, it began in the center of his being—a joyous energy, a radiant lightness, and it expanded and reached to all parts of him. Only then did he realize he had lapsed into a silent chanting of the words, a chanting not of his vocal chords and lips but of his inner being, as when he was preparing himself for discernment. He kept chanting again and again and the feeling grew in intensity, reminding him of his experience that evening long ago and bringing tears to his eyes.

He looked at the book, and a thought crossed his mind: If the chant he had just spoken was *number 1*, what would *2* or *3* or *10* be like? Did the power of the Blessing grow with each successive incantation?

Eagerly he looked at the second *Sefirot* paragraph and started reciting:

TEN *SEFIROT* OF *BELIMAH*, TEN AND NOT NINE, TEN AND NOT ELEVEN, UNDERSTAND WITH WISDOM AND EXPLORE WITH UNDERSTANDING…

The sense of Blessing was not stronger. He skipped to the fourth *Sefirot* paragraph:

TEN *SEFIROT* OF *BELIMAH*, THEIR END IS LINKED TO THEIR BEGINNINGS AND THEIR BEGINNING TO THEIR ENDS, LIKE A FLAME CONNECTED TO A BURNING COAL...

The Blessing of the fourth paragraph was indistinguishable from the first two. "A ceiling effect," he murmured. "The Blessing will not rise above a certain level."

He stopped and felt the feeling slowly evaporate. Then he pondered. It had to be because of this Book that Eliezer and Oleander were meeting in secret. Were they just reveling in the experience? Unlikely. Were they experimenting with it? Or did they have a specific ambition in mind—perhaps to make up for the lost Blessing? No, the Blessing produced by the Book could make no difference to the state of the world. Was it possible the two Councilors were using it in a different, more powerful way, not just chanting it internally but rather... but rather what? Could they be discerning it? Could it be that they were descending to The Depths and actually discerning it at the Edge of the Void?

No. Discerning a text other than the Bible—that was unheard of.

There was a soft knock on the door, but Peprini ignored it. Why would the two Councilors need the Blessing offered by the Book?

Was it possible they, too, were attempting to become Vessels? That they might have the same goal alarmed Peprini; indeed, they might be ahead of him! *The two were going to snatch from the Peprinis the fruits of three generations of work and sacrifice.*

The telephone rang, then stopped, then started ringing again. Then an idea came: The Book of Creation, yes. Yes! Could the Blessing it summoned give him the power—the protection—to reach the Bible World? Could the Book's Blessing—*its shield of Blessing*—protect him from the Void just as it did the Vessels? Perhaps as long as he was reciting the incantations the Blessing would shield him—*perhaps*, he cautioned himself.

His thoughts were in a frenzy now. His impulse was to descend to the Depths immediately and test this theory. But his reason quickly held him back. What if the Blessing from the Book was insufficient protection against the Void? He couldn't afford to die in the Void. The entire Peprini legacy depended on him.

He forced himself to calm down and realized how distressed he had become. Obviously, he needed another Keeper to serve as a guinea pig, but who? The person didn't need special capacities; any novice would do.

But what if that person died in the attempt? It would have to be someone whose absence would not be questioned. After Maria's death and Pilar's disappearance, even he would have some difficulty explaining the loss of another.

He reached for the phone.

On the other side of the Atlantic Tiplady answered. "Councilor?"

"Eric, I have a new job for you. I want you in Lucerne at once."

There was a surprised silence on the other end. "What about following Councilors Oleander and Eliezer?"

"The others will manage without you."

"Did I do something wrong? I got you the Book of Creation, didn't I?"

Peprini replied in a reassuring voice, "I am promoting you, my boy."

Now he could sense Tiplady's relief. "Alright, sure, I'll be there."

"Call when you have a flight."

70

At seven-thirty, half an hour before their appointment with the Ishmaelite Prince, the three Keepers entered the goldsmith shop and found Kedar and an older man working. The other Ishmaelite, Kedar's uncle, Nader, asked them to wait in the café across the street.

They took a table. "*And these are the names of the sons of Ishmael,*" Eliezer absently quoted from Genesis, "*by their names, according to their birth: the firstborn of Ishmael—Nevayot, and Kedar, and Adbeel, and Dumah...*" Then he added, "Osnat, did your Kedar say anything about his ancestry?"

"Only that the Prince is his grandfather."

Oleander noticed that Osnat had taken unusual care in her appearance. Her dark gold hair had a brilliant sheen; her clothes while casual were nicer than anything he had previously seen her wear. Her make-up was understated but clearly calculated.

Eliezer turned to Oleander. "What does our historian know about Ishmaelite lineages?"

"Beyond the twelve Princes that rule them?" He shrugged.

"I thought Keepers knew everything about Abraham's descendants."

"Only those that counted."

"Counted?" Osnat asked.

"The Ishmaelites have always been regarded as outcasts—the children of Ishmael driven away into the desert. Keepers wanted nothing to do with them."

"But why?" Osnat protested. "He was Abraham's son. You'd think our ancestors would have regarded him as a cousin."

"He was the one *not chosen*. It was deemed that the bloodline would go through Isaac. Remember, this had been God's decision: God told Abraham to send away Ishmael."

"Still..." Osnat started but was interrupted by Oleander.

"Issa of Alexandria, a Keeper historian who lived shortly after the fall of Rome, said something like: *'For although it was out of jealousy that Sarah, Abraham's wife, drove Hagar and her son Ishmael out of their household, it was God who decreed this to happen. God used Sarah's jealousy as a blade to cut away the rotten fruit, to ensure that the Gift of Blessing would go to his half-brother, Isaac, and to his descendants forever after.'"*

"Harsh words," Eliezer remarked, "given that in all likelihood this historian had never met a single Ishmaelite face-to-face."

The waitress returned with a tray and set the cups and plates of blueberry muffins on the table.

"Eat and drink, children. I don't know how long this evening will last."

Osnat tore a piece from a muffin. "Wasn't there any contact between Keepers and Ishmaelites even in ancient times? Doesn't it say in Genesis that Esau married an Ishmaelite?"

"Certainly," Eliezer said. "*And Esau went to Ishmael and took for a wife Mahlat, the daughter of Ishmael the son of Abraham, the sister of Nevayot, adding her to his wives.* That was the only such intermarriage in the Bible."

"And in history as far as we know." Oleander drummed his fingers on the table. "And it should probably remain that way."

"There he is," Eliezer said, looking out the window. Kedar was crossing the street. He took a last sip, put two twenty dollar bills on the table and the three joined the Ishmaelite on the sidewalk.

"My grandfather will see you now," he announced, and he turned and started walking. They weren't going to the goldsmith shop. Instead, he led them northwest. They trailed silently behind him.

Soon the Keepers realized they were lost. Several more turns found them in a dilapidated pocket of Manhattan. Many of the streetlights were out and the shadows seemed particularly deep. The burned-out shell of a car, still giving off an odor of gasoline and burnt rubber, sat in front of a parking meter.

"The Prince doesn't exactly live in a palace," Oleander muttered.

A few minutes later Kedar stopped in front of a two-story, indistinct cement-block building. Above a door, a single light bulb encased in a metal cage gave an uneven, weak glow. A chain link fence surrounded the property, windblown trash trapped along the bottom. A three-foot swath was missing. They passed through. Kedar led them up some steps to an entrance. The paint on the door was peeling and the windows on either side were barred and the glass clouded in grime.

Kedar knocked, and the solid metal door gave a low thud. "You'll have to take off your shoes when we enter," he instructed them. Oleander looked at the filth and debris on the ground.

The door opened slightly and a man exchanged a few unintelligible words with Kedar and stepped aside.

They were now inside a small room lit by a single ceiling bulb, the walls and floor smooth concrete. Kedar slipped off his shoes and the others did the same. Oleander looked down at the floor and saw it was perfectly swept. A door leading to the interior of the building was closed in front of them. A tall man, wearing a gray suit and white shirt with no tie, inspected them.

He then opened a small side-door they hadn't noticed. Kedar stepped through and disappeared in the darkness. Eliezer and his two companions followed. This door too was heavy, reinforced steel, ringing as it closed behind them.

It was mostly dark. They could feel a soft rug under their feet.

"There's a staircase going down here, a railing's on the right," Kedar murmured.

Holding onto the railing they started down. A dim light came from far below. The staircase turned right and then right again and again. At last the stairs ended. They were standing in a narrow basement. Several paces in front of them was a curtained doorway.

They followed Kedar inside and a bright light assaulted their eyes. A moment later, when their vision adjusted, the three were dazed. In sharp contrast to the building's exterior and first floor, this underground hall, at least one-hundred feet long and sixty wide, was lavishly decorated. Everything was some shade of the desert dunes. The floor was covered with thick rugs of fantastic arabesques whose color accented the sand-white background. The floor melded seamlessly into the walls which were clothed with rich drapes and delicate golden ornaments. The walls were radiant, somehow appearing illuminated from behind. The ceiling, at least twenty feet high, was a pale yellow like the early morning light.

Three figures were at the far end of the room. They were sitting on a slight dais, their feet folded underneath them. Kedar motioned to the Keepers to step forward. Then he walked over to the three Ishmaelites and sat behind them.

Three large pillows were arranged on the floor, apparently for the guests, leaving them a distance from the dais. Eliezer took the center pillow, Oleander and Osnat at his sides. For several moments the two groups appraised each other.

The three Ishmaelite figures all wore embroidered robes the color of sand. On the right was a woman, slender and regal, perhaps fifty or sixty years old, her eyes dark and judgmental, her graying hair pulled into a short ponytail. To the left was a younger, bearded man, his dark hair short in military fashion. Both of them exuded an impressive air, but clearly the weightiest presence belonged to the man at the center. His face was broad, his long hair silver and wavy. But it was his eyes that captured an observer's attention. They were pale blue and unusually large. He seemed like an ancient rock in the midst of the dunes.

At last the bearded man said, "Welcome Keepers." Eliezer nodded and waited. He knew such meetings followed a certain protocol. This man appeared to be third-in-rank. "We wanted to speak with you, Councilor Eliezer and Councilor Oleander. We have a few things we wish to hear from you. And to tell you."

Eliezer did not like the implication they had been summoned by the Ishmaelites to answer their questions. "Then this is a happy coincidence," he said, "because we came here in order to ask you a few questions."

The bearded man frowned. Eliezer apparently had broken one of the Ishmaelite's rules of etiquette.

"Prince Nevayot, the Chief of Chiefs, the *Nassi* of North America, has agreed to see you." The Prince did not move. "Chief Bosmat," the man continued, gesturing to the older woman, "and I, Chief Dumah of the North American Clan, will be at his service today."

Everything pointed to a formal ceremony. Eliezer did not like this. It was possible the Prince would not even speak during this meeting.

Now Chief Bosmat spoke. "Councilor Eliezer... and Councilor Oleander," she added almost as an afterthought. "For seven weeks now you have been reading the Book of Creation and stirring up the world. What do you seek?"

Eliezer fought to control his expression. How did they know this? And how much exactly did they know? Had the vagabonds been reporting to the Ishmaelites?

"You have been following us, Chief Bosmat, and I wonder why," said Eliezer as matter-of-factly as he could.

She turned to Prince Nevayot, who remained still. She did not seem to know what Eliezer was talking about. "In what way have we been following you?"

"You have sent men and women to follow us in the streets. Here and in Jerusalem."

"We do not follow your people. We do not need to."

"*His hand is in everybody,*" Oleander said softly.

For the first time, Prince Nevayot reacted. He looked into Oleander's eyes and nodded.

"Several people have been following us," Eliezer said. "Vagabonds, like your forefather Ishmael of the desert."

"There are many people in the world," Bosmat said, "and many kinds of nomads." She now seemed uninterested.

"Nomads who shadow Keepers? Have you not you noticed them?"

"The Prince's grandson informed us of one who pursued the young lady. They are not Ishmaelites, Councilor."

"They are nauseating to the Keeper's spirit," Eliezer insisted. "They must be of some Biblical lineage."

"There are many lineages in the Bible, Councilor, most of them insignificant. I repeat: They are not Ishmaelites."

There was tense silence in the room. The two Chiefs appeared annoyed. The Prince remained impassive.

Something had been stirring in Osnat's mind, something she had forgotten until that moment: the seven-line drawing she had seen engraved on the vagabond's leg. It seemed important now, though she could not understand why. The need to speak caused her to fidget on the cushion. She tried to catch Eliezer's eyes but his gaze was fixed on the Prince.

"Now," said Bosmat, "as I said, you have been meddling with the Book..."

Osnat could no longer contain herself. *"Excuse me."*

Such an interruption by a mere novice was unheard of, especially in front of a Prince. Everyone looked at her. Even Kedar tilted his head from behind his grandfather to peer at her. Once more she shifted her position on the cushion. "I wanted to say," she swallowed hard, "the vagabonds have a sign... I saw it on the woman... a sort of tattoo. Seven parallel lines. Red lines."

The Ishmaelites were clearly shaken. Oleander turned to Osnat, reigning in his surprise and disapproval. The two Chiefs leaned towards the Prince and exchanged intense whispers.

Then the Prince turned to Osnat and said, "Tell us again what exactly you saw, young Osnat Aviv."

"Several days ago a woman vagabond had been following me for almost an hour in the streets. Then she cornered me in a restroom. I saw she had a dark sign on her ankle, about three inches long. It was a tattoo, or might have been engraved in her flesh. It was made of seven stripes, red stripes, parallel to each other."

Again the Ishmaelites conferred.

"The Sevenfold of the old prophecy?" Dumah whispered.

The Prince nodded solemnly.

The Prince signaled with his hand and the two Chiefs returned to their positions. He looked at the three Keepers. "You have brought us an important piece of information. You have seen the Sevenfold which the old books speak of. This is a grave omen. That is all I can tell you at the moment. But in return for that information, let me give you this advice: Beware of the Book of Creation. It is not meant for what you are doing. You have been tapping into the forces of the Curse."

The Prince's words stirred vague recollections in Oleander's mind. The Sevenfold… the forces of the Curse… *the Curse of the Sevenfold*—he had come across these terms somewhere…

Eliezer was disappointed, certain the Ishmaelites knew much more than they had revealed. Worse, Eliezer had intended to raise the topic of the Vessels' deaths, but the two Chiefs began to rise. Eliezer knew this was the last chance.

"Prince, may I have a private word with you?"

"If you believe this is necessary."

Eliezer moved closer to Nevayot. The two Chiefs disappeared through a hidden door. Oleander and Osnat followed Kedar upstairs.

Eliezer and the Prince observed each other more closely. They seemed to be of the same age and made of the same human material: an inner power hidden by layers of civility, an intensity and determination concealed by a capacity to smile and forgive human frailty, prudence and willingness to risk.

They felt as equals and could shed the mantle of formality.

Eliezer was the first to speak. "The Vessels have been dying recently, Prince Nevayot."

"Yes, Eliezer."

"We are very worried, Nevayot."

"Who can remain indifferent to this catastrophe?"

"Do you know the cause of this, Nevayot?"

The Prince made a slight gesture with his hand, indicating that he had no answer.

Eliezer persisted. "Are these deaths somehow connected to… to what Oleander and I have been doing with the Book?"

"Everything is connected to everything, Eliezer. Every grain of dust reverberates with the entire universe. This is the fundamental understanding of the Ishmaelites. This is how we can learn everything from everything—within the boundary of human limitations, of course. It was said of our forefather that *Yado va-kol, ve-yad kol bo*: *His hand is in everybody and everybody's hand is in him.*"

Eliezer bowed his head, acknowledging the Prince's generosity in speaking of such things.

"In the eyes of an Ishmaelite," continued the Prince, "each thing is just as significant as any other thing. You have seen my grandson selling gold in a store. Selling gold is not further from reality, nor closer to it, than selling hot dogs, and not less nor more significant than sitting in the Pentagon and moving battalions across the globe."

"Still, Nevayot, some things are more tightly connected. Some things reverberate with others more forcefully."

"That is true, Eliezer. As we both know, a handful of obscure men and women, those called Vessels, exert more influence on our world than all the presidents of the nations of the Earth put together."

"Do you think the... endeavor that Oleander and I have been carrying out is somehow connected to the death of the Vessels? And to the vagabonds?"

"That depends on what exactly you have been doing."

Eliezer lowered his eyes and deliberated.

"Will this matter remain strictly between the two of us, Prince?"

The Prince nodded.

"To open a new Gate to the Bible-World, Nevayot, this is our purpose. To replenish the dwindling Blessing, to make up for the loss of the Vessels."

The Prince closed his eyes and was still. "Your aim is lofty, Eliezer. The danger you take upon yourselves is appreciated. I am not capable of seeing everything; no human being can know more than a limited horizon." He opened his eyes. "But from what is revealed to me it appears that you cannot succeed. What you are trying to achieve cannot be done in this way.

"Remember, cousin," he continued, his voice now heavier, "in such matters failure means disaster. The greater the aspiration, the greater the risk and so the catastrophe."

"What kind of catastrophe?"

"When you open a gate, many things can come in. Not only what you have invited."

Eliezer felt anxiety rising in him. "What do you think we should do?" he whispered. "Abandon our endeavor?"

The Prince appeared suddenly older as if he had aged before Eliezer's eyes. "I wish I could tell you more," he said slowly, almost inaudibly. "I am trying to understand, but the signs in front of my eyes are as yet unclear."

For a moment longer the two men sat silently together. At last, they both rose to their feet.

"Come see me in a week, if you please," the Ishmaelite said. I may have more to tell you. And you," and he looked strangely into Eliezer's eyes, "may have more to tell me."

<h1 style="text-align:center">71</h1>

Outside, Oleander and Osnat waited under a streetlight for a taxi he had called. They stood apart, and Eliezer sensed the strain as he approached.

"Well?" the monk asked.

Eliezer recounted the conversation with the Prince. "And we have another appointment in one week."

Oleander turned to Osnat, having lost the struggle to suppress his anger. "And our *novice* here. Just when were you going to tell *us* about the vagabond's mark?"

She turned to Eliezer but saw that he too was displeased.

"You did make William and me appear foolish, Osnat," Eliezer agreed.

"*Foolish*? We looked like bumbling idiots, a novice knowing what we didn't and lacking the respect to tell us first."

"I'm sorry, really I am. So much has been happening the last few days. It didn't occur to me it might be important. Lots of people have tattoos."

"But in the middle of such an unprecedented meeting," Oleander grumbled sardonically, "it suddenly *did* occur to you the mark might be vitally important. It absolutely could not wait."

"Yes, it suddenly felt so important, I felt virtually compelled to say it."

"Another one of your intuitions?"

"Enough, William," the professor said quietly. "In any event, the Ishmaelites were quite impressed with her revelation, particularly the Prince, if I am any judge. This can only help us."

In the cab, Oleander was wracking his brain about "the Sevenfold" and "the Curse." There are many curses in the Bible. In Genesis alone several are mentioned: The serpent who tempted Adam and Eve was cursed, and so was Cain who killed his brother Abel. Noah's flood is described as a curse. Jacob and his mother Rebecca talk about the curse.

And the Sevenfold? He looked blankly out the cab window. Where had he encountered this term? Ah, yes. There was an unsigned entry in the

Council's minutes, shortly before the termination of Vessel Tsatsolnov in 1583. It was very brief: "The Sevenfold was seen again." It was peculiar that there was no elaboration or further mention.

His mind returned to the meeting. The Prince had said that the *Sevenfold* was from the ancient books. The Bible? "Sevenfold" appears a few times in the Bible and always in the same context: of revenge. In Genesis, the word occurs only in connection with Cain and Abel—the same Cain who was also cursed.

Yes, Cain is the meeting point between the curse and the Sevenfold! Cain, the son of Adam and Eve, described in the fourth chapter of Genesis, is cursed by God after he kills his brother Abel. The first murder of a human being. Oleander recalled God's words to Cain: *What have you done? The voice of your brother's blood cries unto me from the ground. And now cursed are you from the ground which has opened its mouth to receive your brother's blood from your hand... A fugitive and a wanderer you shall be on the Earth.*

As for his Sevenfold—that was God's antidote to the curse. When Cain complains to God that, being a cursed fugitive, *whoever finds me will slay me,* God agrees to lessen the force of the curse, saying: *Therefore, whoever kills Cain, vengeance shall be taken on him sevenfold.* And then God goes on to display Cain's protection for everyone to see: *And God marked a sign on Cain so that those finding him will not smite him.*

Was it Cain whom the Ishmaelites had in mind when they talked of the Curse and the Sevenfold?

Not very likely. Keeper tradition was controversial on the subject of Cain and Abel. The first eleven chapters of Genesis, those preceding the story of Abraham, were contentious. One very small faction still held to a literal interpretation of Genesis, including the creation of Earth about 5670 years ago. Under this view, an actual person, Cain, received the sevenfold mark. Another faction in Keeper tradition, one that over the centuries had become increasingly dominant with the growth of science, held that the first eleven chapters of Genesis are not real history. They are meaningful to be sure, symbolic, but not an account of actual historical events.

Oleander thought of the thousands of documents of the Keepers' records which he had been studying for the past twenty years. Cain was rarely mentioned. Ancient Keepers, superstitious as they were, were careful of speaking of the *Curse of Cain.* To speak of it seemed to invite it; Keepers of the old days were in that respect people of their time.

Sitting between the two men, Osnat was thinking of Kedar. As he had guided her out of the building he had placed his hand on the small of her back. She wondered whether he had felt her reaction.

Eliezer dozed, then would awaken, then doze again.

Entering the hotel lobby, Eliezer sighed. "They're fixed, thank God," he said, seeing the elevators.

"You two go ahead," Oleander said, looking preoccupied. "I'll take the stairs. I need some exercise."

Once inside their suite, Eliezer accessed his voicemail.

"Eli," Erna's message said, "Interesting news here. Peprini has convinced the Council that these vagrants we've encountered—you'll hear about them at the meeting—are dangerous to the Vessels. He is moving ahead to eliminate them. Try to arrive a little early so we can talk beforehand."

Eliezer sank into the armchair and waited for Oleander. What did "eliminate them" mean? Were these *vagrants* the same as the vagabonds he had seen?

Ten minutes passed, and then ten more.

"Seven floors may have been too much," joked Osnat.

"I will see what's happened to him."

He found Oleander sitting on the stairs between the second and third floors.

"William. Here you are." Eliezer's voice was undecided between irritation and concern.

Oleander raised his face. "Listen, Eliezer, I have it all now. The Curse of Cain, the Sevenfold vengeance—that's what the Ishmaelites were talking about. They are the Children of Cain!"

"Who are the Children of Cain?"

"The vagabonds. *They are Cainites.* That's why they carry on their body a seven-stripe sign. Osnat saw it on the woman's leg. I'm sure all the vagabonds have the same mark somewhere on their body. It's the Sevenfold sign—*whoever kills Cain, vengeance shall be taken on him sevenfold!*"

"Interesting," said Eliezer. He stooped over Oleander and clasped his shoulder. "Come, get up. We will talk about this upstairs."

"Eliezer, you're not listening. I've got proof. Already eight centuries ago, One-Eyed Isabel said in her diaries that..."

"Tell me as we go." The two started climbing the stairs, Eliezer in front.

"Isabel reported her people seeing five cases of 'the striped curse.' I always thought she was referring to some kind of plague. But a few days later she says she *'dreads the gates to Nod have been opened.'* She asks God for forgiveness if her own deeds had opened these gates. I've never made the connection between these two entries. But now it's clear."

"How so?"

"The striped curse—that's obviously Cain. Which brings us to Isabel's comment on the land of Nod."

"The land of Nod?" Eliezer stopped to rest, leaning on the handrail. "That is where Cain went after he was cursed. *And Cain went out from the presence of God and dwelt in the land of Nod.*"

"Right. But there is no such land."

"What do you mean?"

"Your Hebrew is better than mine. The word 'Nod' means wandering. Cain went to wander in wandering-land, which means nowhere in particular, or nowhere on Earth."

"Mmm," said Eliezer, saving his breath as he started climbing again. Increasingly he was feeling in his body the diminishment of the Blessing following Vessel Hadid's death.

"For some reason, Isabel dreaded that Cain—not one Cain but five—had returned from the Land of Nod. Five wandering Cainites, five vagabonds marked by Sevenfold stripes."

"I see," said Eliezer. "And Vessel Jason terminated during her lifetime."

"She wrote a long poem, an elegy really. At the end of the poem, she says: 'Seven is Cain's number.'"

"Well, this certainly constitutes promising evidence..."

"And I can show you a dozen other Keepers of the past who understood the connection between these vagabonds and the seven-stripe mark on Cain. It's revealed in letters and diaries, but always obliquely."

Eliezer had an inspiration. He still had to justify their delay in departing for Lucerne. No good could come from admitting they contacted Ishmaelites without the Council's permission. "William, can you present your case to the Council tomorrow?"

"Those are the sources I know from memory. I'm sure I'll find more."

"Excellent," Eliezer said. "I think we now have—you have provided—sufficient excuse for our tardiness from the Council meeting."

Some thirty steps later, already near the exit to the seventh floor, Eliezer stopped. Breathing heavily, he asked without turning around, "Does this new idea of yours have any practical implication? It would be nice if we could suggest to the Council a course of action."

"Well, obviously if the vagabonds are Cainites, and if the Cainites have the Sevenfold, then we must not harm them, or in any case not kill them. Because *whoever kills Cain, vengeance shall be taken on him sevenfold.*"

"Oh, no!"

Oleander quickly took hold of the old man. "I shouldn't have made you climb all these stairs."

"No, no. Erna has just left a message." He paused to breathe. "Peprini... the vagabonds... he is going to kill them!"

72

After Eliezer left Prince Nevayot, Chief Bosmat, and Chief Dumah returned to the room. The Prince sat in the same place they had left him. His eyes were closed now. They sat in front of him and waited. At last he opened his eyes. He nodded, indicating he wished now to hear from them.

"The Keepers have been trespassing against the Book of Creation, Prince," said Bosmat. There was resentment in her voice.

"Abraham gave it to Ishmael, to us."

Nevayot gave a faint smile. "Dumah, you know that the Book of Creation is Abraham's book, and so it belongs to *all* his descendants. Recall the very last passage of the Book: *And when Abraham our father, may he rest in peace, came… immediately the Lord of all… made a covenant with him and with his seed after him forever…* Neither Ishmael nor Isaac is mentioned."

"Still," insisted Bosmat, "Abraham gave it to Ishmael, and we have been using it since that time. Were it not for the robbery of our library, no Keeper would know of its existence."

She was referring to the Muslim conquest of Alexandria in the year 641 AD, in which invading soldiers discovered the secret Ishmaelite library. The soldiers did not understand the meaning of the small underground cache and burned it. But a number of books, including a copy of the Book of Creation, survived. Since it was written in Hebrew, it found its way to a Jewish book-dealer, and from there to Jewish esoteric circles which adopted it without understanding its real significance. Throughout the years it had gradually become known to wider circles of scholars and lately to the general public.

"You both know well that Ishmael and his descendants received the Book only as custodians. We are to guard it, as our sacred tradition says, until the children of Abraham are called to bring about a new beginning. Remember again, we are not the only children of Abraham."

"But who is to say the time has come, Prince? And how are we to know that these two *Keepers* are the ones ordained?"

"Dumah, our prophecies say that the signs will become known when the time comes. The first will be unprecedented global upheaval. That is why I wished to speak to these Keepers, and to Councilor Eliezer alone. I needed to learn whether they might be the ones about whom our prophecies speak."

"Maybe the time is coming," said Bosmat, "but I don't trust these Keepers. Councilor Eliezer is dangerous. I could sense it."

"Eliezer is very powerful," the Prince agreed. "Indeed. And he is dangerous for he does not understand what he is doing with the Book."

"And the monk Oleander?"

"He, Bosmat, may be one of the few innocent souls I have encountered. But purity of intention is no protection against the dangers of the Book."

The two Chiefs carefully reflected on the Prince's words. Like all Ishmaelites, they were Knowers, having the capacity to see beyond the horizon of sensible experience, beyond what the ordinary person could know. Yet, some Ishmaelites could see still further. Their rank of Chief indicated that their knowing capacity was much greater than that of the common Ishmaelite. But the Prince's capacity was far greater, and in their reverent minds had virtually no bounds.

"However," the Prince added, amused, "you two failed to notice Miss Aviv."

"How can they tolerate such insolence from a novice?"

The Prince smiled at Dumah. "She has not only the blood of Esau in her veins but also another kind of ancient gift, maybe even the blood of Ishmael. She is a crossbreed."

"A Keeper and an Ismaelite? Is that possible?"

"It is held, yes, that the different gifts cancel each other. But who knows? It was Osnat Aviv I was most interested in seeing tonight."

The special gift of the Ishmaelites was knowing, and they received it through what they called "gifts of knowledge." These were fragments of information which would spontaneously surface in their minds. A particularly strong Ishmaelite could receive several such gifts of knowledge every week, often about events that happened or were happening far away, sometimes about the intentions or feelings of a certain individual, and sometimes even about future events. Some knowledge was pertinent to their interests, some irrelevant, but the Ishmaelites revered all as gifts sent by the Blessing.

Gifts of knowledge usually came uninvited; though when Ishmaelites needed specific information they had a method: contemplation on a question. The Ishmaelite would empty himself (or herself) of thoughts and emotions, allowing self-consciousness to disintegrate. If he was skilled and powerful, then the Blessing would take over and speak through him. This was an arduous task requiring much training and experience.

Prince Nevayot spent the next morning in his contemplation room. Bosmat sat next to him, serving as his attendant. Her task was to read aloud the contemplation-questions he had prepared in advance and to write down the responses he would utter.

Bosmat was sixty-two years old. Forty years ago the Prince had given her the first lessons of the secret learning, and twenty years later it was he, already an old Prince, who had awarded her the rank of Chief. She could not imagine life without him overseeing the Ishmaelite world. She had never married, despite pressures, because she was completely devoted to him.

She reached for the sheet of paper and looked at it. The Prince had written three questions. Formulating a question for contemplation was a delicate art, since the answers were so often ambivalent and illusive, particularly in deeper levels of contemplation. The Blessing was known to speak in riddles.

For this reason, straightforward questions were of no help. Every contemplator knew the story of the fifteenth century Prince of Asia who, in response to the question "What will happen here tomorrow?" revealed solemnly "It will be Tuesday." Prince Nevayot knew how to formulate effective questions. Some Ishmaelites joked that he could confound the Blessing and force it to divulge its secrets.

"Are you ready?" the Prince asked.

"Let the Blessing speak," was the traditional response she knew so well.

His eyes glazed.

To an outside observer, Nevayot's session with Bosmat was surprisingly quiet, with none of the shaking or spasms, none of the ecstatic screams found in pagan oracle rites. Ishmaelites abhorred unchecked emotion. Originally they had been desert dwellers, and although they had left the desert some two thousand years ago to spread across the world, they were still inspired by the racial memory of the desert, this vast ocean of silence.

Some half an hour later, when the Prince was deep in his contemplation, Bosmat lowered her eyes to the page and read the first question, slowly pronouncing each word:

"What in the history of time is the link that connects the Vessels to their pursuers?"

Immediately the Prince voiced something but it was incomprehensible. Bosmat listened attentively, a pencil in her hand. Several clearer words followed.

"Keepers," "The Void of the Book," "Downwards," "The Children of Cain…"

Then a complete pronouncement issued from the Prince's lips: "Once again the lost children of Cain have found half a path to the Earth from the Void, attracted to the blessed like a moth to candle-light, snuffing out their lights one by one, until the great darkness falls on everything." He paused. Bosmat waited. "Or until the coming of a new light."

Bosmat's pencil moved rapidly across the page. This was an unusually long proclamation. But there was no time to think about its meaning. She looked again at the page and slowly read the second question:

"Who listens to the Keepers' recitation of the Book of Creation?"

The Prince's lips moved without sound. Then "Keeper… voyage… below…"

He was still. Bosmat looked at him with concern. Was he alright? His chest was still moving, if slightly. A few minutes passed. It seemed to her as though the old man's soul was traveling across great distances.

He spoke out loud: "Again Keepers are reaching out to the gates of the Bible-World, but falling short, they open the gates of Nod."

Quickly Bosmat recorded the words. Then she read the third question:

"What are the Keepers secretly whispering to the Great Void?"

The Prince did not react. After several minutes she put down her pencil. So that's it, she thought, the session has ended.

But now he spoke in a whisper: "One Keeper has set out to cross the Void, two Keepers to pave a new path through it, and the future is in many hands."

Immediately his body sagged. His contemplative state was now dispersing. Bosmat jotted down the sentence and then turned to watch him with a tense and loving expression. Finally, he opened his eyes and looked around as if waking from a deep slumber. His eyes met hers. He reached for the page and read it. His face grew solemn, and he shook his head in apparent vexation.

He was exhausted. Bosmat put her hands on his shoulders and gently made him lie down. She put a pillow under his head and placed her hand over his eyes, closing his eyelids.

Later that day Prince Nevayot sent Chief Dumah as an emissary to his cousin and most trusted friend, Prince Massa of Bulgaria, the Ishmaelite Prince of Eastern Europe. Dumah was to inform Prince Massa about the three Keepers' endeavor with the Book of Creation—without mentioning their purpose of opening a new gate, as he had promised Eliezer—and to ask him to contemplate on the matter.

Chief Dumah was expected to arrive in Bulgaria in two days, and Prince Massa would not learn of the news for at least forty-eight hours. Nevayot was not bothered by delays. Everything happens precisely when it happens, was the ancient Ishmaelite saying. He distrusted telephones and e-mail and used them only for trivial matters.

73

Peprini was delighted to hear Tiplady calling from the Zurich airport so early in the morning. The Council meeting was scheduled for one o'clock that afternoon, and the boy's early arrival gave him enough time to start his new experiment before the meeting. He was impatient to test his new approach with the Book of Creation and had been doing nothing but examining the book's enigmatic text, pacing his office from end to end, planning the details of the test.

It was ten in the morning when Peprini brought Tiplady to his cottage in the country. He went straight to the point and explained to Tiplady what he wanted him to do.

"Isn't this dangerous?" the Australian asked with obvious trepidation. "I've heard the stories. I don't want to die down there, or lose my damn mind."

They sat side by side in discernment armchairs, Tiplady in the one formerly occupied by Pilar and Maria. The printed pages of the Book of Creation lay on the table in front of them. Peprini knew that he had to maintain his patience if he wanted the young man's cooperation.

"Why should there be any danger, Eric?" he said with as much warmth and assurance as he could.

"Everybody told me to stay away from the Void. It can kill you, right?"

"If you have no protection." Peprini threw his eyes upward in a glance. "Outer space, too, can be lethal, but if you wear a protective suit then it's a grand adventure, the experience of a lifetime."

"And what'll be my spacesuit?"

"The reciting of the Book of Creation, Eric, just as I explained."

"I'm not very good at discerning, Sir. In fact, I was terrible at the Novitiate."

"I said reciting, not discerning. All you need to do is keep reciting the passage you have memorized. The Blessing will surround you, and when the Blessing envelopes you like that, nothing can possibly harm you. You'll float in the Void just like an astronaut. After a few minutes I will

give you a sign, and you will float back to me, to the edge of the Void—
and that's it. Just a couple of minutes, there's nothing to worry about."

"Have you done it?"

"Of course I have, Eric," he lied. "I am considering implementing this
as part of the novice training. Discernment can indeed be dangerous, as
you were rightly told, and there have been serious accidents. In teaching
the recitation of the Book of Creation we will be providing Keepers a safety
measure, should they accidentally slip into the Void during their
discernments."

"Is this what the two Councilors were doing with it? Anyway, I'm not
very good at floating in the Depths, that's what Berg keeps telling me.
Even you, Councilor, told me I barely survived the Verification Exam,
right? I don't have much talent for this. Maybe I'm not the guy you want."

Tiplady reached across the table and pushed the pages a few inches
away.

The Councilor now understood. The boy realized that Peprini needed
him and was being contrary simply because he could. Despite the impulse
to put the boy in his place, Peprini chose the quickest route to the
morning's goal.

"You still haven't asked me about your promotion."

"What is it?"

"You will be my assistant."

"At the old convent?" It was obvious the boy didn't relish bucolic
Lucerne.

"You will undertake a variety of special tasks for me that exploit your
unique talents. All over the world. Aside from me, you will report to no
one."

This brought the expected zeal to his eyes.

"Let's do a quick demonstration, *without* descending to the Void. I
want you to experience the protective cocoon of the Blessing. I think you
will then have no doubts."

He placed the book's pages on a music stand in front of the young man.
"Look at this passage you've already memorized. Calm yourself. Calm
down, breathe just as they've taught you. Focus your mind—don't worry,
we are not descending to The Depths, just sitting in this room. Now, start
reciting in your mind this passage here: 'Ten *Sefirot* of *Belimah*, twenty-two
fundamental letters'... go ahead, recite... not so loud, just whisper it...
good... now start from beginning again... good... keep going..."

Peprini wondered whether Tiplady would feel sufficient Blessing to be
convinced to enter the Void, or whether he would feel anything at all. The
boy was a remarkably untalented Keeper. His aura was dismal, and what
was worse, it had hardly developed since his first day at the Novitiate.

Nevertheless, after some five minutes of continuous recitation, Peprini was relieved to see his aura responding if weakly, and that his face revealed obvious pleasure and surprise.

Peprini let him enjoy the experience a little longer and then placed his hand on the boy's shoulder. He couldn't afford to tire him. "Eric, that would be enough for now. Good. Well, you have just experienced a taste of the Blessing. What do you say?"

"That was amazing! Better than any drug, better than sex."

"You are one of a special few, Eric, who have had the privilege of meeting the Blessing in this manner."

"Are these other incantations more powerful?" He reached for the pages and turned to the higher-numbered passages.

"Not now. But if you descend with me and do as I told you, then you will feel it again. In fact," Peprini added a lie that had just occurred to him, "in the Void your experience will be magnified."

"Really?"

"Oh, yes. What you've experienced was nothing compared to what you will feel in the Void.

Half an hour later Peprini and Tiplady were both at the edge of the Void. The Councilor was dismayed when he realized how awkwardly the boy moved in the Depths. He was like a child who has just learned to walk.

Tiplady started reciting the passage from memory. At length, his aura started glowing. When it reached a steady, amplified state, Peprini signaled to enter the Void.

Peprini held his breath, scarcely able to bear the suspense. Would the Blessing protect the boy? Now was the crucial moment that would determine whether his family's mission would succeed or fail.

Apprehensively Tiplady moved into the Void. Nothing happened. Peprini sighed in relief. Encouraged, the boy continued. He was now hovering in the Void, his face bright with joy. Peprini's skin tingled in anticipation of success. The boy turned one way then another, clumsily zigzagging his way farther into the Void. He had enough awareness to turn once and look towards Peprini.

"Just keep reciting," Peprini urged silently. "Do not stop reciting."

He raised his arm and motioned to Tiplady to return. Surges of the Blessing were exhausting to the inexperienced.

Tiplady, a rapturous smile on his face, nodded. He tried to turn but his body disobeyed him. He started sliding sideways as if skidding on ice. His arms flailed, searching for something to hold on to.

For a moment his face turned towards Peprini and their eyes met. Even from that distance it was clear that something was horribly wrong. The instant Tiplady had stopped reciting the terror of the Void flooded his entire being and his petrified mind could no longer recall the words. In moments he could no longer be seen.

When Peprini opened his eyes, he turned to the lifeless body slumped in the chair. The boy had done his job. Peprini now knew that the invocations in the Book undeniably offered protection in the Void—for how long, that was still unknown. It had been Tiplady's own weakness and lack of discipline, he said to himself, which had killed him.

He put the pages in his briefcase. Then he took his phone and punched in the number for the convent's watchman.

"Tennier. I need you. The country house." He looked at Tiplady once more, recalling the boy had no family, none that would miss him. He truly had been a lost soul. "There is a body downstairs. An unfortunate discernment accident. Make it disappear. And make certain it cannot be identified. Do it now."

74

The Council was to meet at one o'clock, but learning that Eliezer and Oleander would not arrive until later in the afternoon, Julia Erna rescheduled it for six. Once again she tried Eliezer's cellular phone, then Oleander's, with no luck.

It was already five-thirty and she was fuming. Never had she been so angry with Eliezer. Since the last Council meeting she had suspected that he and Oleander were hiding something. Now this was confirmed. She was hurt and insulted. It was bad enough to have Peprini and Sionn conniving without worrying what her friends were plotting.

Peprini. He didn't hide his arrogance and let the fact he was a third-generation Councilor speak for itself. Except for Sionn, himself a second-generation Councilor, Peprini saw the rest of the Council as foot soldiers risen from the ranks. He tolerates us in the best of times, she knew, just as it rankled him each Council member had an equal vote. She grinned at her naïveté. Of course, he would not bow to the democracy of the Council, of course he would go behind her back. Why was she surprised? And what could he be hiding?

Already eight Councilors were in the Abbey. Margaret Connor had set out from Ireland almost three days earlier, intending to arrive well early, but experienced a series of aviation problems. After wandering for forty hours between six airports across Europe, her flight from Budapest landed safely in Zurich, and she had arrived at the Abbey late the previous night.

Rudolf Antioch had decided that the automobile was the least unreliable means of transportation. He left Prague with his assistant driving but encountered a collapsed bridge and three massive traffic jams due to multi-car accidents. They had arrived at the Abbey early that morning.

Sandrine Krystofski's flight from Australia to Switzerland had been delayed due to a minor fire in the Sidney airport's main tower.

Theresa Fournier had made it from her convent in Colombia, South America, without a single delay.

The four Councilors in Lucerne—Menach Peprini, Albrecht Sionn, Annette Goldman, and Julia Erna—had been at the Abbey since the early morning.

At six o'clock the eight Councilors were seated. Conspicuous were two empty chairs.

"Welcome Councilors," Erna opened the meeting. "I've been assured that Eliezer and Oleander are making every effort. But with this constant barrage of mishaps, some delays are unavoidable."

"Thank you, Julia." The weight of leadership rested firmly at Peprini's end of the table. "Though I cannot imagine what could justify their decisions. First, they cancel their earlier flight. It would seem something they are doing is more important than our meeting. I am informed they took last night's two AM flight from Kennedy. Very optimistic planning, even irresponsible, considering the state of the world. Two Vessel deaths, the appearance of the vagrants, and these two feel their time is better spent in New York? Disappointing. William, still quite young, held much promise."

"He still does," Erna said.

"Your Eliezer was on the Council with my grandfather. Such a long time ago. Perhaps too long."

"*I* was on the Council with Alberto as well. As was Rudolf."

Peprini turned to the frail old man who did not seem to realize his name had been spoken and sighed. "Indeed you were."

She was furious at having to defend them empty-handedly. "Alright," she acquiesced. "Let us start."

"Some of us have not been appropriately informed about the results of our investigation."

"By all means, Menach, proceed."

Peprini and Sionn presented to the other members the existence of the vagrants and gave the evidence that their appearance was very likely, if mysteriously, connected to the deaths of the two Vessels.

"And now," Peprini declared, "some new information about the vagrants. In the past ten days we have identified five more: two near Vessel Lessing's home in Scotland, two near Vessel Wyatt's office in New York, and one trailing Vessel Lenoma outside Addis Ababa. Four have been discreetly transported to remote locations—we have tried to avoid killing them in order not to attract the attention of the public and the local police. One, however, was eliminated when he approached Vessel Lenoma as she was playing in a park. This has led to an interesting discovery…"

"How exactly did that *elimination* happen?" Theresa Fournier interrupted.

"I don't have all the details."

"Why not?"

"When the men drove away with the body they slid off the road and the vehicle overturned. All three were killed. Luckily two others drove behind them, but they had not witnessed the shooting."

There was a moment of astonished silence. Throughout history, even minor accidents had been extremely rare in the lives of Keepers.

"Who were these three?" Theresa asked.

"Sam Chan, Pavel Slotsky, and Marvin Smart." The names made little impression since the three had been removed from the Novitiate years ago, very early in the program, before any Councilor could come to know them.

"What is curious," Sionn said slowly, "is that just like the other one killed in Scotland, our Ethiopian once led a respectable life. A wife, two children, a prosperous travel agency."

"Annette, if you would?"

Annette Goldman appeared as though she hadn't slept; her crisp white blouse and blue skirt contrasted with her haggard face. She had been searching all night for information about the dead man in various databases.

"Most of the information," she said, "is unexciting: his birth certificate—he was thirty-five years old, marriage certificate, credit card information, and so on. But two weeks ago he was admitted to a hospital after collapsing at work. The diagnosis was unclear; perhaps an epileptic seizure. He recovered, was sent home, collapsed again two days later, and sent back home again. He had a doctor's appointment scheduled for six days ago but he never appeared. According to the police report, his smashed car was found near his home in a suburb outside the capital. Most likely he had another seizure while driving."

"And the body—missing?" Erna asked.

"Exactly."

"The same pattern as the vagrant from Scotland," Peprini declared. "A normal person collapses, and while he is unconscious—or even at the point of death—his body disappears, and he is later found as a vagrant."

"If we were in the Middle Ages," Margaret Connor remarked, "I would have said the bodies of these two men were taken over by demons."

"You said several had been captured."

"Four, and to answer your next question, Theresa, no, they have not spoken, but they are not resisting the questioning. They are quite unaware of their own condition. Other than the unique foulness about them, and the markings…" He shrugged. "We are still attempting to identify them."

"Which brings us back," Connor remarked, "to the idea of some demonic form of life inhabiting unconscious bodies."

The door opened.

"Whose body?" Eliezer, his face tense, draped his coat over a chair. He surveyed the room, immediately sensing a lack of welcome, and took his seat at the table. A moment later Oleander entered.

"We apologize," Eliezer said. "Security delays in New York and then weather." Oleander took the chair next to his mentor.

Neither Peprini nor Sionn was going to answer Eliezer's question. Erna saw the other members took their cue from them. Ten seconds passed in silence.

"William, Eliezer, it's good to have you back. I'm sure…"

"Yes, Julia, we'll hear of that," Peprini said. "But later, I suggest."

"Our apologies, again. The delay could not be helped."

"Unavoidable, was it?" He stared at Eliezer. "Was canceling your earlier reservations unavoidable as well?"

All eyes turned to the two latecomers.

"What identification were you talking about?" Oleander asked.

Peprini sighed and looked to Sionn.

"I don't know how much you know of recent events. I'll summarize briefly. It's now our conclusion that the deaths of the two Vessels were not accidental."

"I thought we knew from the start that Alifa Hadid was murdered."

Now Sionn sighed. Eliezer and Oleander could feel the impatience from the others. Eliezer turned to Erna who glared back in silence. "Yes, but under extraordinary circumstances. The lives of those two Vessels were… poisoned… by the presence of these people we've called, for lack of a better word, vagrants. These vagrants have also been haunting the lives of the remaining three Vessels. We've concluded the vagrants had something to do with the Vessels' deaths. We are unable to explain just how, but we cannot risk another Vessel."

"And you're *murdering* them?" William said.

"Gentlemen, this is tedious. In your absence, I have already explained that we kill only when necessary."

Oleander stood and began pacing. The news of the killing had stunned Eliezer, too, but he hid this while deliberating how much to say. He had convinced Oleander to say nothing of the Ishmaelites. If other Keepers were to meet with the Ishmaelites, it might come out that he and William had been experimenting with the Book of Creation, and that must not happen. He watched his protégé gather his thoughts, concerned he might inadvertently reveal more than he should.

"William?" Sionn asked. Erna was a stone, and Eliezer knew she would not risk herself to help them again in this meeting.

Oleander stopped and looked at Sionn. "Did these vagabonds ever attack a Vessel?"

"We don't have the time to debate morality," Peprini answered.

"I am not talking about right and wrong, Menach. My point is this: If they are killing the Vessels, they are not doing it in any manner we can grasp. But if so, then have you given consideration to the consequences of interfering with such supernatural powers and killing such beings?"

None had, and the silence around the table was their admission. Oleander looked at Eliezer who gave a small nod.

"Five weeks ago, right after the death of Gregor, Eliezer became aware of a vagabond following him. The man looked like a vagabond, or your vagrant, and wouldn't have been noticed except for the nausea that Eliezer felt in his presence. A few days I, too, found myself followed by a similar vagabond, a woman," Oleander blushed slightly with the lie, "not far from the Metropolitan Museum in New York. Eliezer's vagabond hadn't reappeared, so we both met in New York in the hope of learning more about these creatures.

"Then I remembered something from the Chronicles, and I asked you, Annette, for copies of documents from the Archives. It was about the death of the Vessel Tsatsolnov. In 1583 he left Latvia to be closer to Pope Gregory XIII and stayed in a Benedictine monastery near Rome. During one of his walks on the Abbey's lands, while stopping to bathe in a river, he drowned. One of the Keepers assigned to him, Asti, the Abbot of the monastery, witnessed the accident." He paused. "Forgive me for recounting what we all know, but perhaps there are details some of us have forgotten."

"Go on, William," Theresa Fournier said.

"Asti stated that a wagon carrying pilgrims was stopped by the river where Vessel Tsatsolnov drowned. He noted that one of the pilgrims was 'a filthy brute, more corpse than living being, who made me exceedingly ill, though none else around me.' I now believe that Asti's reaction was the same as the nausea Eliezer and I felt in the vagabonds' presence. And something more. Asti mentions: 'I noticed a strange mark on the leg of the vagabond who pursued me: a seven-stripe mark.'"

"This is all very interesting," interrupted Peprini, "but we have already noticed the mark on our dead vagrants. William, it seems clear you have been doing your own private investigation in New York, without bothering to inform the Security Office and coordinate these efforts with the Council. Further, how does this explain why Eliezer has hidden from us this new novice of his, the Israeli girl, and why she has accompanied Eliezer to New York?"

The skirmish line was clear: Peprini and Sionn on one side and Eliezer and Oleander on the other. The others realized much had been happening behind their backs. Individually they all came to the same attitude: let the two sides fight and see what truth rose with the smoke.

"Osnat is a student of mine," Eliezer replied. "She…"

"Of yours?"

"Yes, Menach, at the Hebrew University. Several weeks ago I noticed her special aura. I tested her, and I discovered she had an extraordinary ability as a Keeper, to my knowledge unprecedented."

"Then she should be brought immediately to the Novitiate to begin formal training." This was a command and a challenge.

"Personal training is hardly a novelty. You yourself were not trained at Frostburg."

"Without permission from the Council? Without informing any of us?" Peprini looked around at his fellow Councilors. "This New York business reeks of secrets."

Eliezer looked to Erna but she remained still.

Oleander stepped in. "Hold on, Menach. You are not listening to the main thing."

"The main thing, William?"

"The vagabonds, the seven-stripe sign—don't you see?"

"Continue, William," Erna said forcefully.

"Yes," Fournier agreed. "Tell us what you found."

"Asti reported that when the filthy pilgrim sat down, his robe was pushed above his knee, exposing his leg. Asti then writes: 'The brute had the seven *strica* below his knee.' *Strica* means streak or stripe in medieval French. Note that he didn't say 'had seven *strica*.' He said 'the brute had *the* seven *strica*.' Obviously, this particular marking had significance to him."

"What you are telling us," Connor said, "is that the seven-stripe mark is not a coincidence, but…?"

"Yes, and there is more. The next day Asti ordered all pilgrims off Abbey lands. Remember, he was denying them the sanctity of the monastery. This was a big deal. You didn't turn away pilgrims without very good cause, especially as they were the main income source for the monastery. Asti justifies this by writing: 'The cursed must be away. Our Father condemned him and his in the beginning, and we are not of them.' Now, what did 'Our Father condemned him and his in the beginning' mean? And 'we are not of them'?"

"He thought they were heathens, perhaps," Krystofski suggested.

"Or demons," Connor added.

Oleander shook his head. "Did our Father condemn heathens or demons in the beginning?"

There was silence.

"Who was cursed in the beginning of the Bible? Cain, of course, for killing Abel. Cain is cursed and is sentenced to wander as a fugitive. According to the main genealogy in Genesis, all humans descend only from Adam and Eve's third son, Seth. Cain has many children but the Bible is clear that his line leads nowhere. That is why 'we are not of them.' What does Cain say when God condemns him to wander as an outcast? *'Whoever finds me will slay me.'* Of course, exile in those days was tantamount to a death sentence. God says to Cain, *'Not so! If anyone slays Cain, vengeance shall be taken on him sevenfold.'* And God puts a mark on Cain so those he encounters in Nod—the otherworld, or the place of wandering—won't kill him. "

"The sevenfold curse," Margaret spoke to herself.

"Sevenfold, seven *strica* or streaks." Theresa Fournier looked at Margaret. "So that would make our vagabonds... "

"Cainites," Oleander said. "And once this realization dawned on me, I could find others who had come to the same conclusion. Seven-hundred years ago One-Eyed Isabel writes: 'By now our people have noted five cases of the striped curse.' There is also..."

"The striped curse!" Rudolf Antioch cried as if fearful it was nearby. It was the first time the old man had spoken, and the others turned as if reminded he was in the room. And it was as though another man had taken his place, not the same one they had known all their Keeper lives. He looked and sounded every day of his 138 years. His head and hands trembled, his eyes were milky and appeared unable to focus. With some difficulty he removed a handkerchief from his pocket and dabbed at his eyes. "The curse, the curse," he said, attempting to shake his head as he trembled.

Peprini lifted the phone and gave a command. He then turned to Oleander. "William, if you would wait just a minute, please."

Seconds later the door opened and Rudolf Antioch's assistant, a large Russian, entered the room. He took the old man by the arm and gently helped him stand, Antioch still clutching the white handkerchief. The remaining nine Councilors watched them leave the room.

"I don't believe Rudolf will be joining us again," Peprini said.

"William, you were saying?" Fournier said impatiently.

"Isabel reports seeing several people with the seven-stripe curse. And a few days later, Vessel Jason of Padua terminated. In her private journal she writes: 'Have the doors to the Land of Nod been opened? This suspicion must remain mine alone until it is known to be true.' Stephan-Magus of Cypress, the 10th century Councilman, says in one of his metaphysical poems: 'Seven is the number of Nod's people and of the

Vessels who remain.' I could give you a dozen such quotations from eminent Keepers. They were all thinking of the Cainites."

The others grimly considered this. Peprini grinned.

"What you are telling us," he mused, "is that a myth about Cainites has been circulating in Keeperdom. A myth, one among how many hundreds in Keeper lore. And you are asking us to accept that our vagrants are children of Cain. Tell us, where have these Cainites been hiding all these centuries? With the witches and trolls and vampires? Or perhaps at the bottom of Loch Ness?" There was venom in his words.

"Menach, right now I'm looking at it practically. 'Cain's Curse' is probably the name of the power through which these vagabonds killed our Vessels. And we can't afford petulantly to dismiss the possibility that if we attack this power, it may strike back."

"Those three Keepers just killed in Ethiopia, and the one killed earlier in England," Annette Goldman said, "could their death be the seven-fold revenge for killing the vagrants?"

"Four is not seven," Peprini objected

"Perhaps the fallout has not concluded," offered Krystofski.

"Sevenfold is not a mathematical term," the monk replied. "In Biblical language it simply means 'many.'"

"Alright," Erna said. "We all are a bit stunned, but we have to make a decision how to proceed. William has suggested that no more vagrants be killed. Are we all in agreement about his?"

No one dissented. Peprini looked at Sionn and nodded.

Erna collected the papers in front of her. "Well, I believe that we have much to mull over. Let's adjourn for the day."

The others started to rise from their chairs.

"One moment," Peprini commanded. "I wish to return to the issue of the Israeli girl, Osnat Aviv. If she possesses the abilities described by Eliezer, then she must be in Lucerne."

"Really, Menach, we have more important issues now," Sandrine Krystofski said as she closed her briefcase. "If they want to train her, let them train her."

Erna looked around the room and saw, as Peprini did, that Eliezer had won.

Later that night Erna and Eliezer sat next to each other on the third-floor balcony of the Abbey. The light wind was cold and they huddled in their coats. They silently watched the cloud-like motion of the Blessing in the sky.

Erna inhaled, then spoke softly. "Eli, you are hiding something from me."

The statement hung in the air for a while. Then Eliezer nodded. "I truly believe this is best for the time being. But, Julia, you are hiding something as well."

"I am?"

"I sense that something worries you, something you can't share with me." He did not mention the conspiratorial glances he had seen her exchange with Annette Goldman.

Erna searched for his hand in the dark, then squeezed it affectionately. "Let's not talk about this tonight."

75

Alone in New York, Osnat divided her time between discernment exercises, reading the history of the Keepers, and taking walks. Twice she stopped by Kedar's jewelry store. The first time his quiet smile greeted her, and they walked around the block and chatted. The second time Kedar met her with a serious look.

"My grandfather has new information the Keepers will wish to hear. Tomorrow night at eight at the same place. I'll meet you at the entrance." He handed her a slip of paper with an address scribbled on it.

"They are still out of town."

"After tomorrow my grandfather says the Ishmaelites might not be in New York."

She saw that he was unwilling or unable to explain. She had not heard from Eliezer and Oleander since they left for Switzerland, but something inside her knew that they would be back very soon.

"They will be there, Kedar."

"Good. And you also. The Prince wants to see you too."

Osnat called Eliezer and Oleander but there was no answer. She called again and again, but could not get a connection. The next day she kept trying, and by mid-afternoon she started wondering whether she should go to the meeting with the Ishmaelites without them. Then something stirred in her awareness—the beginning of a revelation of knowledge. Moments later she relaxed. She walked out of the hotel to the street and found a taxi.

When Eliezer and Oleander exited the concourse at JFK they found Osnat waiting.

"How did you know we'd be here?" Oleander asked, her lovely face causing him to smile.

"I guess I just had one of my special intuitions," she said with some sarcasm.

On the way to their hotel, Osnat told them about her meeting with Kedar and about the Prince's request. "He said the Prince also wants to see me."

"Kedar appears to have quite a crush on you," Oleander remarked wryly. "Or is it the Prince who has his eye on you?"

"Cut it out, Oleander."

Eliezer waved his hand to silence them. "You and Kedar do cross paths quite a lot," he mused. "Are you sure he is not following you?"

"Or the other way around?" Oleander murmured.

Osnat ignored him. "He said it's our last chance. Tomorrow there may be no Ishmaelite left in town."

Later, when they were alone, Eliezer put his hand on his friend's shoulder. "William, you've got to make up your mind: Are you a monk devoted to God, or an available bachelor in competition for the girl? No use beating around the bush."

Kedar met the three Keepers outside the run-down Harlem building and took them downstairs to the Desert Hall, as it was called. Prince Nevayot, sitting serenely on the dais at the far end of the room, greeted them with a slight nod. Chief Bosmat was at his side.

After the mutual greetings, the Prince looked at Osnat. She felt as if his eyes were boring into her soul, but to her surprise, very tenderly. She relaxed somewhat.

"Prince Nevayot, these vagabonds are Cainites, I presume."

"Of course, Councilor Eliezer. But you do not know *why* they have come."

The Keepers waited for him to continue. Eliezer saw that the Ishmaelite would not continue without acknowledgment of this gift.

"That is true, we have no idea. Please tell us why."

"Because you are letting them in."

"We? How?"

"By using the Book of Creation."

"We are listening. Explain your words, please."

"Esau's descendants have a crucial mission on Earth: To discern the Gates of Abraham, to illuminate the twelve gateways through which the Blessing can flow to the Earth. By discerning, they have been illuminating the path to the Bible-World for their cousins, the Vessels, the children of Isaac. For four thousand years, Keepers have been faithful to their mission so that Vessels might travel in their visions to the Gates and bring back the Blessing to replenish the Earth."

"Of course, yes."

"Even in times of plague, of war, of persecution, Keepers have clung to their task, never sparing their own lives. And then four millennia later, two clever Keepers have decided differently. In their arrogance, they decided the twelve Gates of Abraham were no longer sufficient. They wished to open another gate, the Primordial Gate of the Bible. But this most ancient Blessing was intended to be closed."

"Intended to be closed?"

"As you very well know, the Blessing of Abraham replaced all previous Blessings."

"We did it for a good reason," said Eliezer.

"I understand, Councilman Eliezer. More gates, more Blessing. Especially in dire times like ours."

"Exactly."

"A lofty idea. The only trouble was that you did not open the Primordial Gate—that is impossible. God closed it for all eternity. Instead, you opened a different gate—the New Gate—which was destined to remain unopened, according to our old prophecies, until the proper time comes."

"We opened it? Then that is wonderful, is it not?"

"For the Cainites, perhaps, but not for the people of the Earth. Because the gate you have opened leads from the Earth to the Void. You see, it does not reach all the way to the Bible-World. So as a result of your transgression, there is now an open path for those who dwell in the Void to cross the threshold and haunt us here."

"The Cainites? They are from the Void?" Oleander asked.

The Prince nodded.

"Are you saying... *we caused the deaths of the Vessels?* The accidents, the earthquakes, the millions of deaths?" Oleander's heart began pounding.

"Of course. You invited the children of Cain. Where they go, the Curse follows like a shadow. The Curse destroys the Blessing which protects all things, as you well know. The Cainites are attracted to the Blessing like moths to the light. Once they entered, they homed in on carriers of the Blessing—on Vessels, and to some degree on Keepers and Ishmaelites as well."

Oleander gaped. "*We did this?*"

The Prince nodded solemnly. "When the Curse approaches a Vessel, it counters the Blessing that protects him. He is then exposed to any possibility of harm that happens to pass his way, much beyond what every human continually faces. In short, the Curse makes injury and death more probable to all on Earth, but dramatically so to Vessels."

"But how can that be?" pleaded Oleander. "What about Vessel Tsatsolnov who died more than five-hundred years ago? And Vessel Jason seven-hundred years ago? And Vessel Intef three millennia ago? Seven Vessels died before we were born!"

"Unfortunately, Councilman Oleander, indeed you are not the first to interfere with the Void and let in the Cainites. In all ages, there are those who think they are wiser than the sacred laws. So many laws have been broken in so many different ways." He sighed.

"Are you talking about de Montfort?" Eliezer whispered. Vague rumors he had heard in his early years as a Keeper about this mysterious character now started to make sense.

"He too thought himself wise, and was duly punished, after we informed Councilwoman Isabel. Others killed Vessels before you, if that gives you any comfort. But enough of these historical matters. They do not change the fact that you have killed Vessel Mark Gregor. And Vessel Alifa Hadid."

"Come, Prince," Eliezer said angrily, "we cannot be the only ones responsible for the Cainites. We aren't that powerful."

To their surprise the Prince nodded. "That is true. You only opened the gate. Someone else woke the children of Cain from their slumber."

"Someone else?" asked Eliezer. "A Keeper?"

"You see, when Cain was cursed he was exiled to the Land of Nod. For thousands of years he and his descendants have been living there, in that emptiness devoid of Blessing. Without Blessing, life is impossible, of course. But the Cainites did not perish. Sparks of Blessing occasionally fall into the Void, sometimes from Keepers' beacons or from dreaming Vessels as they pass across the Void. These sparks have been enough to keep their souls alive, but not enough to keep them active and awake. Most of the time they were in deep slumber."

"The Cainites have been... dormant?"

"Occasionally an especially large splinter of Blessing would stray and reach them, and they would briefly awaken, but then sleep again. This was so until several months ago. And then something new happened: Someone stirred them up, and now they are moving about like wasps in a disturbed nest."

"Several months ago?" Eliezer appealed. "But we have been discerning the Book for only seven weeks!"

"Someone—not you—awakened the Cainites. And when you started discerning the Book and opened the new gate, they began swarming in. Bodies do not exist in the Void, not as we think of them. But the souls of the Cainites entered our world and came to inhabit the bodies of those human beings who were especially weak in spirit, or at the moment of death when that body's own soul had departed.

"It is only because someone else has stirred up the Cainites that they are now entering the gate you have opened. Had they been asleep the open gate would have caused no harm. But this shared responsibility is of little moment now."

"And who," asked Eliezer, "who awakened the Cainites?"

"Evidence points to the Keeper with the oldest blood."

"Peprini," Oleander whispered.

There was a long silence.

"Why did you call us here?" Eliezer finally asked. "Not just to share the information."

"You are right, Councilman. Your role now is to complete the opening of the New Gate."

"I am afraid I do not understand."

"Like every other gate, the gate you opened was designed to extend all the way from the Earth, through the Void, to the Bible-World. The trouble is that you constructed it only halfway. The New Gate is now open only between the Earth and the Void. You must continue with what you have started; you must make it reach all the way to the Bible-World."

"And then?"

"Once the two ends connect, the gate is completed and is sealed from the forces of the Void. Because the function of a gate is not just to open, but to open selectively. It opens a passageway but also keeps away the Curse. A gate acts like a sieve: Vessels can pass through, discernment beams can pass through, but no Cainite, no cursed creature can."

Eliezer pondered. "We continue discerning the Sefirot until we connect to the Bible-World?"

Nevayot shook his head. "That would not work. How do you know the passageway is directed towards the Bible-World? The Void is vast, and you can easily miss your target."

"So what do we do?"

"You must open the gate on both ends, from the Earth as well as from the Bible. It is like digging a tunnel—you dig from both sides until you connect in the middle. Your discernments so far have been opening only the Earth-side of the gate."

"How do we open the other side?"

"That I cannot tell you for sure. My guess is—but this is only a guess—that in order to open the Bible-end of the gate, you should discern a passage in the Book of Creation that is about the Bible."

Oleander understood immediately. "There is one passage in the Book of Creation that is about a Biblical event—God making a covenant with Abraham."

"That could be. Perhaps. That passage, I believe, whatever it is, would be the opening in the Bible-World. You must discern it at the same time you discern the Sefirot. The Prince sighed. "If you work as quickly as possible, there is a small chance you will seal the Gate from the Void before more Cainites enter, before all the Vessels die, before the Blessing dies and our world disappears."

Eliezer looked doubtful. "So far we did only four Sefirot. We still have six to go. The problem will be time."

"You might not need to go all the way to the tenth. A narrow opening on the Bible-side—two or three Sefirot wide—might be enough."

"How will we know when we have succeeded, Prince?"

"You will know. We all will." He turned to Osnat. "One last thing, Keepers. Let Osnat help you in this task. There is more in her than meets the eye."

Oleander could not contain himself. "But she's not really part of our work. She is with us simply by coincidence."

The Prince smiled. "She is not here by coincidence." Where the Blessing is concerned, do you think such a thing happens by chance? As we say: The Blessing is the master of all coincidences."

They all rose. Oleander and Osnat left the room with Kedar. Eliezer lingered. The Prince approached him. The two embraced. "May the Blessing remain with you... and with all on Earth."

The three Keepers left the building. Chief Bosmat and Kedar turned to Prince Nevayot and waited for his words.

"Noble intentions," he said and sighed. "They have taken upon themselves a tremendous task. But I am afraid the matter is beyond their powers."

"Can we help them?" asked Kedar.

"The time has come for Noah's Ark."

Kedar looked puzzled. "Noah's Ark?"

"You may explain to my grandson now," Nevayot said. "Soon every Ishmaelite will know."

Chief Bosmat stepped forward. "Remind yourself of the story of Noah's flood. *And God said to Noah: the end of all flesh is come before me...*"

"Then God tells Noah: *make an ark of gopher wood.*"

Chief Bosmat nodded. "*And I will bring a flood upon the Earth to destroy all flesh... but with you I will establish my covenant and you will come into the ark, you and your sons and your wife and your sons' wives with you...*"

"So we enclose ourselves in a kind of Noah's Ark to survive the catastrophe?"

"Our forefathers prepared the ark centuries ago. They knew that someday this time would come."

"But… We are just to let them die?"

"That, Kedar, cannot be averted. We can no longer do anything to help them. The Ishmaelite family will close itself off in a capsule, and when life is renewed, God willing, we will emerge again, just like Noah after the flood."

"What about Osnat, Grandfather? We are going to take her with us, aren't we?"

"No, Kedar. She will stay and help the Keepers."

"But she is an Ishmaelite."

"As well as a Keeper, Grandson. And she would be of greater use to them than to us."

Back in their hotel, the three rushed to examine the Book of Creation. Osnat sat by Eliezer and read over his shoulder.

"Yes," Oleander said. "There is just one passage in the entire Book of Creation that can possibly refer to God's Blessing to the Biblical Patriarchs.

"The very last part of the Book, where God is revealed to Abraham."

"It has to be. So if we discern the next Sefirah, the fifth, together with this Abraham passage, that might open the Bible-end of the gate. We'll be digging from both ends."

"And if we're wrong?" Osnat added.

Eliezer moaned in frustration. "We are fumbling here in complete darkness. I can't think of any better idea."

"Good." Oleander had put behind him the guilt he had felt and was now animated by the intellectual challenge. "Our next problem is the code-word for the fifth Sefirah. Without it, we are stuck where we are."

They turned to the first page of the Book and examined the strange formula:

TEN SEFIROT OF BELIMAH, THEIR MEASURE IS TEN WITHOUT END: DEPTHS OF BEGINNING AND DEPTHS OF END, DEPTHS OF ABOVE AND DEPTHS OF BELOW, DEPTHS OF EAST AND DEPTHS OF WEST, DEPTHS OF GOOD AND DEPTHS OF BAD, DEPTHS OF SOUTH AND DEPTHS OF NORTH, AND A SINGULAR LORD, GOD, FAITHFUL KING, RULES OVER ALL OF THEM FROM HIS HOLY ABODE UNTO ETERNITY.

"It has something to do with dimensions," Oleander said. "The dimension of time—beginning and end. The dimensions of space—height, width, breadth."

Eliezer screwed his forehead. "No, something is not... What is 'Depths of good' and 'Depths of bad'?"

"The moral dimension?"

"That's rather forced."

There was silence as the three deliberated. Osnat closed her eyes for a moment and then suddenly sat up straight. "The point at the center of everything," she uttered, opening her eyes.

"Repeat what you've just said," Eliezer said, taking hold of her arm.

"The point at the center—whatever that means."

"Thank you, or thank your 'bubble of knowledge'!"

"What do you mean?" She was still recovering from her momentary disorientation.

"The codeword refers to the center of everything, to the heart of time and space and morality."

"Exactly, William. But what would be this word?"

Now Osnat understood as well. "I see. I can think of three Biblical words that mean 'center': *Emtsa, Merkaz, Tabur*."

"It could be 'heart'—*Lev*," Eliezer added. "In Hebrew, it's another way of saying center."

"Let's make a list," Oleander concluded. "When we discern, we'll have to speak them one after the other, hoping we hit until we hit the right one."

"Assuming the quakes don't kill us first," whispered Eliezer.

The next morning found them eager to begin. Despite her protests, they decided that Osnat was too inexperienced to take an active part in the session, and gave her the role of observer. She would descend to the Depths but remain a distance from the edge of the Void without attempting to discern.

The three closed their eyes and slowly descended to their Inner Depths. Soon they were at the edge of the Void. Osnat stood by as the two men put themselves in discernment mode and started reciting the introductory passage of the Book:

WITH THIRTY-TWO MYSTERIOUS PATHS OF WISDOM ENGRAVED GOD, THE LORD OF HOSTS, GOD OF ISRAEL, THE LIVING GOD, GOD ALMIGHTY, HIGH AND EXALTED, DWELLING IN ETERNITY ON HIGH, AND HIS NAME IS HOLY, AND HE CREATED HIS WORLD WITH THREE SFR'S: WITH SFR AND SFR AND SFR.

They felt the familiar energy gathering around them and soon found themselves in the obscure darkness they had encountered four times before.

Eliezer now continued to the fifth Sefirah:

TEN SEFIROT OF BELIMAH, THEIR MEASURE IS TEN WITHOUT END: DEPTHS OF BEGINNING AND DEPTHS OF END, DEPTHS OF ABOVE...

At the same time, Oleander plunged into the unknown and started discerning the last passage of the Book of Creation:

WHEN ABRAHAM OUR FATHER, MAY HE REST IN PEACE, LOOKED AND SAW AND UNDERSTOOD AND EXPLORED AND ENGRAVED AND HEWED OUT AND SUCCEEDED AT CREATION...

With no warning, Oleander's two companions disappeared from his sight. He felt his field of vision rushing forward into the Void towards the Bible World at a great speed. The words he spoke were few but the time between them seemed extended, each followed by a faint echo.

...IMMEDIATELY THE LORD OF ALL, BLESSED BE HIS NAME FOREVER, WAS REVEALED TO HIM...

The zooming in stopped, and his field of vision stabilized, now containing an ancient scene: A man in white, flowing robes standing in the midst of a whirlwind. The man was familiar from his past discernments of the Bible. And then he knew: It was Abraham. And the whirlwind was the presence of God.

...AND HE PLACED HIM IN HIS BOSOM AND KISSED HIM ON IS HEAD AND CALLED HIM ABRAHAM MY BELOVED, AND CUT A COVENANT WITH HIM AND WITH HIS SEED FOREVER...

Oleander calmed down. Now it felt like an ordinary discernment, like the hundreds of discernments he had done in the past. There was only one difference: In his entire life as a Keeper, he had never visualized this scene. It was none of the twelve Gates he knew so well. This was a different Gate, the New Gate!

AND HE MADE WITH HIM A COVENANT BETWEEN THE TEN FINGERS OF HIS HANDS – THIS IS THE COVENANT OF THE TONGUE, AND BETWEEN THE TEN TOES OF HIS FEET— THIS IS THE COVENANT OF CIRCUMCISION. AND HE BOUND TWENTY-TWO LETTERS TO HIS TONGUE AND REVEALED TO HIM HIS SECRET, HE DREW THEM IN WATER, HE IGNITED THEM IN FIRE, HE AGITATED THEM WITH BREATH, HE BURNED THEM WITH THE SEVEN, HE DIRECTED THEM WITH THE TWELVE CONSTELLATIONS.

There was another curious thing about this discernment: *the perspective.* He was seeing this scene from the perspective of being in the Bible World. He wasn't actually present with Abraham—he knew he was still standing next to Eliezer and Osnat and looking at the Bible World from a great distance, but his field of vision presented the scene as if he was inside it. As he was marveling at this, he noticed a beam of light extending from Abraham into the black of the Void.

Oleander examined the golden shaft in wonder and then understood. He was envisioning himself discerning from the Bible World towards the Earth. It was his own discernment beam he was seeing, a beam that originated in the Bible World.

Across this darkness, from the perspective of the Earth, he knew Eliezer was sending a discernment beam from the opposite side of the Void.

Osnat watched the two Keepers intently, trying to make out what they were going through. Neither Oleander nor Eliezer had moved. Although their fields of vision were separated from each other—Eliezer envisioning from the perspective of the Earth and Oleander from that of the Bible-World—the two were standing next to each other. The three were engulfed by the pulsing energies waiting to be released. It was time for the codeword. Eliezer had four candidates—four Hebrew words for "center."

"*Emtsa!*"

There was a sharp *crack* in the distance and they held their breath. The dark reverberations rolled towards them like thunder. Eliezer turned to Oleander but the monk's eyes were closed.

"*Merkaz!*"

The world around them shook and quivered, and Eliezer fought to maintain his balance. His mind raced. Of the remaining words meaning "center," which was most probable? He felt his hold weakening and knew he had only one more chance.

"*Lev!*"

The quake was sharply more violent than any before. The world tilted, and Eliezer slid sideways into a torrent rushing towards the Void. Oleander felt isolated in a vortex of forces. His vision was obscured by the sudden storm of energies. He struggled to keep his equilibrium and maintain what image of Abraham he could.

Not far from them Osnat was being tossed and battered. In the midst of her desperation and confusion she felt a revelation of knowledge quickly rising inside her: "What land is at the center of the Bible World?"

She struggled to quiet her mind. She focused on slowing her breathing and heartbeat, waiting for the bubble to resolve itself. And then she knew the answer: In the Bible, at the center of the universe stands the Holy Land, the land of Israel, or what the Bible (like modern Hebrew speakers) simply calls *The Land*!

"*Ha'arets*!"

Like the moment after a lightning strike, all was suddenly still and with an air of expectation. She regained control over her movements. Then a great explosion shook her, but it was directed towards the Void. She could see a fantastic wave advancing along Eliezer's discernment beam, and then going farther, boring deep into the empty expanse. Moments passed as she watched the golden wave recede into the blackness.

The great energies subsided, and she saw Eliezer at the very edge of the Void, weakened but alive.

From the other side of the Void, from the perspective of the Bible World, Oleander too saw a wave of Blessing energies rushing along his discernment beam into the Void, boring a passage towards Earth. He had no time for celebration as his field of vision dissipated and he found himself standing next to his two companions.

Before ascending from the Depths they stopped and looked back. The New Gate had not been opened yet—they could not detect any direct line of vision to the Bible World. But they had survived. And the tunnel was now partly open at both ends.

76

Since the man had been shot in front of his eyes, Dr. Soren Lessing had been feeling unwell. Something dark weighed on his entire being. As a practicing psychiatrist, he was well acquainted with depression and angst, but in his personal life he had seemed immune. Recently, though, bouts of anxiety or gloominess or a choking vulnerability would fall upon him. His first headache had struck him, the first in his lifetime; he had to ask his wife where the aspirin was kept. Shortness of breath, out of proportion to the effort of the moment, came upon him now without warning. Being a Vessel, though without knowing it, he had been extraordinarily healthy and high-spirited throughout his life, so much so that his colleagues would joke that he was afflicted with excessive health.

He wondered if it was the psychological shock of witnessing the murder, but he dismissed that idea. Small accidents mounted: burning his hand taking a tray from the oven, a splinter pricking his finger, stubbing his toe on the leg of a table. He slipped on the wet pavement getting out of his car and fell, spraining his wrist. Something was happening to him, and he did not understand what it was.

Thirteen days after the vagrant's murder, Dr. Soren Lessing went to bed with a chest cold but awoke with something much more serious. Against his wishes his wife Kathryn had him admitted to Royal Victoria Hospital in Edinburgh. The diagnosis was pneumonia, but the prognosis was favorable. Lessing, while forty-seven, was in otherwise superb health. This eased some of his wife's worry, though did nothing to diminish the anxiety of his Keepers.

By the following morning, Lessing's condition had worsened. Half of the ten-person *residence* team relocated to a van in the vicinity to prevent any vagrant from entering or even nearing the hospital, each half on twelve-hour shifts. Eckart Blundt, the Master-Keeper in charge, was apprehensive. Last night he had received a phone call from Peprini instructing him to expect a special squad. Blundt hoped it would not be the same men from two weeks earlier. They had been brazen and condescending, and he wasn't surprised they had ended up killing that man.

At eleven o'clock two Land Rovers stopped by their van, and a tall, muscular man got out and stood in the cold rain, rivulets of water running off the dark skin of his shaven head. Blundt rolled down the driver's window.

"You're Blundt?"

African accent, he thought as he nodded. The halo of the Blessing around his head was so weak that he wondered how the man had passed the Verification.

"Thomas Aruba. From Special Tasks. Two messages from Councilor Peprini. One, I am in charge. Two, none of these vagrants should be hurt—under any circumstances. Questions?"

Blundt sighed at the sort of men Peprini chose for Special Tasks, but also felt relieved he would no longer be responsible for a situation that had become criminal and violent.

"What do you want to do with them?" He pointed to a vagrant that was leaning against a tree fifty yards away.

"Leave them be. Notify us if you see them."

Four other men emerged from the vehicles, their Blessing equally faint. Aruba gave orders and they dispersed, one vehicle moving down the street towards the vagrant. One of the men climbed from the Land Rover and, as if inviting the creature to take a ride, opened the rear passenger door and helped him inside. The vagabond was soon tied securely in the back seat.

By mid-afternoon, two more had joined him.

Aruba and his team stood by the Land Rover. "Blundt, go home. We don't want to appear a crowd out here. Leave this to…"

A sharp *crack* froze the air followed by a horrible screeching. A bus— its front tire flat and sparks spraying from the rim—slid with frightening speed on the wet street towards the group. Eckart Blundt would later say that in those moments he had felt a nauseating emptiness invading his being.

When the bus finally stopped, one of Blundt's Keepers along with Aruba and all four of his men were on the ground, their bodies broken.

"How many?"

Blundt moved the phone away from his ear at the harshness of Peprini's voice. "Six, Councilor Peprini. One of mine and…"

"Any injured?"

"The rest of us were able to jump out of the way."

"Six dead?"

"Yes, Councilor."

Peprini hung up and turned to Sionn sitting on the other side of the desk. "Six, Albrecht."

"*Whoever kills Cain, vengeance shall be taken on him sevenfold.*"

"You are telling me Oleander was right?"

"As William said, in Biblical language 'sevenfold' is not a mathematical concept. It simply means 'many times more terrible.' And this may not be the end of the Cainite's vengeance for the shooting of the Edinburgh vagrant. For all we know, Lessing's sickness may be part of it."

"That has occurred to me." Peprini turned his chair to think.

"What shall we do with the Cainites as we collect them?" Sionn asked. "I was thinking we could take them to the old *residence* in Albania. It's secluded and no one has lived there for at least sixty years."

"We need to observe them. We need a better picture of who or what they are. What do you think of the convent? We can lock them in the lower rooms."

"Too close, Menach. Their proximity will disturb everyone. And it might bring misfortune. I suggest somewhere in the vicinity of the convent—the old Granary."

The next day Lessing's condition had further declined. The doctors had no explanation beyond "He isn't strong enough to defeat the disease." His wife and two young sons, his doctors, and his Keepers all watched with growing distress.

77

Peprini's Special Tasks teams quickly arrived at the dwellings of the three remaining Vessels: Wyatt in New York, Lessing in Edinburgh, and Lenoma in Addis Ababa, Ethiopia. Any person seeming homeless or behaving in the manner of the vagabonds found in the vicinity of the Vessel was captured, and if bearing the Sevenfold mark, was taken by private plane to the Zurich airport. Vans then brought them to the convent, and then farther down the old road to the Granary, an ancient building a mile from the convent and twice that distance from the Abbey.

The Granary appeared as a large barn made of rough-hewn granite blocks with a sharply angled slate roof. Like the convent and abbey, it had been built to last centuries. Underground it contained many rooms of various sizes. In different periods of its seven-hundred-year history it had been used by the Keepers as a storehouse, a wine-cellar, an armory, a hospital for quarantined plague victims, and many times as a hiding place. In the past century, however, it had been largely idle.

Sionn and Peprini had decided to imprison the creatures here until... either they knew what to do with them or the last Vessel died.

Though the prisoners were kept deep underground, standing a hundred feet from the Granary was an unpleasant experience, especially for more advanced Keepers whose sensitivity was far greater. Yards of stone and earth couldn't completely block the Cainites' foul emanation. For the first time, Keepers of inferior power were found to have an advantage over Master-Keepers and Councilors. A small group was selected to guard the Cainites, though this hardly seemed necessary. The prisoners appeared not to mind their situation. Pem volunteered to take charge of the Granary.

The next morning, Peprini's four-wheel drive passed through the stone gates of the convent grounds. He turned onto the ancient cart path leading deeper into the woods. The Range Rover bounced over ground that rarely saw a vehicle. He gripped the wheel firmly and Sionn, his passenger, braced himself with one hand on the dashboard. He carefully steered down a small hill into a clearing. Backed up against an aspen and birch forest was the Granary.

Peprini brought the vehicle to a stop an unnecessary distance from the building. Sionn glanced at him though he understood why, already feeling faint nausea. It was a natural if irrational effort to postpone facing the full brunt of the Cainites.

"Any more identifications?" Peprini asked as they walked the twenty yards to the Granary building, turning up the collars on their overcoats and taking careful steps to keep the morning dew from spilling into their shoes.

"A few more details. The recent one from Edinburgh had been a drug addict known to the police. There is no evidence he died. Rather…" Sionn was uncomfortable voicing this conclusion "…his body seems to have been taken over by the Cainite. The woman from New York was an accountant under indictment for embezzlement. Her shoes were found by the Hudson River together with a suicide letter. The elderly man from New York was a heart-attack case. He was brought to the hospital clinically dead and then his body disappeared."

"And the two Ethiopians?"

He shook his head. "All we have to go on are their fingerprints and pictures. In a third-world country…"

Pem waited just inside the Granary door. The two Councilors removed their overcoats and handed them to the Master-Keeper.

"Pem, I've told you there's no need for you to be here," Sionn said.

"Just the same, if you don't mind, Albrecht, I'll remain."

Peprini's face tightened. "I wonder if that putrid presence will ever leave this place. Any news of our guests?"

"Two asked for food this morning." Sionn's eyebrows arched in surprise. "They didn't speak, no. They…" Pem moved his fingers toward his mouth and made a chewing motion.

"Curious. None have spoken at all?"

Pem shook his head.

"Let's have a look."

The stone stairs taking them underground were steeper than what is usual today, each step shorter in height and narrower in depth, the staircase itself much longer. For light they relied on what was cast from the doorway above and the lanterns stationed in the room below. Even through the foulness they could smell the damp earthiness of soil and stone. At the bottom they crossed the large room, once storage for sausages, potatoes, cheeses, grains, apples and other fruits and vegetables to see the nuns and monks through the long Swiss winters. The space still held the smell of their rich fecundity. They moved down a narrow corridor, past several smaller rooms, to another staircase.

Pem took a flashlight from a chair. "I think I should go first. It's a little dicey."

He led them in near darkness. He would move down two steps and then turn and shine the light for the two Councilors. Indeed it was tricky; these stairs had been built from irregular stone slabs.

Midway Pem stopped abruptly and Peprini almost ran into him. He was just about to scold the small man when he felt the wave of nausea.

"It's thick from this point on."

At the bottom there was light from electric lanterns hanging from rusty spikes driven into the stone walls ages ago. Two novices, Alexi Samsov and Natalie Norisot, stood as the three approached.

"Natalie, the door, please," said Pem. The petite Eurasian took a skeleton key as big as a soup spoon and inserted it into the lock on a wide wooden door. She turned the key two full revolutions and then pulled on the iron handle with the force of her body weight. The door grudgingly began to swing open, the metal of the hinges grinding away at the rust.

"The outer door helps somewhat, Sir."

The stench was in fact worse with only the iron bars between them and the prisoners.

"Why don't you two get some fresh air," Pem suggested.

She handed Pem another key. "This is for the gate, Sir."

The two left quickly.

The three Keepers stood side-by-side in front of the bars. Reflexively Sionn brought his hand to cover his nose but found it made no difference; it wasn't an actual *smell.*

There were thirteen Cainites in the room, seven from Edinburgh, and the others captured in New York near David Wyatt's home, and in Ethiopia near the child Vessel Anina Lenoma. There was enough space so two were lying on the earthen floor in the back, and several others squatted on their heels as they leaned against the walls. One was a child, a girl of seven or eight. No furniture was in the room.

"Where do they...?" Sionn's question was answered as he noticed a metal bucket in a corner. There was no detectable odor, none that could overpower the other foulness.

"You said several ate this morning."

Pem pointed out two that stood nearest the gate. "These two. Though they weren't enthusiastic about it. Just a little bread. Nothing of the cheese or the fruit. There is water but few have touched it." He nodded towards two one-gallon plastic water jugs.

"Are they still human?" Peprini thought aloud.

Sionn looked a Cainite in the eye. "What is it you want? Who are you?"

There was no sign of comprehension, of even a realization that a question had been asked. Sionn tried in French and then German. Nothing. Then once more, this time in ancient Hebrew.

Pem looked at Sionn wondering why the Councilor would use a defunct language. Peprini's eyes ran along the visible flesh of the Cainites. One woman had the sevenfold mark on the back of her hand; a teenage boy had it on his neck and cheek.

"This is pointless." Sionn backed away from the iron gate. He turned with Pem in tow. "Menach, are you coming?"

"In a moment."

"We'll be upstairs."

Peprini nodded absently. He was watching a certain Cainite, the most impressive of the group. Behind the eyes of this one, there was... something, a sign of a mind at work.

"Who are you?" He asked in old Hebrew.

Nothing in the Cainite's expression changed. "Why have you come here?" This he tried in Aramaic, the language of Jesus. Still nothing. Then again in Canaanite, the ancient language of the Biblical land of Canaan, spoken by the original inhabitants of the land before the Children of Israel took over and established the Jewish kingdom of Israel. Hebrew and Canaanite were cognates, closer to each other than English and French, and although Peprini's exposure to Canaanite was limited, his fluency in ancient Hebrew enabled him to speak it reasonably well.

A flicker of recognition crossed the prisoner's eyes. Peprini tried again. The Cainite's mouth began slowly moving, his lips forming words but without sound. Peprini moved closer, grasping the bars of the gate.

Again in Canaanite he asked, "Who are you?"

Again the Cainite made an effort to speak without succeeding. But when Peprini looked at his eyes he saw the prisoner had understood him.

"I will return soon. Then we will talk, yes?"

The prisoner gave a very slight nod of his head.

Peprini climbed the stairs to the surface. Pem and Sionn waited outside. Though the atmosphere was still unpleasant, it was noticeably improved.

"How often are you changing the guards?" Sionn asked Pem.

"Every three hours. We had been on four-hour shifts but that was too much." Sionn imagined standing outside that cell four long hours. "Even though most of the guards are novices and don't feel much, they report it's terribly draining. And there have been accidents."

"What's this?" Peprini turned to face the Master-Keeper.

"Nalini Sing fell down the lower flight of stairs yesterday and broke her arm and leg. And the Tremble boy from the Abbey cut himself on a spike while taking down a lantern; a nasty gash that required a dozen stitches and a tetanus shot. Even then the wound became infected. Each of these incidents is extraordinary, of course. Even singly I can remember nothing like this among us."

"Change the guards every two hours," Sionn said. "And when they aren't on shift, they are to be at the Abbey. No one should be here unless it's necessary."

"I will stay if you don't mind, Albrecht. Someone..." Pem was about to say *of authority* but caught himself, ashamed at his arrogance. "Someone must supervise and look after the place."

The diminutive man stood proudly, his muscular body defiant.

"Very well. But I want you as far from the cell as possible. You must be careful in everything you do. You are at exceptional risk while you remain here."

Pem nodded obediently. "Thank you, Albrecht."

Sionn nodded, embarrassed at his evident concern for Pem.

78

The Ethiopian border with South Sudan

The Toyota Land Cruiser sat in the stone-littered ravine, the driver dozing behind the wheel. A young girl was in the backseat reading a book. She was tired and agitated and wanted to go home, away from the dust and the flies. Now and then she looked up and gazed over the area, looking at the door her mother had entered earlier, impatient for her to appear. The single-story brick building was the only one remaining in what had been the village. Tarps were spread in patchwork over the ruins of other buildings making shelters from the sun. Women worked around cooking fires, cleaning up after the morning meal. A cluster of children kicked a tin can up and down the road. Men lounged in the shade, sleeping or talking, rifles nearby.

Inside the building five men and a woman sat on rugs in the center of the floor. The men formed a half moon on one side, the woman across from them. She was dressed as their own women might have been, though her clothing was much finer, and her speech of a class well above their own. Beyond this, she exuded a goodness that soothed them.

The men huddled and whispered. The leader stroked his grisly, graying beard for a long moment, then nodded to the woman.

She opened a leather bag and pulled out a drawstring sack. She turned it upside down and twenty gold Krugerrands spilled onto the rug. The men's eyes gleamed. The leader turned his head and spoke to the door. A boy entered and the man called for tea.

One of the men began talking when the leader silenced him and leaped to his feet, listening. The sound of the aircraft became audible and orders were quickly given. The first explosion shook the ground and brought a shower of dust from the ceiling. Now everyone stood and another blast quickly followed, closer, causing them to lose their balance. The leader told the woman to stay where she was, that she was safest right here. But she ignored him and ran to the door, to her child.

Peprini took off his suit coat and gave it to his assistant on the flight. He settled into the deep leather and closed his eyes, listening to the hum of the jet engines as the Gulfstream taxied into position on the runway then roared in takeoff. Like every airplane passenger, lately he was tense until he was confident the plane was safely in the air.

The image of Una Lenoma, the mother of the Vessel Anina, kept returning to his mind. An elegant woman in her early forties, she possessed a searing intelligence she had learned to conceal unless the situation demanded its display. She was married with three girls, all the near-image of their mother. Una Lenoma had passed the Blessing to her third child, Anina. Una was the Director of the United Nations' World Food Programme in Ethiopia, as well as the smaller Ethiopian Christian Children's Fund. Peprini gave a very large donation to the Fund each year and ensured the Lucerne Rare Book Consulting Co., Ltd. did the same. Each year he received a polite letter of thanks written in her hand.

She was unreservedly a good person. This was something he thought about often lately. What part of a Vessel's goodness is due to the Blessing and what is simply the nature of the person?

He was traveling to observe young Anina Lenoma on behalf of the Council, to assess the Blessing she held, to learn if it was weakening. The Master-Keeper in charge of the Addis Ababa *residence* was capable of this, but the Council wanted a first-hand appraisal. As much as anything it was action at a time when the Council felt impotent.

He closed his eyes, knowing he needed to rest. But the image of Maria Jongsma appeared, wrapped in white, her face still holding vestiges of the pain she had endured in the Void. She had willingly sacrificed herself for the sake of the Blessing. If her death, he thought, was in the service of me reaching the Bible-World and so restoring the Blessing, it was justified. Unquestionably.

A sharp thought jarred him and he opened his eyes. *Am I virtuous enough to receive the Blessing? Could I stand in front of the Patriarchs in the Bible world and be recognized as worthy of His Blessing?* He closed his eyes and surrendered to the deep fatigue that was his steady companion.

The flight attendant spoke softly until the Councilor awoke. "We are preparing to descend into Addis Ababa, Councilor. The pilot has asked that we put on our seatbelts."

Peprini righted himself in his seat and looked at his watch. He had arranged to run into Una Lenoma at her office, a faithful donor taking the opportunity while passing through Addis Ababa finally to meet the Director. He knew that each Thursday afternoon Anina joined her mother after her piano lesson, waiting at the office to return home together.

Though he needed only to appraise Anina, he found himself looking forward to seeing her mother.

The plane landed and taxied to the private terminal. Master-Keeper Kryshar was waiting, pacing next to a Renault. She was dressed in a white long-sleeved blouse and tan slacks, as a Western woman would have been, her head covered in a scarf. She was alone. Peprini came down the stairs and noticed that Kryshar avoided his gaze.

He realized he was scared. She said nothing and didn't move.

"What is it?" Peprini demanded as he got closer.

"This morning she was with her mother at the South Sudanese border where the WFP—the UN's program—has a relief camp with about 20,000 refugees who crossed into Ethiopia to escape the unrest in South Sudan. It's been perfectly safe there. The South Sudanese army has *never* crossed the border."

Peprini's anxiety swelled. "Dammit, Kryshar, what happened?"

"The South Sudanese launched air attacks on a rebel village early this morning. The rebels were camped near the refugees. Anina and Una were in the rebel encampment when it was hit. They both were killed."

"*What in Esau's name was she doing there?*"

"She'd been negotiating to allow food trucks into rebel-occupied territory. You know how she is. The South Sudanese government seizes most of the aid shipments and distributes the food to the military. This was her only way to get food to the people trapped across the border. And Anina often went with her to the refugee camp. It wasn't unusual, it's *always* been safe there, Councilor."

Peprini nodded sharply to say he had heard enough.

"Do you have their bodies?"

"The Ethiopian army is in charge now. It's very tense there. But Yonani and Bedinna saw Anina's body. They dug her out of the rubble an hour ago. There is no doubt. I'm... I'm so sorry, Councilor."

Peprini nodded again, now in resignation.

79

The Rare Book Company offices were empty. Some had gone home for the evening before the news of Anina Lenoma's death. The others gathered across the courtyard at the Abbey as had become the custom lately. All eyes were turned upwards, scanning the sky. The Blessing was already thinner than anyone had thought possible. In some places there were hollow patches of no Blessing at all, a sight never before recorded.

Albrecht Sionn stood in the courtyard and examined the bronze statue of Esau. Faith could survive the death of one Vessel in a Keeper's lifetime. But three? The news of Anina Lenoma's death had a drug-like effect on the Keepers beyond the further diminishment of vitality they anticipated. With this third calamity, they felt themselves at the mercy of an unknown and unstoppable force.

He saw Erna walking with two young Keepers. She stopped mid-sentence and pointed down to Lucerne, the Reuss River cutting the town in two.

"For how long have we looked down upon them," she gestured towards the town indicating normal humanity, "as their world changed unpredictably, content, even arrogantly at the unchanging quality of ours. In the year 1116 the Chronicles record an amazing event, one unrelated to the Vessels. You'll also find mention of this in their historical record. Two of us, monks at a monastery in England, were gazing at the moon one night when a tremendous explosion occurred on its surface, so dramatic it could clearly be seen from Earth. We now know a large meteor had smashed into it. But in their eyes, with this explosion the moon was beginning to disintegrate. *The very heavens were coming apart.* I had always assumed I understood what they must have felt. Now I know I didn't. Until today. How much longer *our* world will exist, no one can say. You may be witnesses to the end."

Yes, Sionn thought. For what is a Keeper when nothing exists any longer to keep?

He walked across the cobblestones, hands in pockets to ward off the chill, and decided it was time to go inside. As he opened the door to the Rectory, Menach Peprini looked up from his chair.

"I'm sorry, Menach. I didn't know you'd gotten back. I'm not interrupting, am I?"

Peprini shook his head. "Of course not." Then he added, "Albrecht, did I ever tell you I met her once? The mother, that is. Una Lenoma."

"When was that?"

"At Cambridge."

"Your visiting lectureship."

"She was a student, though not in my classes. It was strange to walk on the grounds or down a corridor because I'd feel her presence before I would see her. It made it a magical place."

Sionn smiled sadly. "When I was twelve or thirteen, my father took me to Lyon to see Gregor's mother, Vessel Yvette Gregor. She was a small child, playing in the park with her sister Francoise. My father wanted me to perceive a Vessel's Blessing. He knew I could discern... Truth be told, I think he wanted to make absolutely certain I was a Keeper. He didn't tell me which child was Yvette. I had to walk among the crowds of children, dozens of them, until I apprehended which one it was. I wonder now if I'll ever have the chance again."

Sionn glanced through the window at the sky, then quickly averted his eyes as if seeing something obscene. "This sky gives me a feeling that something is dragging our world to its doom, and that it cannot be stopped."

Peprini was silent for a while. He was overcome by a desire to talk and relieve his burden, and by doing so perhaps bring his friend to his side. "What if I said I might know of a way?"

Sionn stared at him.

"It is something I have never told you, Albrecht, or anyone else. A family secret you might call it."

Peprini went on to explain what three generations of his family had learned, beginning with his grandfather's discoveries about Simon de Montfort. He told of the attempts to accompany David Wyatt through the Void, leaving out the fact of the harm to Pilar and the deaths of Maria and Tiplady. He concluded by revealing his intention to be blessed by the Patriarchs and begin a new generation of Vessels.

"And you will be the first?"

"The Peprinis have earned this right; my father died in the effort. We have Esau's blood in special richness. And the Blessing rightfully should be ours as it should have been Esau's. But you, Albrecht, must accompany me at some point. The Blessing is your right as well."

Sionn stood and began pacing. "All these years. All these years you and I have known each other. And you kept your tongue. *What discipline, Menach.* Very impressive. Tell me, did you feel superior to the rest of us?" He shook his head before Peprini could answer. "No matter. I don't see this changes anything."

"The Peprinis will soon complete de Montfort's mission. He might have succeeded, but the Council silenced him and his great vision."

"Why wouldn't they? His ideas were wild speculation. Just as yours are, Menach."

"Still, why not allow him to test his theory?"

"And break the sacred laws? And plunge the world into unknown dangers?"

"Possibly, Albrecht. But I am sure it also occurred to the Council that if some of their own managed to reach the Bible World and be blessed by God, that this would immediately make all other Keepers—even fellow Councilors—lesser creatures. They weren't willing to risk the loss of their status."

"Just to be clear, Menach. Your family started down this path decades ago. It wasn't done in response to these recent catastrophes. You had much grander ambitions."

"All the Vessels will die, if not soon as it now seems, then in a thousand years. We are in the position of having only two remain, because our predecessors hid from their duty. The Peprinis have not shirked their responsibility to the Blessing."

Sionn examined his friend's face for a long time. "You truly wish to become a Vessel, don't you?"

Menach hesitated. "Yes," he whispered huskily, a passion glinting in his eyes.

Sionn examined his friend's face with unease. "Isn't this the most powerful temptation? What would it do to a man to know that he has such a unique and immense power that the entire world depends on him? Wouldn't the knowledge of his power corrupt him utterly, indeed, drive him to madness? Isn't this the reason Keepers have never revealed to the Vessels what they truly are?"

Peprini recalled that evening in his room when, as a young man, he had chanted the magical invocation and felt the Blessing, the same feeling he had experienced again just days ago when he had found the Book of Creation. How could such a gift from God harm anyone? How could I possibly do wrong when filled with such a glorious spirit? He had never shared this childhood experience with Sionn nor anyone else. Though he believed he might turn his friend to his favor by revealing it, he couldn't bring himself to speak of it.

Sionn broke the silence. "When the Council wondered why the vagrants appeared, you had some idea, didn't you? The timing couldn't have been accidental, surely. The same time you begin your experiment the vagrants arrive? Yet you said nothing. Have you caused all this, Menach?"

"Have I caused the appearance of the Cainites? Should I be condemned for taking action when no one else would? In any event, their curse is here. I have stopped my attempt…"

"Only because you were forced to."

Peprini was unfazed. "The Vessels continue to die. Wringing our hands won't help now. I hold the only hope of restoring the Blessing."

Sionn stared at his oldest friend. "I won't go to the Council; not right away. I need to think. I pray, Menach, I pray you haven't condemned the world."

80

Cedar Rapids, Iowa, USA

Mary Donner scraped a light frost off the windshield and quickly got in her car and out of the biting wind. Shivering, she put the key in the ignition and turned. The key snapped. Disbelieving, she stared at the piece still in her hand. She tried to calm down and think. There was still a bit of the key sticking out from the lock. Going back in the house she returned with a pair of pliers and her spare key. She had to work the pliers at an angle to get a grip on the splinter of metal and the pliers kept slipping. Once more she tried, when a jolt of electricity shot from her hand to her shoulder, sending her hard against the seatback. She couldn't move her hand; the pliers were now on the floor but her fingers were locked as if still holding them. There was a ringing in her ears that was matched by a painful vibration from her hand up her arm, and the smell of burning circuitry filled the air. She got out of the car as fast as she could.

Once inside the house, she examined her hand. Black marks discolored her thumb and forefinger. Taking the phone, she sat at the kitchen table and found the Auto Club card in her purse. After fifteen minutes on hold, an impatient voice asked for her membership number. She then began describing the problem when he cut her off.

"Okay, okay. We might be able to get someone out there tomorrow, more likely the day after. But I can't promise anything."

"*Two days?*"

"Lady." She could feel him fight to control his frustration. "For the past ten hours, we've been flooded by calls. Half the city is paralyzed. Look around you, for Chrissakes."

"But two days?" she complained.

"Look, I've called garages in Iowa City, even in Dubuque, but it's everywhere."

"What is?"

"The Third Wave. It's everywhere."

Sao Paulo, Brazil

An uneasy feeling prompted Getúlio Barbosa, manager of the Santa Luzia supermarket, to leave his office at the rear of the store. Since the Third Wave began this feeling was never far away. There was a commotion from the next aisle—the now familiar sound of falling cans. At least three hundred cans of tuna, salmon, and anchovies covered the floor, with no customer in sight. One of his workers hurried around the corner. They looked at each other for a moment and the teenager began restacking the cans.

Barbosa resumed his inspection. A woman with a child hugging her leg was trying to open the spout on the large plastic rice bin. She held the paper bag beneath the spout and jiggled the opening, but it allowed just a dribble of rice.

"Let me help, madam."

"Oh, thank you. Two pounds, if you would."

"Sometimes when the bin is full, the chute..."

He used all his tricks to dislodge the gate with no luck. He could feel the woman staring and the sweat appearing on his face and under his armpits, no doubt staining his shirt.

"Maybe if you..." She saw his aggravation and stopped. He hit the gate with the heel of his palm and a thick plume of rice showered their feet. The small girl began wailing. Barbosa watched as the thirty-pound bin emptied its last grain.

Returning to his office he noticed a frail old man take a cartoon of eggs from the refrigerator section and drop them before he could place them in his basket. The old man stared at the mess, indecision on his face, then opened the refrigerator and took out another carton. He opened the lid and carefully thumbed each egg, checking for cracks. But as he closed the lid, the carton tipped and he juggled it for a moment and then watched as it hit the ground with a thud. Barbosa's irritation faded as he saw the old man's hands shake and his face tighten in confusion and fear.

"Accidents everywhere we turn today," the manager said kindly as he approached. He took out a new carton and carefully placed it in the man's basket.

A few minutes later Barbosa passed the front windows and saw the old man walk stiffly to his car, the bag of groceries firmly in both arms. He set the bag down, took his keys out, and opened the trunk. He reached down and grasped opposite sides of the bag's top and Barbosa felt the mistake before it was realized. The bag was three feet off the ground when the paper on one side tore and the contents fell to the concrete.

The old man salvaged what he could and drove away.

Barbosa found the sign he had used during the Second Wave, saying the store was closing for a few days. He placed it by the entrance door which he then locked.

Nong Khai, Thailand

Kanokvan Daoruang walked down the path from her village to the river to draw water. She stopped at the bank and set down her bucket. The normally clear water was today a dark brown, with a froth she had never seen. She watched a woman on the opposite bank kneel and cup her hand, bringing the water to her mouth. Immediately she spat it out and wiped her mouth repeatedly on her sleeve. The woman looked across the river at Kanokvan and shook her head. Kanokvan picked up her bucket and started climbing the path, wondering where she would now find water.

81

The news from Ethiopia and the subsequent wave of catastrophes intensified Eliezer's and Oleander's sense of urgency, but neither had fully recuperated. Eliezer sat on the couch in their hotel suite and watched the monk as he paced impatiently. "I say we hold a session today. We can't afford to wait."

"And risk everything? Do I need to remind you of what our last session was like? In two or three days we will be strong enough."

In the meantime they continued discussing the text of the sixth Sefirah, trying to narrow the list of possible codewords.

TEN SEFIROT OF BELIMAH, THEIR VISION IS LIKE THE APPEARANCE OF LIGHTNING AND THEIR LIMIT HAS NO END, AND HIS WORD IN THEM IS TO-AND-FRO, AND TO HIS SPEECH THEY RUSH LIKE A WHIRLWIND, AND BEFORE HIS THRONE THEY BOW DOWN.

They knew that the expressions "to-and-fro" and "the appearance of lightning" were taken from the mystical vision of the Biblical prophet Ezekiel. The particular wordings are rare in Hebrew—the original language of both the Old Testament and the Book of Creation—and appear nowhere else in the Bible. Verse 14 of Chapter 1 of the Book of Ezekiel reads: "And the animals run to-and-fro like the appearance of lightning."

The vision of Ezekiel is full of fantastic and enigmatic images. Despite more than two millennia of Biblical interpretation, their meaning is far from clear. Eliezer and Oleander toiled but could not fathom what the codeword could be. The rich imagery suggested too many possibilities.

It was Osnat again who pointed them in the right direction when she emerged from one of her meditation exercises mumbling "animal."

Oleander jumped from his chair. "I think I now have it! Think about it this way: Why does the formula say *their* vision, *they* rush; *they* bow down? Who are *they*?"

"Perhaps the answer is the codeword, Old Monk... Oh, I see what you mean: The formula is like a riddle: 'Who are *they*?'"

"Exactly. And the answer is: animals. Because the vision of Ezekiel mentions four mystical animals, and these animals run to and fro, and appear like lightning."

"But Osnat said 'animal,' not 'animals.'"

"That's almost the same idea, Eliezer. Or... wait... The book of Ezekiel says that each of these animals has four faces: the face of a man, a lion, a bull, and an eagle. So if we take seriously Osnat's 'animal,' the sixth Sefirah could refer to one of these four."

"Well," Eliezer replied, "in the Biblical world 'man' doesn't fall in the category of animal."

"Then one of the other three."

Eliezer deliberated, then wrote in his notebook: 'animal,' animals,' lion,' 'bull' and 'eagle.'

Oleander looked at the list in frustration. "What I can't understand is the rationale. So far we've had 'circumcision,' 'cunning,' 'keep silent,' 'love,' 'the land'—what the devil is the connection?"

"William, as I have said, when it comes to the Book of Creation, logic alone cannot produce answers. It can get us only a certain distance, and from then on we need... let's call it intuition."

"Which is to say, we need *her*." The monk turned around. "Can you tell us anything—*anything*—about how you've come up with these words?"

She was on the sofa, leafing through a book. "I don't have a clue."

The next day, as Osnat calmed her mind in preparation for another training descent to her Inner Depths, she felt a bubble of knowledge rising in her. Instead of embarking on her descent she changed her focus, opening a space for the bubble to fill, and waited. It was small but clear and concise, and when she understood it her lips formed the word *"Hamor."*

Oleander, who was sitting on the couch opposite her chair, raised his head from his reading. "What?"

"Hamor." The bubble was gone now and she opened her eyes. "That's the Hebrew word for Donkey."

"I know what it is. You're not serious, are you?"

Eliezer joined them from his bedroom. "Did I hear you correctly? Are you sure, Osnat, it was *Hamor* and not something that sounds similar? *Yahmur*—elk—maybe?"

"It was definitely *Hamor*."

"A donkey is a profane animal in the Bible. It would be a curse word. I cannot imagine anything sacred to the Jews referring to this animal."

Osnat shrugged. "All I can tell you is what I heard. Maybe it was about something else, not your codewords."

82

David Wyatt normally maintained an even keel. His work demanded a detached mind. But for the past two weeks he had ridden an emotional roller coaster. He would find himself walking down Park Avenue and it would strike him that he, along with a mere handful of others, was specially blessed by God. What was the expression Peprini used? "The Blessing flows through you to the world." And he would nearly laugh aloud at the absurdity of it.

The last wave hit New York hard. A minor earthquake had ruptured gas and water lines in large pockets of Staten Island and Queens. The fires burned unchecked because of the broken water lines. Telephone service was knocked out across much of Manhattan as a major exchange had been severely damaged, but the system of cellphone towers had survived mostly intact. Several skyscrapers had been condemned as city engineers declared there was an unacceptable probability of collapse. The surrounding areas were evacuated as a precaution. The subways continued to experience intermittent power outages for unknown reasons. Rolling brownouts across the Northeast should be expected, officials said, due to damage to power stations upstate and in Ontario. The Stock Exchanges in New York as well as in London, Europe, Hong Kong, Shanghai, Japan and elsewhere were closed for the weekend. There was a rumor that at least some would not open on Monday.

Wyatt stood at the end of the bar in the Anvil House Tavern, a block from his home, and downed the rest of his scotch. Stepping into the cool night he glanced at the pedestrian traffic light, saw that it wasn't working, then crossed the street.

Coming upon his townhouse he saw two men exit a Lincoln sedan and run to the entrance. Then he noticed a woman standing by the steps. The men grabbed her roughly by the arms. Without thinking, David sprinted up the sidewalk.

"Hey!"

The men turned but dragged her to the car. A third man climbed from the driver's seat to open the rear door. Nearing the struggle David realized the scene was odd. These men were well-dressed and neatly groomed, the Town Car new. The woman, however, looked like she lived on the streets.

"*What are you doing?*"

Now that he was upon them the two men stopped and looked at each other.

"Mr. Wyatt, please, you don't know what's happening here," the third man said.

"*What...* how do you know my name?"

"Please. She's dangerous."

"Dangerous? What do you mean? *Who are you?*"

He signaled, and the two others maneuvered her into the car. The leader stood between David and the car, his hands raised to the sides in a pleading gesture. When his hands went up, his leather jacket opened and the pistol in its shoulder holster became visible.

"I have no idea how she got to the steps of your building without us spotting her. Please, Mr. Wyatt, go inside."

"How is she any danger to me or anyone? *And who are you?*"

The man spun on his heels and jumped behind the wheel, and the car accelerated down the street.

The immediate shock left Wyatt and he reached for his phone to call 911. He stopped. Those men knew me and... there was something about the look in their eyes, the tone of the leader's voice. It wasn't respect. It was more. They were servants doing what's best for their master even if he couldn't understand. As if I were a boy-King too young to understand such matters yet still revered. *Yes.* In the next moment he knew: They were Keepers.

He climbed the steps to his door. Inside he went straight to his study and sat behind his desk, already holding the card with Peprini's number.

He picked up the phone. No dial tone. He cursed and tried another line, then remembered the land lines were down. He turned on his cell and heard the tone. He dialed and the English-accented woman's voice on the machine said simply, "Please leave your message."

"Peprini. Something just happened outside my home and I'm betting you know about it. Call me on my cell. I'm sure you have the number."

Peprini was sitting behind his own desk at the Book Company when the relay in London notified him. He was not in the mood to deal with the Vessel, but long ago he had stopped allowing his moods to dictate his actions.

The cell phone rang on David's desk. He picked it up but said nothing.

"You have questions."

"Do you know anything about what happened here tonight? With the woman?"

"Tell me."

David described the event and waited.

"Peprini?"

"It's unfortunate you witnessed that."

"Unfortunate I *witnessed* that? The woman was kidnapped! Did you order that?"

"Without going into more detail than I'm able, she is... she and her kind are... dangerous to you. Lethally dangerous."

"Dangerous? What, she was going to shoot me?"

Peprini sighed. "No."

"Then what?"

"You'll have to trust we wouldn't undertake something like this without extraordinary reason. No harm will come to her. Had we evil intentions we could have simply shot her. But we went to the pains of removing her from your presence."

"What did you mean, 'she and her kind'?"

"We are dealing with Biblical matters, David. Let's leave it at that. I've told you much about my world, but you can't expect a dissertation on Keepers and Vessels over the phone. You called only to ask about the woman?"

He now recalled the look in the Keeper's eyes as he shielded me—he *was* shielding me—from the homeless woman. A peculiar vulnerability came over him. "Am I in danger?" Silence. *"How could I be in danger from this woman?"*

"The immediate threat has been removed."

"Goddammit, tell me how these people can harm me."

"Very well. As you should remember, Vessels are protected by the Blessing."

"That much I know."

"It seems that some of this protection has disappeared."

"What do you mean? How can you tell?"

"Of the five Vessels I spoke of at our first meeting—you being one of these—three have recently died."

"*Three?* How?"

"One woman was murdered by an acquaintance. Another in a fatal car accident. And a child died in... complicated circumstances."

"A child? Three of the other four are dead?"

"Yes."

"That's it? *Yes?*"

"Very well. The woman you saw this evening is cursed. Or she *is* a curse."

"Cursed? As in…"

"Our modern vocabulary is lacking here. We think she and her kind are the descendants of Cain."

"As in *Cain* and *Abel*?"

"We do all that is possible to protect you."

"You get my vote on that. We're talking protection from… I can't believe I'm saying this… a curse?"

"Cainites. Yes."

"Cainites, fine. And how do we do that?"

"We continue to keep them away from you. Physical proximity seems the key. Is it possible for you to remain inside your home for the next several days?"

"If I have to."

"We are hoping you will soon renew the Blessing. This will help protect you."

"From the Cainites."

"Yes."

David was nodding as if the more he did the more reasonable all this would sound.

"Not to alarm you, but the fact the Cainite got so close this evening likely weakened you further. I'll be speaking with your Keepers. They might know, having been in your presence."

"I don't feel any different."

"A diminishment of the Blessing isn't something you would necessarily feel. Not unless you attuned yourself to it."

"So you expect me to have this dream soon?"

"Given that you haven't renewed the Blessing for some time, yes."

"Will Maria guide me?"

"She is still too weak. You will do it as you've done your whole life, on your own."

"Why don't *you* go with me into the Void?" David asked the question because he wanted to understand better, especially now that his very life apparently depended on being blessed. But he was also following an intuition. Often in negotiations he found an urge to ask a question that seemed only tangential to the deal but revealed important clues in the other side's reaction. At this moment he felt he was in such a negotiation with Peprini. "What's the real reason Maria can't go with me?"

"Because she is dead." He held his breath as he waited for David's reaction.

"*Maria is dead?*"

"She is."

"*How?*"

"We don't know if Keepers can survive in the Void even if shielded by a Vessel. The protection you offered Maria was not enough to keep her alive."

Peprini was aware this might make the Vessel feel guilty and hoped this would make him easier to control.

"Christ, why didn't you tell me her life depended on me? If I'd known…"

"It might have helped. We don't know. Surely you must understand by now the seriousness of what is happening."

"You sent her because you were too scared to go yourself."

"In part this is true. But there are more important reasons why I and my fellow Councilors mustn't take this risk. We are, as you rightly point out, the strongest. It is because we illuminate the Bible world that Vessels successfully navigate the Void as often as they do. This capacity cannot be risked."

"You sacrificed her."

"David, we aren't beasts. Maria understood the sacrifice she might be making. She freely undertook the devotion. She felt honored, if you must know." Peprini could hear the Vessel breathing. "For now, you will renew the Blessing on your own. Otherwise, there is nothing for you to do."

"Except stay alive."

"Yes, David, that would help."

83

The following morning Peprini decided to return to the Granary, this time alone. Like Sionn, Erna, Goldman and Krystofski, he had moved from his house in town into a suite at the Rare Book Company offices. There were too many road accidents, and the Councilors decided to avoid unnecessary risks. His wife and children were as safe as they could be on the family estate outside of Lucerne.

He got into his car and contrary to his habit of driving in silence turned on the radio. "Trains also collided at the Zurich Main Station with perhaps a hundred feared dead, though we have only early reports. Locally, emergency crews are also busy battling four-alarm fires at the Riverstrasse multi-cinema and at the 600 block of Schwanenplatz where fires are spreading among a warren of commercial warehouses. At the moment perhaps forty percent of the city is without power, complicating efforts. Authorities are asking that citizens stay off the roads to allow emergency crews to do their work. And to repeat our main story," the announcer continued, clearly affected, "the earthquake which struck the Netherlands with a magnitude of 7.9 on the Richter scale has burst a large number of dikes. The country which is largely below sea level is now mostly underwater. Holland as we've known it no longer exists. Estimates of the numbers feared dead are... well, it is beyond tragic, beyond comprehension."

Peprini turned off the radio and put the car in gear. He steered down the rutted road and turned through the convent gate. The grounds, still littered with fallen leaves (such matters had been neglected in the last weeks at the convent and Abbey), were covered in frost, a faint steam rising in the morning sun.

He found Pem standing outside the Granary in the bright sun, arms folded across his chest for warmth. The Master-Keeper moved quickly to the car and opened the door.

"Menach, good morning. I wasn't expecting you."

"It is careless of you to be outside with no coat, Pem. It should be obvious we must take precautions against such things as catching a cold or flu."

"Of course. I just needed a breath of air."

"Have you anything to report?"

"One addition. A woman brought from New York a short while ago," Pem said, closing the door behind them.

"I will check on our visitors," Peprini said turning away.

"Menach." His appeal stopped Peprini. "May I ask who or what you think they are? Why you think they are here?"

Under normal circumstances, Pem wouldn't presume to ask what the Council obviously had decided not to reveal. Peprini had noticed this change in decorum among other Keepers too. This new behavior never crossed over to insubordination. So far at least, he thought.

"To the best of our knowledge, they are descendants of Cain, or what we are calling *Cainites.*"

"Because of the marks on them?" Peprini nodded. "It is the curse God laid upon Cain and his progeny that is causing the deaths of the Vessels?"

"It would seem so." He moved to the stairs with Pem on his heels. "I won't be needing you."

"Certainly. We've strung new lights on both staircases, and a handrail was installed on the lower one."

"Very good."

Peprini managed the stairs easily with the additional light. Two novices, Jose Pinedo and Lev Bolski, stood as he approached the cell. He noticed their chairs were facing away from the locked room.

"Please open the outer door." Bolski did as instructed. "You may wait upstairs."

Except for the addition of the new Cainite (whom Peprini couldn't pick out among the others) nothing in the cell had changed. Two—he didn't know if these were the same two as the day before—were lying on the floor near the back. The child sat cross-legged to one side, her eyes fixed on Peprini. The one he was looking for stepped forward.

"Can you speak?" Peprini asked. "Who are…"

"*Why do you hate us?*"

The voice was deep and authoritative. Peprini found the guttural Canaanite accent difficult. Of course, he had never heard a native speaker of the language—no living person had.

The Cainite spoke again. "Who are you?"

"We are Keepers." He couldn't tell if the prisoner understood. "And you?"

"We are from Enoch."

He knew from the Book of Genesis that Enoch was the name of Cain's son, as well as the name of the city Cain founded in Nod. "Where is

Enoch?"

"Where is Enoch?" The Cainite repeated. Peprini wondered whether he had remembered the word correctly.

"Yes, *where?*"

"Enoch is... not." The Cainite saw his captor's confusion. He grasped the rusty gate and turned his hands around an iron bar. "Nothing of what is above is in Enoch."

"Above? Where the sun and sky are?"

"Sun?"

"Yes. Above is the sun, the sky, there is light."

"Light. Yes. Above there is light."

"There is no light in Enoch?"

He shook his head. He reached through the bars, and Peprini took a step back. The prisoner stopped, then slowly extended his arm until he touched the Keeper lightly on his cheek. Peprini girded himself against the revulsion of his touch. "This. There is no light."

Yes, Peprini thought, there would be none of God's light! He looked at the prisoner and quoted Genesis Chapter 4: "Cain said to the Lord, 'My punishment is greater than I can bear. Behold, you have driven me this day away from the ground; and from your face I shall be hidden.' From the light you have been hidden, yes?"

"Yes. Our grandfather Cain was sent to the land without light."

"Please, speak more slowly. It is difficult for me to understand."

"Our grandfather was sent to the land without light."

"What is your name?"

"I am Irad, grandson of Cain."

"How did you come to be here, in the land of the light?"

"Something awakened us. We had forgotten. For how long..." It seemed the Cainite was searching for some gauge of time and realized he had none. "Until I saw the one who gives the light."

"The little girl?" This Cainite along with a woman and the child had been captured together near the rebel camp in Ethiopia where Vessel Anina Lenoma and her mother had died.

The prisoner nodded. "And your name?"

"I am a Keeper. Peprini. But tell me now, how did you get here from Enoch?"

"Once awakened I saw..." In frustration he looked around him. His eyes lit upon a tear in the sleeve of his shirt. He pulled on the cloth so the hole made by the tear was more evident. "I saw this."

Peprini gestured to say he didn't understand.

"I saw it. Not with..." and he covered his eyes with his hands for a moment. "With this." He held both hands over his heart. "There was light in the opening. I was called to it. And then we..." He turned and looked at the child and the woman squatting on her heels, her back against the wall of the cell. "We found ourselves in your world, in these." He put his hands on his chest as if remembering the feel of flesh and bones.

"You were given light?"

"Yes, in the opening we found light. Then... here."

Peprini gripped the iron gate. The nausea made it hard to think. He felt vulnerable in both familiar and strange ways.

"Can others speak?"

"I and Ada, my wife, are the only ones completely awake." The others..." He turned and looked compassionately at the rest. "They are as children dreaming. Some might awaken as I did. I do not know. But you make this to them, you make this to them even though they are as children. You make this to my daughter." He turned to the little girl, then back to Peprini. "Now you will tell why you put us in this cage?"

"Slowly, please."

"Why do you put us here?"

"Because you are destroying the light. You are killing the sources of the light in our world."

"Your world? How are we making this? We are so few."

Peprini was becoming dizzy. He now understood that the guards had the chairs from necessity and not laziness. Peprini glanced at Ada, Irad's wife, and saw she was paying close attention to the conversation.

"The grandchildren of Cain are not meant to be in this world," he said more harshly than he intended. "You are not meant to be in the light. God..." He saw that the mention of God brought a strange, distant expression to the prisoner's face "...Cain's own grandfather decided that Cain and his children and their children will live outside the light."

"We cannot remain in this place of light?"

Peprini turned away, finding that even putting his back to them helped somewhat. Once several steps away, he turned to face Irad. "It is impossible!" He calmed himself. "You are destroying the very light you seek."

"Look at us. Without the light, we cannot exist in this place."

"Tell me, why do you believe you live without the light?"

"It has always been. Our grandfather Cain brought us to Enoch."

"But why? *From where?*"

Peprini could see the question affected the Cainite. "It has always been. Beyond Enoch is the land where our Grandfather Cain was born. But we cannot return."

"Why not?"

"Our grandfather told our fathers we can never return. It has always been so. That is why he brought us to Enoch." Irad spoke as if reciting an immutable law of nature.

"I am sorry. You were not meant to exist here either."

"That can never change?"

"How, when your presence destroys the light?"

Irad's eyes seemed to accept this. He turned to his wife for a moment and Peprini couldn't see his face.

"Are there others, other springs of light, like the small girl?"

"Only two now. You destroyed three such sources of light."

"Two?"

"For the moment. Though I cannot say how long they will remain alive."

"And then you will also be without the light."

Peprini thought he saw a faint smile on the Cainite's face. "I must go, but I will return soon."

Irad only shrugged as if it made no difference.

<h1 style="text-align:center">84</h1>

Sionn was sitting with Erna in her office when Peprini returned to the Abbey. The door was open and he walked in and sat across from Sionn, dropping his body into the chair.

Sionn contracted his eyes and was startled to see that his aura was traversed with dark lacunas. "What happened to you?"

Erna likewise inspected him. "Yes, Menach. You look terrible."

"I've been with the Cainites." They waited for him to gather himself. "My God, I don't know how Pem does it. He must have a constitution of stone."

"It is that bad?" Erna had not visited the Granary and saw no reason to.

"We were there only a few minutes yesterday and I was made nearly ill," Sionn said sympathetically. "Did you learn anything new?"

Peprini shook his head. "As mysterious as ever. I told Pem to cancel the guards. There is no point in making our people suffer when the prisoners are behind two sturdy, locked doors."

"I was just telling Julia I've had all Anina Lenoma's Keepers sent to New York and Edinburg. We now have thirty-five of us protecting each Vessel. More would arouse suspicion."

"I can think of nothing else we are not already doing," Erna added. "Though it seems pitifully little."

A malaise gripped all three.

"Menach," Sionn said, "you should get some rest."

Peprini stood. "I believe I will."

Once in his own office, he dialed the Geneva number.

"Anwar's Rare Coins."

"Please tell the Prince that Mr. Peprini wishes to speak."

"This is an extremely difficult time for such a meeting. I'm afraid it's impossible."

"I am sure the Prince will make an exception for me."

"The Prince is seeing no one. But if Mr. Peprini has a message he wishes me to give the Prince, that will be done."

This was the end of the conversation—that was plain in the Ishmaelite's voice. Peprini was surprised by the second rejection of his request for a meeting.

"Tell him: This will discharge you of your obligation." Peprini used 'you' rather than the more respectful 'the Prince' as an expression of dissatisfaction. Peprini disliked mentioning the debt. It was rude of the one owed to speak of it, but an even greater violation for the one indebted to need to be reminded.

"Please wait a moment."

Several minutes passed.

"Councilor Peprini?"

"Yes?"

"The Prince will be available to Councilor Peprini at seven o'clock this evening. The Prince is most appreciative of the Councilor making a second trip to Geneva." Meaning this settles all obligations.

Peprini looked at his watch. It was almost noon. "Please tell him 'thank you.'"

Peprini paused before getting out of the taxi. The train hadn't been restful. Quite the opposite. The corridors were stuffed with passengers from stalled cars and disabled trains, all frustrated and noisy. The air-conditioning system which ventilated the compartments did not work, and he had a headache from breathing the stale air. Several times the train was stopped for long periods, and the waiting was nerve-wracking. What should have taken ninety minutes became a four-hour trip.

Once again the young Ishmaelite with the dark, slicked-back hair waited for him in the shop doorway. A "Closed" sign was in the window.

He turned and Peprini followed him into the shop. Another Ishmaelite stood near the rear, on his belt a pistol in a holster. The glass cases once holding collections of Greek, Roman and old European coins were empty. Do they believe there is no way to stop the deaths of the Vessels? Do they have some place, a retreat, they believe is safe?

The man led him through the rear door and down the same series of hallways and staircases as before, as best Peprini could tell. When they finally reached the large wooden door, the usher opened it slowly, bowing, and then stepped aside.

Some twenty yards into the great room were seated Prince Kedma, and to his left an unknown man. Peprini removed his shoes and walked across the immense dune-colored rug. He sat on the pillows prepared for him. As before, the Prince and the other man were on a slight dais.

"Thank you for seeing me with such little notice, and while you seem to be in the midst of moving."

The other man whispered and the Prince nodded. Peprini couldn't tell to whom the gesture was aimed.

"I am Chief Efron. How may we again help the grandson of Alberto Peprini?"

Ah, here it is, Peprini thought. The Chief was acknowledging the debt and the discharge of it in the same sentence.

"The question I have is this: Do the Cainites come because of a Keeper's transgression against the Blessing? And also: Is there any action a Keeper can take to stop the Cainites' Curse from ending the Blessing?"

"The ways of the Blessing and of the Curse are hidden beyond the horizon at this hour," the Chief said. "Unless you wish to inform us of something we do not yet know."

"I am here to *receive* knowledge. From those who *presumably* have it."

The Chief seemed immune to Peprini's taunt. "Knowledge begets knowledge. If the Prince starts from more, he might see more."

In short, Peprini thought, the Prince has already contemplated these questions and learned nothing. "I am afraid I do not have any knowledge that is related to my questions, Chief Efron."

"It need not be directly related, Councilor. The world is one, and all knowledge is connected."

Peprini reflected. He couldn't tell them about his experiments with the Void. That would be too dangerous. But he could hint at a lesser transgression. "I can tell you this," he finally said. "The Vessel of New York has been informed that he is a Vessel."

The two Ishmaelites stared at him curiously. Again the Chief whispered to the Prince.

"The Prince will contemplate on your question now."

As before, the young Ishmaelite escorted Peprini to the small room that adjoined the meeting hall.

When the door had closed, Chief Efron took a pad and pencil and gave them to the Prince, and then sat still while he formed the questions for the contemplation. Minutes later he returned the pad to the Chief. On it was written:

Where in Keeperdom do the Children of Nod pursue the sons of Simeon and Benjamin?

If every end is a new beginning, how can a Keeper return the end to its beginning?

Efron believed he understood the first. Benjamin's son—or, Benjamin's descendant—was Lessing, and Simeon's was Wyatt, the two surviving Vessels. The second question mystified him.

"Shall we begin?"

"Yes," the Prince said.

The click of the door startled Peprini who was on the verge of dozing. "The Prince will see you now."

It didn't appear that the old man had moved. Peprini resumed his seat on the pillows and then noticed his face was a cadaverous gray, his cheeks and eyes sunken, these changes having occurred in the past two hours. He had changed his robes. Nevertheless, he sat nobly and with no loss of dignity.

"Two Keepers have attempted to open the Primordial Gate," the Prince began. "A passageway to the Void is now open. Through this passageway the Cainites are coming to pursue the fountains of Blessing in our world. However..."

A sense of relief and spiteful delight invaded Peprini. "Two Keepers tried to open *the Primordial Gate!?*"

The Prince nodded.

"Are you able to know who they are?"

"The professor and the monk. However, this new passageway would not have been enough to cause the disasters. This is the message I received in my contemplation."

"I do not understand its last sentence, Prince."

"Here is the way to understand it: The new passageway would not have been enough because similar passageways are opened every once in a while because of stray discernment beams. They stay open for several days, sometimes weeks, before the barrier heals. Such temporary passageways do not bring in the Cainites, and do not harm the Earth."

"Why not?"

"Because the Cainites are dormant. They sleep in the Void and do not notice the opening. Only this time, something—or someone—has awakened them. They noticed the passageway to this world and entered."

"And why were the Cainites awakened?"

"Because, Councilor, someone has been focusing his discernment beams directly into the Void, into their dwelling." Peprini froze, and the Prince continued. "Someone has been discerning the Void against the old laws. Cainites sleep because they lack sufficient Blessing to stay awake. The beams of Blessing awakened them."

Peprini could feel his face become pale and his hands shake. "Do you know," he said hoarsely, "who that discerner is?"

"I believe I do. But it is not our business to chastise. Our business is to know."

Peprini swallowed hard. "There are still two Vessels alive ..." he mumbled.

"The end of the Earth as we know it is now probable. But the door is open for a noble Keeper to bring about a new beginning, though at great risk."

"At great risk to whom? To what?"

The Ishmaelite ignored him. Chief Efron helped the Prince to his feet. "Though you did not ask, you might wish to know you are not the only Keeper to speak with an Ishmaelite Prince in this time of turmoil."

Peprini's face tightened.

"Yes," the Prince murmured. "The professor and monk."

"Thank you, Prince Kedma."

The old man turned to face the Keeper squarely. "And I thank once more your grandfather. He was a great man, and helped my father when he had no obligation to do so."

85

Eckart Blundt of the Edinburgh *residence* bought a bouquet of flowers at the shop around the corner from the hospital. He wrote a get-well message on a card, adding an illegible signature. Minutes later he took the elevator to the hospital's third floor. Every hour a Keeper made a pass on the floor to check for Cainites. In what had become instinct he scanned the floor for any of the strange creatures though he usually felt their presence before seeing them.

As he neared the room the Blessing was coldly unfamiliar. He knocked on the open door and took a few hesitant steps into the room. His eyes were drawn to Lessing in bed with an oxygen mask strapped to his face and an IV line in his arm, an array of machines around him.

"Yes?" Mrs. Lessing looked up from her book, her pale, freckled face and green eyes displaying an innate kindness.

"Flowers for the patient."

She stood and he handed them to her. "Thank you."

She turned and looked for something to hold them. Blundt lingered a moment, unable to take his eyes off the unconscious Vessel, a man he had watched almost every day for the last eleven years.

Kathryn Lessing noticed he was still in the room and set the flowers on the bed. "Oh, forgive me."

She took her purse and he said, "*Please, no.*" Then realizing he had been dramatic about the small gesture, added, "It's not necessary." He turned, taking one last look at the Vessel, and left the room.

Later that afternoon, on an unusually clear November day in Scotland, Soren Lessing, the last of Benjamin's line, the last of an unbroken chain of 187 Vessels descended from the twelfth son of Jacob, quietly died.

The news of Lessing's termination was received in Lucerne with what could have appeared calmness but which was actually shock and paralysis. Another Vessel's death in just six days—the minds of the Keepers could find no emotional response appropriate.

Erna, upon hearing of the death from Sionn, only emitted a muffled, "Ah... Well, then..."

Annette Goldman, receiving the news from Erna, returned her gaze from her friend's face to the computer screen and continued with her work as if nothing had been said. She felt that if her mind could not hold onto something concrete, it would virtually disintegrate.

"Annette. What do we do now?"

"We wait," Goldman said quietly, her fingers punching the keyboard. "Like someone with no immune system waiting to be killed by the next passing virus."

The impact of the death upon the Earth started seven hours later, when a series of tremors was felt on every continent. The tremors were mostly mild, causing some damage and few fatalities, but their main effect was to arouse a sense that *the very planet* was changing. Geologists noted with surprise that the quakes mainly struck regions with large populations— London, Mexico City, Beijing, Los Angeles, Tokyo, Lagos, and Buenos Aires. It was as if the quakes were directed against humanity.

Hours later a tidal wave hit the western shore of South America, from the southern tip of Chile to Peru. Everything and everyone from the coast to two miles inland was gone.

86

The President liked to be seen leaving the United Presbyterian Church in Washington D.C. with one hand holding that of his wife, and the other holding an oversized Bible. It was so obvious the man had selected the book to stand out in any photo that the press was preempted from making snide comments. Jerome Hunnicutt, the President's Chief Science Advisor, watched as his boss caressed that same Bible while sitting behind his desk in the Oval Office. It was no prop of political theater now. The man worried the leather cover as if it were one big rosary bead.

The President surveyed the others. "None of you has anything to say?"

The Science Advisor looked around the room. The National Security Advisor, the Chairman of the Joint Chiefs of Staff, the President's Chief of Staff, all turned to Hunnicutt, even though the Reverend Shelby Moorecroft, the President's spiritual advisor, had sat up in his spot on the couch and was getting ready to speak.

At that moment the now-familiar primeval shaking of the Earth arrested them. The first time Hunnicutt had been in this room, a similar quaking had dislodged a portrait of President Lincoln from the wall. No doubt everything was fastened down now. He saw that the Reverend in his panic had gripped the knee of Admiral Syznecki, who removed it as if picking an insect from his trousers.

"Mr. President, nothing has changed in our analysis."

"What analysis? Your people have given me nothing. Shelby?"

"God's intentions will become clear in time. We must wait as his humble servants."

"He's not abandoning us?"

"Certainly *not*, Mr. President! What would faith be if it couldn't stand a trial such as this? The mere faith of a child. Our understanding will come, all in *His* good time."

"Well, it's about that time, I'd say," said Grace Railton, the National Security Advisor.

The minister swiveled his head, his fleshy neck contorted by the collar of his shirt. "Blasphemy! If you want an explanation, Sir, you need look no further than the absence of faith on display here."

"Alright, alright, enough." The President sighed.

"Sir, as I've said, we have knowledge of only a small percentage of the geological faults in the Earth's crust." Hunnicutt was repeating his earlier explanations. "Some of these faults have been inactive for hundreds of years, just as we'd expect. Others are newly known to us. That we are just now learning of them in no way suggests there is anything *supernatural* about them. Nor is it surprising these quakes would influence one another. The shifting that takes place in one location—and that reduces the built-up stresses in that area—might also increase stresses and susceptibility to realignment along other fault lines."

"Leading to Earthquakes in other places," the President said.

"Exactly, sir."

This explanation, familiar to the President, served to calm him, reminding his rational side that natural events had natural causes. Still, it was plain to Hunnicutt that his leader's mind was lately a battleground between this rational side and the part of himself that was ready to abandon science and reason and turn to religion for comfort, if not answers.

"Mr. President," the Reverend said, "the people will not be satisfied if you respond again to this emergency by saying that..."

"Shit happens?" said the Admiral.

No one used profanity in front of the Reverend, and for several moments he was apoplectic. He gestured with his chin at both the Admiral and the Science Advisor as if both explanations amounted to the same thing.

"Admiral, are all land-based nuclear weapons systems offline now?" Walt Lott, the Chief of Staff, saw that the meeting was degenerating, something that was becoming common as everyone's nerves were ragged.

"Most. A web of missile silos in the Dakotas and Nebraska was damaged and we're having trouble reaching the weapons."

"Is there any danger?"

The Admiral grinned for just a moment. "Relatively speaking, no. We just haven't been able to disarm the warheads. We'll get to them. I'm more concerned about having sufficient troops to enforce martial law. With the difficulty getting planes in the air, it's damn slow getting our people back from overseas."

"It seems wise we did not order the evacuations, sir," The Chief of Staff advised. "Our projections suggest more would have died in the ensuing chaos than in the quakes we've had since."

"Statistically," said Hunnicutt, "what is much more *confounding* is the conglomeration of what we could term 'negative events' in the past several weeks. These have been far outside of standard deviations."

"Go on, Jerome." The President massaged his graying temples with his fingertips.

"As you noted yourself in speeches to the American people, the world has become inexplicably more dangerous. Accidents of all kinds, what we might call failures of technology, illnesses of virtually any variety, transportation accidents, murders… you name the trouble and the rates of occurrence have jumped, Sir."

"You can't pass this off as just some quirk of nature, Dr. Hunnicutt. Human beings are doing this. This is people causing evil and suffering. This is a fundamental change."

"On the contrary, Reverend. It's no more difficult to account for these than the quakes. It's an instance of mass hysteria, even mass delusion."

"That's absurd."

"Human behavior is much more malleable than other natural phenomena. In short, if people expect they will succumb to illness more easily than previously, they will. If they expect to injure themselves more easily, they will. If they expect driving to be more dangerous than it used to be, there will indeed be more accidents. Frustrations mount, tempers are shorter, there is a breakdown in the rules. To a significant degree, this becomes a self-fulfilling prophecy."

"People are being *more careful*, Jerome, not less. How does this lead to more accidents?"

"Sir, even excessive caution driving a car can have the opposite of the desired effect. The vast majority of us suppress the rational appreciation of how dangerous driving a car is. This suppression is the only way we could get ourselves to brave the highways. But if that ability to suppress the danger leaves us…the anxiety can be crippling."

The Admiral smiled faintly. "My mother. It got to where all she could think of while driving was that strangers she wouldn't trust to watch her dog were hurtling down the road in steel boxes, one hand holding a cellphone. She froze at the wheel in the parking lot of her church. Never drove once after that."

"Extend this phenomenon across all aspects of society," joined the Science Advisor, "and you have our present state."

"Why is science so afraid of acknowledging human evil, of acknowledging the work of Satan in human affairs? I've never understood this fear of acknowledging that so much of our world is beyond our understanding, I've never understood this *faith* in science." The reverend's voice was now shrill with passion.

"Shelby, I don't think this is helping."

"It's fine, Mr. President. Science isn't fearful. Rather, there's no *need* to introduce supernatural causes to explain these events. The burden of proof in these matters is on religion, Reverend, not on science."

"Are you willfully blind to this? We are told time and again in the Bible that punishment will be due those who turn away from God, who deny God and who turn to evil. We are reaping what we have sown. The Lord brought the plagues upon Egypt and the Pharaoh because of their sins. We are told in Exodus 7: *Moses and Aaron did as the Lord commanded; in the sight of Pharaoh and in the sight of his servants, he lifted up the rod and struck the water that was in the Nile, and all the water that was in the Nile turned to blood. And the fish in the Nile died; and the Nile became foul so that the Egyptians could not drink water from the Nile; and there was blood throughout all the land of Egypt. But the magicians of Egypt did the same by their secret arts; so Pharaoh's heart remained hardened and he would not listen to Moses.'* Sir, Egypt was once the most powerful nation on Earth, and we are now as Egypt was. Do not harden your heart to what you are witnessing, to these plagues, these signs from God. Do not allow these magicians…" and he turned to the others in the room, "to harden your heart."

"And you would be Moses in this drama?"

Reverend Moorecroft turned to Grace Railton. "I have recognized the sin of pride and arrogance in myself, Miss Railton. Have you?"

"Perhaps, Shelby, perhaps." The President stared at the Science Advisor and it seemed he detected something in the scientist's face. "Jerome. Shelby put his cards on the table. Now it's your turn. I've heard your professional position. Now I want to hear what *you* really think."

Jerome Hunnicutt, in fact, hadn't told the President what he truly believed. The physicist had spoken of it only among fellow scientists, and friends at that.

"What I truly believe, Mr. President? The laws of probability no longer apply to our world. Gravity hasn't changed. The laws of nature haven't changed. But the frequency with which specific events occur, this has changed dramatically. And these changes in probability seem to favor the adverse occurrence. The bad result."

"The world is having a run of bad luck?"

"No, Mr. President. Luck implies an eventual return to normalcy, to the laws of probability as we've known them." He leaned forward from his seat on the couch. "What you must understand, Sir, is there is no *reason*, no *natural law* that babies don't slip from their mothers' arms and fall more often than they do; that people don't choke to death while eating more often than they do; that people in the heat of an argument don't kill each other more often; that mechanical failures don't happen more often;

that plagues or earthquakes don't strike more often than they do. The world just is that way—or rather, has been that way over human history. It's *that world* we were born into, it's *that world* we've come to accept as natural, as necessarily so. But that world isn't the way the world must necessarily or naturally be. What I'm trying to say is that that world apparently no longer exists. And because we have no grasp of why this changed, we have no idea if the ordered world we remember will ever return.

87

Early that morning Oleander awoke feeling that at last his powers had been restored, and that he was ready for the next discernment session on the Book of Creation. Eliezer examined himself inwardly, then inspected the monk's aura, concluding that their strength was far from replenished. Still, he thought, they couldn't afford to wait any longer.

"Alright, William. We've narrowed down the list to four: 'animal,' 'lion,' 'eagle,' and 'bull'—assuming 'animal' and 'animals' count as the same word. I say we take 'eagle' off the list. I've been looking through the Old Testament and the impression is that birds were not regarded then as 'animals.' Sound reasonable?"

"I don't anticipate we will have the chance to finish the list. I would say we'll have two chances. Maybe a third."

"You'll be lucky if you survive one wrong guess," Osnat thought.

Oleander now turned to her. "And you. You were lucky last time; all of us were. But this isn't the Wild West where you can shoot whenever you feel like. If you say the wrong thing down there, you threaten us all."

Eliezer tried to soften the tone. "You did wonders last time, Osnat, but remember, your role is to support us in case of emergency, not to replace us. If you feel you know the codeword, motion to us and wait until we give you the sign to speak it."

Just when the three were getting ready to sit around the table, Eliezer's phone rang. "I was about to turn it off," he murmured. "Oh, it's Julia."

"Eli. How are things?"

"Not good."

"I'm calling because I feel it is crucial that we shouldn't give in to a spirit of resignation. We must all persevere in our discernment duties as well as we can. I can't imagine that you and William, of all people, should be reminded?"

Eliezer, aware that he and Oleander had not done their customary discernment for several weeks because of their endeavor, felt a pang of guilt. But he also was baffled by her words. Councilors' discernment duties had always been a matter for their own discretion. Reminding a Councilor to discern was a gross insult.

"I am sure you know we are doing our best."

"Yes, of course. Of course. And... are you planning to discern again soon?"

Coming from anyone but Julia he would have been indignant. "What are you trying to say?"

"Nothing, Eli, nothing. I was just wondering whether you've sensed any change in the Depths since Lessing's termination. This is unknown territory for all of us."

"Ah, yes," he said. He nevertheless thought her questions and tone strange. "As a matter of fact, I was preparing to descend just when you called."

"Let me know if anything looks unusual, will you? I'm afraid I'm just searching for some stability amidst all these changes.

"Which reminds me, Julia, why did no one bother to tell us Lessing was ill?"

Erna explained that Peprini had not wanted to cause needless alarm, but Eliezer sensed that she was no longer interested in the conversation and was trying to end it.

"The arrogant bastard." He hesitated, then made up his mind. "Listen, Julia, I need to tell you something about him."

"Peprini again?"

"This must remain between us."

"Alright, go ahead." There was weariness in her voice.

"Two weeks ago his men tried to kidnap Osnat Aviv. In Central Park."

"That's ridiculous."

"We identified one of them. Eric Tiplady, a new novice. According to Joanna Crumb, Peprini removed Tiplady for his own purposes. The boy mentioned Peprini by name."

"It makes no sense. What would Menach want with her? And why didn't you bring this up at the Council meeting?"

"I didn't think the others would believe us." He now regretted speaking, realizing it sounded so bizarre that it was not only an accusation against Peprini, but begged questioning his own activities. "As well, I..."

She waited. "Eli?"

"Please take care of yourself." There was an unexpected tenderness in his voice. "You know you are all I have in this world."

"And you... don't do anything foolish."

Each listened to the silence for a moment and hung up.

Despite their somber mood, the two Councilors did not waste time discussing the conversation with Erna and quickly descended to the edge of the Void. Osnat closed her eyes and soon joined them, stationing herself just behind the two.

Eliezer started discerning the introductory passage which they now knew so well:

WITH THIRTY-TWO MYSTERIOUS PATHS OF WISDOM...

Darkness fell around them, and Eliezer continued slowly. When he finished he continued to the sixth Sefirah:

TEN SEFIROT OF BELIMAH, THEIR VISION IS LIKE THE APPEARANCE OF LIGHTNING AND THEIR LIMIT HAS NO END, AND HIS WORD IN THEM IS TO-AND-FRO, AND TO HIS SPEECH THEY RUSH LIKE A WHIRLWIND, AND BEFORE HIS THRONE THEY BOW DOWN.

They could feel the energies gathering; it seemed that this should have been accompanied by sound, though the silence made it more threatening.

Oleander began reciting the Abraham passage.

WHEN ABRAHAM OUR FATHER, MAY HE REST IN PEACE, CAME, HE LOOKED, AND SAW, AND PROBED, AND UNDERSTOOD, AND ENGRAVED, AND CARVED, AND COMBINED, AND CREATED, AND THOUGHT, AND WAS SUCCESSFUL...

Oleander felt his field of vision drifting towards the Bible World, and he could no longer see his friend beside him. Although intellectually he knew that Eliezer was still with him, a sense of aloneness engulfed him. He waited anxiously as his field of vision kept zooming in faster and faster. At last the zooming motion slowed down, and now his perspective was from the Bible side of the Void. He could see again the wondrous scene of God blessing Abraham. He knew he was not in the Bible World like a Vessel, that it was only a trick of perspective, for he was seeing the Biblical scene from afar just as he always had as a Keeper. But his visual field had now shifted to include the Void from the opposite direction, and he marveled at seeing Abraham against the background of the darkness that enveloped the Earth. He could see his own golden discernment beam emanating from Abraham, penetrating into the Void, its tip a golden sphere, towards Earth, towards, he hoped, the beam Eliezer was creating.

IMMEDIATELY THE LORD OF ALL, MAY HIS NAME BE BLESSED FOREVER, WAS REVEALED TO HIM, AND HE PLACED HIM IN HIS BOSOM, AND KISSED HIM ON HIS HEAD, AND CALLED HIM 'ABRAHAM MY BELOVED,' AND HE MADE A COVENANT WITH HIM AND WITH HIS SEED AFTER HIM FOREVER.

Meanwhile, Eliezer had finished his recitation of the introductory passage. It was now the moment for the codeword. He readied himself to face the wild torrents in case the first guess was wrong.

At the same time, Osnat felt a powerful bubble of knowledge inside her. Hardly had she had time to sense it when a word exploded in her mind with self-evident certainty: "Hamor"—Donkey again!

And as Eliezer was opening his mouth and taking a deep breath, Osnat shouted, "Hamor!"

There was a commotion behind the thick darkness. Then the walls of energies surrounding them collapsed, torrents rushing around them and past them and disappearing into the Void as if a vacuum seal had been released.

The two Councilors continued discerning into the Void, Oleander following the golden sphere receding into the distance towards the Earth, and Eliezer watching a similar shaft of Blessing boring its way towards the Bible World. An explosion appeared at the end of each beam, a golden fireball which swelled for a few seconds before dissipating.

Oleander stopped discerning and once again stood with his companions at the edge of the Void. Together they scanned the emptiness... Yes! A small dot of light in the ocean of darkness. Was the Hidden Gate open? It was doubtful; the light was too dim. Still, it seemed like an opening, because through it they could make out... *something*.

They waited, hoping to see Oleander's beam emerging from the darkness. But no. The spot of light might have indicated a passageway across the Void, but even if so, its dimness showed that it was still too narrow to serve as a Gate.

They turned and started making their way back to their respective Inner Depths. As Oleander passed by Osnat he looked into her eyes with a mixture of reproach and admiration.

Some time later Oleander opened his eyes. He understood that they had succeeded thanks to Osnat—thanks to her disobedience—and his anger evaporated. He saw that Eliezer's face was pale: he was spent. The monk leaned across the table and touched his arm. The old man slowly raised his head.

"Just rest."

Osnat had nearly emerged from her Inner Depths but had noticed a second bubble of knowledge forming. It was slowly shaping itself, growing in clarity and size, maturing. She knew now to be patient.

The bubble opened and its content reverberated.

"The Ishmaelites," she spoke softly, "are sailing away in Noah's Ark."

Oleander turned to her. "What?"

She opened her eyes, still regaining her orientation.

"What did you say?" the monk asked.

"I think it was something like: 'The Ishmaelites are leaving in Noah's Ark,' wasn't it?"

"What the hell does *that* mean?"

"I don't know."

"But they were your own words!"

"No, not mine. They spoke through me."

Eliezer opened his eyes at this exchange, and the two Councilors examined her pensively. By now they accepted she had unusual paths to knowledge. They could no longer dismiss her words.

"I suggest we go to Harlem and check up on our cousins," Oleander said. Glancing at Eliezer he added, "tomorrow morning, after we sleep."

After Erna finished her conversation with Eliezer, she reached to phone Annette Goldman to inform her that Eliezer was about to discern. Then she stopped. No, spying on him with a third person seemed worse than doing it alone. She sat in her discernment chair and closed her eyes.

She waited at the edge of the Void, scanning the vast emptiness, relieved she could detect nothing. But then a beam appeared against the darkness, strong and steady. It was directed at the Bible World, and, as in her previous sighting, seemed to wane and disappear mid-way across the Void. But no—*this time it did not disappear altogether*. A thread of light, barely visible, continued all the way to the Bible World. She had never seen such a beam. A beam was always a unified line; its size and intensity never changed in the middle of the Void.

A few minutes later, when Erna emerged from the Depths, she called Peprini, then Sionn. And when she heard their voices, her fear came true: It had been Eliezer.

88

The cab ride from the hotel to Harlem was painfully slow, winding between abandoned cars and debris of all kinds. The twenty-mile-per-hour limit was strictly enforced by the New York Police and National Guard. Sitting in the back, the two Councilors interrogated Osnat about what Oleander called her "prophetic pronouncement."

"This is awfully similar to what I understand Ishmaelites do. I've taught dozens of novices and have never seen anyone like you. Just who or what are you?"

"Oleander." Eliezer softly scolded him.

"I've discerned. Isn't that proof of what I am?"

"Who said others can't discern? Who knows what the children of Ishmael, or of Lot, or of Melchizedek can and can't do?"

"No, Oleander," Eliezer said, turning back. "The old books say discernment was given to Esau alone." But he looked at her with a new curiosity.

The taxi dropped them off by the now-familiar building. They made their way through the gap in the chain-link fence and up the steps. Oleander knocked several times. Nothing.

They walked around the building and tried to peer through the cloudy windows.

"There aren't any bars on the ones on this side." Osnat thumped a window frame with the palm of her hand. "The latch on this one is loose. I think I... Eliezer, do you have your pocketknife?"

He handed her a small Swiss Army knife, and with a little jiggling she opened the window.

"Such carelessness is not like them," Eliezer said, taking a step back and scanning the building.

"Hello? Kedar?" Osnat shouted. There was no answer.

She took a crate from a pile of discarded lumber and turned it upside down. Using it as a step she climbed through the window. "Meet me at the side door."

"Good girl."

Moments later the door opened and Eliezer entered. Oleander hesitated. "This is breaking and entering."

They found themselves in a small room with a hardwood floor. If there had been furniture, it was now gone. Oleander flipped the light switch but nothing happened.

Eliezer turned to Osnat. "Would Kedar leave without saying goodbye to you?"

She was puzzled and a bit hurt at that thought.

There was a single interior door. It had no knob. She knocked. "Ouch. Steel."

Oleander was eager to leave. "Let's try the jewelry store."

They had to walk three blocks before finding a taxi. The goldsmith's store was closed, the iron grating securely in place. It was dark inside and nothing could be seen through the soaped windows. The shoe store next door was also closed—"temporarily" the sign said—and they then inquired at a bodega two doors down.

The Korean shop-owner pulled the paper medical mask from his face, letting it dangle against his throat.

"The jewelers? They didn't open this morning."

He looked up from habit at the mirrors in the corners of the ceiling, then his eyes returned to the newspaper and the bold headline: "Eastern Fever in New York." The second headline read: "Earthquakes kill 30,000,000 more in China and West Africa."

"Were they here yesterday?"

"Maybe they just had enough. If I could afford it, I'd shut the door. It's getting crazy out there. Me, I was robbed twice last week. And these weren't punks either. Regular people. As regular as anything is anymore."

"Indeed," Eliezer said.

"You have masks?" He tapped a box with dozens of the white paper surgical masks neatly stacked. "Only four dollars, cheap insurance. It's here now, you know. The fever. This is my last box."

"We'll take our chances," said Oleander.

The shop owner glanced again at the mirrors and pulled the mask back over his face.

They had to wait twenty minutes for a taxi and then drove in silence back to the hotel. Standing in the lobby was Kedar.

"Here you are," Eliezer said pleasantly. "We were wondering where you all disappeared to."

"What's wrong?" Osnat said.

Only now did the Councilors see that he looked worried. "Here I am, but I'm supposed to be elsewhere. With the rest of my people."

"Which is where," asked Oleander, "if the great secret can be told? Noah's Ark?"

Kedar was taken aback.

"Where or what is this Noah's Ark, Kedar?" Eliezer inquired.

"It's a space we've managed to… insulate from the rest of the world."

"Insulate how?"

"Let's say—behind a wall of improbability. That's how it was described to me."

"In short," said Eliezer, "you are escaping the upcoming catastrophe just as the Biblical Noah escaped the final flood in his Ark."

"We'll come back after God creates a new world on the ruins of this one, as the ancient books tell us he's done many times before. Or, if this world survives, when things have achieved a new equilibrium."

"And you say this so casually," Oleander said with clear disdain.

"I've come to invite Osnat to go with us."

"She belongs here. She has Esau's blood."

"But also Ishmaelite blood. Haven't you wondered why my grandfather has taken an interest in her?"

Eliezer shook his head. "No, Kedar. She is a Keeper. I have witnessed her discerning."

"She is a Keeper no doubt. But also an Ishmaelite. You must have seen she has the gift of knowledge."

"Aha…" Eliezer looked at Osnat. "Is it possible? A Keeper and an Ishmaelite? Canon has it that a person cannot belong to both lineages. The bloodlines annul each other."

"That's what makes her so special."

"So the Prince," Oleander said, "has sent you with this tale of mixed lineages. Go back and tell him she's staying where she belongs."

"My grandfather? You don't understand. He would be infuriated to learn I was here. He told me Osnat should remain with you and help."

"Help?" Eliezer wondered. "I thought you said the world is doomed."

"My grandfather believes there is a small chance. He is by nature optimistic. But it would be safer for Osnat with us."

She moved between the three men. "You are arguing over me as if I were the family dog. I'm not going anywhere without Eliezer and William."

"I expected that. I'm sure my grandfather won't object if they come along. We'll need good Keepers in the next world."

"And let our world be destroyed?" Eliezer said. "Leave how many people—possibly all of them—to die? No, Kedar."

Oleander nodded. "We'll finish what we started. We've almost opened the passageway through the Void to the Hidden Gate."

"More likely you'll die if you stay."

Eliezer and Oleander stood firm.

"Then you leave me no choice."

"Meaning?"

"That I defy my grandfather and remain with you three."

Osnat turned and her eyes pleaded with Eliezer. He saw a young woman in love, even if she had not yet realized it herself. He took a small step towards Kedar and placed his hand on his shoulder. "Welcome, Ishmaelite." Then he looked questioningly at his friend.

Oleander tried to think but his mind was blank. He glanced at Osnat—he felt a pang in his heart—she was achingly lovely. Then an answer to his prayers arrived at the moment most needed. From the core of his being came the truth: I have devoted my life to the Blessing, I am it and it is me.

His face softened. He extended his hand to the Ishmaelite.

Kedar smiled, obviously relieved. "I have some things I need to do. It may take me a day or two." He took out his wallet and removed a card and handed it to Osnat. "My number."

89

Peprini awoke refreshed in his Lucerne home. The 130-mile train trip back from Geneva had taken a day and a half. Collapsed bridges, power outages at many stations, computer failures, all had made a simple and direct trip impossible. He had decided to rest in Lucerne before returning to the Abbey.

Despite these obstacles, and even in the face of Lessing's death, an optimism and renewed sense of divine purpose pulsed in him. He drove into town delighting in knowing that Eliezer and William were the cause of the Vessel deaths; at least that was the only interpretation he could give the Prince's words. Of course, he had known that they had been up to something, but opening the Primordial Gate? Their audacity was difficult not to admire. Of all the Council members, only Eliezer (not Oleander, not alone) or Peprini himself would dare confront the Primordial Gate. But this admiration wouldn't keep him from exposing the offenders to the Council and witnessing their downfall, no doubt their execution. It occurred to him, of course, that he was guilty of a similar offense, but he believed he had a birthright to violate the rules. Further, Eliezer and Oleander had failed, and history would judge the rightfulness of these acts by their success.

This dark satisfaction wasn't the only source of his new sanguineness. He felt the elements of a plan forming in his mind. The Ishmaelite Prince's pronouncements foretold what would be, insofar as could be known: "*The end of the world is now probable, but the door is open for a noble Keeper to bring about a new beginning, though at great risk.*"

A noble Keeper, he thought. Who else but me? Who else had the nobility, resourcefulness and daring to "bring about a new beginning?"

He drove into town to his favorite café. He settled at a table near the only other patron, a woman engrossed in *Le Monde*.

The woman, dressed in a fashionable blue business suit, gold earrings and bracelet, read the newspaper with a worried expression. Peprini had seen the headline at the news-stand: "Eastern fever spreads to Australia and North America." Millions had died in Indonesia and Malaysia, and it had quickly spread across Asia. The United States, Japan, Canada, Britain, and the European Union banned the few remaining flights from Asian countries, but despite these measures, cases appeared in Germany and in Canada in the Vancouver area, and the first cases in the United States had just appeared in New York, Miami and Los Angeles. Named by scientists "CPVI" or "critical pulmonary viral infection," the public simply called it "Eastern fever." With the means of transmission still uncertain, so were the necessary precautions. Parents began keeping children home from school. Surgical masks worn in public drew few stares, and shaking hands was reserved for those one knew, and even then done uncomfortably.

The woman looked up at Peprini, as if suddenly aware she was breathing the air exhaled by him.

"C'est la fin." She smiled wanly.

"La fin, oui. Armageddon." He returned her smile, and she put her eyes again in the newspaper.

The Keeper's thoughts turned to the Cainites in the ancient Granary. He knew Irad might prove important, and that other Keepers mustn't know of him. But important to me how? How could I use Irad to bring about a new beginning? Everything about the Cainites was deadly to the Blessing. Still, he knew that their meeting was fateful.

He finished his coffee and croissant and smiled to himself as he left the café, anticipating his next conversation.

A short time later he entered the Rare Book Company building. Erna's secretary told him she had been at the chapel all morning.

"The chapel, Ingrid? A newfound ritual?"

"She said she needed to think."

He walked across the courtyard cobblestones to the Abbey and found Erna meditating in the chapel. The handful of Keepers present kept a respectful distance from the Councilor. He sat down on the bench beside her. Leaning forward inches from her ear, he whispered:

"Your Eliezer and William have opened the Primordial Gate. It is they who let in the Cainites."

Her face drained of color. She took a moment to gather herself before standing. Without looking at him she left the chapel, feeling him following. Once in the hallway, she turned.

"What did you say?"

"Eliezer has caused the deaths of the Vessels. He and William have opened the Primordial Gate."

"How do you know?"

"So you were ignorant of this?"

"Of course I knew nothing!" she said defiantly, struggling to keep her voice down. "Do you honestly think I would permit anything that reckless?"

"I know of your loyalty to him."

"The Primordial Gate! My God. Are you sure? How did you learn this?"

She seemed less surprised than he had expected. "An Ishmaelite Prince. I spoke to him two days ago."

"It sounds like you too have much explaining to do."

"Then I suggest you call a meeting of the Council. Immediately."

As if having given an order to an underling, Peprini turned and strode down the corridor.

90

All morning Erna tried to phone Eliezer but couldn't get through. She wanted to hear their side of the story. But Peprini's ultimatum had expired. He would inform the Council if she did not. Finally she got through, but the call went to voicemail and she was forced to leave a message.

She could think of no defense. The anomalous discernment beams belonged to Eliezer and Oleander; of that she was certain. If Peprini's allegation was true, then their transgression was the worse crime imaginable.

Peprini entered her office just after noon. He tapped the face of his watch.

On the other side of the Atlantic Eliezer listened to the message: "Eli, Peprini claims you and William have violated the Primordial Gate, that it's you who have brought the Cainites. He says he has proof from an Ishmaelite Prince. And I must admit I have evidence you have discerned in forbidden ways. Oh, Eliezer, tell me this isn't true! If ever you listened to me, you will arrive on the soonest flight. And be prepared to defend yourselves."

The monk dropped onto the couch. "Oh my God."

Eliezer began pacing. "We go forward," he declared, stopping in his tracks. "This changes nothing."

"*Nothing? They will have us executed*! Or will you deny what we've been doing?"

"I do not plan on putting us in the position of defending nor denying, William. The moment we arrive in Lucerne we will be taken into custody. Nothing then could save the last Vessel. Even if we explain our work and plead we must continue, by the time the others finish debating..." He spread his hands in a helpless gesture.

"We can't stay here," Osnat said quietly.

"I am glad one of us is still thinking," Eliezer said. "They might not wait for us to turn ourselves in. I am sure Peprini knows where we are."

"Kedar will know a place."

Neither Eliezer nor Oleander liked turning to the Ishmaelite but knew she was right. She called from memory his number and spoke for a minute.

"He'll meet us in the lobby in an hour. He said to pack our suitcases but leave them in the room. Just bring what can't be replaced and come down."

He was waiting when they finished walking down the stairs from the seventh floor—the elevators were again out of order.

He led them from the hotel to a waiting cab, opened the rear door for the others and then climbed in the front. "Go north on Park Avenue. I'll direct you. And fast as you can, please."

The Indian cabbie raised his hand as if to silence him. "Twenty miles per hour is the new law."

Kedar handed him a fifty-dollar bill.

The driver pushed Kedar's hand away. "Taking away my license— that's just the beginning of what they'll do to me. They have new special courts, summary courts, that's what they are called. To bring back security to our streets is what the mayor says."

Kedar looked at his new friends. "At least no one else will be going any faster."

91

Erna secluded herself in her office. All afternoon Ingrid had tried to phone Eliezer and Oleander. Other calls to New York had gone through, and several calls had been received from the New York *residence* team. The lack of any communication from the two was an admission of guilt.

Ingrid knocked softly and opened the door. "Councilor, it's time."

She was the last to enter the Council Chambers in the Abbey. Only Rudolf Antioch, under a nurse's care in Prague, and Eliezer and Oleander were absent. All had taken their customary seats, Peprini at the opposite end of the table. She took her chair. He let several moments of silence pass to affirm his authority and the solemnity of the circumstances.

"We gather for a purpose unique in 4000 years of Keeperdom. What question has plagued us these past weeks? 'Why are the Vessels dying in numbers unknown in the history of Abraham's Blessing?' Again he paused.

"Get on with it, Menach. Julia said you spoke with an Ishmaelite Prince."

"Yes, Theresa. I asked myself how we could learn why they are dying. Only one means came to mind: I recalled that the Ishmaelites have certain powers of knowing."

"That is legend," Sandrine Krystofsi protested.

"He may be right," Annette Goldman said. "There are several allusions to their gift of knowledge in the Keepers' Chronicles, too many to dismiss it as myth."

"My mentor," agreed Theresa, "the late Councilor Leonard Levi, mentioned this once to me. And he knew the Chronicles in and out. But we all know the Ishmaelites keep to themselves. Are you telling us they let you speak with them? And that they *gave* you this information?"

"My grandfather had a special relationship with this Prince."

"I don't recall your father ever mentioning this. Does anyone?" Sandrine Kystrofski looked around the table and then glared at Peprini.

"He never said anything to my father, as far as I know, nor to me," Sionn said, looking pointedly at Peprini. "It seems that a great deal, both past and present, has been going on behind our backs."

"The Council does not exist to be a confessional. My grandfather had occasion to assist this Ishmaelite Prince many years ago. It had nothing to do with Keeperdom. The Ishmaelites abhor being under obligation to outsiders, especially to Keepers. And as neither my grandfather nor my father ever asked anything in return, the claim on the Ishmaelites passed to me."

"So you asked the Prince why the Vessels are dying?"

"Exactly, Sandrine."

"I want to hear everything."

Peprini began with a lie of omission, withholding the fact of his first meeting. "This occurred several days ago in Geneva. The Prince received me, and I said I wished to know why the Cainites are entering the Earth and killing the Vessels. I asked the Prince whether Cainites are coming to our world because of anything Keepers have done. With no prompting from me, the Prince answered, and I quote, 'Two Keepers have attempted to open the Primordial Gate. A passageway to the Void is now open. Through this passageway the Cainites are coming to pursue the fountains of Blessing in our world.' When I asked him who those two Keepers were, he said: 'The professor and the monk.' Can we suppose another interpretation but that Eliezer and William are the transgressors and have opened the Primordial Gate? Further, it is obvious that by ignoring the summons from the Council they have admitted their guilt."

Eyes turned to the two empty chairs.

"It is so hard to believe," Fournier finally said.

"How is it *possible* they opened the Gate and survived?" Margaret Connor wondered aloud.

Annette Goldman threw a sidelong glance at Erna who was sitting next to her.

Sionn turned to face Peprini. "This Prince said nothing about illicit activity by anyone else? You're certain, Menach, the Vessel deaths were caused by the opening of the Primordial Gate and that Oleander and Eliezer did this? There is no other explanation, no other... *contributing factor?*"

Peprini held his breath. He had put their confrontation in the Rectory after Vessel Anina Lenoma's death in the back of his mind. "Whatever else might have occurred in the turmoil of these last weeks, Albrecht, there is no doubt the Cainites have entered our world through the Primordial Gate, and that our fellow Councilors are responsible for opening this Gate."

"What is going on here? For God's sake!" Theresa Fournier had risen from her chair, her imposing presence dominating the table. "There will be no more secrets! Have we learned *nothing*? Menach? Albrecht?"

The eyes of Sionn and Peprini were locked on each other. "I have no secrets," Sionn said coldly. "For many reasons, we must be certain of our facts before we make our next decisions."

"Menach?"

"We have all the necessary facts."

The Colombian Mother Superior wasn't satisfied but resumed her seat.

Sandrine Krystofski interrupted the silence. "Do we know where they are right now?"

"New York. Harlem."

"They must be brought here at once!" Krystofski's naturally olive skin was flushed, the change heightened due to her white-blond hair. The relaxed posture she assumed among her equals at the table was replaced by the authoritarian presence she naturally had in the outside world. That this Council, the Council of which she was a member, would be forever known as the one presiding over three Vessels deaths, burned in her. The shame brought upon her by the transgressors would live forever in Keeper history.

"I will have our people in New York apprehend them," Peprini stated. "There will be three. It seems Eliezer has recruited this Osnat Aviv and she has willfully joined their transgression."

"And when they arrive? We will give them a chance to explain themselves; certainly we must do this."

Peprini shrugged at Connor's appeal. "They will either admit the truth or they will lie."

"And what then?"

"One moment. Let me understand." Krystofski calmed herself to some degree. "The Primordial Gate is at this moment open? The Cainites are continuing to enter?"

"Yes."

"Can the Gate be closed? Is there time?"

"Who can say?" Peprini replied. "I doubt Eliezer and William thought that far ahead. A further sin of irresponsibility."

"Can you ask the Ishmaelite Prince?"

"That is impossible. He is no longer under obligation to me. And they are gone by now I'm sure."

"Gone where? All of them?"

"It was apparent during my visit that they were making preparations to leave their facility in Geneva. I have no doubt they are taking refuge from what might come to pass if and when the Blessing ends."

"We must speak with Eliezer and William and find out if the Gate can be closed."

"I'm sure, Sandrine," Erna said, "they are working frantically to do just that. I'm not excusing them—*I cannot excuse them…*" She felt the anger and hurt churn inside her. "But knowing them as I do, their good intentions…"

"Their *intentions* were a cardinal violation in every sense," Peprini said. "Of course, we must take them into custody at once. The full Council can decide what if anything can be done about the Gate. Clearly, our two fugitives demonstrated they know tragically less than they believed they did."

"And after we have their confession?" Margaret Connor asked.

Peprini continued to stare at Erna. "Tell us, Julia, what is the proper punishment for those who have brought an end to God's very Blessing on humanity? Imprisonment? Execution?" Peprini shook his head. "For ordinary human crimes, perhaps. But for the highest treason against God and Keeperdom? Lacking a punishment commensurate with the crime, we must be satisfied with their deaths."

Sandrine Kystofski stared at Peprini, then nodded. Theresa Fournier searched her mind and then her heart for a reason to object, but found none. And turning to Margaret Connor, the only person she had ever met without malice, she saw the young woman also nodding, as was Annette Goldman. She then followed.

"Albrecht?" Sionn nodded once. "Julia? Will it be unanimous?"

She turned to the window. The Blessing in the air was virtually imperceptible.

She faced the others. "It is unanimous."

"It is done then. The order will be to take Councilor Jeremiah Jacob Eliezer, Councilor William Xavier Oleander, and their protégé Osnat Aviv into custody immediately and returned here under the charge and conviction of treason, then to face execution. If they resist, all necessary force will be used. If necessary, they will be killed. The risk of them escaping and continuing their destruction is too great."

Peprini had no intention of allowing the three to leave New York alive. Under no circumstances could they be permitted to speak to the Council. Prince Kedma had said the monk and the professor also had spoken to an Ishmaelite Prince. If they had been told about my violations, and if they revealed this to the Council…

92

Erna returned to her office and locked the door. Moments later Eliezer's phone began ringing. As expected he wasn't answering.

"Eliezer, I hope you pick up this message soon. The Council has found you and William guilty of treason. You are ordered to Lucerne. The punishment... you have been sentenced to death."

The three Keepers were in the back of the taxi, Kedar in the front passenger seat. Eliezer listened as the message recorded, hearing the injury and guilt in her voice.

He picked up the phone. "Julia?" he said softly.

"Eli. We... the Council."

"There was nothing you could have done to stop it."

"Have you and William truly opened the Primordial Gate? Has all this been your doing?"

He said nothing.

"Then Peprini was right. *Oh, Eli, why?*"

"To save the Blessing. Of course, things did not go as planned. We are working as fast as possible to close the Gate. You realize we cannot return while there is hope we can finish."

"You may not have the chance. We've ordered your arrest in New York—yours, William's and the Aviv girl's. If you resist..."

"The sentence will be carried out wherever they find us."

"I'm sorry."

The line crackled and for a moment he wasn't certain she was still there. "Julia?"

"*Run.* You and William must leave New York."

"We need to find a quiet hotel," Oleander said. Kedar looked at the driver but the man had put in earbuds and was listening to an Indian folk song, rocking slightly forward and back, clearly an attempt to quell his anxiety.

"I have a better idea, Kedar said. "We go underground. No one would find us there."

"Do you mean literally *underground?* Is that where the Ishmaelites live?"

"Some, yes. Most choose to live above ground..." He was about to say *'with your kind'* but caught himself. "But in New York our underground dwellings are extensive."

"Would your brethren welcome us?" Eliezer wondered.

"Fortunately," said Osnat, "there's nobody left to ask."

"She's right," Kedar said wryly. "They've all gone to Noah's Ark."

"Aright. Alright. Where to, Kedar?"

"To the same building where you met the Prince. That's the nearest entrance to the Ishmaelite underground. Oh. Give me your phones." He answered their looks. "GPS." In turn, he removed the batteries. "We don't want to make it easy for them."

The taxi driver took small streets where possible. The four passengers checked now and then, but it was impossible to tell whether anyone was following. The traffic, though excruciatingly slow, was chaotic. Several times the taxi was forced to stop as stalled cars were pushed out of the way. Across one street a fissure had opened and a line of cars formed, each coming to a near stop as the drivers inched and bounced their way over the crack. In another place, a water main had broken and all traffic had to back up. Bumpers knocked, causing shouting matches between angry and frustrated drivers. Only the presence of the National Guard kept matters from escalating.

Kedar had the driver stop three blocks away.

"We'll walk the rest. We can tell better if anyone is following."

It was turning dark and as they neared the building the only remaining streetlight came on. Someone was leaning against the lamp pole.

"My God, that's Dina!" said Osnat.

Eliezer was astonished to recognize the young woman from the Frostburg House. His eyes narrowed, and again the extraordinary aura of Blessing about her appeared. "You know her?"

"This is the third time I've run into her this week. In very different places."

The group entered the lamplight's circle.

"Osnat?"

"Dina, what are you doing here?"

She had removed her shoe and sock and was looking where a blister had formed on her heel. A cold wind whipped at her short hair, her cheeks now a rosy color.

"I took a ride over to Columbia. My alma mater. Since then I've just been walking. I try but I can't sit still."

Oleander looked around nervously, aware they were under a spotlight. "Let's not stand in the open."

He and Kedar moved through the swath that had been cut from the chain-link fence surrounding the building. Eliezer stared at the young woman as she replaced her sock and shoe.

Osnat turned to him. "What about Dina?"

"Bring your friend inside," Eliezer said after a moment's deliberation.

They moved up the steps, and Kedar unlocked the door. The front room was dim, only weak light from the outside making it through the cloudy windows. The moment they closed the door a car turned onto the street with a screech of tires. The dark Mercedes slowed as it moved past the building. Kedar and Oleander watched until it was out of sight.

"Dina, these are my friends…" Osnat began.

"This is Dina Carlini," Eliezer interrupted her. "One of the new novices."

She shook her head. "After the initiation ceremony, they changed their minds and said I didn't belong after all." Seeing Eliezer's and Oleander's reaction, she added, "They were surprised too. But I never was able to pass the tests."

"I see. Will you excuse us for a moment, my dear?" Dina moved over to the window.

Eliezer turned to Kedar and lowered his voice. "Ishmaelite, you are our Knower. Do you have any idea why she is here?"

"If I contemplate I might learn something."

"Osnat, you have proved yourself a Knower as well. Any inkling?"

"No, but can it be by chance she is here? First, she gets from who knows where to Harlem. Then her shoe begins hurting her, and she just *happens* to stop in front of *this* building? It's as if we're tied together in some way."

"Ishmaelites don't believe in coincidence," Kedar commented. "Either someone sent her, or she is a gift from the Blessing."

"Either way, she has to go with us. What do you think, Old Monk?"

"Agreed."

For the first time in several weeks Dina felt hopeful.

They descended the long staircase to the Great Hall. There were no lights, and the group moved slowly, using Kedar's and Dina's phones for light. Kedar stopped and opened a circuit box on the wall.

The lights in the Great Hall glowed again. "These are on a different system." Gone were the beautiful rugs and draperies and golden ornaments. The walls were bare concrete, the floor a scarred hardwood. They had not taken off their shoes, and Kedar's heels clacked against the planks. The Ishmaelite approached the wall, pressed a recessed button, and spoke several words in a language Oleander had never heard. A previously unseen door opened with a click.

"Voice activated," he explained and walked in.

They followed him into a dark hallway.

They approached another door. Kedar spoke again, and a magnetic lock clicked. He held the door for the others.

The four passed through and stopped in awe. A cavernous space surrounded them. Obviously, they were no longer in the building, but nor were they inside another. It was as if they had entered a huge cave.

"This way."

They followed along a narrow cobblestone street. The walls, fifty feet to either side, were of unpolished, rough stones and reminded Osnat of the old houses of Jerusalem. The rocky ceiling arched high above, just visible in the darkness. Strangely, the air was fresh and almost breezy. Illumination came from lamp poles spaced intermittently.

Kedar turned and they walked along a broader brick road. The ceiling was even higher in this area, perhaps four stories above their heads. The walls were dark and majestic, sparsely embellished with intricate golden designs. There were large doors on both sides of the street, leading to what seemed to be houses carved from the rock. Here and there were small round windows.

"This is the Upper Quarter," Kedar explained.

There was much decorative brickwork. On the wall twenty feet above their heads was a ceramic-tiled arch with the words 'Hancock Station' spelled out. "Most of the inhabitants are old families. Each door leads to a clan dwelling."

"And you live here?"

"I don't, no, Dina. Few of us do. It's mainly kept as a retreat from… well, from what is above. And certain ceremonies are held here. You might be able to feel that it has a special atmosphere."

"How the devil did you manage to construct all this without being detected?" Oleander found it hard to believe what he was seeing.

"The short answer is we didn't. Much of it is natural. Even New York City has caves. But the city dug this tunnel over 150 years ago. It was to be part of the subway system, but the route was changed after they finished this spur. Instead of filling in the space, they just bricked it off." He pointed to the far end of the street. "And in time they forgot about it. No public entrances had been constructed by the time they abandoned this portion. Once it was walled up, the only way in became through our own entrances. The ventilation shafts still existed, though we had to buy the properties where they exit the surface. We had to make sure they didn't get blocked. We acquired over time all the property above us; we couldn't take the chance someone would start digging. We added a filtering system." He inhaled deeply.

They continued along the winding road—what would have been the path of the subway train—until the towering walls slanted into a narrower street. A large space opened on their right with benches and a fountain surrounded by a small pool. In the center was a statue of a man dressed in Biblical robes.

"Our version of the town square. With it empty... even I feel strange here."

They entered a dead-end alley and stood in front of a tall door. Kedar pulled and it slowly opened. "No need for locks here." Kedar turned to Osnat. "This belongs to my family."

Inside, the rooms were large and open, with only a few delicate designs on the walls for decoration. The furniture was sparse, and everything exuded a formal atmosphere. They climbed to the second floor and Kedar gave each a room. A minor rumbling of the Earth affirmed their arrival.

93

Peprini left the Book Company offices and went searching for Sionn. His friend's insinuations at the Council meeting worried him.

While crossing the courtyard, he saw Sionn coming from the chapel. The two met at the statue of St. Loedger.

"Any news?" Sionn asked.

"Nothing. I have no doubt Eliezer and William are in hiding."

The two men in unspoken agreement moved towards a stone bench with a thick backrest. They took seats, Sionn with a loud sigh.

"Do you remember when we played on this as children? It seemed enormous." He paused. "It occurred to me this morning, Menach, that I've known you longer than I have anyone. It's been fifty-three, no, fifty-four years."

"And I you."

The warmth of the stone seeped into his body, and Peprini felt himself relaxing, though with the fatigue now always present.

"Where is Maria Jongsma?" Sionn asked. He saw his companion's face tense. "The last time she was seen was at your father's cottage."

He saw Peprini's quizzical look. "Rudolf. I learned only because I read the reports on all the Council members, including myself, after his collapse. He left them in his office. I see you didn't realize Rudolf was still taking such an active role."

Peprini snorted. He had underestimated the old Russian.

"Rudolf believed it was a tryst. The security personnel followed when you left the cottage and reported that Maria wasn't with you. They assumed she stayed behind for whatever reason. But later that day you returned to the cottage and met Dr. Loyev. A coffin was put into a van. Rudolf questioned the doctor later and was told it was a discernment accident, a case of a novice slipping into the Void. Rudolf thought little of the incident beyond surprise that you'd personally bother with the details." Peprini frowned. "I suppose he reasoned you kept her death quiet because of the questions it would invite about her relationship with you. Rudolf always was prudish. Had he been less so, who knows what questions he might have asked?"

Sionn buttoned his coat. "I had occasion to stop by the Frostburg House yesterday. I didn't realize Pilar Constantine was staying there. I've always liked Dr. Loyev, you know, even if he is a bit caustic. When I asked what exactly was wrong with her, he said her heart had undergone a great strain; though he had no idea how she came to be this way—at least that he would say." Sionn shifted on the bench, placing his hand flat on the granite. "It always fascinated me as a child how the stone held the sun's heat even on a cold day."

"Maria is dead."

"Your... experiment?"

"Yes. Pilar survived it."

"Something of her did. Why she and not Maria?"

"Pilar was the first attempt. Vessel Wyatt, for reasons even he does not understand, spent only a short time in the Void before returning. For the same unknowable reasons he spent a much longer time while Maria accompanied him."

"She never returned?"

"Her soul... that which went with the Vessel into the Void..."

"You *are* cold-blooded, Menach."

"She had a clear appreciation of what we were attempting and why."

"So that you could become a Vessel."

Peprini did not answer immediately. "That is true. And you would judge me for this? The Blessing was ending even before Eliezer and William began their recklessness. Someone had to act. I did."

"No, Menach. *You* did not. You sent young women to test the safety of the bridge before you would cross." He examined his friend's face. "I don't know if you are capable of shame. If you ever were."

A breeze came from the mountains, and even in the bright sun each man's body contracted against the cold.

"I did not cause Gregor's death. Eliezer and William opened the Primordial Gate."

"But you—Pilar—entered the Void *before* Gregor died."

He had spoken on a hunch and was daring Peprini to lie.

"Yes. But the Ishmaelite Prince at our first meeting did not say I caused Gregor's death."

"A *first meeting?* More secrets, Menach? You can't help yourself, can you?"

Sionn, and perhaps only he among all who knew Peprini, even his own wife, perceived the unaccustomed anxiety and uncertainty on his face. His fondness for his childhood friend soothed his next words. "Do I have your word you are finished with this scheme of yours? Please tell me another young Keeper doesn't need to die before you admit it has failed."

"It is finished."

Sionn felt the first step towards the reconciliation of their friendship. "Perhaps the Gate can be closed again. Perhaps David Wyatt's line will continue for centuries yet."

"Perhaps."

"The Cainites are still coming? I haven't looked at the reports since the day before yesterday."

"Yes, but for some reason in fewer numbers. We have sixteen in the *dungeon.*"

He rose to his feet, and Sionn stood too. "I'm very glad we spoke, Menach. I've missed our friendship. Especially at this time."

"As am I, Albrecht."

94

Tennier stepped from behind the stone fence to open the gate for Peprini's Range Rover.

"You can leave it open. I won't be long."

The Councilor bounced over the rutted road, driving more quickly than was prudent, and parked directly in front of the Granary. It had taken some time to accept that the stench of the Cainites didn't manifest as normal odors do. Although he could already sense the ugliness infiltrating the car, he knew that once he left the property nothing of this would linger.

He had told the truth to Sionn. It seemed pointless to send another Keeper with Wyatt. Also, another death would surely prompt Sionn to go to the Council. They were not in a forgiving mood. His plan was at a standstill unless he was willing to accompany David himself. And he wouldn't—that much he had already decided. What would Father and Grandfather suggest I do now?

He pulled open the Granary's heavy main door. He found it difficult to think as he fought his body's impulse to turn away, stiffening against what was to come as he made his way down the smooth stone steps, across the main storeroom, and then down the winding chain of awkward slabs to the lowest level. The lights had been left on, whether for the sake of the Cainites or the next Keeper to venture, he didn't know. The heavy wooden door was wide open. The barred gate alone held the prisoners. Peprini had ordered the door be left open to allow air from above to circulate through the underground passages.

Irad had come to the bars at the sound of Peprini's footsteps. "How long since you were here?"

His ability to speak had much improved, though Peprini still strained to understand the ancient Canaanite language.

"Two days, yes?"

"Days, yes. And food? Water?"

"I will bring more."

Irad nodded and the two eyed each other.

"Tell me more about Enoch."

"Why should I do this?"

"Ah. Interesting. You would like what in return?"

"To be free of this cage. To be above."

"What you want is impossible. I think you understand this." Although Peprini had told him this on the earlier visit, Irad seemed to need to hear this again.

"Let us talk about your land. Perhaps we will learn something that can help you."

"Then ask your questions."

"How did your grandfather Cain arrive in the Void, in Enoch? Cain was at one time of my world, of the world above." Peprini glanced up. "When God..." he didn't think the prisoner understood the word, "...when Cain was cursed by his grandfather, he was banished from his presence. That was his punishment. But he was given the mark of seven. Your grandfather was still of my world. Otherwise, it would make no sense to give him that protection. So I ask: How did *your* people come to be not of this world?"

Irad looked away, whether to form his answer or only to try to remember, Peprini couldn't tell. He said something to the woman Ada, his wife, but in a voice that Peprini couldn't quite make out.

"Our grandfather," the prisoner began, turning back to the visitor, "took his family far away. After much wandering, he found a place. It was green...so beautiful. But once we set up our tents, everything wilted. The flowers died... The trees died... The water became foul. We moved to another place... and everything wilted again. I do not remember how many times we moved like this. Then our grandfather decided to stop wandering. We built our houses on a hill... He named this place Enoch. Everything became a desert around us. I remember... hard rock surrounded by desert. Yes."

"Continue, please."

The Cainite hesitated. "It is hard to remember those times... The land around us became distant. Enoch was...separated. We were no longer on the Earth. And then there was only the emptiness around us... around the rock, around Enoch. Grandfather said the Earth had vomited us."

Peprini recalled a legend he had heard many years ago about Cain traveling to Nod—the Void. It was not a topic that greatly interested Keepers. But once as a child he overheard the Abbot at St. Ignacio saying to his father: "Like rotten fruit, the Cainites eventually fell from the tree of life and were absorbed into the bowels of Nod."

"In time we...," the Cainite continued, shaking his head, "...*changed*. We did not need the soil anymore. We did not need food. We could survive only with bits of light."

"Light? You mean rays of Blessing? Like rays of the sun?"

The Cainite nodded hesitantly. "Blessing. Is that the name? There would come a ray of light and we would be nourished. It was enough for us. Then...."

"Yes?"

There was silence as the prisoner recalled the ancient memories. "Enoch too changed. There was no longer enough light for all of us. We became more and more... We became," he turned and looked at his companions with compassion, "like a city of ants. Few are like the Queen; few are awake as I am now. Perhaps it was necessary in order to survive. Perhaps this is the true curse of Grandfather's grandfather."

"Did anyone try to escape?"

"We could see the old world far in the distance. It was a very beautiful sight. And sad. Some of us went across the emptiness to the old world. Most who attempted the journey returned, always with the same story. They could get very near, but something, something they could not see, barred them from passing into the old world. And the pain of being so close was too much. Some did not return. Who knows if they succeeded?"

"If the path to my world was closed to your grandfather and his children, how is it possible you are here now?"

"I am to have an answer for each of your questions?" He gripped the bars tightly and Peprini saw his fingers turn white, then regain their color as he loosened his hold and the blood rushed in. "Several times something stirred among us. Something new. A great ray of light came, like the moment the sun climbs above a ridge. A very powerful light, and some of us were stirred from our sleep."

"When did this happen?"

"What happened long ago and what happened yesterday... these are hard for me to separate. But my memory is that this first happened very long ago. And several times since. The last was almost as if yesterday, yes. The great light woke us."

The great light—with a start Peprini realized that the Cainite was referring to a discernment beam directed towards Enoch itself. Yes, only a direct beam could have given the Cainites "a great light." These must have been occasions when Keepers discerned not on the Bible World but directly on the Cain passage: *And Cain went out from the presence of God, and lived in the land of Nod...* His father, Marcus, had done this, and most recently he himself had.

Peprini shuddered at the thought that he had awakened the Cainites from their torpor. Was he responsible for the death of the Vessels? He felt his knees weakening under him, and his eyes searched for a place to sit.

Irad's voice brought him back to his senses. "The great light appeared several times. At first, some of us awakened and floated in the emptiness. Then we saw a… where the emptiness ends and your world starts."

"The edge of the Void?"

"Edge, yes. But something prevented us. We could not leave, and so we returned. And then, what feels like only a short time ago, we were awakened again by the great light. In the emptiness we floated." He turned to his wife and daughter. "We arrived at the edge again. But this time, a door was open."

"A door?"

"An opening, where the light could be seen."

Peprini assumed that this must have been the Gate which Eliezer and Oleander had opened between the Earth and the Void.

"Some of us were drawn to this opening. And… then we were among you."

"But how?"

Irad shrugged. "It was like going inside myself."

The Inner Depths, Peprini thought. The Cainites descend to their Inner Depths to go from the Void to our world, while we Keepers descend to our Inner Depths to go from our world to the Void. A mirror image.

"The rest I don't know." The Cainite lowered his eyes and looked at his body. "I found myself in this body. I did not choose it. And they," he pointed with his chin to the woman and the child, "in these bodies"

It was fortunate, Peprini thought, the three of you surfaced together at the same place. The three bodies had been traced back to a family killed in an earthquake in Ethiopia. They must have been coordinated in some way, just as Keepers coordinate our auras to emerge at the same place in the Depth.

"Can you return to Enoch?"

"You say we are bad for this world. You say we cannot live here. And you would have us go back." Irad turned and walked to the rear of the large cell. He inhaled deeply and ran his hand down the rough stone wall. Again he looked at his kin. "To live in your world, to be awake, to see the day and the night, to smell the Earth, to feel its coolness and moistness, to feel the warm wind, to look in another's eyes… To be awake is what it means to live in your world. Yes?"

Peprini nodded.

"To be awake in my world would be the beginning of the curse. To see Enoch as it truly is." He strode forwards and took hold of the cell bars. "To return to that? But then the fullness of the curse would come. I fear, I know, we would start to lose what I have now, what she has." He turned to the squatting woman who then looked at Peprini. He saw hatred in her black eyes. "To become numb again." He now looked at his daughter. "To forget she even exists." He dragged his palm across a burr on a crossbar. An inch-long line appeared. Slowly it became red and grew larger. A rivulet of blood ran down to his wrist and fell to the floor. "To lose even this."

"There are laws... laws that govern our worlds. They are not for us to challenge." Peprini didn't know if the Canaanite word for "law" was meaningful in the sense he wanted.

Irad smiled darkly. "I think you do not believe your words. He stared at the Keeper. "You know what I want. What I want for my people. Perhaps it cannot be. But you have said nothing of what you want. I see how repulsive you find us. Is it only your curiosity that makes you stand here?"

"I asked if you could return to Enoch."

"Can we return? Yes. The door is still open. I can close my eyes and, if I am very still, I can go there through my mind."

"You imagine it?"

"No. I go there, leaving this..." he looked down at his chest "...behind. It is still uncomfortable being... having a body and one not as mine once was. I am not completely of this body."

Of course, Peprini thought. If Keepers have the ability to descend inwardly, leaving their bodies here and traveling to the Void, then Cainites should be able to do the same. Only they don't have a material body as we do, not even in the Void. Looking at the semi-conscious Cainites in the cell, he asked, "Can the others return also?"

"Most are not awake enough to do this. But as I said, we will not return."

Peprini looked at the drone-like Cainites at the back of the cell. "But what if for some reason you wanted very much to return to Enoch. Could you? Would you be able to see from there..." he spoke slowly, wanting to make sure he was understood to be referring to the Bible World, "the land of Cain's birth?"

"Yes."

"And could you travel to that land?"

"I told you that when we awoke, we entered the door to your world. But that was not the first thing we did." Peprini leaned forward as if to ask a question. "Yes. We went to Grandfather's home." Now Irad was in his memory. "Ada and Rina our child... we thought we were finally going home. But we could not enter. It was so close, but we could feel nothing of this, of what is in this world. So we followed the light here."

Peprini thought he understood. Irad had tried to enter the Primordial Gate but was barred. Was the Gate closed between the Void and the Bible

World? Or was it only the Cainites, cursed as they were, who were barred from entering?

"So it is possible."

"You still have not told me what you want. Not simply for us to return?"

Peprini paced in front of the cell. "Because of you, my world is losing what is most valuable. That cannot be undone. Only one source of the Blessing... do you know this word?"

"You told me it is the light."

"Only one source of the light remains. I want to bring a new source into this world, for my people." He stopped and looked at Irad. "Do you understand? I want to go to the land of Cain's birth and return with a new source."

"Is this possible?"

"I do not know."

"You want to return with us?"

"Yes."

"And then you would travel to the land of Grandfather's birth?"

"Yes."

"It is painful to turn our backs to the light here. Why should we want to suffer this? And why should we help you and your world?"

Peprini bit his lip and forced himself to make the offer. "One of the laws I do know is that the source of light, we call him the Vessel, can enter your world and survive. I would give him to you. You would then have your own light."

"If we are no good for such beings—you say we killed four—would not this one also die if among us?"

"He is perhaps unique among the Vessels. He has been immune to your presence." The Keeper thought of Wyatt's injuries from his fall weeks ago but continued. "Can I guarantee he will survive? No. But if he lives, think of what Enoch might become!"

"Why would you, you who protect the source, give him to us?"

"Because I would return with an even greater light for our world."

"But you worry you cannot pass through the opening with us and survive in our world, even for the time it would take to travel to Grandfather's home?"

Peprini ignored the question and stepped back from the cell in order to think more clearly.

"What was it like to pass through the opening? Was it violent? Difficult?"

"No. We are... protected in our world. The mark protects us."

"How do you know this?"

"I have been thinking of this much. So many memories are returning. Grandfather's grandfather gave him this mark to protect him in our world, in Enoch. We carry with us our own protection from what would harm us, what could harm you." Peprini found himself holding his breath and exhaled. "The smell we have… Yes, what you find so ugly, this is what protects us. What destroys the light in your world protects us in ours. It allows us to survive in Enoch."

Peprini nodded, excited now; he was on the cusp of understanding something crucial. "Go on."

"You say you want to go with us? But you believe you cannot survive the journey." He waited.

Peprini saw he wouldn't continue until the Keeper acknowledged this fact. "Yes. I cannot survive in your world."

"I believe you can. If you are with me, under the protection the mark gives me."

"How do you know this?"

Irad shrugged. "I know. The same…" Irad searched for the word, "…thing that repels you in this world will protect you in mine. Just as that light makes it possible for me to live in your world, what we possess…" and he turned to the others, "would make it possible for you to live in ours. For a time, at least."

"You would escort me through your world to the land of Cain's birth?"

"You would give us the source of light?"

"If I must do this in order to secure for my world an even greater light, yes. It would be my duty."

"Duty. So many words I did not know were in my mind. It would be my duty to return to Enoch with the source."

They looked at each other. "We have the makings of an understanding, I believe. I give you our source of light, this man. You and your people, the Vessel, and myself, all of us enter the Void, enter the path that leads through Enoch to the land of your Grandfather's birth. But: What assurance do I have that once we are in your world you will follow through with the bargain? What assurance do I have you will not simply abandon me once you have what you want?"

"That I tell you I would not do this, is this not enough?"

"My world will depend on my returning with a new source. I have a duty to be certain."

Peprini noticed that Irad and his wife Ada looked at each other continually. The Cainite woman was kneeling next to the young girl, coaxing her to drink water from her cupped hand. Ada dipped a finger into the water and spread it over the girl's lips.

"Here is what I propose. You, I, and the Vessel, we will enter your world. But some of your people will remain behind. Ada will remain here in my world. If you fail to honor our agreement, you will never see her again. If I do not return to my world, Ada will be killed. Your daughter, as well as the others, all will be killed. My people will do this."

Irad continued to look at his daughter and his wife. He turned to Peprini and nodded. "I agree. You will be protected in my world. As long as the door to this world remains open, you will be able to return. But you must make sure the path remains."

"I need to make preparations. We must travel some distance in my world first. It will be unsafe for us to begin our journey from here." He stepped back from the cell. "For now, I will bring fresh food and water."

"And this cage?"

"There is only so much I can do." Irad closed then opened his eyes in understanding.

Peprini returned to the main floor of the Granary where two boxes of food and a number of gallon jugs of water had been left. He put into one box a mix of cheeses, fruits, bread, and nuts. After taking this to the dungeon, he returned with several gallons of water, and this time he included a half dozen cups. Neither he nor Irad spoke, though the expectation between them was electric.

Before leaving the Granary he stood by the main door. "Human beings can adapt to virtually anything," he thought aloud. "I could stand this presence for as long as necessary."

He got into his car and drove up the hill over the old track and left the convent grounds, watching in the rearview mirror as Tennier closed the gate behind him. When he reached the fork leading to the Abbey he pulled to the side of the road.

Irad must be speaking of the Primordial Gate, he thought. *Ironically, Eliezer and Oleander may have made it possible for me to complete the Peprini legacy.* If I entered the Void, it would not be randomly, as happened with Pilar and Maria, as happened with Father. It would be through a passageway of Blessing created by Eliezer and Oleander. That Blessing would protect me. *It should*, he cautioned himself. I would further be protected by the Cainite curse. And also the Blessing aroused by reciting the Book of Creation. Three sources of protection Maria and Pilar lacked. Peprini knew he would be breaking a fundamental law of these worlds. But so was opening the Primordial Gate. And while that law was broken, perhaps other laws could be bypassed. This plan was possible only as long as the Primordial Gate was open. He knew that Eliezer and Oleander were working furiously to close it.

He put the car into gear, and even this small act reminded him of the sluggishness his body fought against as the vitality that was his birthright diminished. Once David Wyatt was dead, it would be even worse. He would have to live the rest of his life, if indeed life was still possible, every day feeling the loss of his protection and divine vitality. To be a Keeper no more.

95

Camulshu at the New York *residence* answered on the third attempt to reach him.

"He is well?"

"He hasn't left his townhouse all week, Councilor. There have been no Cainite sightings in two days."

Peprini wondered when and how Camulshu had learned they were Cainites. "There will be a plane waiting at Teterboro airport in New Jersey tomorrow morning. You are to escort the Vessel to the airport and see that he is put on the plane. I will email the details." Though it wasn't his obligation to provide an explanation to the *residence* leader, he did. "We have decided to move him to an isolated location where he can be more easily protected. In New York too many avenues exist for Cainites to reach him. I will arrange this with the Vessel. He will be ready at eight."

"We will have him there."

"Good."

His next call was to Wyatt.

"How are you enduring your confinement?"

"How much longer will this be necessary?"

"That's why I'm calling. We have decided to move you to a safer location while we solve the problem of the Cainites."

"Where?"

"Algeria."

"*Algeria?*"

"There are reasons, be assured."

"Fine. I'll pack for the Sahara."

Peprini was relieved. He hadn't been confident the man would agree.

"At eight tomorrow morning our people will knock on your door and have a car ready to take you to Teterboro."

"It will be good just to be out of here."

"Fine then."

He left his office at the Abbey and went down the stone hallway to Sionn's. His friend was leaning back in his desk chair with a damp cloth on his wide forehead. He sat up and the chair squealed at the weight of his six-feet-six frame.

"Albrecht, you don't look well." Now that Keepers, too, were starting to contract illnesses, they had an additional worry which previously had been the lot of only ordinary people.

"I just finished discerning. Has it been this exhausting for you too?"

"More and more."

"What we do has never been more important. Yet it seems almost futile."

"Almost. Wyatt has not died yet."

"Of course you are right." Sionn turned the compress over to the cool side and leaned back again with a squeal from the chair.

"On that matter of the Cainites. I have concluded it is unnecessarily dangerous to have them near the Abbey. We don't know if their effects extend beyond our ability to sense them. I propose moving them to an isolated location."

"That makes sense. Where do you have in mind?"

"The archive in Algeria." This was one of the places where copies of the Chronicles were stored.

"That's as good a place as any. Would you like any help with the arrangements?"

"Fortunately, they are as docile as when captured. I'm going to escort them myself and ensure all goes smoothly."

"Thank you, Menach. You know I don't relish more contact with them."

"I'll phone once I have them secured at the archive."

He had new clothing purchased for each of the Cainites. Several Keepers bathed, groomed and dressed those unable to do this themselves. Two vans were arranged to transport the Cainites to the airport. Hopefully, as the vans unloaded and they boarded the private plane, they would draw little notice.

Irad and Ada were in the rear of the plane, several rows behind Peprini. Taking no chances, the Councilor had three men and one woman armed with tasers occupy the rows between him and the Cainites. His main concern was their reaction to air travel. When captured, none had been capable of appreciating their surroundings, seeming to operate on the vague memories and instincts of the previous inhabitants of their bodies. But several had become more aware with time spent in this world. The trip in the vans to the airport had been harrowing for those more-or-less conscious, some closing their eyes in terror or holding each other, fighting vertigo. Peprini had decided to make the trip at night and took the further precaution of having all the windows of the plane covered.

The take-off had been alarming, but once the aircraft leveled out they calmed down. Irad and his wife whispered most of the flight, their daughter between them. Four other Cainites occasionally mumbled to one another; the other nine sat still or seemed to sleep.

In the confined space of the aircraft cabin, the foulness was nearly overwhelming for the four young Keepers. One of them took out a small jar of mentholatum and dabbed a bit just below her nostrils. She handed the jar to her companions who did the same. It served only to distract them from the more profound stench of the Cainites. Silently each wondered how the Councilor could appear impervious. Peprini had begun to think of the odor as a divine protection he would soon need.

The plane landed in Algiers at midnight. Two vans and a Land Cruiser waited on the tarmac. In minutes the vehicles wound through the maze of airport access roads and climbed onto a surprisingly modern highway, the sky thick with stars down to the horizon.

An hour later the monotony of the night sky was interrupted by the outline of a grove of trees. A large house, the plaster of the exterior white in the moonlight, stood in the center of the stand of date palms. The archive was a former French Governor's summer retreat from the heat of Algiers, as much respite as could be found anywhere in the country. The Keepers had quietly acquired it after the French left the country. The Chronicles were stored underground and would not be found even if someone were looking. Keepers had 4000 years of experience in hiding them.

They arrived in the gravel courtyard. Peprini instructed the four Keepers to move the Cainites to the room that had been prepared. Master-Keeper Maxon, the *residence* leader, waited at the entrance and guided the strange group down to the holding room. This was deep underground and had served as the wine cellar for the former Governor. Peprini had arranged that the room be made more comfortable than the dungeon at the Granary. Cots were supplied, though no modern toilet facilities were available in this area of the building. He imagined the Cainites would not understand how to use these anyway. As Irad surveyed the room, Peprini reminded him it would be only for a short time, no more than a day or two.

This time there were no cell bars, only a door. He closed and locked it. Maxon waited for the Councilor in the library.

"Sit. He arrived without a problem?"

"None, Councilor. He's asleep in the north master bedroom."

Peprini saw she wanted to say more. "What is it?"

The woman, sturdy without appearing unfeminine, ran her hand through her black hair. Peprini noticed what beautiful hands she had, long graceful fingers, with short unpainted nails, highlighted by the ruby ring she wore as a Keeper. "If I may ask...?"

He nodded.

"Why have we brought the Vessel and the Cainites together in the same place?" He realized there was no questioning of his decision. That she trusted his wisdom was obvious. She simply wanted to understand.

"Mr. Wyatt has displayed remarkable resistance to the Cainites. How or why we do not know. But more importantly, this is only temporary. He will be moved to a new location in the next twenty-four hours. I will accompany him. You will remain here to supervise both the Archives and the Cainites. I've brought four others to help in that regard. You will find it necessary to spend only short periods in close proximity to the Cainites. And anywhere in this house is close, as I am sure you've already noticed."

She was doing her best to appear unaffected by their presence, but took his comment as permission to let some of her discomfort show.

"I'll set up a schedule."

"Fine. Now, if you will excuse me, I believe I will retire."

"I'll show you to your rooms. We have the master suite on the east side of the house prepared."

"Very good."

As Peprini climbed the stairs, he felt the leaden fatigue in his legs. He noticed Maxon also moved with what he imagined was an unusual effort. At the top, he looked down the hallway to the room where the Vessel slept. Tomorrow.

96

There had been minor earthquakes during the night, and he had slept fitfully. But the unease he felt had a deeper cause. *Today he would travel to the Bible World.*

He showered and shaved with even greater care than usual. If things went badly, this is the condition in which Keepers would find his body and how he would be remembered. He bore that in mind as he dressed, selecting a white shirt, gray summer suit, and a subdued blue polka-dot tie. His handmade shoes were comforting as he pulled them on. He placed on his wrist his father's watch, then his wedding ring, and lastly the heavy ruby ring that had been his grandfather's.

Maxon, apparently waiting, met him at the bottom of the staircase.

"Good morning, Councilor."

"Is he up?"

"On the veranda having breakfast, Sir." She turned and gazed out the French doors to the patio.

David looked up as the Keeper stepped outside. The marble table was under the veranda, but even in the shade it was hot already at seven-thirty in the morning. Peprini squinted in the bright light.

"Yogurt with figs. Not bad."

Peprini sat down. He inspected his aura and found it the same as when they first met.

"How do you feel?"

"A little jet lagged. Other than that, good."

"Good, good." He knew he was procrastinating. "You have proven unexpectedly resistant to the Cainites. Or you might simply have been lucky to this point. This luck might change."

"So what's the plan?"

Peprini smiled at the American bluntness. "I will need you to accompany me into the Void. You, of course, will as always be perfectly safe. I will need your protection, the umbrella of your Blessing."

"You tried this with the two girls. It didn't work."

"I am hopeful it will be different in my case. I am… shall we say, much stronger." That is the plan. May I count on your help?"

"I'll do my part, of course. But I can't tell you when I'm going to have the dream. It could be days."

"I've been thinking about that. The dream comes upon you involuntarily. But I have a means that would make you less inhibited, even at an unconscious level. There is every reason to believe that it would open you to the experience more quickly."

Peprini took out of his breast pocket a tiny silver case, opening it to reveal a dozen small pills.

Wyatt looked at it suspiciously. "Drugs?"

"Simply a tranquilizer of sorts. It will lower your resistance mechanisms. It is something that Keepers on occasion use to improve their discernment, especially when they are stressed. It is absolutely safe."

"And if it doesn't work?"

"Then no harm done. Shall we give it a try?"

"Alright," Wyatt said after some hesitation.

The Keeper sat in a leather armchair facing the bed. Wyatt put a pill in his mouth and washed it down with a couple gulps of water. He then stretched out on the bed.

"If you have the dream, I want you to wait for me at the edge of the Void. Soon I will join you. Then we will proceed into the Void. Do you have any questions?"

Wyatt searched the Keeper's green eyes for dishonesty or uncertainty. But he detected only worry and commitment.

"Need I remind you which of us is leaping into the abyss for the first time?"

"Ready when you are."

97

The following morning Eliezer and Oleander told Dina about the deaths of the Vessels. Briefly they described their work on the prohibited Gate, Peprini's actions, and the imposition of their death sentences, without going into unnecessary details. At this point it seemed futile to hide what they were doing. She knew, after all, of the Primordial Gate; all novices did. No doubt soon all Keepers would learn of their violation.

"How do I fit into this, why did you bring me?"

"In all honesty, my dear," Eliezer told her, "we don't know who or what you are. But of this we *are* certain: you are no mistake.

Later that afternoon they gathered in the living room.

"This waiting is killing me." Oleander paced behind the couch where Eliezer sat. "But I figure it will be another three or four days before we'll be ready for the seventh Sefirah."

"Perhaps a bit longer in my case, I'm sorry to say." Eliezer wore his overcoat, feeling chilled much of the time recently. He pulled the collar tighter around his neck.

Kedar cocked his head. "I hope you are not serious."

"It is not by choice, my young Ishmaelite. The sixth Sefirah was only four days ago. Even in normal circumstances, we would need nearly a week to recuperate. But in our weakened state, and with the awful forces we've been encountering…"

"Three days? What's going on up…"

The furniture began to vibrate and the rock on all sides shook. They held their breath. A mist of dust fell from the ceiling. Seconds later the rumbling subsided.

"Don't you think we'd do it this minute if we believed we could?" Oleander said sternly. "If we die trying to open the gate, then the gate stays closed, open only to the Void, for the Cainites to come in. And that would mean the end of everything."

Kedar sat down. There was a tense silence. From above came faint sounds of car alarms.

"I think there is a way to do the seventh session today," Osnat said.

"And what does the novice know that we don't? We waited nine days before the sixth Sefirah, and even so barely made it." The monk now appraised Eliezer, and for a moment was caught by the weakness of his aura. "We won't survive those forces in our present condition."

"Exactly," she said.

Oleander rolled his eyes. "You deal with her."

Dina left the group, feeling out of place in the heated discussion. The old man had a headache and had to work to be patient. "No riddles today, Osnat."

"I'm new to this, I know. You feel weak after discernment because your efforts depleted your personal Blessing, right?"

"Yes. Please get to the point."

"You told me that chanting the formulas of the Book—just chanting, not discerning—gives you an infusion of Blessing. Now, that doesn't do anything—you said this yourself—for the benefit of the world. It's too small, it's only for the individual. But that's just what you need right now."

Eliezer began to grin. "I knew there was a reason I brought you along, young lady. So if we recite one of the Creation formulas before we descend to the Depths… William, your thoughts?"

"It's worth trying. If it does replenish our personal Blessing, then I say we begin reciting now. Do as much as we can before we sleep. By tomorrow morning we should be ready."

"It won't help. The increase is only temporary, an hour at the most." Kedar answered their looks. "The Ishmaelites have always used the Book to boost our personal Blessing for short periods."

"So you are saying, Kedar, that reciting the formulas will not help unless we do this right before we discern, as Osnat suggested."

"And hope the boost lasts long enough."

"Alright everyone," Eliezer commanded as he stood. "To the kitchen. We are hungry and tired. We eat and then we sleep. Tomorrow morning we will try Osnat's trick—her inspiration. And yes, Kedar, let's hope it is enough."

"That's one problem solved," Oleander said. "Hopefully. But we still don't have the codeword for the seventh Sefirah. We're stuck until we have that."

Eliezer retrieved his copy of the Book from his coat pocket as he sat at the kitchen table. Dina filled a pot with water and set it on the stove, taking out a smaller one. She then began looking through cupboards.

"We have looked at this formula a hundred times. But if we look at it again, maybe someone," Eliezer glanced meaningfully at Osnat, "might give us a hint." He then read aloud:

TEN SEFIROT OF BELIMAH AND TWENTY-TWO FOUNDATION LETTERS: THREE MOTHERS, SEVEN DOUBLES, AND TWELVE SIMPLES, AND A SPIRIT IN EACH ONE OF THEM.

"As I had already told you," Eliezer said, "the standard interpretation is that the text is talking here about the twenty-two letters of the Hebrew alphabet. The seven doubles are those letters that can receive a stress, which is designated by a dot in the middle of the letter. The idea is that stressed letters are pronounced more strongly as if they were doubled. Next: The ancient Rabbis said that 'the three mothers' are the letters *Aleph*, *Mem*, and *Shin*. The rest of the letters are simples."

"Why Aleph, Mem and Shin"? Oleander asked.

Eliezer shrugged. "No one knows."

"There aren't seven stressed letters in Hebrew," Osnat said. "If the text is talking about so-called 'weak stress,' then there are six stressed letters, not seven. And if it's talking about 'hard stress,' then almost all the letters of the Hebrew alphabet can be stressed."

Oleander examined Eliezer's face. The monk's knowledge of Hebrew, while excellent for a non-native speaker, was not up to either that of Osnat or Eliezer. "In ancient Hebrew could it have been seven and not six?"

"She is right. The interpretation seems... forced."

Osnat closed her eyes and after a few seconds began speaking. "Setting aside the 'seven doubles' for the moment; if we are talking here about the time of the Biblical Patriarchs—and we are, right?"

"We are," Eliezer said.

"Then 'mothers'... what if we're not talking about letters? What if it literally means *mothers*?"

"I think I see where you are going."

"'Mothers' must refer to the Patriarchs' wives. 'The Mothers'—every Hebrew-speaking schoolgirl knows that's how they are called."

"But we know that the Book of Genesis says there were four mothers, not three," Kedar objected, setting down the box of pasta he had begun to open. "Sarah, the wife of Abraham; Rebecca, the wife of Isaac; and Jacob's two wives, Leah and her younger sister Rachel."

"Yes," Osnat continued with the same inspiration. "So THREE MOTHERS... could this mean the *third* mother?"

"Eliezer?"

"A grammatical stretch, William, but given the poetic and confounding style of the Book, not unreasonable."

Kedar turned to Osnat. "The third oldest Mother, after Sarah and Rebecca, was Leah."

"Okay, so THREE MOTHERS is Leah," Oleander said.

"Now." Osnat's eyes were again closed. They waited for her. "TWELVE SIMPLES—what are the twelve?"

"*Who* are the twelve. If we're now talking about people and not letters, then it must be Jacob's twelve sons." Oleander tried.

"If we are abandoning the theme of letters in the interpretation, then yes, only Jacob's sons as the TWELVE SIMPLES makes sense. And that leaves us with what—or *who*—are the SEVEN DOUBLES."

"Twins?" Oleander suggested, immediately shaking his head. "None of the twelve sons were twins."

"There is a story in Genesis about the sons of Judah. They were twin boys..."

"No, Kedar. I think we need to stay with the children of Jacob."

Osnat's eyes were still closed.

"Seven," Oleander said, "may mean seventh. Just as 'three' meant third. Leah's seventh son. But..."

"Yes, William, Leah only had six. Of Jacob's twelve sons only six were from Leah."

Dina had just opened a jar of spaghetti sauce. "But she had a seventh child—my namesake."

The three Keepers and Kedar turned to her.

"It would fit," Eliezer admitted.

"Good, *Dinah* then," Oleander agreed. "Now we're left with seven or seventh DOUBLES."

"DOUBLES." They turned to Osnat who sat perfectly still, eyes closed.

Eliezer held up his hand asking the others to be silent. After ten seconds she opened her eyes. "'Double.' 'Double' as in 'second.' The second gender—girls."

"So," Kedar concluded, "if I have this right, what the seventh formula says is this: the seventh child, a daughter, of the third mother?"

Eliezer turned to Oleander who nodded. "It has a certain logic."

"But what is AND A SPIRIT IN EACH ONE OF THEM?"

"What else could 'spirit' mean except the Blessing?" Kedar said. "Obviously, Jacob's twelve sons—the 'twelve simples'—each had the Blessing."

"But... but Dinah too?" said Dina.

Oleander looked doubtful. "In the history of the Keepers, she was never mentioned as having received any kind of Blessing. Nor is there any mention of this in the Bible."

"Nevertheless," Eliezer said, "I think our best guess is that the codeword is indeed *Dinah*."

They had gone to bed when a shout was heard from Oleander's room. The others hurried out of their rooms.

Oleander appeared in the doorway. "I have it! All of the codewords are found in Genesis Chapter 34!"

He handed the Bible to Eliezer. After quickly scanning the passage, the Councilor then read it again aloud.

*And **Dinah** the daughter of Leah, whom she had born to Jacob, went out to meet the girls of **the land**. And Shechem, the son of **Hamor**, the Hivite, the prince of the land, saw her and took her and lay with her and tormented her. And his soul clung to Dinah, the daughter of Jacob, and he **loved** the girl and spoke to her heart. And Shechem spoke to Hamor his father: "Take for me this girl for a wife." And Jacob heard that he had defiled his daughter Dinah, and his sons were away with his cattle grazing, and Jacob **remained silent** until their return... And the sons of Jacob answered Shechem and Hamor his father, speaking **cunningly** because he had defiled Dinah their sister. And they said to him: "...with the following thing we will consent to you, that you will be like us, **circumcising** every male..."*

Eliezer patted the monk's shoulder. "Brilliant. And I am willing to wager that the codewords of the rest of the Sefirot formulas are from this chapter too. How did you figure this out?"

"The codeword 'Dinah' reminded me of the story of her rape. Then it struck me that 'Hamor' was not supposed to mean 'donkey' but a person's name. The rest was simple."

"But that leaves this question: What is the connection between the Book of Creation and this chapter? Why *this* chapter?"

Oleander knitted his brow in confusion. "There is plainly no Gate in Chapter 34. There is no hint of God's Blessing to anyone. The opposite. It's a horrifying tale."

98

David Wyatt's mind felt like a bowl of glass that had been shattered. He wanted to beg Peprini to take away the drug, but couldn't find his mouth. He wanted to open his eyes and see if the man was still at his bedside, but couldn't find his eyes. His mind was floating away from him.

Peprini was sitting by his bed, monitoring his reactions to the drug. Eight hours after the pill, Peprini gave Wyatt another dose in order to prolong the effect without interruption, this time through injection.

During that time, twice the Councilor had entered his Inner Depths and stood at the edge of the Void, waiting. The first time he saw nothing, and eventually returned to the room. The second time he saw Wyatt at the usual place at the edge. The Vessel was floating aimlessly, his eyes closed, tossing slightly once in a while as if by invisible waves. He was clearly no good for a journey to the Bible World. But he was in perfect conditon for Peprini's purpose. Peprini left the Depths and returned to the bedroom.

He now knew what he had only suspected: disabling Wyatt's self-control made him extremely responsive to the Blessing, without the psychological clamor that normally curbed and even drowned this responsiveness. His thirst for the Blessing pulled him into his dream and to the edge of the Void. But once there, he was unable to undertake a voluntary trip towards to Bible World. Wyatt was now under his control.

He checked his watch and calculated the time for the next attempt. Then, narrowing his eyes, he saw how meager the Blessing in the air had become. Since the drug started working, twelve hours ago, the Blessing had been slowly diminishing. Evidently, in this state the Vessel was a poor conduit for the Blessing.

Good, he thought. Excellent. Soon another Wave will hit the Earth. The Council will be utterly unforgiving of Eliezer and Oleander, and that will be their end. Whatever the Ishmaelite had revealed will die with them.

99

Four storms of unprecedented magnitude glued the scientists to their monitors at the National Weather Service office in Miami. One inched across the screens towards the Dominican Republic and Haiti, another just made contact with Honduras in Central America, a third approached Trinidad and Tobago and the coast of Venezuela, and the last edged onshore at the southern tip of Texas. Together the four swirling masses blocked out the entire Caribbean and most of the Gulf of Mexico. The meteorologists didn't speak, numbed as they were at the loss of certainty in what they had believed was possible.

Corpus Christi, like each city in the path of the storms, endured alone. When the storm finally moved away, survivors ventured to rooftops or windows in the upper stories. It was now a city after the battle, destroyed, both armies having moved on. Bodies floated in the floodwaters, caught like flotsam against debris. Decay began. Arriving first were the vultures and crows, brazenly feeding on the corpses, mocking the humans who watched without food and water. After the second day, people stopped shooting at the scavengers and left the dead to the beasts. The sun baked the survivors on the rooftops, the cloudless sky an insult.

Television reception was spotty even in the most modern countries. Satellite and cable systems increasingly experienced outages or failures, and radio was only slightly more reliable. People were compelled to talk with one another. Denied vivid images of these events, they were forced to use imagination. "What have you heard?" was the question of the moment.

Trading in the financial markets was suspended indefinitely in Hong Kong, Shanghai, and Tokyo, allegedly because of technical malfunctions in the hardware; others claimed it was to prevent their complete collapse. The Western markets—the stock exchanges, commodity and foreign currency exchanges—were frozen until "order and a modicum of reason" could be restored, as the British Chancellor of the Exchequer put it. Insiders leaked that the computer systems which ran the financial systems of the developed world—indeed, which *were the financial system*—had begun crashing.

In the United States, it began with a local bank in Buffalo, New York. A branch office closed at ten o'clock on a Wednesday morning, the hand-drawn sign on the front door saying: "We are temporarily out of cash. Please check tomorrow." They had to lock the door because customers entering the bank on other business demanded, after seeing the sign, to withdraw money from their accounts. Rather than keep dealing with disgruntled customers, the bank manager closed early. By late that afternoon, lines began to form at ATMs across the country, small lines making passersby curious, leading to longer lines. Most machines ran out of cash that evening. The following morning brought lines of customers at banks, savings and loans, and credit unions. The majority of these institutions saw their currency reserves quickly exhausted, and shut their doors.

Federal Reserve Chairman Raymond Gillespie announced that this was not a "Depression-era run on the banks" but a simple logistics problem. The modern economy, he reminded, was no longer a "cash and coin one," and so banks did not keep large cash reserves on hand; there was no need. The Federal Reserve Banks in conjunction with the Department of the Treasury were at that very moment working to replenish supplies of cash to the banks. There was every reason to remain confident in the U.S. banking system, he said.

But the promised deliveries of currency did not happen. Confidence was not restored. With cash not readily available, and with the technology of credit either out of service or suspect, the rules of daily commerce changed. "Only CASH accepted" signs appeared on the doors of most stores still open. Credit and debit cards became only slivers of plastic.

The President declared martial law, calling up National Guard as well as regular Army, Navy, Air Force and Marine units to maintain order. Congress passed a resolution allowing the temporary suspension of the *Posse Comitatus* Act of 1878, which prohibited uniformed troops of the federal military from being employed for that purpose. The same was done in most countries with varying degrees of force and cooperation from their populations.

Eastern fever had now been identified as a strain of influenza related to the Spanish flu of 1918, which killed more than twenty million worldwide. The Centers for Disease Control and Prevention in Atlanta said there was no vaccine for this strain. To produce a vaccine would take months. The existing supply of influenza vaccine was in very short supply, and there was no evidence it would prevent Eastern fever. People nevertheless crowded into pharmacies and physicians' offices demanding a flu shot. The supply was exhausted in days.

The disease struck the young and the elderly most hard. Schools closed as a public health measure. Sporting events, concerts, and other large gatherings were canceled. A cough or a runny nose or bloodshot eyes brought stares and a distancing. Many businesses shut either because too many employees were out sick, or for fear of bringing the healthy ones together in a mixing bowl of possible contagion.

Estimates were that more than 15 million had died in India and Pakistan, and twice that number in China. South Korea placed the count at over five million. Communications with Indonesia, known to be the origin of the virus, were especially poor, but one-tenth of its population of 350 million were believed dead or ill. Flickering video images from Jakarta appeared on television and the Internet showing trenches, each the size of a football field, three stories deep, bodies bulldozed over the edges, gasoline trucks spraying fuel over them, and flares setting the mass alight.

Africa, except for Egypt, South Africa, and Algeria, slid into silence. Communications, always poor in the interior, were reduced to the isolated short-wave radio transmission.

A plague was upon the Earth.

100

After breakfast, Pem left the Abbey to check on the Granary. Halfway to the building he stopped. From that distance he shouldn't have been able to feel the debilitating effect of the prisoners, yet he could feel a weight settling on him. He heard someone behind and saw Sionn coming up the dirt track.

"Pem, did any of the Cainites get loose?" he almost shouted, still thirty yards away. He waited until they were closer before adding, "I thought I could feel their stench in while lying in bed."

"I've been wondering the same thing, Councilor. But I think it's not them. It feels like something else."

Sionn raised his eyes to the sky. "*Oh, no.*"

"Councilor?"

"It's not the Cainite's curse. It's the Blessing."

The Keepers most attuned to the Blessing became aware of it first. It was as if they had suddenly been denied oxygen, and only then grasped they had lived amidst a sea of air since birth. Keepers looked up from their work or prayer, perhaps noticing that others had ceased what they were doing, then in a jolt understood.

Sandrine Kyrstofski appeared beside Erna in the Abbey courtyard.

"Oh, Sandrine, you surprised me." The two women crossed their arms tightly against the cold.

"It's like the hush before a tornado. The air becomes unnaturally still as though it all had been sucked away by the coming storm. I haven't felt this since I was a little girl." Sandrine pulled the collar of her sweater closer. "Do you think he's dead?"

"I've been trying to get through to New York."

Erna looked at the walls of the ancient Abbey. Pieces of the slate roof had fallen, and a number of cracks traveled the walls. The statue of St. Leoger in the center of the courtyard now tilted to one side and patches of cobblestones bulged.

Our ancestors did their jobs, they *kept* the Blessing. *What have we done?*

Peprini left the Vessel and went to the old wine cellar. He found Ada, Irad's wife, sitting beside the child sharing bread broken from a loaf. She stood and joined her husband, her hand still on the child's shoulder, looking warily at Peprini. Most of the Cainites were lying on the cots, asleep or in their inert state. Four had sat up as he opened the door. They were obviously conscious.

"Good morning."

Irad nodded. Ada didn't move.

"Were you comfortable last night?"

"As comfortable as captives can be." He stared at Peprini. "How long will we be here?"

"That is what I have come to discuss. The last piece of our plan is in place. The sooner the better, yes?"

"I see no need to wait."

Ada glared at Peprini. This was understandable, as Peprini had threatened the lives of her child and husband, as well as her own. Irad bore these facts more stoically.

"Fine." He turned as he was opening the door. "One more thing. I must make sure that Ada and those of you remaining behind do not follow us to the Void."

"Why would any of us wish to leave your world?"

"Perhaps. But still, I must make sure you will stay behind in these bodies." Peprini now addressed Ada. "If I did not, what would stop you from following your husband, taking the source of light, and abandoning me in the Void?" He didn't wait for an answer. "I will require that Ada and those of you remaining behind be..." He realized he didn't know the Canaanite word for "drugged," if there was any. "I must give them something, something like very strong wine, to ensure they sleep and do not follow us as soon as we enter the Void. About this there can be no bargain."

Irad nodded.

"You are to wait for me at... the great shore, where you left Enoch and entered the door to our world. I will bring the Vessel—the light. Yes?"

"Yes."

"I will see you shortly."

He closed the door behind him and became lightheaded, bracing himself against the wall. When he had left Lucerne he had kissed his wife and children, saying goodbye with a warmth even the two children noticed. Of course, he didn't say where he was going or why; they knew little of his life as a Keeper. He absorbed the finality of what he was going to do. He had anticipated that when the time came to accompany Irad and Wyatt into the Void that he would be nervous, and he expected the many mental rehearsals he had undertaken would have calmed him. But now his anxiety attacked. He struggled to regain his balance as he made his way up the stairs, forcing his legs to climb each step, clutching the handrail.

He found Envot, one of the Keepers who had accompanied him from Lucerne, standing outside smoking a cigarette. "Go down to the Cainites. Take Zdenek with you. Administer the sedative to the woman Ada and the others. Do not touch Irad or the other four that are conscious. Make certain you give them enough so they will be completely out. I want them in a dreamless sleep for at least 24 hours. If you are uncertain, err on the side of giving them too much. Do it now."

Peprini stood still. His eyes were drawn to David Wyatt's drugged body that lay on the bed. This was a leap of faith, a leap with immediate and possibly eternal consequences. It was not the thought of dying that froze him. If he became lost in the Void, what would become of his soul? What had happened to his father's soul? This went beyond the faith of believers. He was going where no human—none but God's chosen Vessels—was intended to go.

He found his legs shaking. But the inculcation of three generations of Peprinis was enormously powerful, and he felt the permission and destiny that had come to fruition in him. Yes, he thought. Our family is unique in 4000 years of Keeperdom. If the Blessing is to survive, it would be because the Peprinis have existed and willed it to survive.

He sat in the armchair and closed his eyes. The familiar sensations of slipping into his Inner Depths barely registered with him, and so practiced was he over a lifetime that even distracted it went quickly and smoothly, and he found himself at the edge of the Void.

David Wyatt's inert body was there, hovering on the edge. The Councilor moved toward him. Suddenly they were among the five Cainites. Peprini felt relieved that he could sense their foulness, their protection. Irad gestured and everyone followed. He stopped and pointed into the Void. Peprini looked but saw nothing. Irad pointed again and motioned for Peprini to move closer. Now he found that if he stood at just the right angle he could see a tunnel of golden light. He marveled at the sight, at the fact Eliezer and Oleander had constructed this, at their accomplishment.

They moved to the very edge. Irad went first, then another Cainite.

It was Peprini's turn. He could see the normal chaos and flux of the Void. He guided the Vessel with one hand. Under his breath he began chanting invocations from the Book of Creation, beginning with the first. Immediately the Blessing gathered in him. From his discernment training he had the ability to focus his mind simultaneously in two distinct directions. One part continuously chanted in his thoughts the formulas from the Book of Creation. With the other, his heart pounding, he stepped off the edge. He started to lose his balance and panic gripped him.

He was encouraged when he realized he had been correct. The passageway was infused with Blessing, though he could also tell that only Vessels, and not mere men, ought to be here. The beam had a viscous quality that made movement awkward though not difficult. The Cainites seemed not to have this trouble. He took another step. There was nothing underneath his feet, or rather, there was nothing more substantial beneath his feet than to any side or above him. Gravity didn't exist here. He collected himself, calming his breathing. Turning to Irad he nodded, getting the same in return. The other Cainites joined them. The odor of the Cainites was different now. Here it felt natural and oddly comforting, not contrary to the cocoon of Blessing that held him.

Irad turned, and all seven moved together. They traveled, yet there was little sense of distance. There was nothing to use as perspective. Periodically Peprini had the impression of having crossed a great distance, though without being able to describe what had been traversed. He sensed time had passed, though the perception was beyond description.

The Keeper noticed the Cainites looking below and to the right. He tracked their eyes. Enoch. Everyone stopped. It appeared as a distant encampment though in heavy shadow. The darkness made the Keeper strain to see and wonder how much he was imagining.

Irad looked questioningly at Peprini, then at the Vessel. Irad reached through the wall of the beam and his wrist and hand were bent in the way an arm half underwater appears crooked from above. He pulled it back, turned again to Peprini, and waited for an answer. Peprini nodded.

Two Cainites took the Vessel gently by the arms, and they passed through the golden-hued wall. As if shot from a cannon they were suddenly away, soon cloaked in the shadow of the encampment.

The golden tunnel continued into the beyond. Irad had claimed it went to the Bible World. Peprini felt the anticipation of the Blessing, of what would soon be his, of what he would bring back to humanity. He looked at Irad as if to say, "I kept my word. Now it is your turn."

The Cainite turned and all four moved farther into the tunnel of light towards what promised to be the Bible World.

They traveled along the passageway for an unknown time. Finally, Irad stopped and moved next to Peprini. He pointed and the full-moon disk of the Bible World was in view.

"Do you see it?" The Cainite asked.

He could hear the Cainite's words, although the sounds reverberated strangely, and the accompanying echoes made them barely decipherable. It was an odd experience; he had never before heard speech in the Void, even his own chanting of the Book of the Creation had been silent. The powers of the curse, he thought.

The Keeper had been concentrating on reciting the incantation of the first Sefirah, his eyes down to prevent himself from losing focus. That focus had become increasingly difficult to maintain as the chaos of the Void clawed at him continuously despite the protection of the passageway of Blessing, of the Cainites, and the incantations from the Book of Creation. Now he stopped and looked up. What he had seen only in his discernments, far from the other side of the Void, was now close, larger than the Keeper had ever imagined.

"Yes," he said. He marveled at his own voice, which sounded as strange as the Cainite's. I too can speak in the Void, he thought. The powers of the curse are in me also.

"It is near."

"I see it, yes."

"Do you wish for me to take you the final measure?"

Looking into Irad's eyes he saw that the man was making a gesture, like a guide allowing the mountaineer to make the last pitch to the summit alone. He felt his weakness cloud his thinking. Despite the protections, Peprini's body and mind spoke the truth that Keepers were not meant to be in the Void. *But who knew what was meant to be?* This thought bolstered him, and he felt the force of his entire life as a Peprini, as a grandson of Alberto, and son of Marcus. Shall I limp into the Bible World all but carried by these cursed exiles? And what if I appear at the Gates of the Bible World accompanied by those once cast out? Would the curse they carry keep me from entering?

Something made him turn. The passageway behind them had begun dissipating. The change was faint but unmistakable. He could not change his mind and return now even if Irad could be persuaded to take him back. He would not survive the trip.

"I will go alone."

Irad nodded. "My wife and child, and the others?"

"I will release them when I return."

"And if you do not live?"

"They will be allowed to return. I know my people. Your family will be awakened. Your wife, Ada. She knows how to leave her body and return to Enoch?"

"She does." He waited until Peprini nodded. "I will wait for her there then."

Peprini looked down the passageway at the Bible World. What had beckoned to him since he had been a child was so near.

"Then our bargain is complete."

Irad moved just inches closer, looking at Peprini. Then he glanced towards the Bible World.

"May you find what you seek."

Irad and the three Cainites moved through the wall of the passageway and instantly were gone. He did not watch them after that. He felt a nauseating blanket fall over him. The loss of the Cainite protection. He closed his eyes and began his recitations again. In a moment of fear he opened them and looked over his shoulder. The passageway was disappearing even faster now. He began moving forward, reciting from the Book, the nausea and weakness making it difficult to move, to remember how to move.

101

The first of the dawn light touched the upper stories of the Manhattan skyscrapers. Far below, the five refugees slept.

A severe quaking roused them from their beds. Kedar was the first to assess the damage. New, larger cracks appeared on the walls of the living room. He could stick his hand in the widest one. The furniture had shifted and a heavy urn of golden sand, a customary ornament found in every Ishmaelite home, had been shattered.

"Something's changed," Oleander said. His eyes cast about the room anxiously.

"What do you see?" asked Kedar.

"It's what I don't."

"The Blessing is gone," Eliezer announced as he entered the room with Dina and Osnat, narrowing his eyes, searching, finding nothing.

A second tremor shook the house, knocking them off their feet. A tall bookcase broke from the wall and pieces of rock showered the room. Kedar found himself rolling on the floor in Oleander's arms, while Eliezer fell on the sofa. Dina was thrown against the wall but remained on her feet.

Only Osnat remained sprawled on the rug, her eyes closed.

"Osnat?"

Kedar knelt beside her. She moved her head and coughed.

"But where is the Vessel?"

Again her lips moved, the words tumbling out: *"The Keeper has taken the Vessel into the emptiness."*

Her eyes opened wider and she tried to sit up. Oleander and Kedar helped her to the couch.

Eliezer sat beside her. "A Keeper has taken the Vessel into the emptiness?" He turned to the monk.

"Peprini," Oleander exclaimed.

"It has to be."

"He's taken David Wyatt into the Void."

They assembled around the dining table.

"If Wyatt is gone, if he is dead..." Eliezer shifted his aching body.

"We don't know what's happened. We have to assume he's alive."

"Yes, yes, of course, William." Oleander put his hand on Eliezer's shoulder.

"Assuming we do open a new passageway to the Bible World," Osnat said, in part to herself, in part to others, "would this New Gate yield any Blessing? What if there is no longer a Vessel to carry the Blessing back to Earth?"

"Oleander and I have discussed this matter," the old professor replied. "It is our hope that this New Gate would work differently; that it would require no Vessel; that it would exude Blessing directly to our world like an open faucet."

"But we simply don't know."

Eliezer continued. "The New Gate must be a different kind of gate. It is not part of the known twelve, so there must be something special about it. I cannot say I know for sure that we won't need a Vessel, but I am entitled to have faith. Otherwise..." His words trailed off.

"Otherwise, our entire endeavor will have been worse than pointless," Oleander said with conviction. "*It is a New Gate*. We have to try."

"The Blessing would not have assembled us here for no reason," Kedar said cautiously but firmly. Oleander nodded.

Eliezer stood. "Thank you both. We will now finish what we started."

Osnat stood hesitantly, "Should I...?"

"You don't think we would try this without you, do you?" Eliezer held out his arm, a concerned, weary smile on his face.

All doubts and fears were now beyond the three Keepers. They dimmed the light and sat at the small kitchen table. Taking deep breaths, each began reciting a formula of the Book of Creation. Soon they felt a warm and powerful energy filling their bodies, inhabiting that place near the heart where every Keeper holds the Blessing most closely.

Oleander gave a small smile to Eliezer, and now both closed their eyes, Osnat following. Their breathing and their heartbeats slowed and their attention turned inward. Confidently they sank deeper and deeper, below the surface of their consciousness, below their selves, to the edge of the Void.

A few moments after they emerged in the Depths. Osnat appeared behind them. Eliezer began:

WITH THIRTY-TWO MYSTERIOUS PATHS OF WISDOM ENGRAVED GOD, THE LORD OF HOSTS, GOD OF ISRAEL, THE

LIVING GOD, GOD ALMIGHTY, HIGH AND EXALTED, DWELLING IN ETERNITY ON HIGH, AND HIS NAME IS HOLY...

A whirlpool of energies engulfed him, gripping and grasping, and he felt again how easy it would be to falter and be lost in those torrents if they spoke the wrong codeword. But there was no fear in his heart.

...AND HE CREATED HIS WORLD WITH THREE SFR'S: WITH SFR AND SFR AND SFR.

Oleander waited until he could feel the gales quivering around him. Then he turned to the Abraham section:

WHEN ABRAHAM OUR FATHER, MAY HE REST IN PEACE, LOOKED AND SAW AND UNDERSTOOD AND EXPLORED AND ENGRAVED AND HEWED OUT AND SUCCEEDED AT CREATION...

Oleander sensed a flicker, and though he was still standing beside Eliezer, his vision telescoped into the distance. He felt flung across the empty vastness, away from his companions, blind to what was happening to him. The movement then slowed, and he felt his field of vision come to a stop. The familiar ocean of foreboding emptiness appeared before him. He knew he was seeing the Void from the other shore, from the side of the Bible World.

He could see his discernment beam extending into the darkness. Further into the blackness was a point of light. *This must be Eliezer's discernment beam reaching out towards his own. Would they meet this time?*

Walls of an unseen force kept building around him. This was the Blessing, but of a raw and pure form he had never experienced.

"...IMMEDIATELY THE LORD OF ALL BLESSED BE HIS NAME FOREVER, WAS REVEALED TO HIM, AND HE PLACED HIM IN HIS BOSOM AND KISSED HIM ON IS HEAD AND CALLED HIM ABRAHAM MY BELOVED, AND CUT A COVENANT WITH HIM AND WITH HIS SEED FOREVER..."

It now seemed to him that the point of light was growing in the distance. That sight bolstered him, even as he had to struggle to focus on the words as the walls of Blessing closed around him, threatening to consume him. As the pressure of the Blessing increased, he felt the borders of his being begin to dissolve. He made a stand against this and spoke the words given to Abraham.

"...AND HE BOUND TWENTY-TWO LETTERS TO HIS TONGUE AND REVEALED TO HIM HIS SECRET, HE DREW THEM IN WATER, HE IGNITED THEM IN FIRE, HE AGITATED THEM WITH BREATH, HE BURNED THEM WITH THE SEVEN, HE DIRECTED THEM WITH THE TWELVE CONSTELLATION."

At the same time Eliezer spoke the words of the Seventh Sefirah:

TEN SEFIROT OF BELIMAH AND TWENTY-TWO FOUNDATION LETTERS: THREE MOTHERS, SEVEN DOUBLES, AND TWELVE SIMPLE, AND A SPIRIT IN EACH ONE OF THEM.

The old man imagined his younger companion envisioning from the other side of the emptiness, waiting for him to utter the word.

"Dinah."

A whirlwind of energies rushed around Eliezer and into the Void. A brief feeling of exaltation rose in his mind, but he pushed it aside, fighting the currents pulling at him. He managed to look at Osnat. She was unsteady but in control. Then he glanced at Oleander. The monk's presence was still beside him. The old man turned back to the emptiness and waited.

A luminous globe exploded in the distance, and a moment later a wave of light pulsed towards him, rushing along his own discernment beam. He was locked in its path. The wave arrived in a blinding flash. The Blessing that struck him coursed through his body with an intensity he had not known, reaching into parts of his being he had not known existed. He was being set afire from within; he was evaporating into a greater reality.

Eliezer found himself standing at the edge of the Void, and before him was a clear passageway that extended all the way to the Bible World. The golden tunnel shimmered in the pure blackness surrounding it. *The New Gate!*

Oleander watched the same sight from the other side of the Void. Soon the sight vanished and he felt himself flung back to the familiar scene beside his two companions.

The three stood captivated by the vision of the New Gate. For a while they savored this magnificent sight—no Keeper had witnessed the glory of a new Gate opened. Eliezer was the first to realize that his strength was gone. He gave a last, reverent look, then made his way to his Inner Depths and started rising to the surface.

He was back in the Ishmaelite room. He glanced at Osnat, her eyes closed but her chest moving with her breath, then at Oleander. The monk's face was pale and glossy with sweat. That was the last image Eliezer had before losing consciousness.

Some minutes later the three Keepers awoke, one by one. The two Councilors looked around them and immediately knew that their faith had not been fulfilled. The tremors still shook the Ishmaelite dwelling. In fact, they were stronger. The New Gate did not seem to give out Blessing by itself.

They joined the others in the main room. The faces of Dina and Kedar were marked in fear and resignation. Eliezer and Oleander now understood: Though the new passageway was open, nothing had changed.

"We did what we set out to do. We opened the New Gate," Eliezer said. "But...I was wrong. A Vessel is needed after all to bring the Blessing to the Earth. And if Menach has taken the last Vessel..."

Eliezer sat down. The responsibility that had been weighing on his shoulders for months dissolved. Things were no longer in his hands; there was nothing more he could do. One wish filled his heart: to hear Erna's voice again.

"Kedar, do cell phones work down here? With all those tons of rocks above our heads..."

"There is a satellite phone that connects to an antenna up top. I talked to the Prince last night." He answered Eliezer's look. "It's my obligation to keep my grandfather informed. But I can't promise it still works."

102

Papers on the table started flying about the room, caught in an invisible whirlwind. Eyes automatically searched for an open window—but in the Ishmaelite underground there were none. Then a coat rack in the corner began wobbling and tipped over.

"When winds are born of nothing," Kedar quoted in a mournful voice, "and objects totter unprovoked; when the impossible begins, the end must be at hand."

The five sat in the great room, eyes extinguished of hope.

One of the flying pages landed at his feet, and Kedar rose to pick it up. But his foot caught on the rug and he tripped and fell. He got up and rubbed his elbow. "Better not to move in this kind of world."

They sat quietly, only the occasional tremors and cracking noises from inside the walls breaking the silence.

"I wonder," Oleander said, "what it's like up there. All my adult life I've worked to give them the Blessing, to protect them. Excuse me, Kedar, but if these are my last hours… I don't want to spend them in a cave."

"Well, then," Kedar stood with a sudden surge of energy, "let's go. It can't be any more dangerous than here." He watched a delicate shower of rock and plaster dust float from the ceiling.

Eliezer nodded. "Alright." He stood and Oleander and Dina followed. "Let's hope the way out is not blocked."

"There are six exits. One should be clear."

Oleander, Eliezer, and Dina followed the Ishmaelite towards the door. They didn't notice that Osnat remained behind.

For several minutes she had been aware of a bubble of knowledge expanding inside her. It was still wordless, an embryo. Tenderly she held it in her mind, knowing she must nurture and protect it until the words could form. Premature birth or eruption would mean losing it. She tried to breathe in tune with its pulsing. It seemed to say something, to express an urgent message—but it was still too vague, now trying to rise from her and evaporate unheard into the world. She strained to keep it from escaping while not crushing it.

All her muscles were working to maintain the enclosure of her inner being, and her breaths became short and heavy. She was approaching the limits of her endurance. The bubble was maturing slowly, too slowly, resolving itself into more and more distinct features. Not yet... *please, one more moment...* Then she could see it very clearly in her mind's eye, and in that second she comprehended it all.

"Dina! Eliezer!" She had to give voice to her understanding before it faded.

"Osnat?" Kedar moved towards her but Eliezer grabbed him from behind, covering his mouth. "Let her speak," he commanded in a stern whisper.

Kedar turned to look at Eliezer, astonished at the speed and strength of the old man. They all now watched Osnat.

"Dina must sleep, she must dream, Dina must dream her dream."

Dina looked questioningly at Eliezer who only shook his head and put his finger to his lips.

"She must sleep now."

Upon her last word, Osnat awoke from her trance. She examined the four puzzled faces. "What did I say?" she asked hazily.

Eliezer was the first to see. "That Dina must travel to the Bible World," he replied. "She must visit the New Gate."

"But I don't understand." Dina looked from Eliezer to Oleander and then to Osnat.

"I do," said Oleander. He turned to Eliezer who had the same hopeful smile on his face that Oleander knew was on his own.

103

Everywhere people stopped what they were doing. They left their meals, they quit sweeping floors of debris or boarding up windows or trying to fix cars or generators, they put down phones. They emerged from apartment buildings, tenements, schools, suburban homes, basements, straw huts, desert tents, and office buildings. They hobbled out of hospitals. They walked out of police stations and army bases and guerilla camps. They gathered in the avenues of New York City, in the streets of Rio de Janeiro, on Kenyatta Avenue in Nairobi, in Piazza Navona in Rome, along the Nile in Cairo, in Tiananmen Square in Beijing.

The menacing rumble from the bowels of the earth had grown during the last few hours. Deep fissures had opened. Cars were strewn along the streets. Debris from rooftops, broken glass, and fallen branches were everywhere. Hospitals and morgues and schools—now makeshift clinics and refugee camps—overflowed with victims. The last intact telephone connections ceased, the remaining radio and TV stations fell to static, and all but a few power stations had failed.

It was no longer possible to pretend the world might return to normal. Like an overheated engine that slowly approaches its maximum workload and suddenly seizes, humanity reached the limits of its capacity to fight the growing chaos and to hope. It let go of all struggles and now awaited the end. What they apprehended without understanding was the extinction of the Blessing.

There was solemnity in the air among the endless crowds that had gathered. Though the quakes had come from below, most eyes now turned to the sky, to the heavens, in a last appeal for redemption, a last attempt to understand why.

The rumble from deep below was constant. People prayed or held their loved ones, their eyes caressing the sky, the human faces around them, the world that had been home. New tremors began, causing buildings to buckle, knocking down trees. Few tried to flee. There was nowhere to hide.

104

Osnat's pronouncement agitated an already nerve-wracked Dina.

"I want you to lie down," Oleander said. "Please, Dina."

"I'm telling you I won't be able to sleep."

Nevertheless, she kicked off her shoes and lay on the bed.

Oleander began calming her. His intention was to bring her to a relaxed state and then to hope sleep would come. But would a dream, *the* dream, follow? He whispered to her as he would to a small child, and the purity of the Blessing enfolding her almost brought tears to him. He closed his eyes and spoke to her as if in prayer.

He opened his eyes, listening to her breathe. She was asleep. He stood and gently closed the door behind him.

The four were waiting downstairs.

"It's up to her now."

Dina found herself hovering in an ocean of emptiness. She vaguely remembered having been here before. But something was new. In front of her was a glorious passageway, radiant with light, leading into the emptiness and far away.

A wave of joy carried her along the golden path towards the horizon. She found she could move as she wished. Yes, she was now certain she had been here many times. In the past she had been barely conscious, but now she was fully and intensely awake; not exactly "awake" in the ordinary sense—curiously she knew she was asleep, but at the same time she was awake in some deeper way.

For what seemed a long time she flew across the vast nothingness, following the passageway of light. A small disc glowed like a distant sun beckoning to her.

This light became brighter and brighter still. She was blinded by its intensity and yet felt caressed by its warmth.

Words whispered in her mind: *And Jacob arrived unharmed in Shechem… and he put his tent there…*

The words of the Bible, she realized.

And Dinah the daughter of Leah, whom she had borne to Jacob, went out to meet the girls of the land. And Shechem the son of Hamor, the Hivite, the prince of the land, saw her and took her and lay with her and tormented her.

Dina shuddered. She wanted the words to stop—she didn't want to hear the rest. She knew it ended with pain and blood and murder. Against her will the words continued to materialize in her mind, only now she found herself not merely visualizing the Biblical story, but actually *inside it.*

The brilliance cleared and she was sitting on top of a hill in the low mountains. At the foot of the hill was a cluster of tents beside a stream. She knew this was Jacob's camp. The rocky hills were green and lush. In the distance, she could see cattle grazing. Beyond was the town of Shechem.

She had seen this before. She had told Father Binino of these dreams.

Something stirred in the camp below her. A girl—Dinah, Jacob's daughter—left one of the tents. She wore a light blue robe over her slender body, and a wreath of chrysanthemums adorned her head. With her dark hair and innocent face she was so lovely that Dina, watching from above, could not help smiling. She followed her namesake leaving the encampment and walking along the path across the green fields.

But her smile faded. Because from her vantage point she could see what the girl could not: a young man walking towards her on the other side of the hill. It was Shechem.

The girl had to be warned. Dina rose to her feet but then stopped, now remembering: every time she had dreamt this terrifying scene she had longed to intervene but had always been powerless. Time and again she wished to stop the terrible course of events but always failed. No wonder she would awaken from the dream crying.

But today something was different. For the first time she could think clearly. And she realized the path of events could not be changed. This was, after all, part of the eternal story of the Bible. Dinah's rape was an already-established fact, as rigid and unchangeable as the past.

She sat down again on the rock, distraught. Her eyes followed the girl as she walked joyfully, not suspecting that her life was about to change. She buried her face in her hands. The words, in the meantime, kept whispering in her mind, steadily progressing towards the bloody ending.

And his soul clung to Dinah, the daughter of Jacob, and he loved the girl and spoke to her heart. And Shechem spoke to Hamor his father: "Take for me this girl for a woman."

And Jacob heard that he had defiled his daughter Dinah, and his sons were away with his cattle grazing, and Jacob remained silent until their return. And Hamor, the father of Shechem, went to Jacob to talk with him. And the sons of

Jacob returned from the field, and when they heard they were saddened and were greatly angered because an evil deed had been done in Israel, to lay with Jacob's daughter, something that was not to be done.

Dina fought her tears.

And the sons of Jacob answered Shechem and Hamor his father, speaking slyly because he had defiled Dinah their sister. And they said to him: We cannot do this thing, giving our sister to an uncircumcised man, because it is a disgrace for us. But with the following thing we will consent to you, that you will be like us, circumcising every male.

Jacob's sons cunningly agree to give Dinah to Shechem for a wife on condition he and his people circumcise themselves. The townspeople of Shechem agree, and while they are still aching from the surgery, two of Jacob's sons, Simon and Levi, attack the city and slaughter everyone. Dina cringed at having to witness again the massacre, how Simon and Levi would burst into one house after another and stab everyone they see; how terrified women and children would run into the streets, pursued by the two brothers.

The plot unfolded in all its horror. But slowly a new understanding illuminated her mind. She could not alter the stories of the Bible, *yet there was something for her to do*: to pour out her compassion upon those tragic events, upon Dinah as well as Shechem, upon Simon and Levi as well as their innocent victims.

Dina stood and looked down at the smoke rising over the burnt city of Shechem, at the bodies strewn in the streets, at Simon and Levi returning to camp with bloody swords, at Dinah crying in her tent. She spread her hands towards the entire world and felt an ocean of blessed love filling her heart and radiating in all directions, caressing every wound and every tear. She was a fountain of the Blessing now, and through her the Blessing shone to every corner of the human heart.

"You no longer belong to yourself," she heard something speak inside her. "You are now a Vessel of the Blessing."

"Amen," she replied. "Here I am."

Dina felt filled with joy almost beyond her capacity. "Here I am," she repeated. Tears of gratitude blurred her vision. The Biblical scenery around her started dissipating, and she felt herself being carried back home.

Eliezer, Oleander, Osnat and Kedar had been unable to wait downstairs and had entered the room and watched over her. Now Dina's body stirred and her lips parted slightly. She opened her sleepy eyes and looked at the four faces.

She was glorious, overflowing with Blessing. Neither Eliezer nor Oleander, certainly not Osnat, had ever witnessed a Vessel awakening after receiving the Blessing. Even the Ishmaelite, though no Keeper, was moved in her presence. This was no longer the Dina they had known. She was now a fountain of love, of life.

"Do you understand now who you are?" Eliezer said to her, reverence in his voice and kindness in his eyes.

Somewhat bashfully she nodded. "I think I do, yes." She sat up. "How long... does this last?" She was trying to give a name to what she was feeling.

The old man could only smile.

"Listen!" Kedar said.

It took them several seconds to grasp what it was. "The tremors have stopped."

"Eliezer," murmured Oleander. His eyes inspected the room, noting what only Keepers could perceive. "It's returned."

"The New Gate has been opened. And a new Vessel has returned with the Blessing."

"A new Vessel," Oleander repeated the words, smiling at Dina. "It is still only one. But with one there is hope."

105

All six Councilors-in-residence had gathered around the table in the Abbey Chambers. Julia Erna, Albrecht Sionn, Sandrine Krystofski, Annette Goldman, Margaret Connor, and Theresa Fournier sat in their customary places, the other four chairs vacant. The oval table had been bolted to the floor, and as a tremor shook the ancient building the six held onto the edge in what had become a universal human practice in the last weeks.

"Have you been able to get through to Algeria?"

Sionn turned to Fournier and shook his head. "There may be no phone service left by now in the entire world."

"If David Wyatt returns from the Void, perhaps things will stabilize, such as they are."

"We can hope, Margaret. We can hope." But Erna's thoughts were on Eliezer, wondering where he was and if he was still alive.

"Menach." Fournier no longer was angry. A new sense of wonder about the world, about human beings and her own ignorance of what they were capable of, had taken hold of her in the last hours. "How long do you suppose he'd been planning this?"

Sionn spoke softly. "Apparently the plan, the idea *for a plan*, goes all the way back to Alberto, to about 1930. Marcus took up the work, and when he died, it was then passed down to Menach."

"So Marcus' death while discerning was no ordinary accident after all. Yes, now I see, this makes much more sense," Krystofski nodded as if finally learning the solution to a mystery. "I'm sure it pained Menach—more than we can imagine—to have all of Keeperdom believe his father was clumsy enough to die in routine discernment. I'm ashamed to say I always thought of Marcus as something of a…"

Fournier slowly shook her head in amazement. "They sat at this table, grandfather, father, and son, for over seventy years. And not a word." She saw the pain in Sionn's eyes and grasped the particular betrayal he must feel.

Sionn had stood and was looking out a small window, the glass of uneven thickness, perhaps two centuries old. It had stopped snowing. The sun had broken through the low clouds, and he felt its warmth and life-giving force push through the glass upon his face. He closed his eyes.

"How much longer will this last?" he thought.

He opened his eyes to look at the sun. It was a glorious sight, pure and good and constant, the same sun thousands upon thousands of generations of human beings had stood under. It shone upon the east orchard, causing the snow and ice on the trees and ground to sparkle like jewels. It struck him as odd that even without the Blessing the world could be so beautiful. He allowed himself to enjoy the dance of light.

At first he thought it was nostalgia, his memory of the countless times since a boy he had looked upon the hillside and apprehended the Blessing swirling among the apple trees, imbuing the landscape with magic and goodness. How he had taken for granted the sight, the feeling, the promise the Blessing lent to his vision! As he looked, something stirred in him, and he resisted this, fearing it was false, that it was the nostalgia tempting him. But he couldn't deny his eyes, that part of himself which was not merely a human being but a Keeper: It was undeniably the Blessing he was perceiving!

It was Fournier who first noticed the queer expression on Sionn's face as he turned from the window to face the group.

"Albrecht?"

He felt the smile on his face. "It's returned."

"What?"

"*Outside*. Look!"

All moved to the windows.

"But is it just what has lingered, before completely dying out?" Margaret Connor was scared to hope.

"No, Margaret," Erna said, the joy filling her heart. "This *is* a return. No, *this Blessing is new*."

They all watched with their Keepers' eyes, witnessing the renewal, being renewed themselves.

"So Vessel Wyatt must be alive," Margaret said. "He must have found his way back from the Void. He must be safe."

For several minutes they watched and gained sustenance from the sight. Soon they noticed that other Keepers had emerged from the Abbey, bathing in the new Blessing.

Everywhere the tremors stopped. Some people held their breath, fearful of allowing their fragile hope to return, but as they waited the silence persisted. Without being able to explain how, most felt the danger starting to move off into the distance. What they sensed without knowing was the return of the Blessing. It was the Blessing that removed their fear and anxiety, replacing this with the hope and promise that is inherent in the Blessing. The skies cleared and the sun came out. Hesitant smiles returned to faces that had grown unaccustomed to cheerfulness. Parents held their children and were able to say truthfully, "It's over now. Everything will be fine."

106

For the first time in millennia, Enoch was in commotion. The city had been asleep since Cain's descendants had arrived after years of wandering in the Void, having been exiled from the Earthly realm. How long they had been asleep was beyond even the knowledge of the Ishmaelites.

One by one the Cainites awoke. The memory of who they had been slowly returned. The city was cast in wondrous radiance. A small light in perfect darkness shines all the more brightly; in the same way, the Vessel amidst the natural absence of Blessing made his presence that much more luminous. The people rejoiced. Mothers were rejoined with children, husbands with wives, brothers with sisters.

As with all exiled peoples, the Cainites had a prophecy of their return to the homeland, and with their awakening they remembered it. They understood the time had arrived. They knew the path back to the Bible World had been opened. They turned towards the shining passageway of Blessing and flew to the New Gate. What had been closed so long ago now received them.

The city of Enoch was empty of Cainites, its cells and winding passages deserted. Only one creature remained. David Wyatt wandered confused through the maze. The forces of the Curse were still inside him, darkening his mind. "This is a nightmare," he kept saying to himself. "I have to wake up."

At last he found an opening. Peering outside, he stared at a dark, boundless space, marked only by a thin shining path. He vaguely recalled that he had been brought here by two men.

"If this is a dream," he told himself, "then the laws of nature no longer hold, and I can fly in this space."

He stepped from the door and hovered in the Void. He found he could control his movements. Despite his many years of navigating in the Void in his dreams, his confused consciousness could not recall those experiences.

"Well done. Now, where do I go from here?"

He scanned his surroundings. He could see nothing but empty space, interrupted by the faint beam of light. He hesitated as something caught his attention. Off to his right a figure approached gliding along the beam. It was a young woman, looking intently into the distance where the beam led.

Her figure became larger. She turned her face towards him and their eyes met.

She slowed, hesitated, and then, as if succumbing to a drive stronger than herself, continued along the path towards the distant Bible World.

David Wyatt followed her figure disappearing in the distance.

"If this is a dream," he said, "then she might still return."

Dina sat on her bed and looked at her four companions. It made her uncomfortable to be regarded with such respect. She recalled how years ago the strange visions started plaguing her and making her fear for her sanity; how she had consulted Father Binino, to be then invited to the Frostburg Institute, to be told by the Director himself that she was a Keeper, to feel accepted, only to be discarded... And now—was it possible? But the facts were undeniable: right after her dream, the tremors had stopped. More importantly, Eliezer had told her: "You must trust what Oleander, Osnat and I perceive—the Blessing that now surrounds you, the Blessing that we see has returned to the world."

She was no longer the shy and insecure woman who cared little what happened to her. She stood tall in the middle of the room, a soft radiance of Blessing surrounding her figure, her face exuding a mixture of tenderness and intensity.

"Now that you have brought back the Blessing," Oleander turned to Kedar, "I imagine the Ishmaelites will be coming back too?"

"The Prince no doubt understands what has happened here. I'm sure they are on their way."

"Alright, then. Kedar, lead the way if you would," Eliezer said as the group headed outside the dwelling.

Dina did not move. Osnat examined her. "Dina? Are you ready?"

She wondered what was keeping her from moving. Vague memories of her dream returned: the journey through the Void, the Biblical scene of Shechem and Dinah, the destruction of the city, and then the trip back through the Void...

"Not yet."

She now realized why she couldn't leave: she had to return to the Void. But why? She searched her mind, wondering. She had left something in the Void, yes. But what was it? Something she had seen while moving across the Void towards the Bible World.

"I have to go back to the dream. There is still something I need to do."

Surprised, the four gazed at her. The confidence and authority in her voice stopped them from asking why or what.

Eliezer broke the silence. "Will you be able?"

"I have to trust the Blessing to take me."

107

Dina felt too excited to sleep, but closing her eyes she found herself pacified by the Blessing. She submitted to it and soon found herself again at the edge of the Void.

She plunged into the blackness and followed the golden path as before. After a while, she noticed a dark spot in the distance, against the background of the Bible World. Something or someone was flying there. Relieved, she darted towards it.

As she approached, she was disappointed to see that this dark spot was actually a cluster of men, women, and children drifting toward the Bible world. She understood: These were the Cainites that Eliezer had mentioned. They had awakened and their curse lifted. They were gliding with joy, some holding hands, some children playfully chasing each other. Her heart swelled and she wished them a happy new life. Curiously, she felt that her wish was not merely words but imparted on the returning Cainites a true Blessing.

She turned and again scanned the empty space. The passageway of light she had been following was fading. The figure of a solitary man moving inside the passageway caught her eye. She moved towards him with hope. Still some distance away she stopped, disappointed. Though she could not see his face clearly, she knew this was not the same man. There was something bleak and cold about him. Even in the radiance of the passageway he seemed dark. Her disappointment turned into worry: Where was the other man? Would she ever find him again? And why was he so important to her?

Moments later she saw him, inert in the blackness. She took his hand and followed the sparkling traces of discernment beam that Eliezer and Oleander had created earlier.

They arrived at the edge of the Void. Emerging from the chaos seemed to revive him.

"When you wake up, look for me," Dina said.

"*Where? Who are you?*"

"My name is Dina."

He found himself lying on the couch in the Archive library. A woman was stooping over him, examining him with obvious concern.

"My name is Roberta Maxon," she said, visibly relieved. "How are you feeling?"

David tried to sit up. "Where is Dina?"

"I am sorry, Mr. Wyatt, there is no Dina here. You must have dreamt."

She stood and turned to a young man standing in the doorway. "Get him some water, Sam. He is virtually dehydrated."

"Where is she?" David pleaded.

"I don't know who you have in mind. You are in Algeria. You are safe."

Some three thousand miles away, in the compound beneath New York, one hundred men, women, and children entered the corridors of their city, happy and relieved to see their home again.

"The Ishmaelites, I presume," Eliezer said, hearing the voices. He, Oleander, Osnat and Kedar moved outside. Leading the large procession down the cobblestone street was Prince Nevayot.

"Greetings, Prince." He was about to offer an explanation for their intrusion but the Prince waved aside his words.

"Where is the New Vessel?" the Prince asked eagerly.

"Asleep. On a journey to the Void."

"Let her rest. You and I, Eliezer, have much to discuss."

Dina opened her eyes. Many people stood on one side of the room, watching her with concern and admiration. She recognized Osnat among them, then Eliezer and Oleander, then Kedar.

An old man in a suit with no tie stepped forward. His figure seemed authoritative and powerful. Dina sat up.

"Congratulations, Vessel Dina. We have you and your four friends to thank for the safety of us all."

"Thank you. But who are you?"

"We," the old man motioned at the crowd, "are the Ishmaelites, and this is our home. I am Prince Nevayot," he bowed slightly, "and I am very pleased to meet you."

Dina nodded courteously. "I am honored to meet you, Prince. But where is..." she paused, embarrassed. "I just met a man in the Void. Do you know who he is?"

Prince Nevayot smiled.

"You do?"

"I am an Ishmaelite and my task is to know. But I will let someone else tell you."

He turned to Osnat. "Osnat Aviv, please answer our new Vessel."

Osnat recoiled, confused. "Me? I don't..." She faltered.

"The knowledge is in you. You only have to let it speak."

She looked at Eliezer for help. His eyes were reassuring. Oleander, who stood by him, nodded.

Osnat understood: This was a test, a most important one. The Prince was testing her, but why?

She breathed deeply and forced herself to be calm. All looked at her expectantly. The room was absolutely silent. She closed her eyes and searched inwardly. A long moment passed, and then she felt something stirring inside her.

"The knowledge is inside me," she whispered.

The Ishmaelites chanted something in a low voice, the words guttural and strange. The soft chanting went on rhythmically, and Osnat realized she was in the midst of an ancient ceremony. In some mysterious way, the Knowledge inside her resonated to the chanting, and soon she felt a bubble vibrating in her and growing. She clasped it inwardly and was amazed at how fast it was swelling.

She watched it carefully, waiting for the right moment... now! She let the bubble open and felt the Knowledge spread through her. She now knew the answer to Dina's question, for she carried it within herself.

She turned to Dina and felt words escaping her mouth. "*It is Vessel David Wyatt who was in the Void, where the Cainites are no more. He is also in the desert, with a Keeper at his side.*"

The Prince smiled approvingly. Behind him, Chief Bosmat and Chief Hadad looked at each other in amazement. Such a detailed and precise pronouncement was extremely rare.

"So it is true," Chief Hadad whispered to his comrade.

Chief Bosmat whispered in response, "I've never seen anything like that; except, of course, with Prince Nevayot."

"It is true, Osnat Aviv," The Prince announced. "You are an Ishmaelite. One of us."

She glanced at Eliezer, who seemed delighted. "A Keeper and an Ishmaelite. It turns out that these two do *not* contradict each other as we have always assumed."

Kedar took a step towards her, an expression of pride on his face. But she was not yet ready to talk to him. There was another, greater Knowledge still inside her. The Prince motioned curtly to his grandson to return to his place.

She closed her eyes again. Another bubble was stirring inside her, so great that all those in the room felt its immensity and unconsciously shifted backwards. The Prince felt it most clearly, and he gestured to his people and they renewed their chanting.

Osnat followed the magnificent bubble inwardly. It was rapidly becoming beyond her capacity to contain it, greater than this room, greater than what she would have imagined to be possible to exist within herself. She could not control it. She was now suspended in it.

And then it was ripe and she felt herself speak. Her voice was so deep and vibrant that all those present braced themselves. "*The era of the twelve sons of Jacob has ended; a new time has begun. Man and woman will now reign together, our two Vessels and their descendants.*"

Osnat felt spent. With her eyes still closed, she sank into the armchair beside her. She understood. She had been honored by the Blessing to announce the new era.

Prince Nevayot understood too. He stepped into the middle of the room. "The old prophecies are now fulfilled. Blessed be Vessel Dina and Vessel David, the new mother and father of the Blessing!"

The room thundered in response: "Hail!"

The Prince now turned to Osnat. "One more matter: Greetings to our new Ishmaelite Prince, Prince Osnat! For a long time we have been waiting for the right person to appear and fill the empty post of Prince of the Middle East, which was vacated by the late Prince Samua. Our search has now ended. For the first time in Ishmaelite history, at the dawn of the era of woman-and-man, we are proud to have a woman as one of our twelve princes!"

The applause, accompanied by calls "Prince Osnat!" left no doubt about the sentiments of the Ishmaelites.

108

In the ancient walls of Jerusalem is the Gate of Mercy. It dates to at least the sixth century B.C. Its other names are the Gate of Gold and the Gate of Eternal Life. It is found on the eastern side of the Temple Mount. The Gate of Mercy, or *Sha'ar Harahamim* as it is called in Hebrew, is one of eight gates or entrances, and is the one closest to the site of *Bet Ha-Mikdash*, or the ancient Temple that had been built by King Solomon, now long destroyed. It is unique among the gates because it has no opening, and was apparently originally built like that. Yet the gate features an elaborate double arch indicative of an entrance of special importance, with twin pillars reputed to have come from the Temple. Several legends tell of the meaning of the gate with no door. One is that the Muslims held that the Messiah would come through the Gate of Mercy. To prevent this they bricked up the entrance with large stones. Another legend held that the Divine Presence, or *Shechinah*, at one time appeared at this gate, and would at some time in the future appear again. Until that time the gate would remain closed and must not be opened by human hands.

Just before sunrise, in the gap between night and day, Rabbi Ehud Ben-Galay gingerly knelt on arthritic knees in front of the Gate of Mercy. He bent forward, his back aching, and kissed the ground. This morning it was to give thanks for the answer to his prayers of the past weeks. The cold stone was painful, but the small suffering he ignored. By the time he finished his prayers and stood, bowing his head towards the gate, half the sun was visible above the horizon. But the morning light was still very poor and appeared to play a trick. He craned his head to look more closely.

He put on his glasses and stepped closer to the stone wall. The post that separated the two bricked-up archways had moved forward somehow—or so it seemed. He couldn't remember it sticking out this far. He moved to the side for a different angle. The post had not moved forward—the wall had moved backwards! There was now six inches of blackness, of space, between the entrance wall and the post. He hurried to the other side and saw an identical opening. *The Gate of Mercy was open!* Had the quakes jarred them open? But did it matter, he thought? For were not the quakes too the hand of God?

In the days that followed, as power and communications returned with a speed and ease exceeding the most optimistic estimates, many opinions were offered about the events of the previous weeks. Albrecht Sionn watched the news at his home in Lucerne, his wife nestled next to him on the sofa, while their two girls were doing their homework on the floor at their feet.

"We can break down what occurred in the last many weeks into two categories," stated Dr. Wilson Hardison, a prominent physicist from the Jet Propulsion Laboratory in Pasadena, California. "The first group is comprised of those events outside of human influence: the earthquakes and the various storms. We know there were substantial and extraordinary changes in the Earth's magnetic field. These changes in the magnetic field were significantly responsible, we think, not only for the earthquakes and storms, but for the chaos in the telecommunications and computer networks, as well as the systemic breakdowns of automobiles, planes, and everyday electrical appliances. Then we have a second group: those events in which human psychology and behavior played a role. And in this category I include all other events, from the increase in traffic accidents to plane crashes to increased rates of various illnesses. The increase in accidents and illnesses falls under the umbrella of 'mob mentality.'"

"Mob mentality?" questioned the host.

"You must realize the power of belief. We're all familiar with the placebo effect: a patient is given a pill and told it is a medication that will cure him or relieve his symptoms. And with a frequency not explicable by chance, the patient does indeed get better. Why? Because he believed the pill—in this case made of plain sugar—would cause him to get well. The human mind—belief—literally altered the chemistry and structure of the body. We know the opposite psychological effect occurs as well. A patient believes he will not get well, and he continues to get worse. We saw this, I believe, to a degree with the Eastern Fever."

"Sixty million died because they imagined they were ill?"

"Of course not, Tom. But given the wildly heightened sense of fragility in the world at the time, the psychological effects no doubt caused many to become ill, and many to die, when otherwise their immune systems would have fought off the disease."

"And the plane crashes? How do you explain those?"

"Unpredictability in weather patterns played a role in many instances. The alteration in the magnetic field, as well, I noted, played a part. In others, pilot error was the likely cause. In still others, mechanical failures through faulty maintenance or poorly constructed parts. Human causes."

"How do you see this, Dr. Melah?"

The psychologist from Stanford did not look comfortable on camera. "Dr. Hardison is essentially correct, I believe. The statistical models we have for these events are quite limited. The amount of new data is enormous. It will be some time before we can offer a well-studied conclusion."

The host looked dissatisfied and now turned to Cardinal Rowland of the Philadelphia diocese. "Cardinal Rowland?"

"We have learned—I hope we have learned, how small our role on this Earth is. Obviously, the power of nature did and should humble us. And I agree with my fellow guests that much of what happened can be attributed to human failings. We have been arrogant in our belief we could bend nature to our will, and even in the belief that we are masters of our own actions. We became complacent and too proud, and have been reminded not to take God's grace for granted."

Sionn pulled his wife closer and looked at his two girls, their faces fixed in concentration on their studies.

109

Gathered in the St. Ignacio Abbey Council Chambers were the eight remaining Councilors plus five guests: David Wyatt, Dina Carlini, Prince Nevayot, Kedar Ishmael, and Osnat Aviv. The introductions were warm. Eliezer and Julia Erna stood side-by-side, as did Osnat and Kedar, and with less comfort and familiarity, Dina and David.

"You must forgive us, Miss Carlini," Theresa Fournier said, her eyes drawn to Dina. "It's remarkable. You are a new species, as it were."

"You know," Erna explained, "that all the original lines of the Blessing came from Jacob's twelve sons. From males. Your line of the Blessing began with a woman, your namesake. It never occurred to us there could be a line of Vessels unknown to us, and so that might appear to us differently. I'm sure Keepers at some time in history encountered one of your ancestors. But their reaction was likely the same as ours: bewilderment."

Theresa Fournier was turning the idea over in her mind. "We humans see what we expect to see. Keepers are no different. But the fact is that we have always had a clue that something like this might happen—in the Chronicles. It's the history of the Keepers," she explained for the guests' sake. "I am thinking of one of them—in fact, the most elaborate legend on this topic."

She began to smile, and the others waited for her to continue. "It concerns the episode in Genesis where Esau and his army encounter Jacob and his family. Still resentful of Jacob's trickery, Esau makes a bargain with his brother. Even though he and his army can destroy Jacob, he would allow Jacob to live on one condition: that the Blessing Jacob would give his eldest son be split among *all* his sons. This would greatly reduce the importance of the gift and so the power of Jacob's family line. Think of an Earl or Duke dividing his estate among twelve sons. What each received would be dramatically less significant than what the father possessed, diminishing the importance and power of the family. Jacob agreed; he had no choice. Though it remains a mystery how he did the splitting."

"Jacob had special powers," the Prince reflected. "As one of the three Patriarchs, he received his Blessing directly from God."

"But Esau forgot something. Or someone."

"Yes, William," Theresa Fournier agreed. "As a man of his times, I am sure it did not occur to Esau that Jacob would give his Blessing also to his daughter, to Dinah. Daughters were ignored in matters of inheritance as we all know—or assumed. Jacob kept his word. He stuck to the letter of the agreement he made with Esau."

"Jacob would have made a good lawyer," David commented.

"Indeed. Jacob divided the Blessing that would have gone to his eldest son, Reuben, among all his sons—precisely as they had agreed. And so we had the original twelve Vessels. But Jacob also passed on some of his Blessing to his daughter Dina."

Sandrine Krystofski ruminated on this. "So for four thousand years her ancestors possessed—what, *the potential of the Blessing*? Because, if I understand what Eliezer and William have done, this New Gate had never been opened. Maybe it's the only one through which she can carry the Blessing from the Bible World."

"Clearly, the Blessing works differently in her case," Sionn agreed.

"Please, would you mind not speaking of me in the third person? I feel uncomfortable enough as it is."

"I'm sorry, dear," Erna said. "Bear with us. Perhaps you know there is no precedent for this communion of Keepers and Vessels. It's very strange for us to talk of this with two Vessels in the room, as well as our Ishmaelite cousins."

Erna opened her notebook and carefully removed a small note written on parchment. She read it aloud. "*Please, Isabel... A higher death must have a higher reason, even if that reason has chosen a miserable man like me as its tool. Recall the poem we sang together at the novitiate: 'When the flowers in the Lord's garden begin to die, a much greater life starts budding elsewhere.' This ancient verse must surely mean something!*"

She had their full attention. "I found this note hidden or lost in the Archives. It is from about the time of Jason of Padua's termination in 1239, and the author seems to be Simon de Monfort. But it's starting to make sense to me now. The Vessels have died, and life—what is life but the Blessing, after all?—life sprouts elsewhere. In Dina."

"Was this all ordained? Was it inevitable?" Margaret Connor looked about the table.

"Was it inevitable," Theresa Fournier replied, "that Menach would enter the Void and awaken the Cainites, precisely at the same time that Eliezer and William open the New Gate for the first time in history, causing the deaths of all but the last of Jacob's line? That the line of Vessels that began with Dinah would survive to this day, and that Dina would have been drawn to us?" She shrugged.

"As we say," Prince Nevayot commented, "in matters of the Blessing there are no coincidences. Yet, we know the Blessing is not guaranteed us."

Sandrine was visibly perplexed. "We know Jacob's Vessels received one-twelfth of his Blessing. But what did his daughter receive?"

"We'll just have to wait and see how the world behaves," said Sionn. "But judging by what has happened since she returned from the New Gate, I would venture that it is more than what was granted each of the original twelve Vessels. Perhaps much more."

Oleander leaned forward in his chair. "Something else intrigues me. When Osnat made her declaration about the coming of the new era, she said we will depend on the loving energies of our Vessel-woman and our Vessel-man and their descendants." The words: 'their descendants,' do they refer to Dina's and David's *separate* lines of children and grandchildren, or to their *mutual* line? And what Blessing might their children possess?"

A new astonishment came to the faces of the Keepers. The two Vessels, sitting side-by-side, moved uncomfortably in their seats. David cleared his throat, trying to wave off the suggestion with a joke but found none to offer.

"What of Menach Peprini?" Eliezer's question tamped down the festive mood.

"He is alive, though in a coma," Sionn said. "He is in the sanitarium in Berne. There is no perceptible brain damage, but the coma is apparently quite deep."

"His… soul?" Margaret asked. "Is he lost in the Void, wandering?"

"That we cannot say. We can pray for him, although somehow I think Menach would prefer that we do not."

"What now?" David disliked feeling the ignorant one in the room.

"I would think you two should return to New York," Theresa said. "There is nothing for you to do here."

"And? What, just pick up where I left off?"

"I think you and Dina will have plenty of time to discuss your future," Goldman remarked, smiling mischievously. "You will have a long plane ride together."

"I'll need a tutor to teach me the ways of the Ishmaelites," Osnat said, glancing at Kedar.

"I believe," the Prince said, "that my grandson would prove useful to you, Osnat."

"I would say that we all have earned a rest," Eliezer sighed, feeling the ache in his bones. "Our Ishmaelite cousins no doubt have much to repair, as does the entire world. Keepers shall do what we have always done. We will keep the Blessing, we will discern. We all must learn to discern the New Gate, the Gate of Compassion, if Dina is to continue to renew the Blessing."

Erna put her hand on Eliezer's arm. "You and William must remain here, in Lucerne, to teach all Keepers how to do this."

He took her hand. "There is nothing I would like better."